SOMETHING H̶̶̶̶̶̶̶̶ ̶̶̶̶̶̶̶̶ ̶̶̶̶̶̶ HER FEEL SUDDENLY WANTON

Anna ran her hands from Joshua's stomach to his neck, and felt him quake at her touch.

"It's been a long week," he said, swallowing hard.

"Forever," she whispered as she traced the curve of his ear with her tongue. "Mmm, you taste luscious."

Joshua had to focus on his knees to keep them from buckling.

"It's claustrophobic," Anna said as she unknotted his tie and flung it into a corner. "It's too hot," she teased, slipping off his shirt. "Too binding," she declared as she unbuckled his belt, drawing it languorously through its loops before pitching it on a chair.

Joshua was nearly naked. As Anna stepped back to study him, her sudden distance made him feel even more urgent, more aroused. He reached out for her, but she took another step backward.

"Let me look," she pleaded. "I thought I'd never see you again."

Dear Reader:

We are very excited to announce a change to Harlequin Superromances effective with the February releases, title numbers 150–153. As you know, romance publishing is never static, but is always growing and innovative. After extensive market research, we have decided to slightly shorten the length of the four Superromances published each month, guaranteeing a faster-paced story.

You will still receive that "something extra" in plot and character development that has made these longer romance novels so popular. A strong well-written love story will remain at the heart of a Harlequin Superromance, but with the tighter format, drama will be heightened from start to finish.

Our authors are delighted with and challenged by this change, and they have been busy writing some wonderful new stories for you. Enjoy!

Laurie Bauman

Laurie Bauman,
Superromance Senior Editor

Maureen Bronson

TENDER VERDICT

Harlequin Books

TORONTO • NEW YORK • LONDON
AMSTERDAM • PARIS • SYDNEY • HAMBURG
STOCKHOLM • ATHENS • TOKYO • MILAN

Published January 1985

First printing November 1984

ISBN 0-373-70149-7

Printed in Canada

CHAPTER ONE

JOGGING THROUGH THE CITY, Anna reached the court-house steps and stopped. A glance at her watch assured her she had plenty of time before work to cool down in the crisp morning breeze. Panting, she threw her head back and gulped at the tangy salt air. Dressed in an azure tank top and shorts, she was oblivious to the fact that she made a captivating picture framed against the gray granite stones of the old judicial building.

Taxi drivers trapped in the bustling Seattle traffic tooted their horns and businessmen paused, smiling broadly at the portrait she made with her hands on her hips, accenting her small waist. Even when the hub-bub was punctuated by a wolf whistle, Anna was bliss-fully ignorant of being the center of every visible male's attention. Unlike women who are acutely tuned to every nuance in a glance aimed at them, Anna was indifferent. She didn't invest any energy in her looks and therefore thought her looks were unremark-able. Her energy was directed, instead, toward being professionally competent and physically toned. Con-sequently, she was blind to the effect her beauty had on others—especially men.

"Ouch!" she yelped aloud. A brief grimace of pain creased her clear but slightly tanned face. "I guess I shouldn't have pushed so hard," she grumbled as she kneaded her right calf. "Looks like I'm going to pay for it."

Anna's mother called her talking to herself a "wrinkle" in her character. Anna knew it was her way of not so subtly hinting that she was turning into a lonely old maid. To mama and papa, who were Russian immigrants, a female who was thirty and un- married was a woman to be pitied.

But Anna rejected her mother's premise that she was a doddering old lady. Her days were filled with her career, teaching and running. She couldn't possibly squeeze one more thing into her life. Loneliness? It was preposterous. Mama would just have to learn that not everyone needed marriage.

Slowly bending over, Anna began to stretch her leg muscles before the cramps became worse. With her back to the street, she didn't notice a cab pull up behind her, depositing two men on the curb just a few feet away. One, a tall rugged man outfitted in a perfectly tailored tweed sport jacket, took several steps backward as he carelessly swung his briefcase.

"Okay, Charlie, I'll be on my best behavior today. I promise no theatrics. I definitely don't want to get on the wrong side of the old curmudgeon."

Anna heard the old-fashioned diction and found her curiosity piqued by the odd combination of an ar- chaic English noun and an obvious Northwest ac- cent. She wondered who in the world still used a word like *curmudgeon*.

Just as she was starting to straighten up to look, she felt a sharp blow to her backside.

"Ow!"

Anna didn't realize the swinging briefcase had inadvertently connected with her posterior. The momentum catapulted her forward onto the steps and she scraped her elbows on the concrete.

Flinging his case down, the stranger instantly lifted her from the steps and started brushing her off with warm gentle hands.

"I'm so sorry," he said. "I had no idea you were behind me."

"That's obvious," Anna snapped as he held her wrists up to look at her elbows. "But why are you continuing to maul me?"

He released her wrists and pulled out an immaculate handkerchief, pressing it against her right elbow. He succeeded in stopping the blood that was trickling down her forearm.

Anna felt foolish for having mistaken the man's concern. Embarrassed, she turned her attention to her injury.

"I think I'll be all right now," she said. "Sorry for jumping all over you like that, but you startled me."

Not wanting to appear rude or unforgiving, Anna stared directly into the man's face to thank him for his kindness. A pair of the brightest blue eyes she had ever seen met hers. His gaze was so intense she had to force herself to keep her head up and not lower her eyes. Behind the blue sparkle of the man's gaze was a hint of caged mirth.

Anna quickly scanned his face. He had attractive angular features, a thick trim blond mustache, and she detected two large dimples struggling to appear around his expressive mouth. She realized he was fighting back a broad grin. Knocking her flat on her

face did not seem like it should be a source of pleasure for anyone—blue eyes or not!

"I'd thank you for your kind ministrations," Anna said acidly, "but one, you caused the damage, and
two, I sense you think there's something amusing
about grinding me into the pavement." She yanked
her arm out of his grasp.

"Whew! You're certainly no whimpering lady in
distress," he whistled. "Well, Spitfire, I have to admit I've always wanted to pick up a beautiful lady,
but it never occurred to me to knock her down first."
He grinned at her like a mischievous little boy caught
red-handed in a prank.

"Listen," Anna said, "if you're that desperate, go
find some willing victim to broadside." She spun
around and stomped up the courthouse steps to the
elevators. Her aching calf muscle prevented her from
running.

"Hey, wait a minute," the stranger called out as he
bounded after her. When he caught up, he put a
powerful hand on her shoulder to stop her. "Listen,
please. I'm really sorry." His eyes penetrated hers
and this time they concealed no mirth. "It was stupid
of me and careless."

In his strong grip, hearing the deep sincere regret in
his voice, Anna felt herself melting.

"Honestly," he implored, "I wasn't making fun
of you back there."

Anna's irritation vanished. "Thank you," she said
on a sigh. "I'm sorry, too, for being such a witch
about a little accident."

He burst into a smile and grabbed her upper arms
with both his hands. "You're a good sport, Spitfire.

Let me buy you a drink after work. A toddy to mend the spirit and the body." He rechecked the improvised bandage on her elbow.

"Toddy! Curmudgeon!" Anna laughed. "Do you always use such antiquated words? And who is this cantankerous person you were hollering about when you toppled me?"

He grinned and, as if on cue, his dimples appeared. "Just an ogre I have to deal with today. But I don't want to talk about it now and spoil a lovely morning and what promises to be an even-better evening. So how about that drink?" he cajoled as he twirled her auburn-colored ponytail with the tips of his fingers.

Anna studied him for a minute. She was definitely attracted to him. He talked like a polished Shakespearean actor but had the air of a contemporary rascal. A compelling combination. Unorthodox perhaps, but fascinating.

Anna realized that he was studying her as intently as she was scrutinizing him. Breaking their locked eye contact, she sauntered over to the elevators.

"I might like a drink after work," she said as she pushed the Up button.

"Great!" he called after her. "What time does your boss unlock your cage?"

Anna was stung. Seething, she twirled on him and snapped, "What makes you think I don't own my own keys?"

She hated the fact that some men made such blatant assumptions, automatically placing all women in stereotyped roles. They left no room for the woman who wanted to break away from conventional occupations. Why she had even considered spending any of her precious spare time with this obnoxious creature puzzled her. The sooner she got away from him the better.

"Don't get riled," he soothed.

Anna watched him come closer, using a gait that perfectly blended power and elegance. Too bad, she sighed to herself, that his personality doesn't match his good looks. But that could be a lethal combination! At least with such a basic personality clash as theirs, there could be no chance of him being anything more than a pretty face in the crowd.

Nearly on top of her, he extended his arm above her shoulder and leaned his hand against the marble wall behind her. She could smell a trace of light spice emanating from him. It was pleasant. She detested overpowering cologne on men.

"I didn't mean to offend you," he said in a coaxing voice. "You probably have a very important position. Are you head of a legal-research department or a court reporter? You certainly appear to be fast enough to qualify for any number of jobs."

Anna heard that mocking tone return to his voice. She tensed. His close proximity made her uncomfortable and she silently wondered when an elevator was going to arrive. Probably one of them had broken down again. Perfect timing! If her leg hadn't been killing her, she would have taken the stairs.

"Please go away," she demanded. "Your transparent patronization is offensive. You have no idea who or what I am and I find your assumptions about me insulting."

"Touchy, aren't you, Spitfire?"

"And you can quit calling me that ridiculous

name,'' she ordered. Finally she heard the elevator bell. Ducking out from under his arm, she pivoted and said firmly, ''For your information, I have a proper name and a very proper title and Spitfire isn't either.''

As she stepped into the car, he tried to follow her. Forcefully placing her hand against his chest, she pushed him out and said, ''No way. This is where we part. It's been a short and miserable relationship. Goodbye.''

''What? No drink?'' he pleaded as he stepped back into the foyer.

''Not today. Not ever,'' she said as the doors started to close. ''I think I'll just keep my cage locked up for tonight.''

He stood there looking chagrined as the doors slammed shut.

Good, Anna thought. *Impertinence, assumptions, aggressions, they all need to be...to be...what? Quashed! That's the word he would have used. Quashed.*

She got off on the fourth floor and passed the double doors of Courtroom Four. She strode briskly to the heavy oak door of Judge A. Provo's chambers. Tenderly her fingers traced the raised brass letters. Taking a deep breath to regain her equanimity, she squared her shoulders, put a wide grin on her face and opened the door. With renewed composure, she was ready to face the day.

''Good morning, Miriam,'' Anna said as she opened the door.

''Good morning, Judge,'' her secretary called back. ''Did you have a nice run? It's a perfect morning for jogging.''

"I guess you could say my day has been invigorating in a perverse sort of way." Opening the door to her private chambers, Anna asked, "Are those notes of mine ready?"

"They sure are. Right here," Miriam said, handing them to her.

Anna perused them swiftly and laid them on her desk for a thorough reading later. Carefully unwrapping the handkerchief from her elbow, she checked to see if the bleeding had completely stopped. Fortunately it was only a bad scrape and would heal soon.

She palmed the soiled cloth, debating whether to have it laundered and returned or to toss it in the wastebasket. Return it to whom? She had no idea who the stranger was or where he worked. The logical thing to do was to dispose of the handkerchief.

She felt an inexplicable twinge of regret that things had not gone better between the two of them. A soiled piece of linen marked with the initials JB was her only link to those startling blue eyes. The man had been polished, urbane and an impudent rascal, as well as a patronizing klutz. But yet, there was a certain charm and an air of gentle caring detectable beneath the bravado.

Realizing she was investing too much time on a man she would never see again, Anna marched off to the shower.

Half an hour later, while donning her somber judicial robes, Anna dismissed the unsettling thoughts that had destroyed her composure. She was not a person who took the authority that had been vested in her lightly. Her sole focus now was to see that the laws she had taken a pledge to uphold were honored. She had recaptured her calm sense of purpose and, with a fresh attitude, opened the door to go to work.

As she majestically swept into court, the bailiff loudly proclaimed, "All rise. King County Municipal Court is now in session. The Honorable Judge Anna Provo presiding."

The first case on her docket was the *State of Washington* v. *Samuel T. Barnett*. Anna heaved a sigh as she noted that old Sam was back again. Poor fellow! He'd been before her several times and she assumed that this preliminary hearing would be no different than the last. Sam's feeble attempts to gain someone's attention—anyone's—constantly resulted in his being hauled into her court. He was seventy-eight years old and had a habit of shoplifting. In plain sight he would slip some small article into his jacket and then be promptly arrested.

Sam meant no harm. He enjoyed the limelight he was in when the public defender's office scurried around preparing his case, begging the court to be lenient.

Anna's gaze scanned the partially filled courtroom to take inventory of who was defending Sam, and immediately her eyes were riveted to the figure seated at the defense table next to the old man. She quickly glanced at her docket to find his name. Joshua Brandon. The JB on the handkerchief!

So I'm the old curmudgeon, she realized.

From the startled look he wore, Joshua Brandon was plainly as surprised as she was. He had obviously not counted on finding himself pleading his case in front of the "cute little clerk" he'd met downstairs.

Anna sensed his discomfort. Momentarily she considered prolonging his turmoil but her better judgment prevailed and she stared evenly at him, trying to silently reassure him that their prior encounter would not be a factor with which he would have to contend.

"Gentlemen," she addressed the attorneys, "are you ready to present your evidence?"

"Yes, Your Honor, the state is ready."

"Yes, Your Honor, the defense is ready."

"Then please proceed," she directed.

Joshua took a deep cleansing breath to try to calm the rapid pounding of his heart. He could not believe his incredible luck nor his unerring misfortune. To smash a woman into the ground wasn't bad enough—he had to pick a judge. And not just any judge. Oh, no, that wasn't good enough for him! This was his first case for the public defender's office and he had ground his first magistrate into the concrete. What a way to start his career in criminal law.

He silently gave himself a brief pep talk to still the anxiety that was threatening to engulf him. If she was magnanimous enough to ignore their first meeting, she would be a true professional. Most probably she would not let her personal bias influence the case.

Putting his feelings aside, Joshua directed his full attention to the prosecuting attorney's words. While listening carefully, Joshua began to institute the strategy he'd so carefully formulated.

At law school, Joshua had come to the conclusion that all first-year students finally reach. In essence, he learned that it wasn't the law he was dealing with but people. Each case had two definite sides to it and an attorney ran a fifty-fifty chance of winning or losing every time he entered court. It was the way one presented the facts and what precedents had been unearthed to defend one's position that determined the outcome. A good trial lawyer should always be an actor, for the judge and jury was the audience who evaluated how well he did on stage.

Joshua had spent a great deal of time preparing for this case. Even though this was only a preliminary hearing to establish if there was enough evidence to show probable cause, he felt strongly that Sam deserved proper representation. He genuinely felt sorry for the old fellow. Something had to be done about the forlorn man's predicament. But what?

Joshua's opportunity came.

"Your Honor," he spoke solemnly, "Mr. Barnett consented to the law-enforcement officer's search willingly, but he was not fully aware of the nature of the search and the legal implications."

"Objection, Your Honor," Tom Randolph, the prosecuting attorney, parried. "Voluntary consent is a waiver of one's Fourth Amendment rights."

"But Your Honor," Joshua countered, "given my client's past history, I can see no way the state's allegation can stand. Mr. Barnett is a repeat offender. Doesn't that imply he should have known what the implications of his voluntary consent would mean?"

"I'm fully aware of Mr. Barnett's previous offenses, Mr. Brandon," Anna replied. "What was your client's motive for submitting to the search?"

"Objection, Your Honor," Tom Randolph interrupted. "Mr. Barnett's motive is not the issue."

"Mr. Randolph," she scolded, "this is only a preliminary hearing. Our purpose is to weed out groundless or unsupported criminal charges before trial."

"My client had no motive," Joshua stated. "Mr. Barnett simply did not understand. He is quite elderly and is frequently confused."

Anna examined the facts superficially to determine whether there was a strong enough case to hold Sam Barnett for further proceedings. The prosecution presented its evidence in order to determine probable cause—circumstances sufficiently strong to warrant a cautious person to believe that an accused person is guilty of the offense with which he is charged. She judged that the facts properly supported the state's allegation against Sam Barnett.

"Please see the court clerk for an arraignment date," she instructed Joshua Brandon and Tom Randolph. "Court dismissed."

Joshua neatly gathered his papers and placed them back in his briefcase. He intentionally slowed his movements so that he could observe Anna as she waited for her next case to begin. When she removed her glasses, he noticed her enormous topaz eyes. He wondered why she shrouded their beauty behind spectacles. Why not wear contact lenses and flaunt them, he wondered.

He was pleased that he had skillfully represented his client and hoped that she had formed a new opinion of him. He wanted to prove to her he was more than a bungling oaf who was bent on bruising the bench.

Anna tried to discreetly watch Joshua Brandon as Tom Randolph approached him and introduced himself. The two men were a study in contrast. Her old friend Tom appeared rumpled and disheveled next to the polished bearing of his adversary. She wished she didn't find Joshua Brandon so attractive. It was disconcerting and she was annoyed with herself. Unfortunately, she was going to have to work with him again. Perhaps by the time the arraignment rolled around she would have brought her silly preoccupation with him under control.

CHAPTER TWO

For the next four weeks, Joshua Brandon punctuated Anna's life with his random appearances. One evening in the midst of a crowd, both inadvertently reached for the same magazine at Benny's Cigar and Newsstand in the lobby of the courthouse. It was the last copy of *Esquire*. He was a gentleman and allowed her to purchase it.

"May I borrow it after you have read it?" he asked.

"Certainly," she answered, as poised as possible. The way the light played off his sun-streaked hair was unsettling and she avoided looking directly at him.

"Did you read last month's article on the drought in Africa?" he asked.

"I tried but it was too dry for me," she quipped as she dropped her money on Benny's counter and hurried away.

His robust laughter echoed after her. Her attempts to discourage even such a friendly and harmless overture had boomeranged. There was no way to escape his pronounced effect on her.

After she rapidly exited the lobby, Joshua smiled to himself. He was amused by Anna's keen wit and appreciated the verbal jousting she obviously used as a defense. He was looking forward to future matches.

But Anna made a point of avoiding him whenever

she saw him in the crowded courthouse halls. Still, it was impossible to boycott him completely. She frequently had breakfast in the cafeteria and would catch his eye across the tables. He was usually seated with other attorneys from the public defender's office and she felt secure sitting alone while he conversed with his colleagues.

One morning she was relieved to see that he was absent from his usual seat and she carried her laden tray to an empty table. She was busy reading the morning paper and didn't look up to see who was joining her.

"Good morning, Judge Provo."

She recognized Joshua's distinctive voice and barely lowered the top of her paper to look at him.

"May I join you?" he asked.

"If you must," she grudgingly consented.

"Yes, unless you expect me to eat standing up?"

Anna glanced around the room. All of the tables were full. She had no option but to let him share her table. But she wasn't obligated to be friendly, so she nodded toward the empty chair and resumed reading the newspaper.

"Tom tells me you two are old friends," Joshua said, trying to engage her in light conversation.

Anna deliberately folded her paper, stood up, looked down at him imperiously and said, "They're the only kind I want."

He grabbed her by the forearm and detained her. "Don't worry, they're likely to be the only kind you'll ever have."

Smarting from his snide remark, she marched from the room and decided to stop eating in the cafeteria. It peeved her that she had to relinquish her usual mealtime retreat. She knew she was allowing him to encroach upon her life.

Anna managed to avoid Joshua for only a little while. Finally, about four days later, she had to face him in court again. Sam Barnett's arraignment was scheduled as the first item on her agenda.

Looking every inch a magistrate, Anna steeled herself and took her place behind the bench. The state presented its formal charges against defendant Samuel Barnett.

"How do you plead, Mr. Barnett?" Anna asked.

Joshua Brandon responded for his client. "He has agreed to enter a plea of guilty in exchange for a promise by the prosecuting attorney to recommend a light sentence."

"Mr. Randolph," Anna addressed Tom, "are you willing to accept this proposal?"

"Yes, Your Honor."

"Mr. Brandon, do you have a recommendation for the court?" she inquired.

"I would like to see my client receive a deferred sentence in exchange for his community service," Joshua answered.

"Mr. Randolph, is this acceptable?"

"Yes, Your Honor."

"Do either of you have any objections to taking a short recess and reconvening in my chambers at, say, eleven o'clock?" she asked the attorneys.

Neither man dissented.

Back in her chambers, Anna began to instigate her tentative plan. She could not allow old Sam to repeatedly clog up the system with his antics. Cases were backlogged too far already to allow this type of time-consuming charade to be repeated with such irritating regularity. Sam's pilfering a $1.19 can of snuff every other week had to stop.

She knew that there was a whole host of social services available and somewhere there had to be one that could provide Sam with the type of attention he needed. There had to be a program that would keep him out of her court.

The time rapidly slipped away and at exactly eleven Anna finally got the answer she was searching for. The Council on Aging had just instituted a new service that ran a foster-grandparent program at Children's Orthopedic Hospital. Sam would be required to show up everyday to read stories, help feed and play games with the children who were hospitalized. Some of the young patients spent months recuperating from their diseases or operations. Having a constant caring companion was a vital ingredient to their recovery. Sam wouldn't have time to make his bed, much less shoplift! It was an answer to her dilemma.

Anna pressed the buzzer of her intercom and asked Miriam to send in Mr. Randolph and Mr. Brandon. Within seconds, the two men walked into her chambers.

"Please be seated, gentlemen," she said as she gestured to the chairs arranged in front of her desk.

With the trained eye of a careful observer, she took particular note of how well Joshua's clothes molded to his broad shoulders and tapered waist. Obviously he had money, so why was he working for the public defender's office?

She carefully avoided making any eye contact with Joshua as she raised her head and acknowledged

Tom's presence. Her friend's face lit with pleasure as she reached out and gave his hand a squeeze. She noticed that he was wearing his curly brown hair a bit shorter. The style minimized his slightly impish appearance.

"Hello, Tom. How are you?" she asked.

"Just fine, Anna. Yourself?"

"I can't complain. Mr. Brandon?" she said, acknowledging Joshua.

As she extended her hand to shake his, she felt the warm pressure of his grip and was surprised to find that Joshua's palm was sprinkled with thick calluses. He held her hand a trace longer than was necessary. She looked into his eyes and read a clear message of gratitude for considering his proposal.

Joshua wished they were alone so he could privately say thanks. Instead he had to search her large amber eyes for warmth, an indication that he had successfully and subtly communicated his understanding of her position. He wanted to let Anna know he was grateful she'd been able to rise above any personal antagonism she felt toward him.

Joshua felt a sense of pride in the profession he'd chosen for a career. Changing to criminal law had been a good move after all. Now he was convinced more than ever that his decision had been a wise one.

"Tread softly, Joshua," Tom advised. "Even though Anna and I go back a long way, I've lost too many cases before her to be able to count on the fact that friendship enters into her decisions."

Joshua smiled. "I have already learned how well she handles herself."

Discomfitted, Anna said, "Now that we have dispensed with the niceties, can we get down to business?''

She proceeded to outline her plan and watched the men for their initial reactions to her solution. It was obvious Joshua was in favor of her idea and would urge his client to accept her sentence. After answering a few mundane questions that Tom presented, Anna felt secure that everyone would approve the plan. Tom's only request was that Sam be put on probation for one year to ensure that he did not slip back into his old ways. She assured Tom that she had fully intended to make that stipulation.

''Let's go back into the courtroom and make this official,'' she said.

Tom hauled himself up out of his chair and said he had to speak to his supervisor first. Anna agreed to give him twenty minutes.

On the way out the door, Tom flashed her a lopsided grin and said, ''Good job, Anna. I think this will work.''

Joshua lingered behind in her chambers and Anna felt uncomfortable being alone with him. They'd covered their legitimate business, so what else could they possibly say to each other? An odd sort of tension existed between them. Anna defined it as almost scintillating, but it wasn't a pleasant feeling. Frankly, it was unsettling.

''Is there something else, Mr. Brandon?'' Anna asked curtly.

''Yes, Your Honor.'' He stroked his mustache and hesitated. ''But it's personal. I'd still like us to make a fresh start. My offer to buy you a drink is still open.''

''Mr. Brandon,'' Anna said, her voice edged in ice,

"this is neither the time nor the place for personal business."

"Oh, it's not strictly personal," he argued. "It has its professional ramifications, too. A new public defender can't afford to insult a judge."

Anna furiously restacked some papers and folders on her desk before she responded. "A bribe, Mr. Brandon?"

"Certainly not!" his voice almost roared, angry at the insinuation. "A courtesy, Your Honor!"

She threw the stack of papers down with a ferocious thud. "You are forgetting yourself." She enunciated each word angrily. "These are my chambers and this is my court. I'll brook no grandstanding by attorneys. I thought Tom made it very clear that I'm adamant about keeping the decorum of my court within traditional bounds."

"Grandstanding? A simple peace offering is suddenly distorted into bribery and grandstanding? Clever," he seethed.

"I advise you to edit your words," she warned, "and not indulge yourself in any antics."

"Now it's antics!" Joshua put both hands on her desk and leaned toward her.

Anna felt his blue eyes pierce her like a lance. None of the congenial good humor he'd displayed earlier showed in his handsome face. Instead his jaw was rigid and his full mouth was unyielding.

"It was your tone of voice I found offensive, Mr. Brandon," she said, trying to take the bite out of their confrontation.

Joshua drew himself up to his full six feet two inches and shifted his weight. He flexed his shoulders, stretched his thick muscled neck and said, "Then I apologize for my tone, Judge Provo. However, my offer was an innocent one."

"Then forgive me, Counselor, for taking offense," Anna conceded.

Joshua's eyebrows raised in surprise and a smile crept back into the corners of his mouth. His dimples were back home where they belonged.

She watched him stroll languidly to the door. She decided he was interesting and easy to handle.

He stood in the open doorway for a second to look at her and then said before closing it, "Good job, Anna, but I don't think it'll work."

She almost ran after him and demanded to know what he meant. What wouldn't work? The plan for Sam? She remained rooted in her office. Anna instinctively knew that Joshua Brandon was not referring to the case they were handling. He was blatantly stating that her attempts to fend him off were pointless.

His audacity was incredible and it made her laugh aloud. One minute he wanted to throttle her and the next he was making a pass. She felt her resolve melting and, against her better judgment, she entertained the thought of having a quiet cocktail after work with this enigmatic man.

Dismissing the idea, she glanced at her watch and noted that she had ten minutes left before she needed to reappear in court. Lacking any definite task to occupy her spare moments, she drifted over to the window and thoughtfully scanned the uneven Seattle skyline. Her emotions matched the buildings. High and low. High and low.

Watching the small figures on the street below

scurry back and forth, her thoughts were lazily drawn back to another young lawyer who had caught her attention long ago. She remembered another morning when she had wandered the vacant city streets of Seattle in the bright dawn.

She and Sean had been out all night at a graduation party at the Olympic Hotel. They'd saved their money for months and, as a reward for finishing law school, pooled their limited resources and rented an opulent room at the posh hotel.

The warm afternoon had gone by in a rapid whirl of graduation activities coupled with family commitments. Each of them had posed for countless pictures snapped by beaming relatives. On the surface they had both seemed calm and self-assured, but underneath was a consuming passion to escape the strict confines of the family and indulge in an afternoon of unrestrained lovemaking.

Even after all these years, Anna could feel her cheeks grow warm as she recalled the wild abandon she had experienced in Sean's arms. How lovely it had been to respond to his playful kisses. Sean had made her feel so vibrantly alive.

They had been lost in a world of their own and had by silent agreement leisurely wandered the quiet streets until they were staring up at the impressive grandeur of the stately courthouse. Fingers intertwined, they had stood quietly wrapped in private thoughts and fears of what the future held for them.

Sean had broken her quiet reverie by saying, "Someday I'd like to be a judge and have my office right up there on the fourth floor with Puget Sound at my feet."

Anna had nestled into his arms and said, "Let's be the first husband-and-wife team on that floor. It'd be quite a feat. Offices next to each other; the same hours; cases to discuss...."

Sean kissed the top of her head and mumbled, "Don't be silly. You won't have time."

Pulling away from his embrace to look at his face, she'd asked, "What does that mean?"

He patiently began to explain the dynamics of the situation to her as if she was a two-year-old child.

"How do you think you could handle all that work? You'll be far too busy raising our family to even consider becoming a judge. I'd pictured you having a small practice in the suburbs," he said. "Don't you think that's a bit more realistic?"

A sickening pall engulfed her and she tried to mask the panic and confusion she felt.

With a quivering voice, she said, "I have no intention of staying home to raise a family and letting all these years of hard work go to waste."

"But your talents wouldn't be going to waste," Sean argued. "There's always a need for lawyers to handle small civil cases or to specialize in domestic relations. It's a lucrative field."

An edge of irritation crept into her tone. "I don't want to be ensconced in some boring little office dealing with the petty quarrels that men and women become immersed in when they divorce." Building up a head of steam, she added, "I want to carve out a niche for myself in criminal law. The field is financially and mentally rewarding. I've worked too hard to settle for less. And—" she took a deep breath "—where did you get the idea I want a family?"

Sean uncharacteristically guffawed. "Someone as beautiful as you are must want a child to perpetuate your gorgeous red hair." He tousled her mane. "Part of the reason I love you is that I have always had this vision of our little girl looking like her mother."

Anna grabbed his wrist and removed his hand from her head. How had they fallen in love and not discussed careers and children? A chasm as wide as the Grand Canyon was opening up between them.

"Sean," she begged, "please listen. There are two things in my life. Only two. You and law. I don't have time for children."

"I'll help," he insisted. "I want to play an active role in raising the kids."

Sean refused to believe her when she was adamant about remaining childless. They argued for several more minutes as if they were in front of a court presenting opposite sides of a complicated case. Neither would budge.

Finally Sean convinced Anna to table the discussion for another time. She readily agreed. She'd always known that she could not risk having a child but Anna was unable to verbalize her fear. Unvoiced, her private terror could not be dissected and analyzed and found invalid. By leaving her fear unspoken, her secret inner conviction could stand.

They drifted back to the hotel, and eventually they drifted apart—Sean to somewhere on the East Coast and Anna to the highly prized fourth floor. Her reluctance to accept the role he'd written for her and her determination to pursue her own goals had severed their bond. She'd changed direction, made new decisions and gone on without him.

But the same question that always rose to haunt her surfaced again. Had it been worth it?

"Judge Provo." John, her bailiff, poked his head around the corner of the door. "Judge? You're five minutes late. Everyone's waiting."

"Sorry, John. I lost track of time," she answered, wrenching herself out of the past. "I'll be right there."

What in the world had caused her to go digging through the ruins of an old love? *Just because a man waltzes into your court and gives you a lingering glance,* she lectured herself, *you immediately become maudlin.*

Quickly checking her hair in the mirror, she was satisfied to see that it was still neatly drawn back. Papa referred to her hair as cinnabar, a color the Russians treasured. Anna thought of it as red, but she liked the sound of the word *cinnabar* better.

Realizing she was primping, she scolded herself in a mocking tone, "Fickle, aren't you?" and headed eagerly to her bench.

Seated sedately, Anna put her reading glasses on the bridge of her pert nose. She barely needed them, in fact, she could easily have worn contact lenses, but the spectacles provided a barrier between herself and the rest of the world. There was something distinctly professional about a woman who wore glasses.

She made a succinct statement to the floor summarizing the court's decision. For the record she noted that the state had dropped all charges upon recommendation of probation.

"Mr. Brandon—" she peered over the top of her glasses "—does your client understand and accept these terms?"

Joshua stood, squared his shoulders, unbuttoned his jacket and slightly loosened his tie.

"Yes, Your Honor," he responded in almost a drawl.

Anna bit her tongue. She wanted to curtly inform him that this was not an informal parlor debate where dress was relaxed and response was casual. However, she refrained from issuing a reprimand because she sensed he wasn't intentionally being disrespectful. That nonchalant stance of his seemed like second nature to him and was probably not intended to be an affront.

"Good. Court is adjourned," she said and brought her gavel down.

As she rose to leave, Anna was touched by the caring way Joshua bent down to help old Sam out of the chair. He exuded an air of gentle concern and she was puzzled at how he could be so aggressive one minute and so patient the next. But as she turned to leave, she caught him staring at her with a look that stripped her of her robes. He was unabashedly caressing her visually.

Her composure was rapidly fading and Anna made a quick exit. With her hands shaking, she unbuttoned her robes and flung them into a corner. She gratefully sank into her leather rocking chair. Its cool smooth surface felt soothing. But the thought of Joshua, his insolence, his audacity, his blatant ogling, caused her to rock furiously. Putting him in his place some day would be a task that would give her immense pleasure.

CHAPTER THREE

ANNA BENT INTO THE WIND as she briskly walked along Fourth Avenue. The gentle morning breeze had grown into a stiff bluster by evening. It had taken only a day, not a month, for the weather to come in like a lamb and go out like a lion.

She compared her quixotic mood to the sudden wind. She'd started the morning calm, practical and cool. Now she was obsessed with an urbane rascal and she was thrown into an emotional tumult. It wasn't just today's encounter with Joshua that had her disoriented and almost in a state of chaos. She'd been plagued by the thought of him for weeks. Ever since that morning he'd bumped into her on the steps, she'd had to battle with herself to forget him. The thrill that coursed through her when his capable hands had gently picked her up had caught her totally off guard and it had kept her reeling for more than a month.

Despite the nip in the air, Anna could feel a hint of scarlet begin to creep up her face. There was no logical reason for her to be drawn to him. She'd been telling herself all day that any man who had the impudence to look at a woman the way he had looked at her should be forgotten. But she hadn't been able to banish him from her thoughts.

During lunch she'd attempted to distract herself by brown-bagging it to a concert in Freeway Park. When Seattle ran an ugly multilaned, multitiered freeway through its heart, the city fathers had rebelled. So terraces were built, trees were planted, flowers were bedded, grass was grown and ivy was draped to camouflage the concrete. The result was a magnificent park in the center of the business district. Daily concerts lured office workers and executives to the site. Now scores of municipal designers visited every year to copy the park plan.

Anna had listened to Cajun bayou folk songs for almost an hour, but even the intricate and fast-fingered fiddling didn't work its usual magic. She couldn't stop thinking about Joshua.

But that was at noon when the sunlight had still been bright. Now a storm threatened on the horizon. What she needed was a quiet refuge. She increased her pace and soon found herself at Freddy's Pub. The thought of sipping a mug of dark rich ale and munching on some of Freddy's crisp homemade pretzels was appealing. A quiet hour alone was the perfect way to file the edge off a rough day.

The dark interior of the bar was a sharp contrast to the early-evening sunlight and Anna had to stop for a minute to let her eyes adjust.

"Good evening, Anna."

"Hi, Freddy. How are you?"

"Fine, and yourself?"

More tired than she'd realized, Anna sighed. "I'll make it."

"Bad day, huh? Well, I'll heap some T.L.C. on you. I'll take you to a nice quiet corner."

"Thanks."

Even though her eyes hadn't completely adjusted, Anna followed Freddy. As she stepped into the bar's dimly lit recesses, she felt someone firmly take her elbow and fall into step with her.

"So nice of you to be so prompt," a rich sonorous voice said.

She recognized his voice immediately, the way Joshua rolled certain words, stressed some consonants and enunciated particular vowels. The enigmatic Mr. Brandon was propelling her along as if he had expected her.

She stopped abruptly and removed his hand from her arm as if it was something quite disagreeable. Facing him, she could now see perfectly. He looked like someone waiting patiently for a child to make up his mind.

"You're mistaken, Mr. Brandon," she said coolly. "We made no arrangements."

"No?" he feigned shock. "I must reprimand my secretary for misinforming me. She insisted you called and said to meet you here."

Anna heard the playful bantering in his voice and realized that Freddy was waiting to see if she really was meeting this man. Indecisive, she hesitated too long.

"Still," Joshua insisted, "there's no need to waste the evening now that you are here. Let's have that drink I promised you."

He took her arm again and Freddy abandoned her to Joshua. Anna noted again how elegant he was. He was gorgeous enough to display in a showcase! She smothered a laugh. He certainly didn't assert himself like a mannequin, Anna thought. He lacked the docile temperament! In fact, Joshua's whole demeanor was that of a swarthy roughneck ready to do battle.

With catlike grace he nuzzled into her, pushing her against the wall to let another couple pass. With his body pressed tightly to hers, Anna felt how tall and well built he was. At five feet eleven, she normally felt large and gangly, but Joshua made her feel small and defenseless. He had her in a tantalizing pinfold.

"How did you find me here?" she asked, slipping away from him.

"Would you believe I wasn't looking for you at all? That this is a favorite haunt of mine?"

"No, try again. I come here frequently and I've never seen you."

"What if I said I followed you?"

She could see that mischievous grin of his cavorting at the corners of his mouth and a teasing gleam in his eyes. She had to admit that he was certainly charming, but he didn't seem to have any compunction about dogging her all over the city.

"I'd have to demand why," she responded.

"Well, Judge Provo, I decided to stop being so timid and become bold. And it seems to have worked, too. Here we are having an intimate cocktail conversation."

"Excuse me," Anna said, "but I wouldn't exactly call this intimate. It's more like a sparring match."

"Well, now, how about letting me join you at your table and we will turn our sparring match into an—"

"Intimate conversation?" Anna felt torn. If she gave him an inch he'd take the whole mile. Despite her good sense, she capitulated. "Okay, one drink, but let's steer away from intimacies. Just a truce with a quick drink to seal the agreement."

As Anna followed him to a table, she asked herself why this man was so different from any other she'd met before. She was used to working with men but somehow she knew that she and Joshua were becoming entangled. And it frightened her. Somehow he totally unnerved her.

To assuage her qualms, Anna reassured herself that she would have one drink, then she would make a fast exit and head home. She ordered herself not to prolong the encounter by a minute, to stay calm, to maintain an aloof attitude and to let Mr. Brandon know she was an independent woman. Surely she could scare him off.

"This *is* just a quick toast to seal a truce. Correct, Counselor?" Anna wasn't sure if she said that for the benefit of the waitress who came to take their order, or to set Joshua Brandon straight regarding her intentions, or for herself.

"Correct, Your Honor. I'll have a schooner of dark draft and a—" Joshua halted.

"The same," Anna finished the request.

Joshua wasn't sure he liked the position he was in, even though he was responsible for it. This woman drove him crazy. He felt like a pimple-faced adolescent asking out the homecoming queen. *Hell,* he thought, *she acts as regal as an empress. On or off the bench!* The desire to unseat her had become almost an obsession with him.

"So, Mr. Brandon, how do you think Sam Barnett will do in the foster-grandparent program at Children's Orthopedic?"

"Please call me Joshua. Otherwise I will keep looking over my shoulder for my father."

"All right, Joshua."

"I think it was the greatest gift the judicial system could have given the old man," he said sincerely. "I mean that as a personal compliment to you, ah...."

Anna heard the hesitation in his voice. "What's wrong?"

"I can't quite figure out what to call you. Your Honor, Judge Provo and Miss Provo all seem too formal. Spitfire suits you best, but I get the distinct impression you don't appreciate it."

"How about Anna? I think it will solve the problem for both of us, and you're absolutely right about Spitfire. It's not my favorite nickname."

"Well, well, well." Joshua's rich baritone laugh rang out across the bar. "Do you realize that we've finally agreed on something without an argument? That calls for a celebration."

Anna couldn't help chuckling, too. His laugh was pleasant and with the change in mood that settled on the two of them, she felt her spirits soar.

They toasted their first agreement and Joshua took her hand in his. "I have another toast to propose," he said softly. "To a beautiful lady I hope to get to know much better."

Anna felt a tingle spread from her hand to the nape of her neck.

"You realize, Anna, that you are an absolutely ravishing creature, don't you? What nationality do you have to be to get that beautiful red hair?" He let go of her hand and twisted a curl near her temple around his finger.

"Thank you." Anna was flustered and struggled for control. "I'm of Russian descent. My parents came to this country right after World War II."

Against her better judgment, Anna ached for him to kiss her right then and there. She fantasized what he would taste like. Summoning any self-discipline she could muster, she sat back in her chair to gain some distance from him.

"Enough about me." She kept her voice evenly modulated.

"Please," he insisted, "tell me how you chose law as a profession, how you got on the bench so young, how many brothers and sisters are in your family, where your parents live, what kind of music you like, whether you speak any foreign languages, if you're interested in—"

"For heaven's sake! Should we say goodbye right now and I'll go home and write an autobiography?" Anna laughed. "I could fictionalize it, and believe me, it'd be a lot less boring."

"I'm sorry," Joshua said. "I just want to know absolutely everything about you."

"I'm flattered," she demurred. "I'll try to answer your questions if you promise to let me interrogate you."

"Agreed," he said. "Shall we toast to it?" He lifted his mug.

She lightly tapped her tankard against his. "Agreed, but that has to be the last pact. Otherwise we'll be slurring our words and suffering blackouts. Then all this camaraderie will be for naught. We'll have forgotten we buried the hatchet," she teased.

"Agreed," he toasted.

Anna shook her head at his good-natured mockery. "You're incorrigible," she said and hoisted her ale.

"You're right," he laughed. "That's why I have so much empathy with my clients. So how did you get involved with criminals?"

"Well, let's see," she mused. "I don't remember consciously choosing law. I just always wanted to be part of the judicial system." She paused for a second, trying to find the right words to express her commitment to justice. "My parents are immigrants. They love this country and they instilled in me, probably at conception, a great respect for the freedoms America has."

Anna searched Joshua's eyes. He was listening intently. "Corny, isn't it?" she whispered. She felt foolish admitting her obvious sentimentality, her outmoded patriotism.

"Yes—" his lips curved into a soft smile "—and quite enviable."

"Maybe," she hedged. A part of her questioned her motives for choosing law. She suspected that maybe she dove into an almost-male domain to compensate for Niki. Nikolae Alexandrovich Provolosky. . . her retarded brother.

"Maybe," she repeated. "Anyway, I'm not so young to be a judge. I'm thirty and most municipal judges are in their thirties."

"Thirty?" Joshua was surprised. He had thought she was twenty-seven or -eight.

"What's the matter?" Anna was irritated. She thought Joshua perceived her as a middle-aged cast-off.

"Nothing," Joshua raised his hands as if to defend himself. "In fact, I was thinking you're at a perfect age. I've always had a theory that a woman is still an untested child until she's thirty. Then a miracle happens—she blossoms," he said sincerely.

"Truly?"

"Truly," he reassured her. Then he quoted:

> "I am not old, but old enough
> To know that you are very young.
> It might be said I am the leaf,
> And you the blossom newly sprung."

Delighted, Anna applauded his recitation. "You're a renaissance man, Mr. Brandon."

"No," he said seriously, "I'm an anachronism. I should be in the Globe Theatre strutting around in women's clothing and spouting the Bard's lines."

"Why didn't you go into the theater instead of law?" she asked.

"Because," Joshua chuckled, "I'm not a good actor. It's only a fantasy and—" He became somber again. "I'm addicted to certain luxuries and I don't cherish starving in some cold-water flat."

Joshua found himself being more frank with Anna than he felt he should be. He told her that all his life he'd been saddled with guilt about his inherited wealth. Not so guilty he'd misused it, but he had always possessed an uncomfortable awareness that he'd been blessed when many hadn't.

For ten years he'd paid his dues to his family and joined his grandfather's multinational corporation in San Diego. He'd started with a cubicle office in the

law department, worked his way up to a spacious suite
and pleased his grandfather with his legal acumen.
He'd also made and saved his grandfather a lot of
money, which his relative repaid by issuing Joshua
shares in the corporation. To date, Joshua had earned
and now owned a considerable percentage of CAN-
AMER-MEX.

Then Maurice, his younger brother, had finished
law school and entered the ranks of the giant con-
glomerate. He showed a prowess and passion for corporate law. Maurice's enthusiasm gave Joshua his
freedom. He broke the news to his grandfather that he
was quitting and moving back to Seattle to become an
underpaid public defender. His grandfather stormed
and raged about his "altruistic actions," but conceded that Joshua would be happier doing what he
wanted to do.

"You've been competent, damn competent," the
old man had said, "but there's been no joy in it for
you."

His grandfather used the words *altruistic* and *joy* as
if they were dirty expressions. Joshua doubted that his
grandparent had ever really grasped their meanings.
He suddenly looked troubled.

"How long have you been with the public defender's office?" Anna asked, trying to bring Joshua back
from wherever he was. He certainly wasn't with her.

Joshua did a quick double take, yanking himself
back to the present. "Pardon me. What did you ask?"

"How long have you been with the public defender's office?" she repeated.

"A few weeks," he hedged, suddenly not wanting
to talk about himself. Completely changing the sub-

ject, he said, "I have a sailboat. How about crewing for me sometime? Tomorrow after work?"

Again he was pressing for immediate decisions, demanding immediate involvement.

"Sorry, I teach on Tuesdays." Anna was glad to have a real excuse to dodge him. Joshua Brandon was a whirlwind and she instinctively perceived any commitment to him or his life would suck her into a dangerous vortex.

"You teach? Where?" He leaned back in his chair and clasped his hands behind his head.

Anna nibbled her lip debating whether or not to tell him. The conversation was encouraging him to get to know her too well. And that was exactly the opposite of what she wanted.

"You're temporizing," he teased. "Don't tell me you instruct a bunch of housewives how to belly dance?"

Anna exploded. "Yes, that's right, Mr. Brandon. I've spent years in law school so I could bump and grind!"

She expected to him to shrivel in his chair but he didn't. He just continued rocking back and forth with a smirk smeared across his face.

"Spitfire, you need to develop a sense of humor."

"I've told you I despise the name Spitfire."

"How about Tinderbox?"

Anna sputtered incoherently. The gall of the man was unbelievable. Nothing seemed to faze him. She grabbed her purse and started to head home.

Joshua leaped up and caught her arm even though she had quickened her pace.

"Whoa! I was joshing you," he quipped.

Anna stopped, studied the suppressed grin lurking on his face, and finally broke down and laughed at his pun.

"I read once that any man who'd stoop to make a pun wouldn't scruple about picking your pocket," she teased.

Joshua played with the curls that had loosened around her face. "True humor is from the heart. It's not contempt," he explained. "And you're right. I lifted your wallet ten minutes ago."

She laughed and shook her head in disbelief.

Joshua reached out, took her coat and purse and placed them on the bar next to Freddy's cash register. A band had set up and was playing the first tune. It was a slow song that demanded to be danced.

"Come on," he coaxed.

Taking her arm, he guided her onto the floor. He could feel her pliant but firm flesh in his grip. It was as though the only source of warmth in the universe was beneath his fingertips. He yearned to envelop her entire body so he could absorb her vitality, her heat. Gently he encircled her waist, drawing her close. When her thighs lightly brushed against his, he stepped back and imperceptibly loosened his hold. He didn't want to frighten her.

Anna was as skitterish as a kitten. Startle her and she retreated instantly—but not before she took a few swipes with her claws. Yet, like a kitten, she could be enticed to come out and play. Woo her sweetly and he suspected she would eventually curl up in his arms and purr.

He tilted his head close to her hair and inhaled her fragrance. She exuded an aroma of scrubbed soap and water, a lovely relief from the heavy and suffocating perfumes most women wore. She was the personification of natural health and beauty.

Anna found herself to be almost floating. Joshua guided her across the dance floor the way a gentle breeze moves a willow or a chiffon skirt. It was effortless and all her previous anxiety vanished. It was as if he had cast a spell over her and created a whole world that ebbed and flowed in a wispy dream. A dream she wanted to stay in for a long time.

She unconsciously drew closer, wanting to meld with him and prolong the mood. The word *cuddle* came to her mind. Such a nice word, *cuddle*, she mused.

She leaned her head against his broad chest. With each breath he took, Anna was lulled into a feeling of deep peace. Her hand kneaded the muscles of his neck. She wished she could run her fingers along every sinew on his body.

Abruptly, Anna shoved herself away from Joshua. What in the world was she doing? What in the world was happening?

The band was still playing, several more couples had joined them on the floor, but something was terribly wrong. Bright lights were glaring and people were circling the perimeter of the dance area.

"Keep dancing, miss," someone ordered from the darkness beyond the spotlights.

"Hey, it's Anna Provo," another voice said. "You know, the lady judge. Remember, she was nominated for Woman of the Year? We invited all of the candidates to be on one of our shows."

"Yeah. Great shot!" the first voice said. "Don't stop, Your Honor."

Anna was aware that all the customers, including the other dancing couples, were staring at her and Joshua. Summoning as much dignity as she could, she left the floor as quickly as possible. She headed for her purse and coat but Freddy had put them behind the bar for safekeeping.

Joshua was directly behind her. "Freddy, what's going on here?" he asked.

"The band I hired just cut an album that's selling like gang busters all over the country," Freddy explained. "The camera crew and host from the Seattle A.M.' program are here taping for tomorrow's show."

The impropriety of her being shown on television cuddling Joshua hit Anna like a blow.

"Freddy," she pleaded, "they can't use the segment with me in it."

Joshua lightly ran his hand up and down her arm to reassure her. "I'll take care of it."

She followed the trail he made through the spectators and stood by as Joshua tapped the TV host on the shoulder. He was a small man, extremely thin, dressed in finely tailored clothes and meticulously barbered.

"Excuse me," Joshua said. "Judge Provo asks that you edit out the portion of tape with her on it."

"The name's Link Foster," the other man said and extended his hand to Joshua. "What were you saying about the judge?"

"She would like you to edit the tape. Take her out."

"Aw, come on," Link Foster cajoled. "Use a little sugar on her. It's a great piece." He ogled Anna lewdly and then winked at Joshua.

Joshua tightened his jaw. "Cut the con," he

ordered. "She wants it to hit the splicing-room floor."

Link Foster stretched his neck and jutted his chin in a belligerent pose. He looked ridiculous. It was as if he thought the gesture would make him taller, more imposing.

"Who are you, anyway?" he demanded. "Her bailiff?"

In total contrast to the bantam posture of Link Foster, Joshua's mien was that of a puma. Even his golden hair reflected the same coloring in the light as that of a wild mountain lion. His body had a deceiving grace, a relaxed stance that looked as if it hid a powerful ability to pounce.

Anna perceived that Joshua could be dangerous—very dangerous indeed, if angered.

"Listen, you little publicity barker, who I am is unimportant," Joshua intoned in a voice oozing threat. "What I want you to do is vital."

Link Foster blanched. He attempted to mask his intimidation by smiling, but instead it was a weak quivering tremble of the mouth.

"I guess we should work this out," Link conceded, "like gentlemen."

"Then Judge Provo is not a part of your carnival act." Joshua made it clear it wasn't a question but an ultimatum.

"Sure, sure," Link said. "I'd best get back to work." He turned away, obviously relieved.

Anna was aware that the entire pub was quiet. Even the band had stopped playing. The customers were looking at her and Joshua, probably wondering what the hubbub was about.

She let Joshua steer her out of Freddy's and away from the whisperings and mutterings about the two of them.

As they carved a gap in the crowd, Joshua joked, "Think they'd hire us as a team in vaudeville? Let's get out of here and I'll drive you home."

Smarting from the looks thrown at her, Anna just nodded. She was grateful when Joshua held the door open to his car, a restored vintage Jaguar. She slipped in wordlessly.

"Do you remember where you live or do I have to look at your driver's license?" he asked.

"Huh?"

"I guess I could call that talking," he chided.

"Oh, I'm sorry, Joshua," she finally responded. "My address is 1628 Harvard."

"That's better." He brushed her cheek lightly.

As he pulled into traffic, Anna relaxed. The whole incident had been blown out of proportion. There wasn't anything wrong with her dancing or being filmed. What *was* wrong was the scene she felt she had painted. The way she'd danced with Joshua was decidedly too personal for public viewing.

"Maybe I am old-fashioned," she said, "but I don't like being caught off guard."

"Afraid it might jeopardize your Woman of the Year nomination?" Joshua kidded.

"No," she said, laughing. "I lost three months ago."

"That was quite an honor, Your Honor."

"What? That I lost or that I was nominated at all?"

"You're quick. No wonder you are sitting on the

bench at such a tender age. What were you? A legal prodigy? Entered university at twelve and moved on to law school at sixteen?''

"No." She smiled. "I started my freshman year at the university when I was sixteen."

"Precocious and beautiful. Two perfect gifts! That's being blessed twice."

"You make it sound like everything has been handed to me on a platter," she snapped at him. "I've paid my dues. I spent five years in the prosecuting attorney's office." Remarks like Joshua's made her feel like she'd had a free ride. She didn't need the guilt. She had enough when she compared herself with Niki, her brother.

"I've seemed to make a habit of stepping on your feelings," he apologized. "I was simply complimenting you. I was not passing judgment."

He was right, Anna reasoned. She was edgy and defensive and needed a few lessons in diplomacy. "Sorry for snapping at you. It was ungrateful of me after the way you handled Mr. Foster," she said.

"My pleasure." It was apparent he really meant it.

"Aha! I thought I detected a smattering of enjoyment," she teased. "In fact, I sensed a little bully in you."

"Me?" Joshua feigned shock. "There's not an aggressive bone in my body."

Caught up in the bantering spirit, Anna needled, "Yes, I noticed how you begged and pleaded with that TV mogul." She giggled and the sound startled her. She hadn't giggled since she was about thirteen. Joshua's humor soothed her mortification and brought out the little girl in her.

He reached over, rumpled her hair and it fell from its chignon to her shoulders.

"You're loosening up, Spitfire," he said, and he laughed a deep rumbling laugh.

"What happened to curmudgeon?" she asked. "What inspired you to call me that before you ever set eyes on me?"

"I was hoping you'd forgotten," he blanched. "I was the brunt of an office joke. You know, new kid on the block. First case in court. It was a kind of professional hazing."

"Hazing?"

"Yeah, initiation by humiliation. All the guys in the public defender's office set me up," he explained. "Told me I was getting an ugly, fat and vile old sow who ate public defenders for lunch."

"Didn't miss by much, did they?" She laughed convulsively.

"They were about as close as this planet is to Saturn," he said.

The rain started the same second Joshua parked his car and turned off the engine. Unlike the light drizzle Seattle generally gets, the precipitation was a deluge.

They dashed up the sidewalk arm in arm to her condominium. Her unit occupied half the ground floor of a converted Victorian mansion. Wet and giddy, Anna rummaged through her purse for keys. She opened the door, turned to thank him, and caught an expectant look in his eyes.

"Would you like some coffee?" she asked.

Joshua said nothing. He tenderly cupped her chin with his hand and lifted her face. With his other hand he wiped the beads of rain from her cheeks, her forehead, her nose.

Anna felt a clenching desire rise from her chest and she moved closer to him. She silently begged him to consume her.

Joshua quickly reached out and pulled her body up against his. He gently nibbled her neck and slowly worked his way up to a sensitive spot behind her ear. With infinite patience, he traced each curve of her cheeks with his mouth and Anna's knees weakened. He grabbed her firmly, nearly lifting her off the ground, and smothered her lips with his. His beseeching fingers played a provocative pattern up and down her spine, sending small tremors through her. He forced her mouth open and teased her until she thought she'd perish unless he carried her to bed.

"I want you," he groaned. His breathing betrayed the pitch of his passion.

Anna didn't speak. Her desire was so high in her throat there was no room for words. She simply stepped back and took his hand to lead him inside.

A flash of lightning nearly blinded her and almost immediately thunder rolled and roared, rattling the building.

Niki! What about Niki? He would be hiding under the blankets in terror. He hated storms.

And Sean! Hadn't she learned not to become seriously involved? Of course there had been other men in her life since Sean, but they'd all been mild romantic contacts. The rules had been established. She had her career, her commitments. They'd had their professions, their distractions.

But this man, she perceived, would want all or

nothing. Total possession. Or was she reading him wrong? Was she throwing herself at him without setting the same ground rules she'd been using since Sean?

Confused, she released Joshua and forgot her hunger. She couldn't get entangled with him. There was something happening to her she didn't understand. Something she was afraid of.

"I'm sorry," she choked. "I thought I wanted you but I was only kidding myself. This is all a mistake."

She attempted to close the door on him but Joshua put his hand out and stopped it.

"What mistake?" he demanded. "I've never felt anything was so right in my entire life!"

"Well it's not right for me," she yelled back and forced the door closed. She locked it as Joshua pounded.

"Let's talk about it," he stormed.

"No, go away. Just go away," she ordered.

The pounding stopped and she thought she heard his car roar off into the night.

Anna fought back the tears of frustration welling up within her. Desire had almost overcome her common sense. How could one man create such havoc in her life? But hadn't she encouraged the wrecking ball named Joshua Brandon in his virile attempt to smash down her carefully constructed barriers?

Her honest answer was "Yes. Yes. Yes."

With her back pressed against the door, she felt it being hammered on again. Yells of "Anna! Anna!" were nearly buried in a roll of thunder.

Joshua? He was back. He wasn't going to leave without an explanation! He felt it, too. They had to talk.

And suddenly she wanted to talk. More than anything else, she wanted to explain her wild hysteria. She wanted to define her fears to him. Maybe he had some magic solutions that would dissolve her anxieties. Anxieties that encompassed her fears, her conflicts, her doubts, her...what? Mostly her life with Niki. She needed to talk about Niki.

She struggled with the lock, trying to get the door open before Joshua changed his mind. She ended up bungling the latch in her haste. Finally, she swung the door wide.

"I lost my key," her brother said.

Anna stared at him as though she'd never seen him before. Instead of Joshua hammering to be let into her life it was Niki—wet, bedraggled, confused and begging to be taken care of once more.

"Come in, Nikolae," she whispered. She took his cold hand and led him in out of the rain. "You'll catch cold."

Nikolae towered in the doorway. His head barely cleared the opening. He was a giant of a man with thick black hair matted by the rain, a swarthy olive complexion over high classical cheekbones and a patrician nose.

He looked like a Slavic god, reminding Anna once more how often society had a misconception about the retarded. The stereotype that brain damage was always apparent in physical defects was false. Niki was physically perfect. In fact, he was stunning.

She pulled a towel out of the hall linen closet and told him to sit down. "I'll dry you off," she said, noticing his wet cheeks.

He obeyed dutifully. "It's only rain, Anna," he

said. "I haven't been bawling like a baby 'cause I got a little scared."

Anna rubbed his head and face briskly. "Of course not," she said, knowing if she tasted the water on his cheeks it'd be salty. "It's been raining cats and dogs."

Niki grabbed her wrists and stopped her toweling. "How come they say that?" he asked. "All my life they say that, but no matter how many times I look, I never see any cats and dogs falling out of the sky."

She hugged his head to her chest and laughed softly and sweetly. "It's just an expression meaning *hard*," she explained.

"Well, it's a dumb expression," he mumbled, "'cause I keep looking for the dogs and cats."

She let go of him and tossed him the towel. "Here, go take a hot shower, get your pajamas on and I'll call mama and papa. You can spend the night here."

Niki started down the hall but halted. Turning, he said, "I brought you a present." He reached inside his jacket and threw her a small plastic egg.

She caught it deftly and he left. She opened it. The present was a cheap vending-machine capsule, and inside was a warped little ring with a lopsided green stone glued to the top. Niki plied coin after coin into the machines, hoping to get some special little treasure that pleased him. It was another typically childish gift from her thirty-two-year-old brother.

She put the ring on the mantel and called her parents.

"Hi, mama," she said. "Niki's here so don't fret."

"That boy," her mother clucked. "He's going to give me gray hair."

"Mama!" Anna laughed. "Your hair is already gray."

"That's right," she retorted, "and every one he painted."

Anna knew her mother was joking but what she said was true. Niki worried his mother and she was getting too old to be constantly agonizing over him. Anna had tried to take up the slack. More and more Niki stayed with her overnight. Bit by bit he'd moved some of his clothing and his precious possessions into the spare bedroom. Day by day he transferred more of himself into Anna's world. The slow move had taken the burden off her aging parents.

"Kiss him good night," mama ordered, "tuck him in tight and tell him to be on time for work."

"I will," Anna promised. "I will."

"Anna?"

"Yes, mama?"

"Papa and I love you." She hung up before Anna could respond.

ANNA FOUND NIKI snuggled into bed, sound asleep. Anna straightened the covers, folded his clothes and turned out the light.

She tucked herself into bed, ordered sleep to descend and tried to obliterate her feelings. But sleep escaped her and her confused emotions ran rampant.

Earlier she'd been willing, even anxious to talk to Joshua about Niki, about everything. But Joshua hadn't come back. She'd frightened him away and, even if she could find him, she was at a loss to explain her situation. The need to talk was lost under the tangle of her responsibilities. How could she ever make clear the twisted maze of duty she had to her family?

CHAPTER FOUR

ALL NIGHT LONG the storm raged outside but Anna's turmoil within was the greater. Memories came back and haunted her and any snatches of sleep she caught were marred as she relived Sean's rejection.

In the last weeks of their relationship he had continued to stress the issue of having a family. She had been forced to dismantle her guard and expose her fear.

"Listen to me, Sean," she had demanded. "Really listen."

Then Anna had listed the myriad problems associated with raising a retarded child. She'd recounted some of the troubles her brother had unwittingly caused and the agony her parents had endured.

"I'm just too afraid," she told Sean. "I couldn't handle another Niki. That's why I don't want any children. What if we find out Niki's retardation is inherited?"

She'd kept her head down during her speech but raised her eyes to assess Sean's reaction.

Her instincts had been right. The extreme distaste of such a life was clearly displayed on his face.

"I never thought about it, Anna" was his only answer. He seemed to be in a daze. He'd never been comfortable with Niki and Anna had gone to great lengths to keep them apart. For the first time it was dawning on him that Niki would be a part of his family—and worse—that his perfect family might, just might, include a daughter or son who was flawed! "I've never thought about it," he repeated.

"Well, I have," Anna responded.

Just as she both feared and predicted, Sean eased himself out of their relationship. He had tried to make it appear as if nothing had changed, but his phone calls became less frequent and his excuses of being busy more obvious. By the end of summer he had accepted a spot at Harvard's Law School and had moved out of her life completely.

Niki blasted the cartoons on the TV and snapped Anna out of her discordant reverie. She lay in bed exhausted. There would be no jog this morning. It would take all the strength she could muster to drive herself to work.

Only a few weeks ago she'd been content, if not happy, with her life. Then Joshua Brandon had come crashing into it and her neatly constructed world was knocked askew. Here was a man who was ruggedly attractive, witty, persistent and wonderfully vigorous. Yet there was no way she could become involved with him. She couldn't forget that the past wasn't a bad witness. She had nearly lost sight of that on the porch.

Over and over she relived last night. The desperate clinging to each other, the erotic caresses, the hot demanding kisses, and Joshua's cry, "I want you!"

Anna sat up abruptly. Joshua hadn't said anything about caring! He'd only said he wanted her. She'd mistaken lust for affection. What a fool she'd been.

Realizing her error, she sprang out of bed indignantly. A rage swept through her like wildfire.

"How dare he presume I could be used? How dare he woo and humor me just to play with me?" she ranted to the wallpaper.

Abruptly her fury died. "How?" she asked meekly. "Easy. I gazed into his eyes and said, 'Come take me, I'm yours.' What full-blooded man wouldn't take advantage of a stupid woman like that?"

Sheepishly, Anna looked at herself in the full-length mirror and said, "You asked for it, stupid, so stop your caterwauling."

"Where?" Niki asked. He'd come into her room unnoticed with a glass of orange juice for her. "Where?"

"What?" Anna was confused.

"Where's the cat on the wall?" Niki asked, searching every inch of her room. He lifted a curtain and peeked behind it.

"There's no cat. I was using an expression," she snapped at him irritably.

"You and your dumb talking," he said, and plopped her juice glass on the chest of drawers angrily. "Why don't you stop calling me stupid? You're stupid!"

He marched out of the room in a huff before Anna could explain she hadn't been talking to him or about him. Poor Niki. She'd offended him. She certainly hadn't meant to. But wasn't that about par? Didn't she always manage to mess things up?

Disgusted with herself, she showered and dressed perfunctorily. Niki, Sean, Joshua, her own outrageous behavior were forcibly shuttled aside. This was just another day and she was going to go on with her life as if nothing had shaken it. At least there was little chance that Joshua Brandon would ever give her a second thought. After last night he'd never want to cross her hysterical path again.

Anna made Niki a large breakfast to compensate for their misunderstanding. She watched him heap the strawberry jam into his glass of hot tea. He drank the brew in the Russian manner and scoffed at her drinking it in a china cup, black and undoctored.

His colossal hands cradled the glass and she smiled at the image. The giant with his sweet tooth.

"Anna—" Niki looked at her with adoring eyes "—how come you never get scared?"

The question jolted her. How could she explain to him that she was often frightened? Especially of the vague, the unknown.

"I do," she answered.

"Not like me and you're only a girl," he differed. "I'm not talking about storms and mean dogs and things like that."

"Like what, then?"

"Like not knowing the answer to a question that somebody asks," he explained. "Baby things. Like never being sure I counted my money right for the bus or a hamburger."

"Well...." Anna chose her words carefully. She never talked down to Niki but thought out her answers so they would be sensible, sensitive and, above all, truthful. "Well, I worry about other things. People are different. We're not made alike."

"What things?"

"Oh, doing my jobs well. Like preparing good lessons for my class. People ask me questions, too, and I don't always have the right answers."

"Aw, come on, Anna." He chuckled. "You never get the mixed-ups."

She smiled at him and then rumpled his hair. "Oh yes, I do, big brother. I get mixed up all the time."

This morning was a perfect example. She didn't know where north or south was. Would she ever get her bearings again?

She whisked Niki out the door and off to work at the Pike Street Market where their parents had a shop. While she loaded the dishwasher, she thought about Joshua but came up with no answer, except that she'd made an idiot of herself by jumping to all sorts of irrational conclusions about his intentions.

Sighing deeply, she closed the door to her condo and closed the door on her tumultuous interlude with Mr. Brandon. She had her equilibrium back and that was all that counted.

At work, mayhem struck the courthouse. One of the trials down the hall from Anna's courtroom had become a battleground. A felon's brother had smuggled in a weapon and held the bailiff hostage for an hour until a release was made. The entire judicial system came to a halt until order was restored.

By the end of the day, Anna felt wrung out. Violence in the courts was happening too frequently. No judge or court officer was sure whether or not he would be the next victim.

Drawing on her reserves, she found a smattering of energy left inside and threw off her robes. Slowly she stood and got ready to go to the class she taught on litigation for the paralegal program. This was her first quarter of teaching and she was pleasantly surprised at how rewarding it was. She needed something gratifying to offset her fatigue.

Tonight Tom Randolph was a guest speaker for the first half of her class and she wanted to be there early to meet him. He'd been flattered when she'd asked him to speak to her students about the responsibilities of the prosecuting attorney's office and how he approached a case.

Ten minutes later, Anna skillfully maneuvered Elizabeth, her aging Volkswagen, through the heavy downtown traffic on First Hill. As she stopped for a light, Elizabeth wheezed and spewed forth a belch of black smoke. Anna knew she should retire her dilapidated car but found herself unwilling to part with the relic. Elizabeth had served her well for more than ten years and she was attached to the beat-up old girl.

Anna parked in the faculty lot and spotted Tom patiently waiting for her in his car. Forcing a bounce into her walk, she went to greet him.

She saw that Sue, Tom's wife, had probably convinced him to don more traditional attorney's attire than he would be inclined to wear if left to his own preferences. It had been almost twenty years since she'd first met Tom in junior-high school, and he'd been a precious friend ever since. He deserved the happiness he found with Sue. They made the perfect couple. Anna occasionally discovered she was smitten with twinges of jealousy when she compared her sterile life to their chaotic but vibrant one.

Tom gave her a warm hug and asked, "How are you? I heard about this afternoon."

She squeezed him back. "Just fine."

"Sure you're up to this tonight? You could cancel," he advised.

"No, no. Besides, when could I ever catch you on the run again?"

"Okay. Do I pass inspection?" He pirouetted in front of her.

"Smashing. Sue does a good job picking out your clothes."

"Thanks a lot, but what makes you think she picked this out?"

"As fashion-unconscious as you are, you'd never manage to look this good on your own. Right?"

Laughing, Tom conceded, "Right."

"Well, handsome, let's go have a cup of coffee and catch up on some gossip. We've got twenty minutes before class."

"Sounds great. Lead on."

While they chatted about Sue and Tom's one- and two-year-old children, Anna remembered the picture Niki had made for Sue. Last week the Randolphs had invited the entire Provolosky family over for a barbecue. Niki had thoroughly enjoyed the afternoon. He was fascinated by the toddlers and spent hours patiently building block towers, which they loved to smash to the ground. Niki showed an uncanny understanding of young children.

In honor of the occasion and the great fun he'd had, Niki had painstakingly created a penny print from the hand-carved wooden blocks papa used. He'd applied bright colorful inks to depict a scene of Tom and Sue playing with the kids. It was Niki's way of saying thank you. As an artist herself, Sue encouraged Niki's creativity and had prominently displayed some of his other works in her studio.

"Here, Niki made this for you and Sue. I promised to deliver it tonight."

A wide grin broke across Tom's face as he inspected the handbill.

"Tell him thanks and that Sue will love it. He's one of our favorite people."

"Hey, it's time to scoot," she said, noticing the time. "It doesn't look good for the teacher to be late."

He followed her to the classroom and waited for her to take roll call. He was flattered by the glowing but brief biography of himself she delivered. After asking the students to welcome him, she handed the class over to Tom.

"I'm going to attempt," Tom began, "to explain the system the...."

Anna heard the door open and looked up to see who was slipping in late. She was flabbergasted when Joshua slid into a desk chair at the rear of the class. What was he doing here?

Whatever it was, she would set him straight during the break. School policy forbade unauthorized visitors auditing classes. He would simply have to leave.

Without glancing up, Joshua took a notebook from his pocket and began taking notes, acting just like any attentive student. His face was expressionless. Anna couldn't figure out whether he was taunting her, badgering her, or trying to prove some obscure personal point.

She continued to stare at him until she realized several students were watching her with puzzled faces. They obviously couldn't understand why she was so preoccupied with the man in the back of the room. To avoid drawing further attention to herself, Anna gave her full consideration to Tom's lecture.

She kept her eyes forward and for the remainder of the hour never looked at Joshua. Yet she could sense when his eyes were on her. It was as if his gaze alone generated an energy. Was it the warmth of affection? Or, more likely, was he boring holes through her with fury? No matter what it was, she would have to confront him soon. Anna returned her attention to Tom.

"And I would like to thank you for the pleasure of being here tonight," her guest speaker concluded. He was answered by a short round of applause. Anna rose, thanked him and faced the class.

"Now is a good time to take a fifteen-minute break," she announced. "Mr. Brandon, would you please see me about your enrollment?"

"Certainly, Miss Provo. Is right now convenient?"

"Fine," she answered brusquely.

He slowly wove his way through the crowd and she noticed how his light blue shirt accentuated his shoulders. It was unbuttoned at the collar and she noticed for the first time that he wore a miniature gold sextant on a heavy chain around his neck. The gold stood out next to his tan.

"Well, good night, Anna. You have a great group of students here. Keep up the good work," Tom patted her arm.

His patronizing comment and attempt at a swift departure caused her to grab his sleeve. "You're not going anywhere," she hissed through clenched teeth, hoping no one could hear or detect the quaver in her voice. "The only place you're going is to have coffee with me."

She required a good excuse to avoid being left alone with Joshua. And Tom provided an excellent one.

"You wanted to speak to me, Miss Provo?" Joshua's voice didn't even hint that there might be some intimacy between them.

Primly she said, "Yes, Mr. Brandon. Exactly what are you doing in this class? The school policy specifically states there shall be no unauthorized visitors."

"But, I'm not unauthorized. I'm auditing and the dean's office knows all about it. I've filled out the appropriate forms and therefore I'm in complete accordance with the rules." He tipped his index finger toward his own chest, indicating that he scored this round for himself. "Any further questions, Miss Provo?"

Anna seldom found herself at a loss for words, but this man was making a habit of leaving her speechless. It appeared that Joshua was intending to hound her for whatever obscure reason.

"Good. Would you join me for a cup of coffee?" he asked.

"I, uh, promised to show Tom the way to the cafeteria," she stammered. "Maybe some other time."

Usually Tom covered for her, but he ignored her unspoken message.

"Hey, no problem," Tom said. "Let's all go together. My mouth is dry. Guess I talked too much."

Tom headed off to search for something to quench

his thirst. Anna noticed that Joshua didn't seem too pleased by Tom's presence, but he didn't decline the invitation or voice any protest. Realizing there was no way out, she hurried to catch up with Tom. At this precise moment, she would have gladly strangled both of them and had her coffee alone.

After searching for a vacant table in the packed cafeteria, Anna found herself wedged between the two men. An uncomfortable silence descended on them.

Tom broke it and said, "I forgot to ask you, Anna, how's that bailiff doing?"

"He's fine," she answered. "He's a little shaken, but he promises to be back on the job again tomorrow."

"Incidents like that one," Joshua added, his face reflecting the frustration and anger most lawyers feel over the absence of courtroom security, "prove we need more protection."

"The man was taken into custody," Anna said.

"What's going to be done," Tom argued, "about these instances where relatives, girlfriends or boyfriends smuggle in weapons?"

"We've got to increase the protection somehow," Joshua said.

"Enough shoptalk," Anna interrupted, visibly paling. "I hope it never happens again."

"That's the whole point, Anna," Joshua insisted. "As officers of the court we all need to join forces and demand better security measures so this type of menace can be eliminated."

"Hey," Tom said, "why don't we follow through on this? Let's get a bunch of us together and form a task force."

"Great," Anna agreed, "but the break is almost over, Tom, and I have something I'd like to settle with Mr. Brandon. Exactly why are you auditing my class?"

She'd hoped to phrase her question a little more delicately, but her words had just popped out.

Joshua locked her gaze and said quietly, "I've always found that education is never wasted. If a certain subject eludes you, you find a way to capture it and study it more carefully. Also, if you don't understand something you feel frightened by it, but exposure to the subject brings understanding and then the fear is gone."

"I hadn't realized that as a lawyer you had such trouble understanding a basic subject like litigation," she said sarcastically.

"I don't recall saying litigation was the subject I came here to study."

His remark surprised her so much she choked on her coffee. Tom clapped her between the shoulder blades.

"Are you okay?" Tom asked.

"Yes, yes, I'm fine. I just swallowed wrong."

"Have you found some moorage for your sailboat? The last time we talked you were still on a waiting list," Tom inquired. His question gave Anna time to regain her composure.

Joshua grinned. "Yes, I have, at Shilshole Marina. Now I'm working on it and it provides me with a soothing release from the pressures our profession imposes. How do you cope?"

Tom whipped out his trusty supply of snapshots and proceeded to brag about his children. He inadvertently brought out Niki's penny print and it fluttered to the floor.

Joshua picked it up. "You dropped this," he said as he glanced at the crude design. "Aren't your kids a little young to be doing this?"

"Yes, but this is from a special friend of mine. In fact, he's Anna's brother," Tom explained.

Anna kicked Tom under the table, warning him not to say anything more. His intentions were well meant but she didn't want him to go into any lengthy explanation about Niki. She didn't feel that she knew Joshua well enough. She couldn't bear to hear any of the glib condescending comments that she was sure he would offer.

"It's time to start class," she said abruptly and rose. Panic seized her as she walked briskly from the cafeteria, and her stomach performed a pagan dance making her nauseous. These two were hitting it off like long-lost pals. It was bad enough that she was stuck with Joshua for a whole quarter, but she didn't need Tom including him in their circle.

"Hey, wait up," Tom called as he ran after her. He caught her by the arm and steered her into a quiet corner. "Why so huffy? Is it me?"

Instantly contrite, she said, "No, Tom, it's not you." The last thing she wanted to do was alienate him.

"Him?" Tom jabbed his thumb toward Joshua, who was still sitting at the table. "Why are you steamed at him? He didn't say anything. In fact, I would say he was smitten with you."

"Tom," Anna placed her finger against her lips, signaling him to be quiet. "I hardly know the man."

"Don't be coy," he said. "He hasn't taken his eyes off you all night."

"You're letting your imagination go bananas."

"Now you're being defensive," Tom said. "Listen, you spend too much time by yourself and with Niki. Why don't you give the guy a chance?"

"If I choose to get involved with a man, it won't be Joshua Brandon," she snapped.

"Why?" Tom chuckled. "Still carrying a chip on your shoulder about the scene on the courthouse steps?"

Lowering her voice, Anna asked, "How did you hear about that?"

"Hear about it?" Tom smiled. "Joshua told me. He felt like an idiot and asked me how he could go about mending things with you. I told him that I knew you'd never hold it against him."

How could she explain it was something personal between Joshua and herself? She couldn't.

So she offered a lame excuse. "What makes you so cocksure I'm that forgiving?"

"Aw, come on, Anna, I thought I knew you better than that. You're a pro and a pro distinguishes between the job and private life."

"I realize that."

"Then bury the hatchet. Joshua seems like a nice guy. No, a great guy. Why not at least be friends with him?"

"Friends?" She hadn't even considered the concept. She'd thought of him as either an irritant or a lover. Nothing in between.

"Yeah, friends. You have so many you don't need to cultivate another one?" he accused cruelly.

"What's *that* supposed to mean?"

"It means you've become reclusive. You've buried yourself in black robes and musty old law books."

Tom was painting an ugly picture. By making a friend of Joshua would the picture be any prettier? There was no argument that she was isolated. But would Joshua be willing to keep the relationship on a platonic level?

She'd have to make him understand that was all she could handle. After all, what choice did she have? Their paths were destined to cross again and she couldn't battle him at every junction. Tom was right.

"Okay, I'll clean up my act and be buddy buddy with Mr. Brandon," she said.

Tom enveloped her in his arms and squeezed her. "Good. Sorry about being so rough. I know you've had a hell of a day, but you're letting your career sabotage your private life." He kissed her on the forehead. "I've got to go and so do you."

Anna glimpsed Joshua over Tom's shoulder as her friend squeezed her one more time. Joshua was watching them and he didn't look pleased. Hastily, he stood and brushed past them to class.

Joshua folded his long legs up to cram them into the confining space beneath the desk and prepared to listen to Anna's lecture for the next hour and a half. When the rest of the students had taken their places, she began her detailed lesson on depositions and interrogatories. Joshua was instantly impressed with how well she translated the technical aspects of discovery procedures into layman's terms.

Anna was not the type of woman he was normally

attracted to, but he found her trim athletic body a refreshing contrast to the model-slim women he usually dated. Nor did Anna Provo exhibit the same placid temperament he was used to. She was an exhilarating lady!

His life had been dotted with women, but they had been unnecessary to his happiness. They'd been a lovely distraction, but none had held his interest for long. If there was one flaw he could name that had consistently made him reject a lady, it was a clinging dependent nature.

He could never accuse Anna Provo of hanging on him. He was lucky if she even gave a damn if he existed or not.

Sitting up straight in his seat, Joshua halted his musing. She'd probably call on him to see if he was paying attention. It would be like her to try to shame him in front of the other students. He wouldn't give her the satisfaction.

Anna finished the remainder of the evening calmly and with a degree of poise. Fortunately, she had planned her lecture well and was familiar with the material. It kept her from floundering and masked her exhaustion.

The room swiftly emptied and she thought she was alone. She gathered her things in slow motion. The drain of the past twenty-four hours had taken its toll.

When a callused hand reached out and took her wrist, she hardly even reacted. Her hand was lifted off her books then released.

"You're beat," Joshua said kindly. "I'll carry these to the car for you."

He bent over, stacked them in his arms, then looked

her directly in the face. His eyes, whirlpools of blue, held hers.

"You should've cancelled tonight," he said as he reached out and put his arm around her back.

His eyes haunted her. They were pools threatening to draw her into their depths. They were dangerous and she broke off looking into them directly.

"Thanks, Joshua, but I can make it." She knew she didn't sound convincing.

Propelling her along, he argued, "No, it's late and there won't be many people strolling around. It's not safe."

"I'm entirely capable of getting myself to my car."

"I'll escort you regardless of how self-reliant you are."

"I wish you wouldn't," she said, shrugging his arm off. She couldn't afford to be indebted or dependent on this man. The price might mean too much.

"Listen, this isn't a good area and I don't want you to be someone's unwilling victim."

"Why not? I am already."

"What do you mean by that remark?"

"Just exactly what I said. I'm the unwilling victim of your pursuit."

Joshua stepped in front to block her. "Hold it a minute. You gave me every reason to believe you were very interested in me. Then poof, you disappear. What's going on? Is it an amusing game you play with people's emotions? Hot, cold, hot, cold? Why not fill me in on the ground rules and maybe I can play the game, too?"

"This is no game," she insisted. "I don't need some romantic panting behind me."

"You were the one panting last night, lady."

Anna swung her arm to slap him in the face but he caught it in midair. "Uh, uh, that's not ladylike," he growled.

She tried to wrench free but his grip was like steel. He held her arm for a second longer then bent and lowered it behind her back. She was pinned next to him and he clamped her body to his like a vise. Unable to struggle, he gently kissed her, nibbling at her lips, flicking his tongue lightly on the soft skin inside her mouth. He nudged her lips further open and traced her warm moist recesses, and she responded by probing and exploring his.

Breathless, he pulled away and whispered, "Tell me again how you don't feel it."

There was no denying she wanted him. Her whole being reacted to his power.

"Y-yes," she stuttered, "I feel it. But I already have enough commitments."

Joshua released her abruptly. "Is Tom one? You two seemed pretty cozy in the cafeteria."

Anna laughed. "If I weren't so tired, I'd be angry at your cheap innuendo. Tom is an old and dear friend. Period." She tensed, remembering Tom's advice. Fencing with Joshua was no way to deflect his pursuit and turn it into a friendship. "I could always use another. Are you interested?"

She became uncomfortable as he stared at her silently. Now that she had defined the boundaries of their relationship, she was worried he'd reject the proposal. But friendship was all she could offer.

Joshua tried to determine what lay behind her suggestion. "Of course I want to be friends with you.

But I want more. So do you! So why the denial? What's with you?''

"That's not an answer," Anna accused. "That's a battery of questions."

He stood quietly studying her. Here was the skitterish kitten again. She'd just swiped at him with her claws and now she was demanding a bosom-pal détente.

This was not just another woman to be trifled with. She was different. With each passing moment, he became more deeply certain of that fact. But was she worth it? Maybe. For now, he'd accept her offer. What option did he have?

Joshua's prolonged silence led Anna to believe that Tom's suggestion was a waste of time.

"Well," she quietly said, "I guess I have my answer." She took her things from him, turned out the lights and headed out the door before she made an even bigger fool of herself.

"Wait," he hollered from the dark. "I didn't give you my answer." He banged into a desk trying to catch her. "I took a few minutes to consider whether I could keep my hands off you." He caught up with her and took the load of books out of her arms again. "But you win. If the only way I can get close to you is as a friend, I'll accept your terms for now. I'll warn you first if I want the rules amended. Sound fair?"

Weighing his frank statement, she finally said, "Fair." She stood still briefly, unable to look at him. She'd both won and lost something. "Let's get out of here."

Unlocking Elizabeth and placing her things in the back seat, she realized Joshua had been right. The dark parking lot was empty except for her car and his. She was grateful he'd be walking with her after each class.

"Thanks for the escort," she said, getting in and revving the motor. The acrid smell of exhaust wafted over Joshua, causing him to cough.

"I see you're into antique cars, too," he teased.

Anna eyed his sleek Jaguar and said, "There's a difference between antiques and junk."

"I just spent some time and money restoring mine. You could do the same for your Bug."

"I've never considered restoration. Everyone just nags me to scrap her. I should fix her up and keep her to be ornery and spite them."

"Tell you what—" Joshua leaned on her window "—I'll pick you up after work one night later this week and take you to a special place on Vashon Island. A man I know owns an auto shop there. He did my work. I'll call Martin and see what his work load is like."

Anna wasn't sure. Going to Vashon would make the third night she'd spent with Joshua. Could the relationship stay on a platonic level with so much exposure? He'd given his word, so why not? Besides, rehabilitating Elizabeth would be a joy.

"Perfect," she agreed. "I can't say exactly what evening would be best. Why don't you leave a message with my secretary and I'll get back to you? We can work out the logistics then."

"Fine." He straightened and took two steps but came back to her open window. "Sleep tight, *pal*," he said, then chucked her under the chin. He smiled impishly, his dimples like parenthesis.

Before she could say anything, he sprinted to his car and was out of earshot. She ran her knuckles across the spot he'd touched. Pals? Well, it was certainly preferable to being lovers. Or was it?

CHAPTER FIVE

AFTER RUNNING an extra mile, Anna still found herself brimming with energy. The waterfront had been particularly lovely this morning. When she was jogging along Pier 62, she'd stopped to watch the fireboats practice their drills. They sprayed giant plumes of water into the air, dousing imaginary dock and shipboard blazes. Their arching streams created crystalline droplets, giving the air a pure clean quality.

The streets were fresh with no litter marring their surfaces. The crowds of tourists hadn't appeared yet. So the steady pace she liked to keep was not interrupted by the browsing hordes that were attracted to the colorful waterfront.

Just before she turned up Marion Street to the courthouse, she caught a glimpse of the ferry, *Hyak*, cruising across Elliott Bay, and she smiled. She was eager for tonight when she'd climb aboard one of those lumbering vessels with Joshua.

Panting a little, Anna bounded into Miriam's office and cheerfully said, "Good morning."

"Good morning, Anna. You certainly have sounded happier these past few days than you have in ages," Miriam remarked. "I'll bet it has something to do with the surprise sitting on your desk."

"What?"

"Go look for yourself."

Anna quickly opened her chamber door and there on her desk was a huge wicker basket full of shiny red apples. Pinned to a plaid bow on the handle was a note. She grabbed it and ripped open the envelope. Inside was a small card.

Charming women can true converts make,
We love the precepts for the teacher's sake.

George Farquhar

This quote has been running through my head.
Call me at 555-6111 at noon!

Joshua

Anna rubbed an apple on her sleeve, polishing it. It glistened like a huge ruby and she bit into its juicy meat. At that minute, life seemed just as nice, just as sweet.

Munching on the crisp fruit, she marched off to shower and prepare herself for another busy day. Instead of just hurriedly cleansing herself, she took special pains with her grooming. She hauled out her French-milled soap and carefully scrubbed her skin until it tingled.

After applying her makeup, she stepped back to admire her handiwork. She was appalled at the painted face that glared back at her. A solitary groan escaped. That wasn't Anna Provo in the mirror but someone she hadn't seen before and no one she ever wanted to meet again. Snatching up a damp washcloth, she furiously scrubbed all the painstakingly applied cosmetics from her face. Then she reapplied her usual light touches of blush and lip gloss and smiled.

Momentarily she considered how flattering it would be if Joshua really found her attractive, but she dismissed the thought. Friendship wasn't supposed to be based on physical appeal. Wasn't she trying to put a stop to their sexual attraction?

A maelstrom of conflicting emotions swirled in her heart. Could she be just good friends with Joshua? What about those broad shoulders of his? His lingering kisses? His inviting arms?

For several minutes she wallowed in a world of seething desire. Wouldn't it be lovely if he found nothing in her life that he couldn't deal with easily? Wouldn't it be wonderful if he was capable of accepting her limitations? Wouldn't it be marvelous if. . .if what?

Anna thought of her limitations. She believed she was inadequate outside of anything but law. Who wanted a woman who wouldn't have children? Who could deal with her hot temper, her single-mindedness about her family and career? It was unreasonable to expect anyone to tolerate her lack of maternal instincts, her busy schedule. What man would put up with being wedged into her busy life?

She realized she was dreaming and goaded herself back to reality. If she didn't hurry, she'd be late. Slapping her hair into a neat bun, she left her chambers.

Her schedule for the rest of the day would run typically. New cases, old paperwork, pleas, objections, clarifications, overrulings, instructions, evidence introduced, statements withdrawn, decisions, considerations, warnings and finally sentences to be handed down. By five o'clock, she'd be ready to flee.

LESS THAN A MILE AWAY, Joshua bounded into his office, jerked the phone up and impatiently barked, "Hello."

"Well, hello to you, too," came a raspy reply.

Instantly, Joshua recognized the voice. "Sorry, Douglas. Didn't mean to bite your head off."

"I should hope not. I was goin' to invite you to lunch today but I don't know now. Think you could be civil?" Joshua's friend's voice was tinged with humor.

"Promise I'll do better, if you're buying," Joshua agreed.

"Fine, son. What's a good time for you?"

"Come check out my new cubbyhole at eleven forty-five. It's in the Smith Tower."

He gave Douglas exact directions and then carefully replaced the receiver.

Swiveling around in his chair, Joshua basked in the morning sun streaming through the window and absently ran his hand through his tousled hair. He had sent Anna the basket of apples, but would she phone? The time was going to drag, waiting for her call. But the prospect of seeing his oldest friend, Douglas, brightened Joshua's mood considerably, and he forced his mind back to the myriad of tasks crying for attention.

Joshua's first and foremost concern was to corral his investigative intern, Tiffany, and go over the new cases that had been assigned to him. He needed to review one in particular and get her to deliver a subpoena. Joshua would be underpaid as an attorney with the public defender's office, but he could already see the work was going to be much more rewarding than the corporate law he'd been practicing.

Joshua heard someone typing in the next office and the noise pulled him out of his conjecturing and into the present. With a shake of his head, he forced himself to get to work.

After calling Tiffany into his office, he went over three new cases that had been handed to him and outlined the approach he was going to take. He gave her the subpoena and instructed her to check the records on yet another client to see if he had any prior arrests or convictions. Tiffany was a young and eager paralegal who was helping out at the public defender's on a work-study program. Her skills were limited, but with his huge case load, he knew he'd be able to keep her busy researching, running errands, filing petitions and interviewing witnesses. It would relieve him of the many necessary but time-consuming and mundane activities that are part of criminal law practice.

The morning whisked by and before Joshua was aware of it, a wizened man strode into his office. Surprised to see Douglas so soon, Joshua glanced at the clock and said, "Eleven forty-five already?"

"Just a-fritterin' your time away, eh?" Douglas teased in a rich brogue. Born in Ulster, his voice had a distinctive lilt.

"I guess. I can hardly believe the whole morning's gone," Joshua said.

There was so much to tell Douglas that Joshua hopscotched from one subject to another, trying to fill in all the spaces.

"By the saints," Douglas said with a whistle,

"you're a bundle of nerves. What's got you so rattled?"

Chagrined that his apprehension was so obvious, Joshua made a monumental effort to calm down. He failed. Instead he poured out his plan for the evening—if and when Anna ever called.

"I'm hoping to take her to the island tonight," he confessed. "Any chance you could whip up one of your scrumptious meals?"

"Intendin' to impress her?"

"What better place than Doug's Island Inn?"

"I see. A little wine, a bit of my Dun Laoghaire tart with its smoked salmon, a ladle of Ballyconneely soup, a slice of soda bread and a dollop of colcannon. Most important—" Douglas winked "—the brass lantern turned down to a suitable romantic glow."

"Can you manage all that?" Joshua taunted goodnaturedly, knowing full well that Douglas always provided a feast suitable for a king.

"Ever known me to let you down?"

"Never, old friend."

Douglas had always been a part of Joshua's life. Hired by his parents before Joshua was born, Douglas was the jack-of-all-trades on the Brandon estate. He had mended the gutters and put Band-Aids on Joshua's knees. He'd cleaned the terraces and washed Joshua's face, as well as his brother Maurice's. He'd consistently trounced the boys' father in a mean game of chess until the elder Brandon had refused to play anymore. Then Douglas had taught the boys how to play cribbage. He'd slyly let them win until they finally caught on to his trick.

No, his oldest and dearest friend had never let him down. Neither had his birth father. But Douglas J. Casey, his surrogate father, his constant childhood companion, had nurtured, loved and disciplined him. Douglas's caring was something Joshua felt he could never sufficiently repay.

When the boys grew up and went to university, Douglas moved on to start his restaurant. He chose Vashon Island because it reminded him of the Emerald Isle he'd left behind. But Joshua sensed he was not really content. Overseeing a business was not the same for him as raising two rowdy boys.

"Mind tellin' me a bit about this girl? I've yet to see you so worked up," Douglas commented. "Is there a hint of seriousness in all this plannin'?"

"No, I'm only bringing her over so Martin can spiff up her car." Joshua chuckled. "Besides, don't use the word *planning* within earshot of her. She'll balk. Anna seems to put a high price on her independence."

"You can count on me to keep my trap shut," Douglas whispered in a conspiratorial tone. "So, tell me how practicing this kind of law suits you."

"It's funny," Joshua said, "but the word *practicing* always makes me think seriously."

"How's that?"

"I'm a practitioner. Right? What does that mean?"

Douglas thought about it for a moment before answering. "Someone who is skilled in a profession. Someone who has perfected it."

"I've spent ten years executing paperwork, juggling contracts and participating in heady negotiations. It wasn't what I had in mind when I chose law as a career. Maybe I was naive, but law to me meant helping men and women. It meant the art of using the law so that people benefited.''

"Do you feel as though you've wasted your time?" Douglas asked.

"No," Joshua answered, doodling on a scratch pad. "My corporate servitude wasn't wasted. I've taken my earnings and invested well. I'm proud of that. It's money I earned. Not the Brandon family money I've always been uncomfortable using simply because I was born to it.''

Douglas smiled. "So you've proven yourself. You've carved out your independence. There's no more strings attached to you. You can do what you want without permission, without guilt.''

"Guilt?" Joshua didn't like the sound of the word.

"Yes, guilt. Admit it." Douglas laughed. "You always were a supersensitive lad. You thought the world was going to judge you as just another spoiled wealthy kid living off his rich parents.''

"You're right," Joshua answered. "But it wasn't just money. The problem was I was never needed. Here in the public defender's office I am accessible to those who need me. People who can benefit from my talents.''

"Don't tell me," Douglas cautioned, "that you grew up feeling unloved?''

"No, of course not," Joshua said vehemently. "You know my parents and grandfather certainly loved me. But as a kid they also didn't depend on me to mow the lawn, dump the trash, make my bed or tune up the car for dad. I just never felt necessary.''

"So you think this new job of yours will make you feel necessary? Will it fill in the gaps?"

"Maybe," Joshua responded absentmindedly.

He was thinking about Anna. Did she need something he sensed that only he could give her? Was that her appeal? Another maybe.

But she was more. There was a stunning beauty to her that completely mesmerized him. The way she moved stirred him beyond description. When he watched her, there was an ache in him that could only be silenced by touching her. It was incredible. Of all the beautiful women he'd ever known and touched in his life, none had ever whetted his desire as Anna had.

But what Anna had was more than beauty and some elusive need. She had an essence about her. Was it wit? Was it some exquisite feminine strength? He definitely sensed a power in her.

Douglas cleared his throat, politely interrupting his distracted thoughts. "You're a million miles away, son. By the smile on your face I venture to guess you were thinking about Anna."

"That's a safe wager," Joshua laughed. "The lady is a mystery. She's tempting but I haven't figured out if she's worth it yet."

"I've known men married for forty years who still haven't answered that question," Douglas said. "What is—"

The strident ringing of the phone cut Douglas off in midsentence, but Joshua waited three peals before answering it. He didn't want to act like an overeager schoolboy.

Calmly and with forced self-restraint, he picked up the receiver and said, "Hello?"

"Hello, Joshua. This is Anna Provo. I got your note."

"I'm glad you called. Would you be able to make it tonight?"

He heard a slight hesitation before she finally said, "I can't see any problem. The cases on today's docket should be no trouble. How about meeting in my lobby about five o'clock?"

"Great," Joshua said nonchalantly. "See you at five."

"Oh, Joshua—" a warm inviting sigh brought an audible caress to her words "—thank you for the basket. Unique quote, too. Where'd you get it?"

Maintaining an indifferent tone, he answered, "Just something I dusted off to honor the occasion."

There was a pause before Anna responded, "Well, thanks. Bye."

"Bye, Anna."

After making sure the receiver was securely in place, Joshua turned to his friend and said, "Come on, Douglas. Let's go to lunch."

"Hold it," Douglas interrupted. "I have this very special lady comin' for dinner and I have to get back to my stove. How do you expect me to create a masterpiece claptrappin' with you all afternoon?"

With that the wizened man turned on his heel and briskly walked down the corridor to the elevators. As the doors of one closed, he tipped his cap and gave Joshua a broad grin.

ALMOST FIVE HOURS LATER, Anna tacked the last note to the file in front of her, sat back and took a deep breath. The day was over and everything had been neatly taken care of.

Miriam popped her head around the corner and asked, "Anything else?"

"No, Miriam. See you Monday."

"Oh, by the way," Miriam added, "I put the package from the pharmacy in your bottom drawer."

"Thanks," Anna said, opening it to find her birth-control pills.

"How's that new prescription working? Has it straightened out your cycle?"

"It's working great. Thanks for recommending your gynecologist."

Humming a cheerful passage from her favorite classical work, Anna hastened into her private bath to freshen up. She chose her new jeans with their faint white pinstripes. She liked the feel of them, and they hugged her hips nicely and fit snugly at the waist. She pulled on a bright blue cowl-necked sweater that was fashionably long and stretched to her thighs. Quickly she slipped on her low cuffed suede boots and grabbed her Windbreaker. The outfit was perfect for a cool late-spring evening. Her hair was tucked up under a beret that matched her sweater.

After locking up her office, Anna glanced at her small gold watch and realized she would be right on time. Being prompt was a small obsession with her. It stemmed from her parents' old-world tardiness. "If invited to dinner at six," her mother explained her lackadaisical timing, "it's not polite to arrive until seven. Never appear too eager." Her mother's rationale had driven Anna crazy and now she overcompensated.

She was excited at the prospect of spending the entire evening with Joshua. Anna knew she shouldn't be seeing him so much or so soon, but she excused her behavior by convincing herself it was for Elizabeth's sake.

Tapping her foot impatiently, she silently cursed the snail's pace of the elevator. At this time of night it seemed to take so long to get to the first floor. Finally the doors opened and she exited from the crowded and stifling car into the lobby. Almost immediately she picked out the tawny-gold head of hair she knew belonged to Joshua. He was scanning the crowd and it pleased her to know he was searching for her. He didn't see her, so she threaded her way through the mob of people scurrying like troops of worker ants toward home. Suddenly he spotted her and cleared a path through the throng.

"Hi," he said. "Where's your car? I hope it's close."

"Elizabeth's in the basement garage across the street. I brought her in before I went jogging this morning," Anna answered.

"Elizabeth? You named your car?"

"Don't say 'car' in front of her or she'll lock her doors on you," Anna teased. "I have this penchant for naming machines."

"What have you dubbed your microwave? Monty?" he chuckled.

"Heavens no," Anna laughed. "She is a liberated woman. I call her Melinda Micro."

"Right." Joshua smiled and shook his head. "Let's hurry or we'll miss the five fifty-five ferry."

"You sound like the white rabbit from *Alice in Wonderland*. To make you feel at home we'll take the walking tunnel under Second Avenue. We can avoid the lights and traffic. It's longer but faster, and I feel like stretching my legs."

As Anna led the way, he couldn't resist asking, "Who is your mother—the Queen of Hearts?"

"No," she answered, "but mama plays a mean game of croquet."

After starting the car, Anna tried to ease Elizabeth gently into reverse without causing the customary screech that followed when she shifted gears. But the car remained true to character and gnashed her cogs.

Joshua grinned as he flinched. "I see Martin needs to do some minor transmission work."

"Minor?" Anna laughed. "What are you, the master of understatement?"

"Am I on the witness stand?" he joked.

"Yes. The truth and nothing but the truth. Does Elizabeth qualify for a new life?"

Joshua reached forward and patted the dashboard. "Everything has the right to live the best life it can. No exceptions. No defects, no scars, no hidden flaws or supposed injuries should disqualify them. But sometimes it's expensive. Are you willing to pay the price?"

Anna had the distinct feeling Joshua wasn't just talking about her car. But she didn't let on that she caught his double entendre. It would have given him permission to pry into her life. "So you're saying your friend, Martin, is an expensive body-and-fender man?"

"Yes. Is that a problem?"

"No. It'll be cheaper than buying a new car and I'll appreciate not having to part with her."

"Just so you're willing to allow him the freedom to do the job right."

"You don't know me very well yet, or you'd realize if I do something, I do it right. Otherwise I'd rather not start a project. I just hope Martin is as optimistic about Elizabeth as you are. I hate to part with my friends."

"Does that apply to human friends, as well, or only to cars?" he asked.

Anna left his question unanswered. She was engaged in the delicate task of guiding her vehicle through the narrow maze leading onto the ferry. A husky attendant was frantically directing vehicles to their proper spots to enable the maximum number onto the deck. During peak hours the cars, trucks, trailers and tractors, buses, motorcycles and vans crammed like sardines on the mammoth ferry decks and not one square inch was wasted. The State of Washington had the largest ferry vessels and fleet in the world and at rush hour it still wasn't enough. This tight spacing made Anna nervous and conversation halted while she slowly inched forward until she nudged the bumper of the car in front of her. With a sigh, she gratefully turned off the engine and started to belatedly answer Joshua's question.

Expecting to retort with one of her flip comments, she was startled to see the serious look on his face. He was looking for a straight answer.

"What did you mean?"

"I mean, if I abide by the rules of friendship, can I count on you to return the sincerity of my efforts? I don't enter into any relationships casually and I'd like to know that you respect that. Time is too precious to waste on dead-end encounters and unimportant people."

"Who are unimportant people? People with no influence or money?" Anna had heard the rumors that he was the son of society—money, power, education and an old family standing in the community. She was just a struggling girl-child of first-generation immigrants who ran an ethnic craft shop in the market. He could buy and sell her and her whole family for a pittance. But she wasn't for sale. "What do you do, run a ticker tape through your social register? Who's important? What constitutes a dead-end contact? How do I rate? Today Provo is up a point. Tomorrow Provo is down two points?"

Insulted, Joshua snapped, "Absolutely not! And cut out the histrionics. I may be a lot of things but I'm not a snob. Unimportant people are those who only clutter your life and offer no positive input. Money and power have no bearing on who is admitted to my private world. Yes, sometimes it does affect my public image. Believe me, I keep those two distinct and different worlds quite separate and it works very well. You have only seen my public life. I'd like to show you a small segment of my private life."

Anna regretted her nasty accusations and was profoundly touched by his honesty. She understood what it meant to have two different lives and she wished she could let Joshua into her private one as easily as he invited her to enter his.

Contrite, she apologized. "I'm sorry. I understand what you just said. You explained perfectly why I've insisted on only a friendship, even though you tempt me sorely, Joshua Brandon." She had to fight the urge to reach out and run her fingers along his strong jaw.

Joshua kidded, "Why, Spitfire, you surprise me. Do I look like the kind of man who would tempt you?"

"Instead of evaluating your character, let's go up on deck and get some fresh air."

"Excellent idea. I've been cooped up all day and I want to shed the city."

"Shed the city?"

"Come on, you'll see what I mean." He grabbed her hand.

After winding their way up to the top deck, they stood at the rail and watched the Seattle skyline disappear. The brisk breeze whipped at their clothing and Anna could feel Joshua's eyes take stock of her. She saw the easy gentle smile on his face as he obviously liked what he saw. The cool air was refreshing as it washed over her, and she understood what he meant by shedding the city. It was as if the wind had peeled the gas fumes away, the tension of milling crowds, the accumulated irritations that clung to the spirit. She felt good.

To get a better view of the approaching island, she strolled out to the walkway, which was suspended over the bow. The wind was much stronger there. Suddenly a strong gust blew past her and virtually yanked her beret loose. Titian locks were flying in wild disarray and she desperately made a frantic attempt to capture her hair and tuck it back under her hat.

"Please don't," Joshua begged, and removed her

hands from her head. "You look lovely with your hair down. With a low-cut gossamer gown and bare feet, you'd make a perfect figurehead for a brigantine. I don't understand why you wear it pulled back all the time."

"To present a dignified image in court," she whispered. "People, especially men, seem to take me more seriously when I wear it in that style."

"But there's the small matter of this being a ferry boat, it's after five o'clock and I asked nicely. As a favor, would you leave your hair down? It isn't often I get to escort a beautiful woman on a cruise to the Isle of Vashon."

Anna's better judgment told her to stop this sudden turn in the conversation, but she found herself immensely flattered that Joshua found her appealing. She enjoyed it when a man paid her a sincere compliment.

"But what will Martin think when he sees a wild redhead come chugging into his shop in a beat-up VW?"

"His only complaint," Joshua said, touching her upper arm lightly, "will be that I found you first."

To avoid any further such comments, she said, "Don't you think it's time to head back to the car?"

"What's wrong?" Joshua countered. "Can't you accept a genuine compliment? Just because we're working on being friends doesn't mean I'm blind. You're beautiful, Anna."

"This type of conversation wasn't quite what I had in mind."

"What did you think friendship entailed?" he questioned. "That it implies neutering? I suddenly become a eunuch, oblivious to your marvelous feminine appeal? That you ignore any redeeming masculine traits I possess?''

''Of course not,'' she conceded.

She knew that Joshua was deliberately offering a challenge. She knew that his offer of a platonic relationship was merely a pretense, but she had encouraged the whole arrangement. She had set the rules. On the face of it he was keeping his end of the terms—but was she? Every move he made, every word he spoke threw her nearer to the brink of melting into his arms. She was drawn to him bit by bit, and was close to violating her own restrictions. Yet she still held out the belief that theirs was only a fleeting type of attraction that would pass quickly if she just got to know him better. Magic often fades in the daylight.

Joshua watched the change of expressions on her face and he couldn't resist rubbing her creamy cheek with his thumb. She was frightened, he could tell, but he firmly believed that he would cast a spell on her this evening. Her reticence would vanish. He devoutly believed that there was enchantment under the stars.

CHAPTER SIX

THE FERRY BELLOWED two short blasts, alerting the passengers it was about to dock. Heading down the staircase, Anna dreaded the maneuvering of Elizabeth out of her parking stall on the car deck. Whenever she came to one of the islands, she and Niki rode their bikes. It was a lot less nerve-racking.

"I feel like a lemming," she joked to break the tension caused by the mass exodus.

"Toss me the keys," Joshua said, "and I'll drive."

"Thanks." She gratefully threw the key ring to him and he deftly caught it.

"Besides, I know the way and it'll save giving a lot of directions," he explained.

Edging out of the constricted spot, Joshua drove off the ferry and began the scenic route around to the west side of the island. Anna watched him out of the corner of her eye, finding pleasure in the companionable silence that fell between them. He pushed Elizabeth a bit faster than Anna ordinarily would have, but the car responded well and Anna admired Joshua's instinctive knowledge of the vehicle's limitations.

Rhododendrons in full bloom flaunted their spectacular mauve, red and pink heads along the roadside. Oregon grape and sword fern blanketed the forest floor, a carpet at the feet of the regal Douglas fir and red cedar. The dense undergrowth never failed to amaze Anna. A person couldn't walk two feet without being halted by a wall of foliage. It was a temperate jungle.

The forest disappeared and lush pasture rolled by their car. It was astounding to think that the pioneers had cleared the forest to make these grasslands for their dairy stock, for they had done it with only primitive tools and back-breaking work.

Grazing on a knoll were a pair of llamas.

"Look at them," she almost yelled. "What are they doing here?"

"Several people keep them as pets. They're gentle and shy creatures. Would you like to see some first-hand?" Joshua asked.

"Yes, but how?"

"A friend raises them as a hobby."

"You mean Martin?"

"No. Another friend whose name is Douglas Casey."

"Do you think he'd mind if we just dropped in on him?"

"Doug never objects to company. His motto is The More the Merrier." Joshua coaxed the sputtering Volkswagen up a steep grade before adding, "Besides, he's expecting us."

"Oh?" she said suspiciously. "What plans have you concocted for the evening?" He always seemed to be brewing up something. It was as if he had to be in control. She wondered if anything spontaneous ever entered his measured life and knocked him off guard.

How would he react when and if the unpredictable occurred? Anna knew from well-tried experience that people and happenings didn't always fall in with plans. Niki had taught her that much.

"Doug owns a restaurant," Joshua explained. "I thought we'd stop for a bite after Martin's."

"How did you meet this auto artist?"

"Martin? Oh, we go back to our school years." Joshua chuckled at the memory. "That kid could fix anything. I mean *anything*. Toasters, washing machines, typewriters, and especially cars."

"Mama would adore him," Anna said, laughing. "Papa can't even repair a little leak in a faucet."

"That's not so bad. My mother can't cook," he said. "Not even toast."

"Really?"

"Really. But I was telling you about Martin and how we became friends. We had a few classes together. I had a reputation for hitting the books hard and, outside of his ability with cars, he was known for using books only to sit on. You see, Martin's a little guy and he sat in the back of the room so he could sneak in late or escape early. Anyway, he used the books to give him some height over the kids in front of him."

"Not your straight A type?" Anna asked.

"Not with books. But the auto-shop teacher said Martin was a genius with a capital *G*."

"So how'd you two become pals?"

"Well," Joshua said with a smile, "my parents went to Europe for a couple of weeks and left my brother and me with the household staff. I filched dad's prized possession...his brand new Maserati... and took it for a spin. I spun right into a tree.''

''You mean—'' Anna faked outrage ''—I'm having dinner with an ex-juvenile delinquent?''

''And ex-race-car driver whose career ended at the trunk of a blue spruce.''

''So Martin fixed the car before your dad got home?'' She'd pieced together the rest of the story.

''Yep. I couldn't take it back to the dealer or admit my crime to the insurance company. My father would have instantly heard about it. So I made a deal with Martin. I'd tutor him through high school and he'd save my skin.''

There was something about Joshua's story that hit a responsive chord in her. Hearing about his childhood, his adolescent indiscretions, his friendships, stirred a warm feeling in her. Joshua was becoming three dimensional; no longer just an engaging lawyer popping in and out of her court; no longer a potential lover furiously trying to woo her. He was sharing parts of himself that friends share. Their whole charade of friendship was turning into a sincere camaraderie.

Anna shivered slightly. She could handle lawyers. She could fend off suitors. But she had to...wanted to...cherish a friend.

''Cold?'' Joshua asked, breaking her reverie.

''No,'' she answered. ''Only a few goose bumps when I think about Elizabeth being reborn. I'm just excited.''

There was no plausible way she could say, *You scare me, Joshua Brandon. There's more to you than meets the eye!*

"How long will Elizabeth be laid up?" she asked.

"One, maybe two weeks. Is that a problem for you?"

"No, no problem. If there is somewhere I can't jog or walk to, I'll hop a bus."

"Stoic to the last," he teased and patted her shoulder the way a football coach would pat a tackler who's playing a good game. "Deprivation is good for the soul and all that, eh?" he laughed.

Anna found herself laughing, too. He seemed to be able to bring out the best and the worst in her. He triggered the temper she normally kept bridled; he stirred up the fears she fought to subdue; and he made her feel special, carefree and alive, which she treasured. But most of all, he intrigued her. The more she was with him, the closer she wanted to get. But getting closer meant letting him into her life, and she wasn't prepared to allow that.

The thumping of the car as it bobbed up and down a rutted driveway jarred Anna out of her introspection.

"Are we there?"

"Yes," Joshua answered.

He pulled up to a huge garage that appeared to be deserted. After several short toots on the horn, a slightly built man peeked around the corner and ambled over to greet them.

"Hi, Josh," he said as he leaned languorously on the driver's windowsill.

Joshua unfolded his long legs from the cramped interior of the car and rose to greet his friend.

"Hello, Martin. This is the lady I was telling you about," he said as he leaned against the Volkswagen's fender and draped his arm on the roof. "Elizabeth—" he patted her top "—meet Mr. Baker."

"Josh, you devil," Martin chastised him as he surveyed Anna's flowing auburn mane and lithesome figure. "This is the lady I want to be introduced to." He wiped his hand on the back of his coveralls and extended it to Anna. "How do you do?"

"Just fine, Martin. I'm Anna. Anna Provo."

Grinning, Martin said, "Right now I wish I'd liked school better and was a doctor. You're a much prettier patient than this VW."

"Thanks," she murmured. She always found taking a compliment a difficult task. "But I'm not sick. Can you fix Elizabeth? She's no Maserati."

Martin was taken aback and colored. "He told you that? It was supposed to be a permanent secret. His dad would probably still have a conniption if he found out about it." He eyed her critically. "It's a mark of Josh's trust if he told you that story."

Instantly, Anna liked Martin. Really liked him. His frank appraisal and unspoken approval touched her deeply. There was an old-fashioned, special quality about him. It was apparent that Joshua had excellent taste in friends.

"Joshua explained your policy of either repairing a car completely or not doing the job at all," she said. "You have total freedom. Do whatever is necessary."

"Great," he beamed. "Josh, take Anna upstairs and offer her a cold beer. Give me a few minutes to look this baby over and let you know what kind of job we're talking about."

"Come on, Anna. Let's give the master some working room," Joshua said.

Grabbing her hand, he led her to a steep set of stairs at one end of the building. The steps were narrow and as they climbed, they kept bumping and brushing against each other.

Even such innocent contact affected Anna. She felt a warmth so pleasant she could easily abandon all caution. But it terrified her that Joshua's touch could evoke such a response.

At the top of the landing, Joshua sported a Cheshire grin. It was apparent he expected some reaction from her when he opened the heavy carved door to Martin's apartment.

The interior was striking if not downright outlandish. Cedar tongue and groove paneled the walls and ceiling. It was a lair, not a home. Nailed to the walls were hundreds of miscellaneous car parts, many probably dating back to the invention of the automobile. Wooden Model-T wheels, shifting levers, gear cogs of various sizes, distributor caps, headlights—brass lanterns to mercury-vapor beams—an array of gaskets and more, much more. Most of the collection was a mystery to Anna.

Aware she must look awestruck, she tried but couldn't mask her bewilderment. Martin had two sofas but they were really just seats taken out of some luxurious old limousine and mounted on casters. The matching sofas were made of soft doeskin leather dyed a pale baby blue. His coffee table was a red hardtop, probably from a '50s vintage T-Bird convertible, she guessed. Placed atop it was an ashtray that had formerly been a piston. A polished hubcap now served as a fruit bowl.

"Unique, huh?" Joshua whispered in her ear.

"It's a museum!" She gasped. "Or a mausoleum."

"Here—" Joshua walked to a window and pointed "—see this?"

Anna nodded at the gray velvet shade edged in silk tassels.

"It came out of an old Stanley Steamer," he said.

"A Stanley what?"

"It was a car that had a boiler for an engine. You just stopped by the side of the road, chopped a little wood and dipped into a bubbling brook for some water, and then went on your merry way."

"You're joking," she said. She couldn't visualize the scene he was painting.

"He's overdoing it a bit," Martin said from the doorway. He sauntered into the room and over to the window where he fingered the shade lovingly.

"The Stanley was a masterpiece. Did you know that in 1898 it broke the world's speed record? It went almost twenty-nine miles per hour. It could negotiate a 30 percent grade. By 1906, it went a hundred twenty-seven miles per hour with an engine that had a pressure in excess of one thousand pounds per square inch. Think of it! Something no other car could do at that time!"

Anna didn't know what to say. What could she add? She knew absolutely nothing about automobiles. A comment from her would be like telling Leonardo da Vinci that Mona Lisa was cute.

"If we went back to steam engines now, we'd eliminate all the pollution generated by the internal combustion engine. The effects on the atmosphere would be—"

"Whoa, pal," Joshua halted him. "You'll short-circuit Anna's brain with all your expertise."

"Sorry," Martin apologized. "Now I'm overdoing it."

"No, no," she reassured him. "I think it's wonderful. I think your place is wonderful and so are you."

Martin blushed crimson. He wiped his hands nervously on a purple grease rag.

"Got a sister as nice as you?" he joked.

Joshua broke the uncomfortable silence by asking how much work Elizabeth needed. The three of them discussed details and costs until most arrangements had been settled.

"I took a quick look at her, Anna," Martin explained, "but it's going to take me longer to give you an exact estimate. How about if I call you tomorrow and quote you a price?"

"She's that bad, huh?" Anna laughed. "Tomorrow will be fine."

"You two want a ride to the dock?" Martin offered.

"Thanks," Joshua said. "Drop us at Doug's place. We're going to dine in style this evening."

"There's no better grub in the country," Martin agreed.

Joshua's friend led them outside and to the back of the garage. Anna stood stock-still as she eyed the vehicle Martin was going to chauffeur them in. It was a dilapidated tow truck with bashed doors, peeling orange paint and huge cancerous holes of rust mottled over its body.

"This," she asked incredulously, "is *your* transportation?"

Self-conscious, Martin stuffed his hands into his coveralls. "The shoemaker's children, you know. Or the carpenter's house is never finished?"

The cab of the truck was packed to the hilt with batteries, cables, chains, a case of oil, numerous tools and a veritable stock of new auto parts like spark plugs, air filters and others. There was barely enough room for Martin to drive, never mind adding any passengers.

Joshua stacked packages to the center of the seat to allow room for himself. After climbing into the cab, he extended his hand to Anna. She was going to have to sit on his lap.

He saw the wariness in her expression and he didn't blame her. The situation certainly looked contrived, but he couldn't just dump all of Martin's expensive gear out and then expect him to come home and reload it. All that aggravation just because he was nice enough to give them a lift?

"I promise to be a perfect gentleman," he coaxed her.

Anna hesitated, then took his hand. She stepped onto the running board and gracefully swung herself up and onto his lap. She tried to take some of her weight off his legs by bracing herself with her elbows on the dusty cluttered dashboard. It was bad enough to have to be so close, but she was determined not to crush him!

Martin gunned the engine and it roared. The truck's body might be diseased but its heart was healthy. They jolted down the washboard driveway and finally glided onto the smooth surface of the main road.

Joshua purposely kept one arm stretched across the back of the seat and the other along the ridge of the door's armrest. He yearned to wrap them round Anna's delicate waist and draw her comfortably back against his chest. But no, she was making a monumental effort to keep as much distance from him as she could. He had to respect that.

He concentrated on the scenery. The towering Douglas fir stretched as far as the eye could see. Green. Everywhere there was green. Multiple shades of the color flashed by as the trio sped across the countryside. Emerald, jade, reseda, olive, Granny Smith apple. All of it so verdant!

"Southern California has parched me," Joshua told Anna and Martin. "It'll take years for me to absorb enough of the Northwest to dispel the arid residue."

"A good weekend of camping would help," Martin suggested.

Trying to ignore the closeness of Anna and the splendid scent of her hair only inches from his face, Joshua forced his thoughts back to the times he and Martin had escaped the city and gone camping in the Cascade Mountains together. They'd had some special times. Particularly the weekend Martin had taught him some folk songs. After that, they had spent many a night huddled around a campfire harmonizing.

Joshua was startled when Martin's clear resonant tenor rang through the cab. It took him a second to realize Martin was singing now. He had almost thought he was remembering those nights so long ago. His friend must have been reading his mind.

"Greensleeves was my true love," Martin soloed.

Anna shifted her position and looked at the little man behind the huge steering wheel singing one of her favorite ballads. She was astonished when Joshua's baritone blended in with exquisite clarity.

"Greensleeves was my delight, Greensleeves was all my love."

Joshua sensed Anna's shift, both in her mood and her body. She'd forgotten to be defensive and tense. He relaxed accordingly.

"Do you two hotshots know 'The Maid Freed from the Gallows?'" she taunted. Folk ballads were one of her hobbies.

Joshua sat up straighter, juggled her slightly on his knees and sang lustily. "Oh what will you leave to your father dear?"

Anna answered in her mezzo-soprano. "The silver-shod steed that brought me here."

Martin pretended to jockey the battered tow truck down the road as if it were the silver-shod steed. He questioned her with the next line. "What will you leave to your mother dear?"

Anna put her hands behind her head and seductively lifted her thick tresses from the nape of her neck. Coyly, she trilled, "My velvet pall and my silken gear."

In tandem, Joshua and Martin sang, "What will you leave to your brother John?"

Clapping her hands with glee, she responded throatily, "The gallows tree to hang him on!"

The three of them whooped an unchecked roar of delight. Joshua hugged Anna without even considering what he was doing and she reciprocated by throwing her arms around his neck and hugging him back.

Martin continued to drive the back roads of Vashon and a companionable silence filled the cab. Anna snuggled closer to Joshua and rested her head on his shoulder. She felt him lightly squeeze her upper arm. The message he telegraphed was warm and sweet and not the least bit threatening.

They arrived at Doug's Island Inn and Anna disembarked from the truck reluctantly. Still no one had spoken and she didn't want to break the lovely quiet. She walked around to the driver's window and Martin took her hand without a word. He raised it to his lips and lightly kissed the back. Letting go, he put the truck in reverse and drove away.

Joshua stood behind her and rested his hands in the cradles of her shoulders.

"I want you to meet another precious friend," he said, nodding at the shingled building in front of them.

The weathered exterior of the inn gave no clue to the warmth and charm that lay inside. By skillfully arranging furniture, each group of diners had been given an individual retreat looking out over the mazarine bay. Plants and antique sideboards created a cozy atmosphere. Whoever had planned the decor had created the impression of many small private dining rooms within the large rambling structure.

A craggy face peered out of the kitchen and Joshua leaned down and whispered to Anna, "Doug has spotted us."

She watched with fascination as the spry-looking man bounced across the room. A grin engulfed his face.

"Hello, son."

"Hi, Douglas," Joshua answered. "This is Anna Provo."

"Ah, pleased to meet you," he said. "I see Joshua inherited my penchant for flaming beauties."

"Inherited? Are you and Joshua related?" Anna was confused. Joshua hadn't said anything about Douglas being a relative.

"No," he said, stroking his chin as if he was contemplating a very serious question. "No, we're not kin. We're closer."

It was an amazing thing for someone to say. Anna mulled the statement over as Douglas seated them at a table. She waited for him to leave and get the cocktails they had ordered before she asked Joshua what Douglas had meant.

"Doug is my real father, not my biological one. He was hired by my parents to grow and tend flowers, but he really raised and nurtured my brother and me."

"That's incredible," Anna murmured. "Are you bitter?"

"On the contrary. I'm eternally grateful. My parents are wonderful people but absolutely incapable of raising children firsthand. At least they had the good sense, or maybe it was just the luck, to find Douglas. He is gifted when it comes to handling children."

"The idea of one's parents delegating the responsibility of caring for their children to someone who is hired horrifies me," Anna said. "My parents cherished every moment of the child-rearing process. They would have never abdicated the honor to someone else."

"It would have horrified my parents if they hadn't hired someone," he said with a laugh.

Studying Joshua across the table, Anna reviewed his blue eyes that so quickly flashed humor, his thick blond hair that waved slightly to his ears, the lush mustache that arched over his inviting lips, and she wanted to reach out and stroke his face.

How could he be so loving? she asked herself. How had he grown to be so strong? So happy? How had he learned to laugh so readily? Her parents had been with her every step of the way and yet she had to struggle to keep up with Joshua's generosity and good humor.

"Why so pensive, Spitfire?"

The rankling endearment prodded her out of her reverie.

"Why do you insist on that moniker?" she asked tartly.

"Because it snaps you out of all those serious monologues you have with yourself and brings you back to me." He winked at her as if he really was privy to her deepest thoughts.

Before she could make a rebuttal, Douglas returned with their drinks. Joshua tried to talk him into joining them but the older man begged off, saying he had to monitor the kitchen and a dozen other areas.

Anna guessed the real reason. Douglas wanted to leave Joshua and her alone. It would have been an admirable intention if she had wanted to have a lovely candlelight dinner on a romantic island. But she didn't want to be alone with Joshua. Well, not really. The truth was she did want to have him all to herself but that was what was wrong. The man had cast a spell on her.

Joshua didn't need a mind reader to tell him that Anna was withdrawing again. She almost emitted a flashing red signal that said, "Back off! You're getting too close."

He had never met a woman who was so complicated. There was something holding her at bay and as much as he wanted her, he couldn't push her. She must come to him willingly, and that was going to require his patience.

"Tell me what you thought of Martin," Joshua asked, hoping to find a neutral subject that would ease her tension.

Anna smiled warmly. "You know what I think?" she answered. "He's beautiful."

She reached in her purse for her glasses. Her motive was twofold. One, she wanted to read the menu, and two, she felt a need to hide. Creating distance this way was an old ploy. If she looked studious and intellectual, most men lost interest.

"That's very unusual," he said, pointing to her eyeglass case. "The craftsmanship is wonderful."

"It's made of birchbark," she said. "My father made it."

"He's quite an artist," Joshua commented as Anna picked up the menu. "No need to read that," he informed her. "Everything has been chosen for us."

Douglas served them a delicious hot pie stuffed with smoked salmon and Swiss cheese that steamed aromatically as he placed individual portions in front of them. The soda bread was hot and butter instantly melted on its surface. But the coup de grace was the side dish of colcannon—mashed potatoes with cabbage mixed through the fluffy white mound.

The conversation through dinner was safe and comfortable. The earlier mood of peace and contentment prevailed. Anna found herself slipping into an easy rapport with Joshua and the sense of friendship between them increased.

Folding his napkin neatly next to his empty plate, Joshua asked, "Is your brother as different from you as mine is from me?"

Anna bristled imperceptibly. She considered sidestepping the question but decided it was time to be candid about Niki. It was time to see if Joshua was as flexible as he seemed.

"Yes," she answered tentatively. "Niki and I are like night and day. It's hard to explain, but I'll try."

She took a sip of wine to give her a chance to find the right words. Her eyes caught Joshua's and she saw that he was giving her his fullest attention.

"Niki is retarded," she blurted out. It wasn't the way she meant to say it.

Joshua lolled back in his chair and grinned. "Is that all?"

"What do you mean, 'Is that all?' "

"Hell, the way you melodramatically led up to that statement I thought you were going to tell me the Honorable Judge Provo's brother was a convicted felon or something," he laughed.

Anna was speechless. His reaction was nothing like she'd expected. She'd anticipated rejection, shock, fear and, worst of all, pity. Or perhaps at best, empathy and concern. She was not prepared for his joking! Maybe she *was* being melodramatic. It wasn't something she'd ever evaluated. In fact the whole issue of Niki's retardation was hard to evaluate.

Mama and papa always seemed to skirt the issue. Whenever she'd asked about it they fobbed her off with the statement "God just gave Niki to us."

"Listen, Anna," Joshua said as he leaned forward and clasped both her hands in his brawny large ones, "my brother, Maurice, is brilliant and he's a first-class pain in the neck. Now, I bet Niki is a lot easier to like and get along with than Mudger."

"Mudger?"

"It means milksop and describes Maurice to a T. It's a word Douglas taught me when I was five or six and I've called my brother Mudger ever since."

Anna laughed. "Poor Maurice isn't that bad, is he?"

"No. He has his flaws but I kind of like the kid. How about Niki?"

She stared at Joshua's handsome face a split second before answering. "Despite his handicaps, I love him very much."

"That's nice. It's just the way family members should feel about one another." He smiled and then kissed her fingertips.

As they walked to the ferry dock, less than a block away, Anna knew she and Joshua had succeeded in becoming friends. She also acknowledged that she wanted the relationship to grow more affectionate. So when he held her hand as they strolled down the sidewalk, she didn't resist.

The sky was crystal clear. Not even the moon broke the ebony sheen of the heavens and millions of stars formed a canopy above them.

Anna exercised an old Russian proverb and avoided looking to the west. If a maiden sees Venus, it was said, her fortune is made. If she sees the Milky Way, another year of maidenhood would follow. She wasn't sure what she wanted her fortune to be but she was acutely aware of her looking straight ahead and not seeking out the Milky Way, either.

"If mama was here she'd use a crane to turn my head west," Anna spoke aloud to herself without realizing it.

Joshua was puzzled by her comment and asked, "Private joke?"

"Yes. I was thinking about my mother."

"Why?"

"She's a buttinsky."

"Buttinsky? What's that?" he asked.

"Someone who sticks their nose into your business," she replied. She was about to explain that it was a word that originated in Australia, but as they were walking onto the ramp of the ferry, *Issaquah*, she noticed a young woman taking small excruciating steps. There seemed to be something wrong.

Anna quickened her pace to catch up with the woman who was inching along the vacant car deck.

"What's the hurry?" Joshua called out, trying to match Anna's sudden burst of speed.

"I don't know," she answered.

When Anna was abreast of the woman, she saw that she had long black hair pulled back into a ponytail. Her brown eyes were wide with alarm. It wasn't until she put her hand on her large abdomen that Anna realized the woman was pregnant.

The woman gasped and Anna grabbed her elbow to keep her from collapsing to her knees.

"Are you in labor?" Anna asked.

"I think so," the woman hissed between clenched teeth.

Anna felt the ferry lurch away from the island. It was just as well. Vashon had no hospital. Seattle was the closest place to get help.

"Joshua," Anna ordered, "take her other arm and let's get her upstairs to a padded lounge."

They were halfway up the long staircase when another contraction came; she couldn't take one more step. Joshua scooped her up into his arms and Anna ran ahead to open the heavy metal door at the top of the stairs.

He carefully placed the woman on the lounge and rolled up his jacket for a pillow. Taking out his handkerchief, he mopped her face.

"What's your name?" he asked.

"Julie Hewitt."

"Well, Julie, I'm Joshua, and Anna here is going to the purser and have him radio ahead. There'll be an ambulance waiting in Seattle at the dock. Can he call anyone else? Family? Friends?"

"We just moved here from Florida," Julie answered between the pants she was using to control the pain.

"We?"

"My husband is on maneuvers with some NATO forces. It's survival training near Mount Rainier," she panted. "No radios."

Anna found the purser and he said he'd radio the message. She asked him if he could deliver a baby if necessary and he explained that most of the crew could administer CPR or splint a bone but nothing more.

Swallowing hard to force down the terror she felt, Anna hurried back to Joshua and his charge. She knew absolutely nothing about childbirth and she felt worse than helpless.

"What are we going to do?" she asked him quietly.

A small crowd had gathered to see what was happening. Since it was late at night and not peak traffic hours, the chance of finding a doctor or nurse on board to help was minimal.

"Can anyone deliver a baby?" Joshua asked.

No one answered.

"Then please move away," he said. "Give her some privacy."

People dispersed and Anna watched Joshua stroke Julie's hand. He explained that what was happening was perfectly normal and everything would be fine. He promised to help her if the baby insisted on being impatient.

Anna drew him aside and asked nervously, "Can you deliver a baby?"

"If I have to," he said. "I've taken a few first-aid courses over the years. They covered the basics."

He used his watch to time the spaces between contractions. There were barely two minutes between intervals.

"Anna," he ordered brusquely, "buy several editions of newspapers out of the vending machines. They're fairly sterile and we'll wrap the baby in them."

By the time Anna had dashed back with the papers, a look of confidence dominated his face. It relaxed her to see him so at ease.

"Anna," he instructed, "take Julie's hand and let her know that everything is just fine."

Julie's knees were bent and her legs trembled. Instinctively Anna reached out to help. By drawing Julie's knees to her own chest, Anna calmed the shaking. She gently massaged Julie's upper thigh to relax the muscles.

"What can I do?" Anna asked her.

"Rubbing my leg helps," Julie answered.

"Have you taken any birthing classes?" Joshua asked.

Julie nodded. "My husband was my coach."

"Anna is a quick learner," he reassured her. "She'll help you."

A contraction was beginning, and in her fear, Julie was holding her breath.

"Take nice deep ones, Julie," Joshua encouraged. "Anna, you help by taking audible deep breaths with her. Use a slow and easy rhythm."

Anna had unconsciously been holding in her own breath but she did exactly as Joshua instructed. Inhaling and exhaling, Anna set the pace.

"Come on, Julie, nice and deep," Anna coached.

Joshua stood and stroked the top of Anna's head. "Good job," he told her. "Keep it up while I go wash my hands and find a first-aid kit from the purser."

She watched him hurry off and was impressed by his lack of panic. Julie's contraction was receding and Anna felt her tension ease. It gave Anna a moment to assess conditions. Fortunately, Julie was wearing a long loose summer dress and no panty hose. By tenting the dress over her knees, Julie could be given as much privacy as possible.

The sound of something being rolled in their direction made Anna turn to look. The purser was bringing a portable partition from storage. Joshua was striding ahead of him with a first-aid kit.

A powerful spasm caused Julie to cry out, "It's coming!"

Joshua flipped open the medical box and used the scissors to cut away Julie's underwear. Anna sucked in her breath when she saw the baby's head with its dark curly hair pushing out.

"It's spectacular, isn't it?" Joshua said to Anna softly.

"Yes." Anna smiled. "But what happens now?"

"Hold Julie's shoulders up and encourage her to bear down."

Anna put her arm behind Julie and she curled forward. "Push hard, honey. We need your help," Anna said.

The sweat glistened on Julie's face as she strained to deliver her child. Anna mopped the beads of perspiration with Joshua's handkerchief.

"Come, little one," he coaxed the infant as it slipped into his cupped hands. "There's a wonderful life waiting for you."

Warm happy tears ran down Anna's face. It was a marvelous thing to say to someone the first moment he entered the world. Joshua was stripped of all his bravado. His tenderness was overwhelming. She would never forget the way he looked right now—encouraging a life to begin.

"It's a girl," he exclaimed triumphantly. "A wee little damsel."

Anna lowered Julie's shoulders and took the child

Joshua proudly handed her. She wrapped the baby in newspapers and then swaddled it in her jacket before handing the infant to her mother. An unexpected wrench tugged at her as she put the little girl into Julie's arms. She felt like she'd given birth herself and the child should naturally remain nestled next to her breast.

"What name have you chosen?" Joshua asked Julie.

Grimacing, still not capable of breathing normally, she answered, "We haven't decided."

Concern spread across Anna's face as she watched Julie struggle with another contraction. Anna was frightened that something might be wrong. "Why is Julie still in labor?" she asked Joshua.

"Probably just the placenta," he answered matter-of-factly.

Julie lifted her head up and Anna immediately assisted her back into the curled position. Julie's voice was shaky when she spoke. "I don't think you're right," she gasped. "I may be new at this but I think...." Her words were muffled by exertion.

Suddenly Joshua smiled and Anna wondered what was happening.

"If this next one is a boy," he said with a chuckle, "how about the names Hansel and Gretel?"

Twins! Anna felt the way she had as a child when she played blindman's buff and was the one in the circle with the blindfold on. She couldn't predict what was going to happen next and it left her dizzy. She'd started out the afternoon wondering how Joshua would react to an unscheduled occurrence. Now she knew. He was as flexible as bamboo in the wind. It was she who was as rigid as an oak tree.

Like an instant replay with Anna coaching, Joshua delivered a strapping boy. This time Anna swaddled the baby in the shirt she had taken from Joshua.

He moved out of the way to let Anna sit next to Julie while she held the little boy. He smiled at the maternal love radiating from both women. Anna acted as though it was she who had given birth, and he guessed that in a way she had. They all had. There was a time when he had been frightened and unsure if he could deliver a child. But when the little girl's head had peeked out at him, all his doubts had dissolved. It was probably the sweetest moment of his life and it hadn't even been his own baby. Yet he couldn't have been prouder if it had been.

Joshua watched Anna oohing and aahing over her charge and he smiled at his own reaction. If her maternal instinct was surfacing, his paternal nature was also asserting itself. This was definitely a night to cherish, a time he and Anna would remember together. It was a kind of bonding that only they would understand.

A COUPLE OF HOURS LATER, elated but exhausted, Anna let him walk her up to the door. They'd ridden to the hospital with Julie and her burgeoning family. Joshua had insisted on a private room where the twins could be placed in bassinets next to their mother. The prerogative, he explained, of being a godfather was to demand the best accommodations.

"The entertainment was wonderful," Anna teased him as she searched for her keys.

"It was beautiful," he said as he brushed his lips along the side of her neck. "I'm looking forward to the time when it's my own kids chafing to be born."

His words made her pull away. She'd planned on inviting him in but what he was saying made her reconsider. This was a man who obviously reveled in the lovely process of having children, raising them and cherishing them.

What could she offer him? The idea of having children was frightening. She wasn't sure she wanted them or should even have them. If she and Joshua let their relationship expand and blossom, would she be leading him into believing she had the same desires, goals and needs as he did?

"I planned on inviting you in," she hedged, "but it's been a long night and I'm tired."

His face hardened and he straightened to his full imposing height.

"Someday, Spitfire," he snapped, "I'm going to discover what makes you run hot and then cold. Something really extraordinary happened to us tonight. Didn't you feel it?"

"Of course I did," she whispered. "I'll never forget it."

"Do special moments always make you so perverse?" he asked irritably.

"It's complicated." She weakly tried to defend herself.

"No, it's not. You just choose to make it so."

He pivoted to leave and Anna quickly said, "Call me or I'll call you this week."

Turning back, he said, "Damn right I'll call. You may frustrate me to no end, but I know what I want."

With that he strode off, and for the second time in

her short relationship with Joshua Brandon, Anna let herself into her home alone. Tonight, however, she knew he would be back, and the knowledge both relieved and alarmed her.

CHAPTER SEVEN

IT WAS WITH GREAT RELIEF that Anna found herself alone in her chambers. She had time to fritter away as she waited for the jury to return their verdict. The week had been a long and harried one with little time to evaluate the sudden changes that had catapulted her from municipal court to superior court. There had been even less time to consider what this unexpected career shift could ultimately mean.

But now she had the luxury of kicking off her navy blue pumps and leaning back in her chair. She meant to use the quiet time. Miriam had brewed a pot of Anna's favorite spice tea and the aroma was fabulous. Sipping the special blend relaxed her and allowed her to get things into their proper perspective.

Her thoughts immediately gravitated back to the last free day she'd had. Saturday. Sunshiny Saturday. She'd awakened in a cloud of indecision and mixed feelings. Her evening with Joshua had left her yawing like a ship at sea in a storm. Yes, she'd had a marvelous time! No, she didn't want to lose the budding friendship she'd begun. Yes, she wanted to include Joshua in everything she did. No, she didn't want to make commitments to him she couldn't keep. Yes, she wanted him! No, she didn't want him! Yes, she was going to call him right then and ask him over. No, she was going to ease him out of her life. Back and forth she oscillated.

Finally she impulsively decided to find Niki. He'd been hounding her to take him to the zoo for weeks and it would be a good diversion. The sun was shining and perhaps it would clear the fog in her brain.

He wasn't the companion she preferred, but he could be depended on. Whenever she needed a pal on an expedition to the zoo, the aquarium, or to explore one of the San Juan Islands, Niki could always be counted on. It didn't matter what she suggested or how many times they had been somewhere, he was thrilled to accompany her.

At an ungodly early hour that morning, she went to find him. Saturday mornings were sparked with an electric anticipation at the market. The merchants knew that soon throngs of people would be appearing to purchase their wares. The vibrant colors of the fruits and vegetables formed a giant patchwork quilt in their painstakingly arrayed displays. The enticing aroma of freshly baked breads and pastries drifted out to greet the shopper. And then there were the fishmongers unloading the seafood freshly caught in the chill waters of Puget Sound. It was like coming home for Anna whenever she managed to escape from her closely ordered world and slip back in time to her childhood, which had been spent in the rambunctious market.

She spotted Niki's dark head towering over the rest of the merchants. He was unloading produce from a large flat-bed truck, happily absorbed in his job.

"Hey, Nikolae," she called out to him, "come give your little sister a hug."

At the sight of Anna, a wide grin broke across his face. Like a bull in a china shop, he charged his way through stacks of crates. All six feet five inches of him was concentrating on getting to Anna by the shortest route, and that meant anything in his way was ignored.

"Hi ya, Anna," he said as he embraced her. "Whatcha doing here?"

"I was looking for someone to go to the zoo with me today." She smiled as she began the special game she played with her brother. "Do you know any good-looking fellow that might be free for the day?"

"How about me, Anna? Papa says I look like the Incredible Hulk. Is that good-looking enough?"

"You? I didn't think you liked the zoo. I thought you hated the place."

Niki's face lost its puzzled look as he realized his sister was teasing him. "Ah, Anna, quit kidding. You always take me with you. Did you forget?"

"Can you get off work?"

"Yeah, soon as I finish unloadin' this truck, I'm done. But I'll make sure."

"Okay, you finish up and I'll go say hello to mama and papa. Meet me at the shop."

"Mama's not at the shop," Niki said. "She's at Giorgio's having breakfast."

Anna pictured her mother sitting at a small table enjoying her morning tea and savoring one of the many tempting pastries that Giorgio baked for his customers. Mama and papa took turns leaving the shop for a few minutes every morning to indulge themselves in a daily offering from their old family friend.

"All right, Niki. Meet me at the bakery."

"Okeydokey, Anna. I'll hurry."

Winding her way through the bustling merchants, she spied her mother sitting at one of the front tables, reading the morning paper. *Mama will never change,* she thought. The older woman's gray hair was pulled back in a red babushka and the cotton housedress was covered by a large blue work apron. The seasons changed and the produce at the market with them, but mama never did.

Sneaking up behind her, Anna covered mama's eyes and whispered in her ear, "Guess who?"

"I couldn't possibly guess," mama answered. "I know I have a daughter somewhere in the city but I see her so seldom that I've forgotten what her voice sounds like."

"Come on, mama," Anna begged. "I saw you just last week."

"So sit down and visit. How are you?" her mother replied tersely.

"I'm fine. I came to say hello and take Niki to the zoo."

A knocking on the door brought Anna back to the present, to her chambers, to Friday afternoon.

"Come in," she called.

Her bailiff handed her a slip of paper. "From the jury," he said.

She read their question silently and then quickly wrote an answer. She handed it to the bailiff to deliver. It was one of the many duties she had and, when a jury was sequestered, she had to remain in her office to assist them with any requests or instructions.

Mama had had a lot of requests and instructions last Saturday morning, too.

They'd only been visiting for a few minutes when Niki came rushing up. "All done, Anna. Let's go," he said, grabbing her arm and dragging her to her feet.

"Okay, dynamite, I'm coming. Mama, I'll keep Niki with me tonight and bring him home in the morning."

Her mother slowly walked over and gave her daughter one of her unsolicited pearls of wisdom. Taking Anna's chin in her hand, mama looked into her hazel eyes and said, "You spend too much time with Niki. Why don't you find a nice man to go dancing with on Saturday night? Why always your brother?"

"'Cause Anna likes me, that's why." Niki had answered mama's question better than Anna ever could. He had also ended an all-too-familiar conversation before it had escalated into another row about Anna's lack of a steady beau.

"Niki's right, mama, and besides, the day is too pretty to spend arguing. We're off. See you tomorrow."

Before her mother could start in again, she grabbed her brother and headed for the Metro bus just pulling up to the stop. As she turned to wave goodbye, she saw her mother plunk her hands into the front of her apron and shake her head in disapproval.

Anna could have predicted the next sequence of events because Niki never failed to disappoint her. When they entered the long Battery Street tunnel, she heard a large gulp for air. He was going to try again to make it through the tunnel without taking a breath. He never succeeded but he never stopped trying. Other passengers blatantly stared at him turning a deep shade of purple as he struggled to keep his breath. Then just before they emerged into the bright sunlight, he exhaled loudly.

"I almost made it," he pouted. "You drive too slow," he hollered at the bus driver.

"Ssh! Nikolae!" Anna hushed him. "One more outburst like that and we'll forget the zoo."

Slouching down in the seat, Niki promised, "Not a peep. Not a twitter outta me."

Niki could hardly contain himself when they finally got off at the zoo's entrance gates. His excitement caused his eyes to sparkle and his face lit up like a kid's at a birthday party.

"There it is, Anna," he urged. "Come on. Hurry. I can see the elephants."

The gentle giant broke into an awkward lope as he bounded off to visit the placid pachyderms. Anna sighed wistfully as she watched him in his silent appraisal of his jumbo friends. Niki was such a handsome man and young women were frequently enchanted when they first saw him. Sometimes they were coy, other times they were brazen and flirted outrageously. Anna had to chuckle when she recalled the shocked expression that had swept across a cute brunette's face on their last outing. Niki had made an obviously terrific impression until he'd turned to Anna and said, "Come on, let's go home and play Old Maid 'cause I'm tired."

Days at the zoo or the aquarium with Niki were like a soothing balm after her frantic workday schedule. Niki's innocence and good humor washed away the tensions and worries that lingered. Maybe some people would have found such experiences boring, but she found solace in the peaceful predictable afternoons. She helped Niki but he helped her, too. Theirs was a symbiotic relationship.

Anna shivered and realized her chamber was a little cool. She got up from her chair and turned up the thermostat a notch. Then she asked Miriam to bring another hot pot of tea.

No matter how much she reminisced about the good times she had with Niki, she had to face the fact that he didn't fill her life. In fact, sometimes she felt achingly empty after a few hours with him.

Last Saturday had been typical. Their idyllic day together had disintegrated into a nightmare. Everything was fine until she and Niki had stopped at a minimarket for a quick bite to eat. They'd ordered burritos and a couple of little cartons of milk. After they'd left the store and were out on the sidewalk, a half a dozen ruffians made some obscene remarks to her.

She'd tried to ignore their lewd beckonings and their shrill wolf whistles, but they were persistent.

When Niki didn't intervene but continued to eat, oblivious to what the hoodlums were doing, they began to make fun of him.

"What's the matter, dummy?" one sleazy character taunted. "Don't you know how to take care of your lady?"

The jackals scented a better victim than Anna. They had found a man who seemed to be vulnerable. One after the other took verbal potshots at Niki until he was backed up to the wall, confused and frightened. Someone knocked the food out of Niki's hand and started playfully slapping him around.

Anna tried to get between the attacker and Niki, but his cohorts threw her aside as if she were a feather. She screamed for help as Niki took a nasty blow to the stomach.

Suddenly Anna was screaming for a whole different reason. Her mild easygoing brother was holding two hoodlums by their necks. Their feet were a full eighteen inches off the pavement and Niki was shaking them like rag dolls. If he didn't release them quickly, he would permanently harm them.

"Let them go, Niki!" she commanded. "Drop them!"

The rage in him slowly died and he dropped the gagging men in heaps at his feet. They scampered away as quickly as possible, clutching their bruised throats.

"They hurt me, Anna," Niki said. "They hurt me." He smeared the tears from his face with the back of his hand and wiped his hand on his jacket. "I'm sorry," he sobbed, "but they scared me."

"I know, honey," she consoled him.

And she continued to console him, reassure him and comfort him for the rest of the weekend. All the time she was wondering how any man could adapt to living with Niki in his life.

"Judge? Judge Provo?" the bailiff called. "Another question from the jury."

Anna stopped mentally rehashing last weekend and focused her attention on the present.

Taking the written question from him, she asked, "How's it going in there?"

"They're conscientious, I'll say that for them," he said. "But I don't know how long it will be before they make a decision."

Anna checked her notes on the evidence and answered the jury's inquiry succinctly. The bailiff was right. They were being very careful with the defendant's life and she was proud of them.

Left alone again, she mulled over last Monday morning. She'd come jogging up to Miriam's desk and was startled when Miriam grabbed her arm.

"Anna, get on the phone to Judge Walker right away."

"What's wrong?" Anna asked.

"I don't know, but something big is up. He called here about ten minutes ago and told me to have you return his call the minute you got in."

"Get him on the line," Anna said.

She'd never received a call from Ben Walker before and her stomach promptly knotted in concern. Judge Walker was the official assigned to making routine court appointments for May. The job of overseeing the judiciary was handled on a rotating basis and she wondered why Ben was looking for her. He was the current watchdog but she couldn't recall any action of hers that would elicit a reprimand. The buzzing of the intercom ended any chance for a hasty review of her court procedures or judgments.

"This is Judge Provo."

"Good morning, Anna. Ben Walker here. Sorry to catch you so early but I need to meet with you. Can you make it to my chambers in half an hour?"

"Yes, Ben, but what's up?"

"I'd rather go over it in person. See you in thirty minutes."

Racing into the shower, Anna was terror stricken that someone had filed a motion for an amendment of judgment and now the executive committee was reviewing one of her decisions. Had they found fault with one of her sentences? She racked her brain trying to figure out which of her cases might be in question.

In record time, she was dressed and heading toward the elevators when she said over her shoulder to Miriam, "I don't know when I'll be back. Tell the bailiff to inform counsel that something critical has come up and I've been unavoidably delayed."

Summoning up her courage, she slowly walked across the marble floor to the presiding judge's secretary and announced her arrival.

"Yes, Judge Provo, Judge Walker is waiting for you. Please go in."

Unable to quell the butterflies in her stomach, Anna rapped on the door and entered the distinguished man's chambers. His back was turned to the door and he was engaged in a one-sided phone conversation.

He swiveled around in his chair and acknowledged her presence with a nod. She heard him say, "Yes, Margaret, I'll do that. She just came in, so why don't you let me get back to you."

He rose out of his chair and crossed the floor to shake Anna's hand. "Have a seat. That was the court administrator I was just talking to. We were discussing a problem that's cropped up. Last night Joe Elliot had a heart attack and we've no idea when or if he'll be back to work. That leaves us with a gap in the superior court. How would you like to fill it in?"

Anna found it difficult not to break into a jig. Someone having a heart attack was no cause for rejoicing, but not being chastised for some indiscretion was. Fighting to keep her elation under control, she sank into the proffered chair and said, "Superior court judge? Me?"

"Yes. If we didn't think you were qualified, we wouldn't have offered you the position. Are you interested?"

"Definitely, and I'm very honored. If I'm acting confused, it's because I thought you called me up here to chew me out for something, not to offer me a promotion."

"Heavens no, Anna. We're all quite impressed with the job you've been doing, and it was by unanimous decision of the executive committee that you've been recommended," Ben Walker reassured her. "Do I take that smile to mean you accept?"

She felt overwhelmed by the chance that this quiet gentleman was giving her. Superior Court Judge Anna Provo. The title had a nice ring to it. But could she do the job? A momentary doubt filled her as she considered the responsibility that was being placed on her.

Then she came to her senses. The only difference between municipal and superior court was the type of case she'd be hearing. The basic tenets of justice were the same. Of course she could do it.

"I accept, Judge Walker. Thank you. When do you want me to start?"

"Well, let's see, Anna. . . ."

An hour later, the two of them had made the necessary adjustments in cases and called in a temporary judge to fill Anna's absence on the municipal bench. Out of necessity, the arrangements had been made in a hurry, but Anna's mind had gone into high gear and had dealt with the multitude of details in an organized way. Once again she had proven herself.

THE ENSUING WEEK was a long one because the court rules were different and the precedents for major felony cases, juvenile matters and probate had to be more thoroughly researched. It would take time before Anna felt comfortable in her new role, but she knew that she was handling everything well.

Ideally she hoped to work her way up the rest of the ladder to appellate court and then to the state supreme court. Even though there had been other women superior court judges, she was presently the only one. Her new male colleagues seemed to have accepted her graciously, but she still sensed a hint of reticence in them. She knew it would take time to prove her abilities to them.

Those were her long-term objectives. Her goals for this week had been to get her office and chambers moved to her new quarters. Thank heavens she had been able to take both Miriam and John, her bailiff, with her. Without their loyal support and hard work the transition would have been ten times more difficult.

The first thing she had to adjust to was that her jurisdiction had been expanded. She now heard cases on appeal from the municipal courts, and not only from Seattle. They came from around the county.

Anna absently flipped through the pages of her desk calendar. The days had flown and she'd barely had time to take a free breath. At least now with the jury out for deliberation, she could relax.

Miriam buzzed her intercom. "Mr. Brandon is on the line. Do you wish to speak to him?"

"Ask him to hold for a minute," Anna said.

The week's activity had allowed her the freedom to ignore him. He'd left several messages, but she'd never returned them. Her excuse was that she had been busy, but she actually could have found two minutes somewhere. She had shuttled him aside.

Staring at the flashing light on the Hold button of her phone, she tried to overcome her ambivalence. Nervously she picked up the receiver and punched the button.

"Hi, Joshua."

"So you're alive" was his casual reply. "I've been checking the obituary column every day to make sure I'm not trying to get in touch with a dead woman. Rest assured, I haven't seen your name yet."

"Sorry about ignoring you."

"Many a valiant man would have given up after the first three days. I'm glad to see my persistence paid off. How about dinner tonight?"

She didn't hesitate. "Love to, but I've got a jury sequestered on a felony trial."

"Will they come back with a verdict soon?"

"I hope so but I don't know."

"How about if I leave the time open and you just come over to my place when you finish?"

"I guess that'd work. Where do you live?"

"A houseboat on Lake Union. Slip 43. You shouldn't have any trouble finding it."

"Sure you don't mind waiting for me?"

"It'll be a pleasure. Until tonight."

As the hours dragged by and the jury still hadn't

returned with a unanimous decision, Anna began to feel her patience wear thin. There had been several more notes from the foreman of the jury requesting instructions, but John had not returned with the necessary slip of paper.

As she paced back and forth across the burgundy carpet, she tried to picture Joshua serenely waiting for her. But never having been to his home, she had a difficult time placing him in the proper surroundings.

Just as she was about to call him and cancel dinner, John rapped on the door and poked his head in.

"The jury's in."

"Great. Let's get this thing wrapped up so we can all go home."

It only took a few minutes to finish up the case because the verdict was not guilty.

Just as she was locking up, she spotted her friend Tom stepping into an elevator headed down.

"Tom, hold the door," she called out.

She flashed him a smile as she stepped in next to him. "Thanks. How've you been, stranger?"

"Great. Heard about your promotion. Congratulations."

"Thank you, again. Why are you hanging around here on a Friday night?"

"I had to attend an oral deposition of one of our key witnesses. You know how drawn out these pretrial question-and-answer-sessions can be. To top it off, the court reporter was late. Sorry you asked?"

"Nope. I've bent your ear many times."

"Guess that's what friends are for. Where you headed?"

"To a friend's for dinner."

"Good. I'll walk you to your car."

"No, you won't. Elizabeth is in for a face-lift. I'll catch a cab."

"Nix that," Tom said. "I'll give you a ride."

When Anna tried to object, he refused to take no for an answer. Unable to find a valid excuse, she acquiesced and rattled off the directions to Joshua's.

"Who do you know who lives on Portage Bay?" Tom queried.

Anna was in a quandary. She didn't want to admit that she was visiting Joshua. Feeling rather like a child caught with her hand in the cookie jar, she mumbled, "Joshua Brandon."

"Did I hear you right? Joshua Brandon?" Tom crowed. "I knew it. You two are perfect for each other."

"Can it, Randolph." She laughed. "This is only dinner."

Still laughing, he said, "Wait till I tell Sue."

"If you do," Anna threatened, "I'll tell her that I always pick out her birthday presents."

"Spoilsport," he said with a smirk.

"Uh, Tom. You just passed the right address. I saw Joshua's blue Jag parked back there."

He turned his car around and dropped her off. As she got out, she thanked him and waved goodbye. A bright sunshine-yellow Volkswagen parked next to Joshua's car caught her eye. Wondering if it could possibly be hers, she walked over for a closer look. A large ribbon was taped to the dashboard and a note was attached to it. Written in bold letters was "WELCOME HOME, ELIZABETH!"

Astonished at the bug's metamorphosis, Anna

slowly circled the vehicle for a closer inspection. Martin had kept his promise. Elizabeth was a brand new car. Better than new. Playfully patting her hood, Anna said, "You'll be the envy of every VW in town, old girl."

But Anna's mood was promptly toned down as she passed the ice-blue vehicle next to hers. The contrast between their cars served as a reminder of the many differences in their personalities. *He is a sleek elegant jaguar and I'm a skitterish ladybug. Ladybug, Ladybug, fly away home!* she chanted to herself, smiling.

CHAPTER EIGHT

STILL ROOTED TO ONE SPOT, staring at the cars, wondering what in the world she was doing at Joshua's, Anna didn't hear the soft footsteps behind her.

"What do you think of her?"

She turned at Martin's voice and saw him standing under a lamppost at the edge of the carport. "Elizabeth looks fantastic," she told him. "Thank you."

"The bow was Josh's idea," he said.

"How did you get her done so quickly?"

"I just rolled up my sleeves and went to work," Martin answered modestly.

She walked over to him and put her hand lightly on his arm. "I don't know what to say," she said.

"Why do you have to say anything? Thank you is enough."

"But...."

"We all talk too much. Sometimes it's better just to do something or feel something," he said, looking at the pavement.

Anna added, "Sometimes we think too much, as well." Impulsively, she gave Martin a hug. He squeezed her back and with a gentle smile he left. It was the second time he'd exited without saying goodbye. Anna was beginning to learn it was Martin's way of not ruining a lovely encounter with words.

Warily she picked her way down the slanted wooden walkway and was confronted with a choice. On her left was an imposing shingled houseboat with lights blazing and soft music drifting out from its depths. On her right was an aging cottage someone had long ago stuck on a giant raft and then forgotten. Which one was Joshua's? Her first response was to head for the modern sleek building but something stirred her to walk over to the small cottage on the right.

"Glad you made the correct choice, Anna."

She jumped when she heard Joshua's voice call out from the shadows.

"Where are you?" she asked.

"Keep coming in this direction and when you get across the plank, hang a sharp left."

Choosing her way carefully, she was finally able to make out his tall form among the shadows at the end of the deck.

"I was sitting out here enjoying the night air when I spotted you coming down the walk," he said. "Surprised I'm not living in the posh setup next door?"

Actually, Anna felt relieved. She was glad he didn't live on the modern boat. He seemed more approachable living in his ramshackle cabin.

"No," she answered, "I'm not surprised. You're a man of contrasts."

"We're even," he said. "You're a paradox."

Taking her hand, Joshua guided Anna to the front deck where two wicker chairs were placed among a pile of siding, nails, paint cans and sheets of plasterboard. She sat in one chair but he remained standing, leaning against a railing. He was wearing cutoffs and she tried to ignore the way his tanned thighs glistened in the dim light

"What do you think of your new wheels?" he asked

"She's marvelous, and I told Martin so when we met up on the street."

"He dropped her off since he was coming to town for the evening anyway. If you hadn't accepted my dinner offer, it was a way of bribing you. Want your car, you have to come to me."

She smiled at the conspiracy. "So you and Martin were in cahoots?"

"Like Gilbert and Sullivan," he laughed.

"More like Don Quixote and Sancho Panza," she teased innocently.

But Joshua turned serious. "Am I tilting at windmills?" he asked.

She wasn't sure what he was asking. Was he referring to his career? Or was he asking if she was going to remain elusive?

Her answer was the same for both questions. "No," she whispered. Then to change the subject quickly, she asked, "Remodeling?"

He looked at the stacks of building material and said, "Yes. Watch out for the booby traps on board. The hazards of the job."

It was Anna's turn to take an innocent statement and twist it.

"Do you always overhaul any aging women that wander into your life? Or can some of us rest assured we'll be safe?"

She realized too late that what she intended to be a playful bantering between friends had suddenly changed tone. She watched in paralyzed fascination as Joshua slowly bent down, took her face and, holding her cheeks gently in his bronzed hands, stared into her eyes.

"You'll never be safe with me, Anna," he said softly. "But don't worry, I have no intention of remodeling you. You're absolutely perfect as is."

Hypnotized, she looked into his cerulean eyes. The lights from the house next door danced in the depths of his gaze and she found herself being drawn to him. Without even realizing that she was responding to his touch, she rose up out of her chair and wrapped her arms around his waist.

"Relax," he said and felt Anna's guard dissolve. He began to trace a light pattern up and down the rigid muscles of her back. He could feel the tension in her ebb and he slowly increased the pressure. Without saying a word, he continued the massage, dispelling her ironclad coat of armor. It was the first time she had ever allowed herself the freedom to respond completely to him, and he was on guard against any hint of hurry. He'd waited too long for this moment to take a chance of scaring her off.

"It has been a long time since I've felt so content and at one with the world."

The noise of the bustling daytime traffic had faded, and one of the few sounds that disturbed the evening was the peaceful lapping of the waves against the bottom of the houseboat.

Encircling her small waist, he said, "Dance with me. I guarantee there's no audience." He started to sway to the distant notes of music that floated across Lake Union from the restaurant perched on the western shore. His fluid movements brought Anna's body directly against his and he started to hum the melody of the song.

Anna willingly followed the commands his body gave hers. As they waltzed in the dark, a few stars appeared and the night creatures joined the chorus. Fifty yards or so away from Joshua's moorage was marshland. It was the bass croak of a large bullfrog that broke the tranquil mood and shifted her attention from Joshua's dancing to the crisp evening air.

As if he could read her mind, he said, "It's getting chilly. Let's go inside and I'll pour you a drink."

He kissed her forehead lightly and, without removing his hand from the small of her back, guided her into the house.

The small room was sparsely furnished. Placed squarely in front of the bay window was a large suede couch piled high with an array of soft pillows. She gratefully sank into it, watching as Joshua poured some white Burgundy into a crystal goblet.

Anna played with a paint drop cloth that was draped over a chair next to her. Fingering the paint splattered on it she joked, "Is this a new style of decorating?"

"I thought I'd take up interior decorating if the public defender's office lays me off," he chuckled.

He handed her the glass of wine, and as his hand brushed hers she impulsively reached out and held his wrist, silently inviting him to stay near. Soft evening light filtered through the windows, bathing the room in bouncing shadows. The soft couch became an isolated island adrift on a sea of intimacy.

She curled her long legs up under herself and gently

pulled him down next to her. The shy reticence that had colored all previous encounters with him vanished.

With natural ease, his muscular arm draped over her shoulder and they leaned back onto the pillows. It was comforting to sit quietly sharing the silence. Neither he nor she felt obligated to offer any pat phrases to fill in the conversational void.

Minutes passed with neither of them saying a word. Her head rested on his shoulder and his sensitive fingers lightly fondled the soft skin of her ear lobe. As if by mutual agreement, they leaned forward and set their glasses on the packing crate he was using for a table.

Unable to resist the temptation of Anna's softly parted lips any longer, Joshua began to sprinkle a rain of light kisses across her delicate cheeks. With infinite care, he traced a pattern on her waiting lips and slowly began to increase the pressure of his mouth on hers. His tongue sought the honeyed recesses. A soft moan escaped from Anna and he shifted his weight, allowing himself access to the ivory skin of her long graceful neck.

Beguiled by the soft nuzzling, Anna dropped her head back and encouraged him to explore all of her. He awakened erotic areas of her body she hadn't known existed. His soft mustache played against the satin skin of her throat, causing tiny hairs on her arms to stand up.

Just as she thought she could stand no more, he switched rhythm and centered his attention on her lips once more. Only this time, his kisses were not soft and successive but were firm in their demand as he boldly probed her mouth with his tongue.

Unable to sit passively and merely submit to Joshua's lovemaking, she snaked her arms around his neck and pulled his body closer. They moved together as if directed by a skillful choreographer, and Anna lay back, pulling the full weight of his body onto hers.

She could tell he was releasing a small degree of control. His breathing was irregular, and when she pulled his shirt out of his cutoffs, she heard a sharp intake of air. Reaching her hands up and drawing her fingers across his back, he gave out a small gasp of pleasure.

Spurred on by his response, Anna thrust her tongue into his mouth. He fondled her firm breasts and she arched her body in reply. His fingers fumbled with the delicate pearl buttons of her silk blouse and she withdrew her hands from under his shirt to help him loosen the fastenings.

The suede couch felt warm against the naked flesh of her back as she nestled into its pliant depths. She watched with barely disguised anticipation as Joshua carelessly tossed his shirt to the floor. The soft light framed his torso and her eyes roamed over his heaving chest.

She was caught off guard when he settled back on his haunches and made no move to cover her half-exposed body with his. Embarrassed by his bold stare, she attempted to sit up, but he reached out and tenderly pushed her back.

"Please don't move," he crooned. "I just want to look at you. You're magnificent."

Then he slowly leaned forward and began to explore her skin with his mouth, seeking out every hid-

den spot with his lips. As he slipped the straps of her
bra down with his teeth, she could feel her responsive
nipples begin to quiver. But to tease her and heighten
her arousal, Joshua's tongue repeatedly missed the
sensitive areola and he refused to center his attention
on her nipples. Just as she thought she couldn't endure the marvelous deprivation any longer, his
mouth encircled one pink orb and he began his on-
slaught. While he gently nibbled one peak, he lightly
brushed his callused palm back and forth across the
other.

Her hips shifted under him as her body reached upward. Taking each nipple between thumb and fore-
finger, Joshua continued his seductive teasing as he
kissed her neck and whispered, "Your skin's like
velvet."

Anna felt herself being swept up into his arms and
he carried her to the bedroom. He carefully lowered
her onto the bed, but he did not join her. His hands
slipped her skirt over her slim hips and with delib-
erate unhurried movements he removed the rest of
her clothing.

She felt like a gift being joyfully unwrapped.
Revealed, naked to his appraisal, she deliciously
stretched on the bed, cloaked only by a beam of
moonlight.

Looming above her, he leisurely discarded his own
clothing. She greedily took in his resplendent phy-
sique. His lean stomach was lightly touched with
golden hairs and she could distinguish the white skin
of his torso, which was shielded from the tanning
rays of the sun.

Curving his body over hers and supporting his

weight on his arms, he lightly brushed the soft down on his chest across her breasts. Anna felt like a canvas being painted in delicate watercolors. She reached out to pull him closer but he resisted.

"Not yet, little one," he purred, his voice sounding like rippling water.

Her heart pounded with greedy anticipation as his lips plied their way up her smooth thighs. As he traveled up one leg and down the other, his hands caressed her flat stomach and supple hips with lambent touches. Uncontrollably her hips swayed as his kisses gradually worked their way to the center of her passion.

Placing his hands under the firm flesh of her buttocks, Joshua lifted Anna's hips off the bed and she instinctively wrapped her slim calves around his body. Just when she'd adjusted her breathing and managed to regain a semblance of control, he touched her in a new place, sending her senses careening.

Certain she could no longer contain her hunger, she begged, "Now, Joshua, now."

He abandoned her moist recesses, slid his body up the bed and covered her with demanding kisses. They were no longer gentle as he forcefully took command of her mouth, shoving any remaining vestige of control aside.

Their bodies glistened and tumbled rapturously in the starlight as they fulfilled each other. As he lowered himself into her, she replied with savage upward thrusts of her hips.

They moved in perfect time, each one urging the other on to higher plateaus. "Joshua!" she called out.

"All the way with me," he coaxed as he drew her over boundaries she'd never crossed before.

As she drifted back down from their zenith, Joshua fingered her tangled tresses and her heart slowed its frantic pace. It was several minutes before either one had any inclination to move or speak.

Finally Joshua breached the silence. "If this is friendship, spare me passion," he said, kissing her on the cheek.

Had this comment come from anyone other than Joshua, she might have taken offense. But in light of their earlier pact of maintaining a purely platonic relationship, the unabandoned scene that had just unfolded seemed humorous. She couldn't possibly proclaim they were just good friends now. The absurdity of the notion, or even how she could have ever entertained such a thought, made her smile.

Nibbling her earlobe, he murmured, "Are we still pals?"

"It's not incompatible to be both lovers and friends," she said, resting her head on his shoulder and drawing a whimsical pattern on his chest with her fingernail. His gold sextant with its serpentine chain intrigued her and she touched it.

"This is original. A gift?" she asked.

"Yes, my grandfather gave it to me when I left the family business and moved back here." Joshua smiled at the memory. "He knew I'd purchased a sailboat and said a bum like me needed a talisman."

"Has it brought you good luck?" Anna fished, hoping he'd say she was the best thing he'd ever found.

"The jury's still out." He winked and rumpled her hair. "Have I told you you're beautiful?"

"Yes," she said while her stomach growled. "Did you hear that? It's reminding you to feed me."

"The cook needs some incentive," he said, and proceeded to peck his way up her neck and across her flushed cheeks. Once he made his way to her full lips, he gave her a quick smack and jumped out of bed. Grabbing a pair of faded jeans, he slipped them up over his legs and hastily threw on a sweat shirt.

She contemplated his relaxed composure and an old Russian adage came to mind. "The devil is always dressed in the latest fashion." Well, this devil was gorgeous no matter what he wore.

She lounged in bed for a while, enjoying the warmth of the covers and listening to the pleasant clatter of pots and pans in the kitchen. Feeling guilty for loafing while he prepared their meal, she forced herself up and out of the snug cocoon.

Just as she was about to dress, Joshua popped into the bedroom and tossed her a thick terry-cloth robe.

"Put this on," he advised. "I've some fresh butter clams steaming and I wouldn't want you dripping on your silk blouse."

He seemed oblivious to her nudity as he slipped the robe over her shoulders and pulled her hair out from under the collar. She found no reason to object, so she tied the sash and traipsed after him into the living room.

Carefully arranged on the packing crate in front of the couch were two shrimp-and-artichoke salads. He had covered the box with an ivory-colored linen cloth and the table was set with exquisite china and antique silver. The sharp contrast of elegance and simplicity was touching. He had taken great pains with the dinner. The Tropicana rosebud placed on her napkin was a lovely compliment—to the table, to the evening, to her.

"Thank you," she said as she slowly reached down and picked up the tiny blossom to breathe in its soft scent.

"I'm glad you like it." He sounded pleased. "Now eat."

After they finished their salads, Joshua brought over a heaping bowl of little butter clams and two small cups of drawn butter for dipping.

"I hope you like them." He placed the overflowing container between them. "I also have some Jailhouse bread. Would you like some?"

"I'd love some," was her quick response. "It didn't take you long to find that bakery. What's your opinion of the program?"

"I totally approve," he said. "Giving the prisoners a useful task like baking is constructive. It's an excellent job-training program and, on top of all that, it's darn good bread."

Sitting down on the couch next to her, he buttered a thick slice. "Here." He handed Anna the bread.

"Are you going to let all that marvelous clam nectar just sit in the kettle and go to waste?" she asked.

"Do I dare have any?" He laughed. "Does that sign at Ivar's have any truth to it?"

Smiling at the local joke, Anna leaned back and flashed him an innocent look. She knew exactly what sign he was referring to. The sign warned patrons of the waterfront restaurant that any man requesting more than one cup of clam nectar needed his wife's permission first. The amusing caveat was based on an old wives' tale that claimed clam nectar is an aphrodisiac.

"Let's be brave and find out," she said teasingly.

Ogling her lasciviously, Joshua warned, "I'll not be held responsible for any side effects." He rose to get the clear broth.

They gorged themselves on the fresh seafood and groaned in unison as they pushed their plates away.

"You're an excellent cook, sir. My compliments."

"Thank you. Would you like some coffee?"

"Yes, but let's do the dishes first. Then we can relax without feeling guilty," she said.

"You're on."

After they finished washing and drying the dishes and everything was neatly cleared away, Joshua poured two mugs of freshly brewed coffee. They sat on the couch and entered into an unhurried account of their respective weeks.

"So what took you so long to return my calls?" he asked. "Trying to avoid me?"

Anna felt a twinge of guilt as she acknowledged the truth of his statement. She had been avoiding him. But now they had crossed the threshold of intimacy. It was too late to stop and push him away. Besides, she wanted to draw him closer.

"No," she lied. "I wasn't dodging you. I was truly busy."

"With what?"

"My new job."

"What new job?"

"I got kicked upstairs. You are now having coffee with a King County Superior Court Judge."

After she answered his bombardment of questions, she set her mug down and smiled. "Now do you believe me when I say I was busy?"

"Yes, but from now on neither of us will be too busy to make time for each other," he said.

"Is that so?"

"That's so. Now that we've amended the rules, I'll insist on using the doctrine of stare decisis."

"You mean I've got to stand by our decision?"

"Decision to be lovers?"

"Have we decided that?"

"I don't know about you, but I have," he said, smiling.

"Well..." she started to quibble about how they had other considerations, other commitments, other demands, but he prevented her from speaking.

He locked her eyes with his determined stare and defied her to voice any excuses. He leaned over and kissed her. It was no gentle tender kiss, but a dominating one full of fierce hunger. His demanding lips forced her yielding ones apart and immediately his tongue thrust its way into her pliant mouth.

Unexpectedly he stopped and she was disoriented. She'd been aware of nothing but his lovemaking and didn't want him to stop. Realizing she wanted to be with him as much as he wanted to be with her, she finally nodded her head in silent consent.

"Good," he said. "Now that that's settled, how about a toast in honor of your promotion. Cognac?"

"Please."

"I have a bottle of Courvoisier that I keep on hand for special occasions. I'll be right back."

Anna took the few minutes that he was gone to analyze her situation. This was getting out of control. But the memory of his passion forced all logic out of her mind and she leaned back to simply enjoy the evening. His lovemaking had erased all her doubts and she basked in the extraordinarily warm feelings that washed over her. Could she dare to love this man? Just for tonight she'd throw all caution to the wind and ride with her heart.

As Joshua rounded the corner, he was astonished by the picture Anna made curled on the sofa with her hair spread out like a nimbus behind her. A look of tranquility replaced her normal guarded expression and he was moved by the transformation. He'd started out wanting to conquer her. But now a sense of wanting to cherish her descended on him. He felt shaken. Cherishing implied responsibility.

"Don't fall asleep on me yet," he said as he slipped in next to her. "I want to hear more about your week."

Forcing her eyes open, she raised her head and reached out for the snifter of golden cognac.

"I think we've talked about me long enough," she said. "I want to hear how your week was."

"Well, let's see," he mused. "I've got a really sticky case. It deals with domestic violence and I'm having a devil of a time setting up a defense for this guy. He admitted he's guilty, but only to me. I know everyone is entitled to an adequate defense but I have a hard time stomaching this one. I just wish I didn't have to represent him."

"I know what you mean," she consoled. "I run into the same problem with some of the cases I sit on. I simply work hard at maintaining an objective attitude and don't prejudge anyone. What if you forgot this man's confession to you and took the attitude he just might be innocent. Would you have an easier time?" she asked.

"Maybe." He sighed. "At least I'll try. But let's forget work. I've had it with the legal world for a while."

"You're full of good ideas tonight."

"Talking about ideas," he began, "my parents' fortieth anniversary is coming up. I couldn't think of an appropriate gift until I saw that unique eyeglass case you have. I was wondering if it would be possible to get something done out of birchbark for them? I'm sure mom doesn't have such an original piece."

"When's their anniversary?"

"Not till the end of next month. I just need lots of time because they have almost everything."

"I understand. I have a hard time shopping for my folks. But papa would love to make something for them. We could go to their shop tomorrow."

"Great! I can meet your brother, Niki, too."

"Sorry, but Niki won't be around. He's spending the weekend at Fort Lewis with the Special Olympics," she explained.

"The what?"

"Special Olympics—for the handicapped. He competes in several track events. The athletes go out to the fort and stay for a couple of days. The soldiers share their barracks and the mess hall with Niki and his friends. They have a grand time. Every spring Niki works hard to get in good shape."

"How many people participate?" Joshua asked.

"Oh, I'd say two or three thousand from all over the state. There are hot-air balloon rides, games and lots of other kinds of entertainment. The army even displays tanks and helicopters for everyone to climb on and inspect," she said.

"I'm sorry I'm going to miss him," Joshua said, sounding sincere, "but it sounds like he'll have a ball. I'll have to meet him another day."

"There'll be plenty of opportunities."

"Is that a promise?" he asked, brushing her hair from her face.

"I promise," she pledged. It reminded her of another promise. "Don't let me forget to pick up something for him tomorrow. A new toy or something. That way if he hasn't won a medal, he has some memento to appease him."

"Medals?"

"Yeah, they hand out medals and ribbons. Niki has a board set up in his room that is chock-full of them."

"I'd like to watch one of those meets sometime. Think I could wangle an invitation out of Niki?"

"Wangle? He'd love it. But enough about him."

Joshua's total acceptance of her brother even before meeting him was almost overwhelming to Anna. She'd never expected him to be so open, so tolerant. How could she have misjudged him? And now that she knew what Joshua was really like, was she falling in love?

"What would you like to talk about, pretty lady?" he asked.

"How about what time you're picking me up in the morning?"

"Picking you up? I thought you'd spend the night here."

"I couldn't possibly."

"Why not?"

"Well, I...." She searched for a reason to go

home. Niki wouldn't be waiting on her doorstep and she didn't have to work in the morning. So why not? She wasn't running away anymore. "I guess it's just that I'm not used to sleeping anywhere but in my own bed."

"I'm eternally grateful for that," he teased, "but couldn't you make an exception? Or aren't my accommodations grand enough for a superior judge?"

She laughed at his mock wounded pride. "All right, all right. I'll stay."

"I have a confession to make," Joshua whispered in a conspiratorial tone. "The clam nectar didn't work. I'm beat. Will cuddling up together and being wrapped in my arms suffice?"

Anna ran her fingers through his soft golden curls, studied his haunting eyes and said in a hushed voice, "I can think of nothing that would please me more. I, too, have a confession. I'm exhausted."

Slowly rising, they ambled toward the bedroom with their arms curled around each other's waists. She turned her back to Joshua as she slipped out of his robe and quickly dove under the soft eiderdown quilt. When she emerged from the billowing duvet, she was startled to find him watching her every movement.

"What are you waiting for?" she asked.

"I was hoping to catch more than a fleeting glance of your lovely form, but you're too fast."

His expression had taken on that mischievous look as he carefully pulled off his sweat shirt and stepped out of his jeans.

"Maybe that nectar worked better than I thought," he muttered hoarsely.

He stood framed by the filtered moonlight. He made no attempt to cover his nude body and Anna sensed he was purposely allowing her the opportunity to study him, to prove to herself that there was no doubt that his earlier fatigue had vanished.

With calculated movements, he crossed the small room and pulled back the covers, exposing Anna's willowy form.

"Now it's my turn" was all he said.

CHAPTER NINE

THE MORNING SUN filtered through Joshua's bedroom window, swathing them in a diffused light. Anna shifted her head and dreamily studied his angular face as he slept. There were golden whiskers shadowing his jawline and his hair was tousled like a little boy's.

Her father had a saying, "Morning is wiser than evening." Well, being enveloped in Joshua's arms told her that both the evening and morning were equally marvelous. Spooning her body closer to his, she had no regrets, only a sanguine anticipation of what lay ahead for them now that they had coupled their lives.

She scanned the bedroom looking for a clock. Finally she spotted a small digital on the nightstand and was barely able to make out the time. Five-thirty! Utterly content, she cozied her head on his chest and drifted back to sleep.

"HEY, SLEEPYHEAD," Joshua said. "I thought you were going to take me to the market today."

Passing a steaming mug of coffee back and forth under her nose, he playfully patted her fanny and nudged her out of her world of dreams.

"What time is it?" she asked, fighting off the morning lethargy that still had her trapped.

"It's precisely eight. Time to wake up."

"All right, master, I'm awake. Just give me a couple of minutes for my brain to catch up with my body."

After drinking her coffee, Anna felt ready to attack the day and jumped out of bed, excited at the prospect of introducing Joshua to her parents and all the hidden pleasures of the market.

Dressing, she said, "We need to stop at my place before we visit my folks. It'd look pretty strange for me to show up in work clothes on a Saturday morning. My parents aren't stuffy, but they'd wonder."

"Wonder what? Why you hadn't done your laundry or why you hadn't been a good girl and gone home last night?" he teased.

"Both, so find my shoes and I'm set."

They found them kicked under the couch. Slipping them onto her narrow feet, he glanced up and said, "We'd better get going fast or I'll change my mind and hold you captive in my lair for the entire weekend."

Jumping out of his reach, she scurried for the door and deftly made her way across the deck. He followed close behind and when they got to her car, she tossed the keys to him.

She enjoyed sitting back and watching the familiar scenes whiz by. She seldom was a passenger. Joshua chose to drive through the city rather than jump on the freeway. On the weekends, the city streets weren't too busy, but during the weekday traffic, Interstate 5 provided a much faster way to get through the maze of office buildings.

In just a few minutes they were waiting at a stoplight directly in front of Pioneer Square. The area had been restored to much of its former grandeur. The dominating landmark remained the original triangle surrounded by ornate park benches and covered with an oxidized bronze canopy. At one end of the square was a large Indian totem pole, a testament to the original inhabitants of the area and to Chief Sealth for whom Seattle had been named.

Many of the shops were just opening and café owners were hauling out small sidewalk tables for dining in the late-spring sun. A few blocks farther down, Joshua made a left turn and headed up Jackson Street. Soon they were in the heart of Seattle's large International District. This melting pot of Asian cultures attracted many visitors to its specialty shops and small family-owned restaurants.

Anna glanced down a side street and spied the unimposing front of Bush Gardens, an inviting Japanese inn that was one of her favorite dining spots.

"Let's eat Japanese style tonight," she said.

"Where?"

"Bush Gardens. The food is superb and the atmosphere is cozy."

"More cozy than my couch?"

"I don't know about that, but if we phone for reservations we'll get a tatami room and you'll definitely have privacy."

"You'll be my geisha?"

"If you'll be my samurai," she countered.

Pulling up in front of the Victorian house, Joshua parked the car but left the engine running. He came around and opened Anna's door.

"You go up and get ready. I'm going to the bakery to pick up breakfast. Any requests?"

"A couple of croissants, please?"

She took the stairs two at a time and managed to shower, change into some jeans and a sweater and put her makeup on before he returned. The pale yellow sweater was new. She'd been saving it for some special occasion and was pleased by the casual yet feminine effect it created. While brushing the tangles out of her hair, Anna toyed with the idea of putting it into a ponytail but decided against it. She let it fall around her shoulders in a cascade of gleaming curls. Remembering the amber combs her grandmother had worn, she rummaged through her jewelry box. Fastening the golden flowers made of petrified tree resin in her hair, she recalled the legend behind amber. Russians revered it, believing it was formed from the tears of people who cried over the tombs of heroes. They also wore it to preserve good health.

Anna stepped back to analyze the image in the mirror. She was pleased and knew Joshua would be, too.

Just as the water for tea came to a boil, she heard a rapping on her door and rushed to let him in.

With a wide grin, he thrust a white bag full of croissants and several varieties of Danish pastry under her nose so she could catch a whiff of the freshly baked treats.

"Smells good, huh?" he teased. "But before you can have one, you've got to hold still and let me look at you." He blew a long low whistle as he surveyed her. "You look great."

"Cut out the leering, Counselor," she laughed, grabbing the baked goods out of his hands.

Joshua followed her across the living room and silently admired the simple elegance of her home. The fabrics were all neutral tones, which allowed the natural beauty of the many polished wood pieces to shine. There were a few articles strategically scattered around the large room that hinted at her background. A brightly painted wooden doll was on the mantel. Joshua lifted the top off and inside was nestled a boy, and inside of him was another little girl and then finally a baby swaddled in a painted blanket.

"That's called a *matryoshka* doll," Anna said. "It's a very old one that happens to be Niki's pride and joy."

"What's that?" Joshua asked, pointing to a vase. "Ivory?"

"No, it's bone. Probably deer horn with mother-of-pearl inlay. It was a purely Slavic art form for many years. Papa thinks this piece dates from the mid-eighteenth century," she said. "Are you really interested in all this stuff?"

"Show me more," he answered eagerly.

"Well, this is my modern version of the Russian 'beautiful corner.'" She led him to a niche near the fireplace where a handful of icons in gilded frames were hung on the off-white wall. "Every Russian house had such a spot where the icons were placed and votive candles were burned. The light would flicker on the bright faces of the saints or the *Madonna with Child*, and the pictures came alive. I guess that's why they always referred to it as the 'beautiful corner.'"

"They have an ethereal quality to them even without the candles," Joshua marveled.

"How would you like tea out of a real samovar?"

She set up her large brass samovar on the table out on the terrace. Joshua watched her as she brewed the tea, and she felt a lovely sense of pride in her heritage.

Quietly they sipped their drinks and nibbled on the pastries. Boxes overflowing with spring flowers surrounded the verandah. It was a veritable bower of blossoms and created the impression of a mountain meadow instead of an inner-city condominium.

Reluctantly they cleared the table and headed for the market.

It took them several minutes to find a vacant parking spot but eventually they wedged the car into a stall. The red-brick road in front had been washed clean and its uneven surface cut through the center of the market area like a mahogany-tinted ribbon. They strolled hand in hand through the jostling crowds and Anna found it hard to walk slowly and let Joshua have a chance to leisurely inspect all of the produce stands. She was anxious to take him on a complete tour of all the nooks and crannies hidden away on the lower levels of the market. One of her favorite spots was the spice shop tucked into the corner of the second floor. Locals beat a steady path to the tiny cubbyhole to browse through the wide variety of aromatic herbs, teas and spices the owners crammed into the small establishment.

She would show Joshua the sights too many people missed when they only explored the upper level and didn't venture into the cavernous interior. It would be a rare treat to introduce him to the friends of her childhood and share the special charm of her private world.

But she knew their first stop had to be mama and

papa's shop. If word got back that they went to another place first, she'd never hear the end of it from mama. Anna knew the basis for her reluctance. The only man she'd ever admitted into her life had been Sean. Now when mama met Joshua, she would immediately jump to false conclusions about her relationship with him and the pressure would begin. Somehow she would have to find a way to haul mama off to the side and warn her not to make any comment about wedding plans and lifelong commitments.

Joshua interrupted her silent plotting by asking, "Where's your parents' shop?"

"Just around this bend you'll see a sign reading The Lubki."

"What does *lubki* mean?"

"They are penny prints, handmade broadsides, which are a type of advertisement. Papa still produces them for the local merchants to hand out to passersby. They are printed in bright colors and Niki helps with the carving of the wooden print blocks."

They entered the brightly lit shop and mama let out a cry of surprise and rushed over to greet them.

"So, Anna, what brings you down here? And who is this with you?"

"Mama and papa, this is Joshua Brandon. Joshua, my parents, Eugenia and Alexis Provolosky," Anna said.

"A good name," mama pronounced, "not shortened."

"I've explained a hundred times," Anna argued, "I shortened it for professional reasons."

"Ha!" Mama almost snorted. "Professional reasons! That's all this silly girl thinks of is her job."

Papa ran interference. "Leave it alone, woman, and be polite to Anna's friend," he said.

Mama promptly locked her arm in the crook of Joshua's elbow and began peppering him with questions. "So, Joshua, what do you do for a living?"

"I'm an attorney," he answered.

"Oh? You must work with my Anna. Do they pay you well?"

Joshua grinned. "Actually no, but I like the work."

"So, how long have you been friends with my little Anna?"

"I bumped into her almost two months ago."

Her mother turned and switched her attention to papa and fired a string of directives. "Papa, look at this mess you made. Here we are with guests and your stuff is spread all over. What will they think? And that Nikolae. I told him yesterday to clean up the workshop and go look at it. It's a pigsty. Him and his Olympics. That's all he thinks about."

"Mama—" Anna halted her parent's ranting "—since when am I a guest? The shop looks fine. Relax."

"Yes, but what will your friend think of us?"

Papa put his arm around mama's shoulder and gave her a gentle shake. "*Nichevo*, never mind. Listen to Anna," he soothed. "I'll take Joshua to the back room and show him around. While we chat, I'll pick up the mess. You visit with Anna."

Joshua flashed Anna a perplexed smile and followed the path her father blazed through the cluttered aisles. He walked slowly and carefully for the little shop was full to overflowing with articles and handicraft items, most of which he had never seen before.

On a shelf with caviar and pâtés were other delicacies he couldn't name. Gaily paraded on the walls were Russian clothes ranging from simple peasant styles to elaborately embroidered ethnic costumes. Everywhere he looked there was a different display set up to intrigue the customer. The thing that particularly fascinated him was the rack of books, papers and magazines, all printed in Russian.

Hurrying to catch up with Anna's father, Joshua went through a curtain in the back and wandered into the cluttered workshop of a true craftsman. The workbench was full of tools for carving and shaping birchbark.

The elderly gentleman stumped over to a stool and sat at his bench, well lit by an overhead fluorescent fixture. His gleaming silver hair was worn somewhat long and he sported a full flowing beard. Joshua noted that Anna received her statuesque height from her father. He was well over six feet with long legs and a hardy robust build. His simple clothing was well covered by an ink-spattered printer's apron and his hands identified him as a working artist. His fingers were nicked and scarred and a rainbow of colored inks stained them. He was a commanding man, but his features were softened by the tiny lines that splayed out from his hazel eyes, indicating he probably had a fine sense of humor.

"Like my hideout?" he asked Joshua. "I keep it messy and that way mama gets so frustrated she never comes back here. I love that woman but Tolstoy was right."

"How?" Joshua asked, knowing there was a punch line.

"He said, 'When I have one foot in the grave I will tell the truth about women. I shall tell it, jump into my coffin, pull the lid over me and say, Do what you like now.' "

Joshua laughed at the vivid imagery.

"Till then my workshop stays messy," papa pronounced. "Like my system?"

"Yes, Mr. Provolosky. I think it's brilliant."

"No, no, son. No one calls me Mr. Provolosky. I'm Papa Provo to everyone and mama is just mama. Don't change a good system. Rule number one in this family."

"Okay, Papa Provo. I'm catching on."

"Good. Would you like to see my latest creation?"

Joshua nodded and pulled up a vacant stool. "What's that you're working on?" he asked, pointing to the intricately etched box.

"This is a tea box out of birchbark," papa explained. "The birch tree is one of God's greatest gifts. It can do four things: give life, muffle groans, cure the sick and keep the body strong."

Anna's father seemed to be an endless source of miscellaneous information, oddball quotes and artistic talent. In other words, he was a wonderful character, and Joshua had a penchant for uniquely different individuals. Papa was a bonus to a beautiful weekend.

Fingering the tea box, Joshua asked, "How in the world can you get such delicate flowers and leaves out of birch? They look more like lace."

Papa's eyes glowed as he warmed to one of his favorite subjects. "I take a piece of bark and using a cobbler's awl, I impress my pattern onto it. Then I use a very sharp knife and slice away all the superfluous material," he explained, turning the box so that Joshua could see the different angles clearly. "Don't you think it looks like a fairyland of snow? It reminds me of the old country, and when I get homesick, it helps."

"It's stunning. Would you do up a tea box for me? I'd like to give it to my parents for their wedding anniversary."

"I'd be honored. Is there any special scene you want on it?"

"Use your own superb judgment. Will four weeks be too soon to finish one?"

"Not at all," papa reassured him.

Joshua watched as he wrote in Cyrillic script. Obviously Papa Provo still communicated better in Russian than he did in his adopted tongue. Undistracted by conversation, Joshua tried to isolate the odor that permeated the workshop. It was a combination of the fresh bark shavings that lay strewn over the floor, the acrid smell of thinners, chemicals and inks used for printing, and the musty odor of the piles of paper stored on the far wall.

"Papa Provo," he asked, "would you mind showing me how you use the wooden blocks for printing those broadsides Anna was describing?"

"Mind? Does the sun object to shining?" he preened.

The two men immersed themselves in the treasures of the back room. They were oblivious to the world beyond their realm.

In the outer regions, Anna was answering her mother's barrage of questions.

"No, I'm not in love with him. I introduced him as

my good friend and that's what he is. A good friend. Don't start imagining things that don't exist.''

"But you never bring your friends to the shop.''

"I brought Joshua because he noticed the case for my glasses that papa made and he wants to get something for his parents. That's all there is to it.''

"I saw the way he looks at you, ha!''

"Mama, stop it. I don't want you embarrassing me. You keep your opinions to yourself and let me handle things my way.''

"If I let you handle things your way, you'll be fifty and still single. How will I get grandchildren with you an old maid?''

"Can we drop the subject? I'm having a nice time and I don't want to spoil the day by fighting with you,'' she begged. "We've been over this subject a million times. Case closed.''

"Case closed, ha!''

"Mama, I'm warning you. . . .''

"Okay, okay. I'll be quiet. But I'm warning you, too, little girl. That Joshua is in love with you.''

With a twitch of her head, she scurried off to tend to a customer, but she tauntingly hummed Brahms's lullaby under her breath.

Anna had to laugh at her mother's crude attempt to instill a maternal instinct in her. Her mother was about as subtle as fireworks. Always talking, clucking, scolding, badgering and angrily exploding at her. But, Anna had to concede, always with the best intentions and a huge helping of love.

She wondered how Joshua and papa were getting along. She slipped to the rear of the room and pulled the curtain aside. Standing in the doorway, quietly observing the two men, she saw they were totally engrossed in talking about woodworking tools and what the old-fashioned implements were used for. Time didn't exist for them. The world had stopped to let them revel in their newfound camaraderie.

She could see that Joshua was enjoying himself. Most people would have been bored with papa's conversation, but Joshua had his head bent over the workbench, attentively listening and watching. She felt a sudden flush of sadness. Too bad Niki couldn't completely share papa's world like this. Not that her father had ever complained, but Anna knew the joy it would have given papa if only he could have passed on his ancient skills.

Shaking off the bittersweet mood, she called out, "Are you two going to stay back here all day?"

The men straightened up from the bench with guilty looks on their faces, just like two little boys caught playing in the mud in their Sunday clothes.

"Sorry, Firebird," papa said. "I didn't mean to keep your friend so long."

He walked over and gave his daughter a light kiss on the head.

"Come, Joshua, I think we'd better keep the ladies company."

As the three of them headed to the front of the store, her father waylaid her by wrapping his arm around her shoulder. "That boy is a nice one," he said in a stage whisper.

"He's a man, and don't you go getting any ideas about us," she said. "I've already had this conversation with mama and I thought at least you'd spare me. Can't I bring a friend to meet you without both of you contacting Father Dimitri?"

"Don't ruffle your feathers, Firebird," he cooed.

"I only said that I thought he was nice. Besides, I invited him to go with us on a picnic some Sunday and he accepted."

"Accepted?"

"Yes. Are you coming, too?"

Her father had taken to Joshua completely. What Pandora's box had she opened?

Mama was stocking some shelves when Anna returned. Joshua was chatting amicably with her and turned when Anna and her father joined them.

"Did I hear you call her Firebird?" he asked papa.

"Yes," papa answered. "There is a legend about a humble maiden who is turned into a Firebird by an evil sorcerer. She dies but her feathers continue to live on earth. The feathers are magic ones, which only those who love beauty and who seek to make beauty for others can see and admire. When I saw Anna's fiery hair for the first time, I knew she was one of those magic feathers. She was my Firebird."

Anna's face turned a deep pink as she stood and listened to her father relate the folk tale.

"Joshua isn't interested in Russian folklore," she chastised him. She was trying to shift the conversation away from such a personal note. "Why don't we tell him about the market?"

"I think the story is fascinating," Joshua corrected, "so don't interrupt, *Firebird*."

Anna flipped back her long hair in irritation and stomped off to help her mother.

Shaking his head and vainly suppressing a laugh, papa said, "That girl is so much like her mother. She'll be a wild one to tame. And stubborn!"

Joshua nodded. "I've found that out. Got any helpful hints?"

"Only one. She's worth the aggravation."

"I wonder," Joshua said, then laughed.

The two tall men made their way to the counter where the women were working.

"Are you ready to go, Anna?" Joshua asked.

Pretending she hadn't heard him, Anna kept her back to him and continued to fold some embroidered napkins that were being set out.

"Watch this," Joshua whispered to her parents. "I have the perfect way to get her attention."

"Hey, Spitfire, are you ready?" he called out.

Whirling around, Anna jammed her hands onto her hips and glared at him with snapping eyes. "I'm ready, Mr. Brandon."

Grinning, Joshua gloated to mama and papa. "See, it works."

Anna spent the next couple of hours guiding Joshua through her beloved market. When they finished canvasing the entire area, they headed back to the car. Just as they were almost out of the shopping area, he noticed a small store that specialized in kites.

"Let's buy one and fly it at Gas Works Park," he suggested.

She hadn't flown a kite in years and gladly followed him into the store to pick out a multicolored dragon. Soon they were romping over the knolls of the grassy expanse. The park, which overlooks Elliott Bay, was virtually free of any wires or trees that could ensnare their airborne monster. They rollicked in the afternoon sun like two young puppies.

Inevitably the sun scudded behind some clouds and

a light drizzle began to filter down. They brought in the kite and wandered among the monolithic towers of the old refinery that dominated a corner of the park. There was something pleasant about strolling among the rusty stacks and feeling small but alive next to the decaying structure. It was as if the old gas works was a kind of industrial Stonehenge.

By the time they were heading back to Anna's place, the vigorous activity of the afternoon had taken its toll. It was Joshua who was the first to admit he wasn't up to a lavish meal on the town.

"Anna," he tentatively inquired, "would you mind postponing our dinner at Bush Gardens?"

Anna was relieved that he had taken the initiative and suggested a more relaxed evening.

"Perfect," she sighed gratefully. "Let's just stop, get a pizza and take it home to eat in front of the fireplace. I've got a bottle of Burgundy."

Later, after they had eaten their fill of the rich Italian dish, they lay on the soft carpet watching the flames dance between the logs in the fireplace. Anna's head was in Joshua's lap and he was twisting a lock of her hair with his sturdy fingers.

"See anything in the flames?" he asked.

"Lots of things," she murmured. "I can make out brightly colored poppies, brilliant fall leaves, ferocious monsters and frolicking nymphs."

"Quite a combination. Know what I see?"

"What?"

He lifted her chin so he could look at her. "A bewitching woman who has cast a seductive spell over me."

"Want to break the spell?" she whispered.

"Not in a million years."

He took the glass of wine out of her hand and set it aside. Bending to reach her lips, he began to weave his own sensual spell. Her mouth melted under his firm lips and he gathered her into his waiting arms. His tongue searched out hers and time stood still as passion led them on a journey of fresh discovery and unending pleasure. With patient fingers, he peeled Anna's clothes off, and soon his garments joined hers in a small mound of unwanted impediments. A flush covered her face and it reflected the heat of desire surging within her.

On the cushioned floor, Joshua painstakingly explored every sensual grotto and erotic plateau of her snowy body.

In a husky whisper, he moaned, "I love your fresh and natural perfume."

Intoxicated by Joshua's lovemaking, her fingers outlined his taut muscles. His uneven breathing signaled his growing ardor and she was encouraged to continue her soft probings. His hand guided her to his loins and she tauntingly brought him to the edge only to soothe his need with words of promise.

Mercifully she threw all preamble aside and slowly lowered her waiting body onto his. She had set the mood and he allowed her the right to set the rhythm. Swaying slightly back and forth, she marveled at the intense gratification that rushed through her as he filled her body with his.

Suddenly, feeling as if they had crested a hill, they were transported to a realm of shuddering and total fulfillment. A mutual cry of rapture escaped their lips.

Wondrously depleted, having given the gift of themselves to each other, they lolled back on the pillows to enjoy their shared contentment.

The sound of the telephone ringing was as jarring as a rifle shot and the serene mood shattered. Anna grudgingly disengaged herself from Joshua's arms and walked across the room to answer it.

"Hello?" she answered abruptly.

Joshua rested his chin on his hand and watched her standing completely nude in the shadows. He admired the way her thighs blossomed up into her firm creamy backside. She looked so inviting, so delectable—why the blazes did someone have to draw her away?

He listened to her end of the conversation and tried to divine whom she was talking to.

"Listen, sweetie," she said, but then caught Joshua's eye and lowered her voice, intentionally muffling her words. "I promise to be there tomorrow. Just relax. I haven't forgotten."

Despite her lowered voice, Joshua could clearly distinguish what she said and he couldn't deny his irritation. He felt like a cuckold, which, he instantly reasoned, was impossible. He didn't own Anna, much less have any sort of enduring understanding with her. Still, it was incredible that she'd even carry on such a conversation just after another man had made love to her.

"I love you too. See you tomorrow," she cooed.

She hung up, but Joshua was going to be damned if he'd ask her who it was. If it didn't bother her, it certainly wasn't going to disturb him. Yet he found her behavior ate at him and he was forced to admit he was becoming possessive of her.

Snuggling back up to him, she said, "Sorry. Niki's a little homesick tonight and he was upset about the wheelchairs getting across the soggy center field of the track. That last rainstorm left everything pooled in the middle. I told him to relax, something would work out and that I'd pick him up tomorrow afternoon." Every year Niki took personal responsibility for one of the wheelchair participants.

"Niki?"

Anna didn't miss the suspicion in his voice and she wasn't sure if she should be flattered or angry.

"Yes, Niki. Remember, my brother?" she asked sarcastically.

Joshua nodded, but inwardly he was ambivalent. He believed her. Why shouldn't he? Why would she fabricate a lie? On the other hand, he'd never asked her if there was another man, or men, in her life. Besides, who was he to judge? He certainly hadn't lived a celibate life till now.

Anna had returned to precisely the same spot she was in before Niki called. But she might as well have sat alone somewhere. Niki had inadvertently managed to drive a wedge between them. Once again she could feel the erosion begin to cut away at a relationship between herself and a man.

For the rest of the evening she and Joshua attempted to regain the enchanting mood of earlier. Slowly they brushed aside the pall that had descended on them. Nonetheless, there lingered a slight fissure in their intimacy.

CHAPTER TEN

ANNA WAS UNPREPARED for the profound serenity she felt when she woke to find Joshua's arm slung across her body. They had stumbled off to bed the night before in a somnolent haze and neither had even considered sleeping anywhere but together. His even breathing indicated he was still asleep, but the day was beckoning her.

She eased herself out of Joshua's grasp and sauntered into the kitchen to brew the morning coffee. Content to enjoy the solitude, she bundled up in her heavy robe and sat out on the lanai to sip her coffee and clear her thoughts.

The past two days had been idyllic, but were she and Joshua on a collision course? Their relationship had burst into flower, but how long would the bloom stay fresh? What did they really know about each other? He had gallantly sloughed off Niki's retardation, but then when her brother simply called, Joshua seemed to backpedal. How would Joshua handle Niki when and if they actually met? There were so many questions left unanswered.

Anna still felt she knew very little about Joshua. She wondered what he was doing in a poorly paying job in the public defender's office. She didn't care about money, but she did care about his motivations. So far he hadn't shared that part of himself with her.

Sipping from the mug she held tightly, she looked out over the terrace. She wondered whether or not the carefree time they'd spent together was coming to an end. Today she'd have to drive out to Fort Lewis and pick up Niki. She'd bring him home and Joshua would realize that he had seen only an uncluttered facsimile of her life.

How could she explain to Joshua that their bond, as euphoric and lovely as it was, was as ephemeral as the rare trillium that blooms in the spring?

As she sat pondering her questions, Joshua silently crept up behind her and said, "A penny for your thoughts?"

She took the hand he placed on her cheek and kissed his fingertips. "Good morning, Counselor. Coffee?"

"I helped myself. What were you so preoccupied with that you didn't hear me fumbling around in the kitchen?" he asked.

Loathe to dive into such heavy subjects first thing in the morning, she glibly replied, "Nothing. I was just enjoying the view. Isn't Puget Sound spectacular today?"

"Yes," he said, kissing her forehead. "Do you get the Sunday paper?"

"Look on the front porch."

As he went off to fetch the hefty edition of the *Seattle Times*, she was pleased to have evaded discussing her troublesome thoughts. But she knew in her heart that even though she'd been successful in forestalling the conversation, she'd be forced to clarify her concerns before the morning was over.

Slapping the paper down on the glass-topped table, Joshua promptly ruffled through its contents until he found the Sports section. He buried his head in the latest baseball statistics. Anna chose the front page to scan first and lost herself in the problems that faced world leaders, hoping the news would put some perspective on her own distress.

She was completely absorbed in a long editorial and didn't notice Joshua pick up the pictorial section. His attention was riveted to a lengthy feature on a hometown boy who had been honored by the Supreme Court of the United States. The young transplanted Seattlite, an East Coast lawyer, had been selected to defend a man who was serving a life sentence in Washington State's Walla Walla penitentiary. The man had filed an appeal with the Court in forma pauperis. Joshua knew that it was rare that the Court granted such a request, for it was an admission by the prisoner that he was unable to pay for his own defense and would not be bound by the ordinary rules that applied to most of the cases they reviewed.

When the Court did grant a writ of certiorari, they were in essence acknowledging that the case had special merits and was deserving of their time. Very few people understood that most of the cases argued in front of the Supreme Court are at the voluntary discretion of the members of that Court. They vote on the individual files, and at the most, ten percent of the appeals are granted. But on the special occasion when a writ of cert is granted and it has been filed in forma pauperis, the Court assigns a distinguished member of the bar to represent the defendant.

"Look at this," Joshua said as he thrust the colored spread under Anna's nose. "One of the locals is up before the Supreme Court."

Anna glanced up from the editorial and was faced with a large photograph of Sean. The icy claws of panic clutched at her. What was his picture doing in the paper? His smiling face drove all logic from her mind and she batted the offensive image away.

Trying to regain control, she said, "I'll look at it later. Let me finish what I was reading."

"But this is great. Don't you know what an honor it is to be selected?"

"Of course," she snapped irritably.

Joshua was puzzled by her peevish reply and pulled the paper back up in front of his face. Why had she reacted with a blend of irritation, fear and anger? Scanning the article, Joshua calculated when the man would have graduated from law school and figured that he would have been in Anna's class. Had she known him?

His curiosity was piqued and he asked, "Do you know this guy? He must have graduated with you."

Anna carefully folded her paper and pulled her glasses off. Finally she admitted, "Yes, I know him from my days in college."

Joshua searched her anguished face for an answer to her initial response. Why hadn't she offered the information willingly? The only logical reason was that she had known this man well, very well indeed, and she was reluctant to admit it. Was this man the reason that she was still single and had buried herself in law? If his assumption was correct, it would answer a lot of questions for him, and would explain her aloof posture and unapproachable demeanor.

"He burned you, didn't he?"

Anna felt as though she was backed into a corner and there was no way out except concession.

"Yes," she said quietly. "It was a very long time ago. We had planned on getting married but Niki was too much for him. Sean wasn't able to handle the idea of having a retarded person in his family."

Anna's pain at recounting her past was evident and Joshua felt that if he could have gotten his hands around that man's neck, he would have gladly strangled him. How could he have been such a cad? How could a man reject her love simply because she had a little brother who was handicapped and wheelchair bound? *No wonder she shied away from me,* he reasoned. *She had good reason to be skeptical of any man. And didn't I reinforce her fears last night? Didn't I prove to her that she was correct?*

"You know," he said sincerely, "you're not the only person who's been hurt. We all have a skeleton or two in the closet."

Anna twisted her lips into a mock grin. "Are you trying to say that Sean was different? That other men would react differently?"

"Yes."

"Let's see," she said sarcastically. "Correct me if I'm wrong, Counselor. You were full of trust, and it didn't faze you in the least when I talked to Niki last night? Is that right? The remainder of the evening after he called went on just as it had before?"

So she *had* noticed. He hadn't been successful in masking his response.

"I plead guilty to all charges. But don't let your past sabotage our future."

"We have a future?"

"Maybe. Let's just take it day by day."

"Including all my excess baggage? My complications?"

"Like what?" he demanded.

"Like Niki."

A loud sound of relief escaped from his tightly pursed lips as he said, "Why do you insist on letting that bother you?"

Irritated, she snapped, "You have no idea how much effort goes into caring for my brother."

"Maybe not, but a least give me a chance," Joshua said, standing up and starting to pace.

"Are you sure?"

Was he sure? He stopped his pacing, leaned his hands on the railing and looked out over the water toward the Olympic Mountains. How did he suddenly get into this position? Anna Provo was supposed to be some kind of diversion to fill his nights. Now here he was considering a full-time relationship. Did he want to?

"Yes," he said spontaneously. "I'm sure."

"You say sure now. But what about when you meet Niki? He demands a lot of time and affection."

"I'm willing to make some sacrifices."

"You see, that's the whole problem. I don't want any man making sacrifices. Dealing with Niki shoudn't be considered one. How would you like to be merely tolerated?"

"Now you're twisting my words."

"I'm not. I'm only pointing out a few facts that Sean made very clear to me. Someday Niki will live with me full time. What man wants a ready-made family? And Niki will never grow up and leave the nest."

Joshua thought she argued her position very well, but she wasn't going to scare him off that easily. Joshua admitted the truth. He did want to spend more time with this woman, but what that exactly meant wasn't clear. He only knew that he was becoming deeply involved with her and was willing to test the waters before he made any commitment.

He pulled her out of her seat and wrapped his arms around her waist. "Listen, let's not fight," he said quietly. "I'll admit I came on a little strong. It's a gorgeous day. Let's not spoil it with some silly quarrel."

"Joshua, this is not some silly quarrel. It's very real and very serious."

"How does this sound?" he bargained. "Let me meet Niki and we'll see how things go. Day by day?"

Anna rolled her eyes in frustration at his failure to comprehend what she'd been trying to tell him. "But Joshua...."

"End of conversation, Firebird." He covered her mouth with his and smothered her objection with sweet kisses. Finally he broke free and said, "I have to visit my folks this afternoon. Would you like to come with me?"

"I can't, remember? I have to pick up Niki."

"Sorry, I forgot. What time do you have to leave?"

"About two o'clock."

"Well, let's enjoy the rest of the morning together. You can meet my folks another time."

"Okay, let me check my social calendar," she

teased, trying to ease the spell their heavy conversation had cast. She picked up their mugs and went to the kitchen to refill them with hot coffee.

Joshua pretended to be reading the paper but he was actually a long way away from the want ads he was staring at. What was behind her last remark? Was there someone else in her life? She claimed the problem was Niki, but was that really it? There was no way he could accept that as her only excuse. Many people had retarded brothers and still managed to live happy normal lives. Why was she so distant and secretive? Why was she so adamant that he couldn't cope with her brother? She hadn't even given him a chance to prove that they could blend their lives. Why wouldn't she let him show her it could work? Was there more to this than she was willing to admit?

A battery of questions whirled around in his head like tumbleweed in a cyclone. None of his queries was useful because none had an answer. Anna wouldn't let him put down roots long enough to get a sense of stability in their relationship. She kept him in a constant emotional vortex, and just trying to figure out what was happening made him dizzy.

A bolt of insight cleared Joshua's befuddled brain and another possibility struck him. Maybe there really was someone else in her life and his name wasn't Niki. Maybe Niki was only a smoke screen. After all, he'd only known her for a short time and a woman as beautiful as Anna must have an aggregate of suitors.

The thought threw him off-balance. He didn't know how he would handle a rival. He'd never been jealous in his life. But then, he'd never had a reason to be. No woman had been worth it. The jealousies he'd seen other men display had been silly and child-ish. Would he be such a victim? The idea of throwing himself around in a rage appalled Joshua. Yet he couldn't be sure he'd be rational if another man was the reason for Anna's hesitation.

Joshua knew he was working himself into a lather on mere speculation. She had given him no real rea-son to believe or even suspect there was another man in her life. He was letting his imagination run amok. Calling on his common sense, he dismissed his sus-picion as the conjecture of a smitten man groping around in the dark trying to analyze a difficult woman.

Laughing at himself and his jealousy, Joshua started to read the want ads seriously. He was look-ing for a good buy on a used dinghy for his sailboat.

Having finished leafing through the paper, he glanced at his watch and was amazed at how the time had flown.

"Anna—" he jumped up "—I've got to run. I promised mother I'd have brunch with them at one o'clock and it's twelve-thirty."

"Give me a minute to throw on some clothes and I'll take you home," she said.

"Don't bother. I'll call a cab. No sense in your rushing, too," he said as he tousled her hair.

As she gathered the rumpled papers and tidied the table, the harsh blast of a horn alerted her. She looked down to check the street and saw an impatient cabby waiting.

Handing Joshua his jacket, she said, "You'd bet-ter hurry."

"I have enough time to give you a proper goodbye," he said, curling his arms around her waist and indulging himself in a lingering farewell kiss.

The contact effortlessly annulled any traces of reserve Anna felt. Instead Joshua fanned the fervent need she had for him and she was once again responding to him without any checks or balances.

Patting her shapely fanny in a playful manner, he said, "I really must go. I'll call tomorrow."

Accompanying him to the door, she gave him a final hug. She leaned back against the solid wood as she closed the door, then attempted to regain her perspective. Knowing she had to pick up Niki in two hours did nothing to still the unrelenting conflict that was playing havoc with her peace of mind.

"Who needs this?" she muttered.

Life had been so simple before Joshua—so serene. But she also had to admit it had been barren, too. He had blithely stepped in and filled the void. What would she do now?

"You'll get busy, that's what," she told herself in a firm authoritative tone of voice.

She bustled around the house removing all traces of her evening with Joshua, hoping to restore the order and tranquillity that had been present before he'd bolted into her life and sent everything askew. By the time she was ready to leave, she'd scrubbed, dusted, mopped and folded him to the deepest recesses of her mind.

Martin had installed an elaborate sound system in Elizabeth, and as soon as Anna was in her car and buckled up, she pushed a tape into the stereo. Johann Strauss would escort her to Fort Lewis, instead of thoughts of Joshua Brandon III. Turning up the volume, she filled the car with so much noise there wasn't room left for any disturbing thoughts.

She soon found herself at the entrance gate of the large sprawling army base. Following the guard's directions, she easily located the barracks where Niki was billeted.

Her brother hadn't seen her car since it had been refurbished, so he didn't recognize Anna as she pulled into the parking lot. She tooted the horn a couple of times and waved to him.

"Niki, over here!" she called.

She watched as he galloped across the lawn. Two gold medals on blue ribbons dangled from his neck, and it was apparent that he'd come in first place twice. A huge grin lit his face and he lugged a backpack, sleeping bag and portable radio.

"Get a new car?" he asked.

"No, this is the same old Elizabeth. I just had her fixed up."

"Wow!" He oohed and aahed.

"Put your gear in the back seat and climb in," Anna directed. "I had a tape deck installed and I bought you the new Muppets album. Want to hear it?"

"Yeah." He squirmed around in his seat in anticipation of hearing his favorite songs.

"Okay, but you have to sit still and do up your seat belt."

He followed her instructions and settled down to listen to the music. Later, she asked him about his weekend. He gave her a blow-by-blow account of all the events and before he'd finished, she was pulling up to her condo.

"Here we are, kiddo. Want to spend the night?"

"Can we play Crazy Eights?"

"Only if you promise to be a good sport about losing."

Just as she was fitting her key into the lock, she heard her phone ringing. Hurrying inside, she snatched up the receiver.

"Hello?" she said.

"So you're home, Anna," her mother said. "Where's Nikolae?"

"He's here with me, mama. He wants to stay the night, so I'll drop him off in the morning."

"You don't have any plans with that nice Joshua?" her mother probed.

"No, I don't have any plans with that nice Joshua. Niki and I are going to make dinner and play cards."

"Why don't you bring Nikolae home and do something else?" mama insisted. "Something with Joshua."

"Mama," Anna lowered her voice and hissed into the phone, "you promised to lay off. Besides, he had other plans. He's busy...so cancel your appointment with the matchmaker."

Niki interrupted by blasting into the receiver, "I won two gold medals. Did Anna tell you?"

Anna handed the receiver to her brother and said, "Here, you tell mama all about your weekend while I start dinner."

"Can we have hot dogs?" he asked.

"Yes, but talk to mama first."

She watched as Niki flopped down on the floor and started to twist the cord. *Well, there goes another one,* she fumed. Whenever he used the phone he had the habit of playing with the wire by flexing, stretching and snapping the coils. She'd tried to break him of the nervous practice but no amount of scolding could make him remember from one call to the next. Every time he faithfully promised to keep his hands off, but just as she expected, the next time he picked up the phone the wringing and twirling started.

To hide her irritation, she headed to the kitchen and put a package of hot dogs on to boil. Glancing through her freezer, she pulled out a container of homemade soup and put it into the microwave to thaw. Soup and hot dogs—not gourmet fare but filling, she reasoned.

A pang of longing threatened her facade of calm domesticity. Her dinner with Joshua last night had been so romantic. Lying in front of the fireplace, munching on pizza with a handsome man lolling at her side. Now she was having dinner with another handsome man, but the situations were so different.

As she watched over the hot dogs, she tried to picture what Joshua would be doing right now. But wasting her time thinking about him would only add to her longing, so she turned her attention to the task at hand—preparing dinner for Niki.

Suddenly the qualifying factor in her life thrust his head over the pan of hot dogs and, exclaimed, "Smells good. When can we eat?"

"You set the table and I'll dish up."

"Can I have just hot dogs?"

"No, you can't. You have to have some soup, too. It's full of healthy vegetables and all good athletes eat lots of vegetables."

"All right," he groaned, "but I'm not going to tell you how great your stupid soup is. 'Cause it's not."

"Niki, do you want to play Crazy Eights after dinner?"

"Yeah."

"Then watch it. I don't want any snotty remarks. I'm in no mood to listen to them."

"I'm sorry, I'll be good," he promised in a hurt wistful tone.

"I'm sorry, too. We're just hungry and we'll feel better after we eat."

Niki wolfed down four hot dogs and to appease his sister, asked for a second bowl of soup. She knew if she commented on the additional bowl, she'd be forced to endure a long discussion about how well he ate vegetables, so she ignored the extra helping. But she did smile as she watched him rapidly consume it. The well-tanned face was screwed into a fierce grimace as he shoveled in the steaming broth. He was going to have a second portion but he was going to make darn sure Anna knew he hated it.

"Did you get enough?" she asked.

"I could fit a bowl of ice cream in. Got any?"

"I did have. Where did I hide it?"

"Oh, Anna," he said with a laugh. "You know it's in the freezer." He took off to retrieve the quart of Rocky Road she always kept on hand.

After they played two hands of Crazy Eights, Niki gathered the cards and asked, "What time is it, Anna?"

"I don't know. Go check."

She'd worked hard to teach him how to tell time, but she'd failed until the advent of digital clocks. With them his ability to monitor the hours had been made easy and that gave a tremendous boost to his ego. She constantly tried to reinforce his newfound skill.

"It says six fifty-five," he announced. "Is that seven o'clock?"

"It means five minutes to seven. Why?"

"'Cause the Muppets are on. Can I watch them?"

"Sure."

They watched several programs. When it was ten o'clock, Anna announced it was bedtime.

"Already?"

Niki started to complain that he wasn't tired, but she put a stop to his string of excuses before he had a chance to build a head of steam.

"It's been a long weekend and you need the sleep. It's a workday tomorrow, remember? And I'm tired, too."

Knowing he was disappointed that the weekend was finished, Anna suggested he might like to take her portable radio to bed with him and listen to music as he drifted off to sleep.

Pleased, he kissed her on the cheek and she said, "Good night, dear. I'll check in on you in a few minutes. Sweet dreams."

She poured herself a glass of wine, shut off the blaring television and left on only one small light. Alone, she sipped her drink and thought of both Joshua and Niki, the two most important men in her life. Would they be compatible?

"Anna," Niki's quiet voice broke into her thoughts. "Your radio is broke."

"Broken," she responded. It was an automatic response to correct his grammar.

"Broken," he mimicked.

"Bring it to me and I'll take a look."

He slowly walked over to Anna with the radio in his oversized hand. His head was hanging as he said, "I didn't fool with it. It just quit playing."

She popped the back off and checked the batteries. Things had a way of crumbling when Niki touched them, but that was not the case this time. The batteries were corroded and obviously dead.

"Do we have to throw the radio away?" he asked.

"No, the batteries are shot."

"I swear, Anna. I didn't have a gun," he protested vehemently.

"Niki, Niki." She couldn't help but laugh. "I meant they are worn out. Old."

"Gosh, Anna. I thought you said I shot them."

Hugging him, she reassured, "I'll buy some new ones tomorrow. Back to bed, big brother."

As he trudged off, she gave up trying to carve out a niche of solitude and followed him down the hall. Crawling into her bed, she sprawled under the heavy blankets and waited for sleep to dull her senses and blot out the images that kept surfacing every time she closed her eyes.

After struggling for what seemed like hours, she finally drifted off. But there was no release, even in her dreams. All night long, she and Joshua argued endlessly before the U.S. Supreme Court. Sean sat with the other justices and laughed at her futile attempts to make Joshua accept Niki. When the alarm went off at five-thirty, she felt like she'd run the Boston Marathon.

Once she'd downed her first cup of coffee, she felt just a trifle better and opened the curtains to let in the morning sun. In keeping with her frame of mind, the cheerful spring weather of yesterday had been replaced by gloomy drizzle and thick blanketing fog. Just when she counted on a day being clear, it rained. Natives joked that the rainy season in Seattle lasts from Christmas Day to Christmas Eve. The city, situated between two mountain ranges, is the recipient of moist marine weather off the northwest coast.

Anna decided not to jog this morning. Instead she would ride her exercise bike in the living room and stay warm and dry.

To fortify herself against what promised to be a miserable day, she decided to fix a nice breakfast of bacon, waffles and fresh strawberries. Niki would love it. Throwing the bacon in a pan, she went to wake him.

"Time to get up, sleepyhead." She shook his shoulder to rouse him.

Grumbling, he rolled over and pulled the covers back over his head. "Not yet," he groaned.

"Sorry, but it's rise and shine."

Squinting his eyes against the light, he sat up and rubbed the sleep away. "Okay, I'll get up."

"I've got bacon frying and I'll fix some waffles."

"All right!" he shouted. The prospect of his favorite food brought him flying out from under the covers and racing to the table. "Is it ready yet?"

"No, so why don't you get the paper and we'll do Hocus Focus while we wait?"

Niki went to pick up the newspaper off the front porch. She encouraged him to play the game with her whenever he stayed over. Hocus Focus was two pictures, much the same, but one had certain things missing. The object was to find all the differences between the two.

After he poured himself a cup of coffee laced with lots of sugar and milk, Niki opened the paper and searched for the Coffee Break section.

"Here it is, Anna. Looks like a hard one today."

"You study it while I cook. If you have trouble, I'll give you clues."

He bent his head over the pictures and began comparing the drawings. "I found one," he said. "See, the lady's purse is missing."

"You're right. Can you find other differences?"

He thought the game was great fun but she knew it was good training for him to have to discover what the artist had eliminated or changed. Helping Niki to expand his skills and solve problems was a rewarding experience. He became so excited, so grateful when he learned new things or overcame an obstacle.

They had finished their breakfast by the time he'd finally found the last item.

"I got 'em all," he bragged.

"Good job. Now let's see how good you are at getting ready for work. You take a shower while I do the dishes. Scoot!"

"Okeydokey."

"Don't forget to shave." She leaned across the table and stroked his cheek. He desperately needed a good shave. His dark bristles cast a strong shadow along his jaw and upper lip. "And floss your teeth."

She tired of the constant reminders she issued but there was no other way. Niki would always require guidance, even in the most mundane matters.

Clearing the dishes from the table and scraping them off, she heard the sound of Daffy Duck from the TV. "Niki," she called, "did you turn on cartoons?"

"Yes," he answered in a guilty voice.

"No cartoons until after you're cleaned up. I have to shower too, you know." As an afterthought she added, "You can leave it on but you can't watch it until you're finished."

"Sure thing," he said.

She heard his electric razor begin to whir gently and went back to the dishes. When the doorbell rang, she hurriedly wiped her hands off to answer it but Niki hollered, "I'll get it!"

She was several steps behind him when he threw open the door to face Joshua.

Niki stood there clad only in a bath towel and grinned at him. She glimpsed herself in the entry mirror. Her red silk robe was dusted with flour, her hair was thrown into a twist on the top of her head with spit curls framing her face. Not exactly the way she would have liked Joshua to see her, but considering the early-morning hour, she had to admit she made an intimate and fetching sight.

Joshua stared at Anna icily, and then his nostrils flared at the sight of the scantily clad man.

"I see you're busy." His voice was cold and angry.

"No," Niki answered with his deep throaty good-natured laugh. "We were just playing, and now we're going to take a shower."

"I see." Joshua eyed her brutally. "The judge likes her fun and games on the weekends provided they don't jeopardize her weekday status."

Anna was dumbfounded. Joshua's coarse comments shocked her and she was having trouble fathoming just what he was hinting at.

"Joshua?" she said tentatively. Then the realization that he thought Niki was her lover struck her, and she found the whole situation terribly funny. Unsuccessfully she tried to cover her giggling with her hand. She stepped in front of Niki to introduce them and end the confusion.

Joshua heard her lighthearted laughter and his anger boiled over. "So what's going on?" he demanded, already sure that he knew what was happening. She did have another lover! And he was staring into the man's eyes. He'd been right all along and now he was staring at the tall, good-looking creep!

"Joshua," she laughed even harder. "If you understood, you'd—"

"Since you find this so damn humorous," he roared, "why not let me in on the joke? But before you deliver the punch line, I have a question."

Anna grabbed his arm and tried to interrupt his loud outburst, but he gripped her fingers in his hand and flung them away as if her touch would contaminate him.

"What do you do, Miss Provo?" he sneered. "Line up your male harem for each day off? Or are there notches on your bedposts?"

Anna flinched. How could he be so vulgar? "Mr. Brandon!" Her voice shook with uncontained fury. "It's none of your business what I do with my life!"

"That's right, baby. It isn't. I thought it was. I thought this has to be special. But it just goes to show you what a sentimental fool I am."

Joshua turned angrily and ran down the steps. But before he reached the street, a possibility occurred to him. Could the man in the doorway be Niki? He seriously doubted it. Niki had called about the trouble he was having with his wheelchair on the soggy fields. Still, there had to be a reasonable explanation. He knew he was acting like a fool. Perhaps if he quietly went back and talked with her, they could iron things out. Impulsively, he spun in his tracks and went back up to the stoop.

"Listen, Anna," he said rationally, "why don't we talk...."

"No." She wasn't going to permit him to insult her again. "You went in the wrong direction, Mr. Brandon. Turn back around and just stay out of my life permanently." In a rage, she slammed the door.

Joshua's willingness to talk with her vanished and was replaced by an irrevocable decision. He hollered back to her, "That's the last time you'll ever slam that door in my face."

Jumping into his car, he revved the engine fiercely and spun a U turn in the street. Anna could hear the roar as he wildly accelerated away. She stood there feeling totally empty. Then a horrible sinking feeling flooded her and she couldn't dam it.

"Didn't he want to play?" Niki asked as he closed the door.

Fighting back tears of anger, hurt and frustration, she answered in a choked voice, "No, he doesn't want to play."

Niki left to shower and Anna gave in to her tears and let them cascade down her cheeks. *Well,* she thought, *that ends my problem of how to get my point across.* Suddenly the irony of the whole situation crystallized and she said out loud, "And he said Niki would be no problem."

CHAPTER ELEVEN

THE JUMBO JET touched down on the wide expanse of asphalt and Joshua rummaged under his seat for the flight bag he'd brought on board. When the call had come from his brother, Maurice, early that morning, Joshua had immediately phoned the airlines and checked on the next available flight to San Diego. There had been one cancellation on the 8:00 A.M. flight and he'd wasted no time in packing. He'd simply thrown a few necessities into a small satchel and headed out the door.

Throughout the flight, Anna's laughter loomed up and taunted him, forcing him to relive the humiliating scene at her door. He'd stopped by to quickly tell her his grandfather had had a heart attack and he was flying to be with him. He'd gone searching for her condolence and received her scorn. She stood there in her red robe looking so casual, so unruffled, with her lover draped only in a towel. She didn't even have the decency to act ashamed of being caught in her ugly duplicity. Instead, she laughed at him!

Watching as the plane taxied to the terminal, Joshua forcibly shoved thoughts of her to the furthermost regions of his mind. It was going to take a concerted effort to keep her from his thoughts. He could only grieve over one thing at a time. His relationship with

Anna was over, but he would have to mourn it later. Right now his grandfather deserved his complete attention and affection.

He was impatient to disembark and get to the hospital. He and his grandfather may have had their differences, but he wanted to at least say goodbye to him. Joshua wanted the old man to know that he hadn't left the family business because he didn't approve of or love him. It was just that his goals were unlike his relative's. His decision implied no disrespect nor any animosity toward the family.

When Maurice had called, Joshua had questioned him about the old man's condition.

"I don't know, Josh," Maurice had said, sounding frightened and tentative. "He's awfully weak. The doctor says that it was definitely a heart attack, but they don't know if they can stabilize him and prevent any more."

"I'll be on the first flight, Mudger. As soon as I land, I'll head straight for the hospital."

"Good. He keeps asking for you."

"Tell him to hang in there, I'm on my way."

It seemed like an eternity before he was able to make his way off the crowded aircraft and through the melee of swarming people in the terminal. Servicemen snatched up every available cab and Joshua thought he'd never escape the mass of people all headed for their own destinations with their own urgent needs goading them on. Finally a vacant taxi pulled up to the curb and he rudely jumped in and barked the hospital address to the driver.

After an interminable wait, he was admitted to his grandfather's room and he warily walked over to the bed. His grandfather had always been so dynamic that seeing him hooked up to tubes and monitors stunned Joshua. This man had seemed larger than life and now he was helplessly dependent on a host of machines to maintain what little spark of life he had left.

Gripping the cold white hand in his, Joshua whispered, "Granddad, I'm here. It's me. . . Joshua."

His eyelids fluttered open and in a feeble voice he asked, "Is that really you, Joshua?"

"It's me, granddad. How you doing?"

A faint grin played at the corners of the elderly man's mouth as he said, "I've been better. But did you take a gander at my nurse? Quite a looker."

Joshua was forced to laugh. "You're not very sick. Is this another one of your ploys to get me back into the company? If I see you pinching any lovely bottoms, I'm taking the next plane back to Seattle."

"Never could fool you," his grandfather said in a barely audible voice.

"Rest now," Joshua soothed. "I'll sit here but you have to sleep. You're going to need all your strength to keep Mudger in line."

He quickly lapsed back into a deep sleep but Joshua kept his vigil. He held his hand and occasionally stroked his face lightly with the back of his fingers. The nurse who monitored the intensive care patients tapped him on the shoulder.

"Mr. Brandon?"

"Yes?"

"Why don't you get a cup of coffee? I need to change his IV's. You can come back and sit with him when I'm done."

As Joshua wandered down the sterile corridors in search of the cafeteria, Anna crept back into his thoughts, but he put his feelings for her aside. He would deal with her later. There were more pressing needs just now and he required every shred of composure he could summon to deal with his grandfather's plight.

Absently playing with his spoon in the coffee cup, Joshua was unaware of Maurice's entrance into the room. The younger man slid onto a chair next to him.

"Glad you could make it, Josh."

"Yeah. I was up to see him but the nurse ran me out."

"She told me that I'd find you here."

"Have you talked to the doctor again?" Joshua asked.

"Yes."

"And?"

"It doesn't look good."

"Exactly what does that mean?"

"His heart is simply worn out. He could go at any time."

Joshua took a couple of sips of coffee before answering. "I was afraid of that."

The two men silently headed out of the cafeteria to resume their vigil. As they entered the modern room with its banks of medical apparatus, Joshua dropped back and let Maurice sit down next to the slumbering man. The staff didn't allow any flowers in intensive care, but someone had brought in the faded photograph of the boys' grandmother. Eloise Brandon beamed at Joshua from six decades earlier. She was dressed in an elaborate flapper's chemise and she clutched a dapper young man's arm as they posed for the photographer. The young couple's joy radiated from the picture and transcended the years. It was the last photograph taken of her. She had died the next year giving birth to Joshua's father.

"Poor granddad," Joshua said in a low voice to Maurice. "He never forgave himself for losing her." He pointed to the old portrait.

Maurice glanced at it and shrugged. "It was his choice. There were lots of women who would have had him after she died," he said.

Joshua was stung by his brother's callousness. Obviously he didn't believe in true love. Maybe he was right. There are a lot of women to be found in a lifetime.

The two brothers waited until their parents arrived. The specialist called them into his office and relayed his prognosis. The outcome to be expected was the worst. Trying to comprehend the loss of the man who was the bulwark of the family dazed them all. They decided to go somewhere and sort out their feelings.

Joshua rode with Maurice in his Mercedes and they followed their folks to a nearby restaurant.

"Did you notice dad was wearing a navy blue suit as if he was already in mourning?" Maurice asked.

"Yeah," Joshua answered. "He looked terrible. There was no expression on his face. I feel sorry for him."

"Why?"

"Dad has lived a pampered life but he's never known a mother's love, and he was left with a father who buried his grief in business and ignored his son.''

The relationship between his grandfather and father had never resolved itself, and Joshua sensed that part of his dad's loss was that time had run out for him to ever become really close to the old man. The sad part was that the tradition had been perpetuated. Joshua felt alienated from his father. The Brandons may have known how to cultivate money, but they couldn't nourish loving relationships.

Joshua's mother seemed to run the meeting. She was her ever calm and collected self. A tall woman, always chicly dressed, stunningly coifed and smartly made-up in the most expensive cosmetics, she could only handle life if it was perfectly scheduled and timed like the country-club balls she was forever planning. She organized her house, her servants, her social engagements and her children with rigid and cool regimentation. Beneath the brittle exterior, Joshua always suspected there was a vulnerable woman who would break if her regimen ever eroded. Her security, her peace of mind, depended on a chain of command.

''Who's likely to be elected chairman of the board now?'' Maurice asked.

Listening to Maurice using his cool detached voice exuding elegance and sophistication, Joshua was struck with how his brother had perfectly absorbed the Brandon traits. He was handsome, dark and powerful—physically and intellectually. He was also distant, indifferent and well armored against any feelings that might ruffle his self-composure.

The whole family appeared perfect. But Joshua

knew his parents' and brother's flaws. Yet he loved them. They were people doing the best they could in a world they thought they'd created.

With that analysis, Joshua concluded he probably wasn't much different from his relatives. He had thought he could control Anna. He had believed he could restructure her life to fit his needs. He had assumed she would want what he wanted simply because he wanted it. He had taken for granted, as all the Brandons did, that what he deemed right was right. Still—still she had hurt him badly.

The talk around the table centered, of course, around Joshua Brandon I, the elderly man who had controlled so much and influenced each of them so profoundly.

"He'll never be able to come back to work," Maurice stated matter-of-factly, "even if he survives this crisis."

"Then the interest of the corporation must be protected," Joshua's mother insisted vehemently. "Granddad lavished his devotion on the company and his illness shouldn't be allowed to diminish its strength."

To an outsider, the trend of the conversation may have sounded harsh and uncaring, but Joshua knew it was his family's way of expressing love for the old man. To worry and plot about his enterprises was precisely what his grandfather would have approved of.

By seven o'clock, Joshua was filled to the brim with coffee and with conversation forecasting gloom and death. He needed to feel free of the oppressive pallor, and with little subtlety he excused himself.

Maurice offered to put him up at his apartment, but Joshua declined.

"No, thanks. I want to walk around and then I'll find a hotel." He clapped Maurice on the back to reassure him it was nothing personal. "I just want a little solitude."

Hiking down the road, his thoughts turned back to Anna without anger. More than anything in the whole world, he wanted to feel her arms around his neck and have her lips firmly planted on his. He was lonely and frightened and her warmth would succor his sorrow.

Then the apparition that had filled her doorway came back to haunt him and he rejected the thought of turning to her. "The devil take the hindmost," he ranted to the swaying palm trees. He didn't need that kind of aggravation in his life. There were other women in the world. Faithful women. Who needed Anna Provo?

WHILE JOSHUA WAS PACING back and forth in the San Diego hospital, Anna, too, was pacing. After calming down, she put herself in Joshua's place and tried to view the scene from his perspective. Wouldn't she have jumped to some pretty lewd conclusions herself? She wanted to talk to him and had tried all day to reach him. Each time she called she received the same answer. "Sorry, Mr. Brandon hasn't checked in today. Would you care to leave a message?"

"No, no message," she'd answered.

What would she say anyway? Tell Mr. Brandon he made a mistake? Inform Mr. Brandon he's a pompous fool? Express to Mr. Brandon that Miss Provo would like to slap his smug face for his nasty accusations? Or even better, rub salt into his complacent attitude about accepting Niki into his life? "I told you so," she muttered to her absent lover.

The more she stewed the angrier she became and the less willing she was to talk to him. She was the one who had been maligned. She was the one whose phone should be ringing off the hook. She was the one who deserved some consideration.

But the ridiculousness of the whole morning struck her once more and Anna pondered the funny side of the whole mess. On the ferry it had seemed Joshua could handle any kinks in a situation with aplomb, but now he had a dent in his suit of armor. She found his weakness reassuring. To know that he could be out of kilter cheered her. She wasn't the only one in this duo who had a hard time handling unwelcome emotions. Joshua had plummeted from the lofty heights of perfection to a more realistic level of fantastic human being. His self-assured attitude would be easier to cope with in the future now that he was off his pedestal.

Would there be a future? Not if he had really meant what he'd said. Anna's doubts assailed her. Could one little spat extinguish the passionate emotions they'd lit between them? Could they weather this storm?

Joshua was gone. That empty feeling that had engulfed her on the ferry when she'd handed Julie her baby crept back over Anna once more. Babies! For years she'd glibly tried to spurn anyone's attempts to convince her that she'd make a wonderful mother and jokingly referred to herself as distinctly unmaternal. But the pain of knowing that she'd never hold her own child in her arms brought tears to her eyes.

What was she going to do? Sit here and wallow in self-pity all evening or do something constructive? Deciding that being weepy all night was a grim way to pass the time, she called Julie. She hadn't checked in with the new mother in several days and was curious to find out how the twins were doing.

"They are constantly ravenous," Julie told her.

"Don't they sleep?" Anna laughed.

"They never do at the same time. One sleeps and the other eats," Julie said with a sigh.

"You sound tired."

"I am but I love it. My mother came up from Florida to help. She's a godsend."

"Sounds like you have everything you want," Anna said. "Two babies to love and a doting mother to help."

"Yes. It's funny how things change. I didn't want one baby much less two. Now I wouldn't trade them for all the wealth in Persia."

Anna wasn't sure she'd heard Julie correctly. "You didn't want a baby?"

"No, I didn't. You know how you get caught sometimes," Julie tried to explain. "Suddenly you're pregnant and mad at everybody. I wanted to see the world, read every book, go to concerts and never have any sticky little fingers messing up my clean house."

Julie's reluctance about having a family was different from her own, Anna rationalized. It was like comparing apples and oranges.

"Actually," Julie confessed, "that was all camouflage. I was scared to death. What if I was a lousy
mother? What if my child was imperfect? What if I
couldn't give it everything: clothes, education,
money, lavish vacations? You know."

Suddenly Anna's apples became just like Julie's
oranges and vice versa. Julie had had vaguer fears.
Anna's were based on experience. There was always
Niki to emphasize what she dreaded.

After she finished talking with Julie, Anna decided
to go for an early-evening run. Perhaps the exercise
would free her of the tension she was feeling. When
she was running hard and fast, her mind had little
room for destructive thoughts.

The cool air whipped past her as she worked up to
a rapid pace, but despite her effort, she still could
only think of finding Joshua. They had to talk if only
to say goodbye. There was only one place left for Anna to call.

As soon as she returned home, she scoured the
phone book for Doug's Island Inn and dialed his
number.

Douglas greeted her warmly. "And to what do I
owe this pleasure?" he asked, his lilting voice rolling
over his words like a brook over pebbles.

"I'm looking for Joshua. Have you seen him today?"

"No, he's not shown his dimpled grin around here.
Is somethin' wrong? Does he need another tannin'
for not mindin' his manners?"

She laughed nervously. "We just had a slight row
and I'd like to straighten it out."

"Ignorin' you?"

"I'm not sure."

"He'll surface, Anna. Don't fret. The secret for patient waitin' is keepin' yourself busy."

"You're probably right. I'm sorry for bothering you with my petty problems."

"Sorry? Now that's what friends are for. If I hear from the bounder, I'll send him your way."

Later, nestled in bed, she was reassured by Douglas's words and convinced that Joshua would eventually call her. She knew him well enough by now to know he didn't quit easily. With that thought, she had no trouble drifting off to sleep.

As ANNA PEACEFULLY SLUMBERED in her bed, Joshua walked up and down the silent hospital corridor. His grandfather had taken a sudden turn for the worse and the family had been called back to the hospital.

"Mr. Brandon?" A nurse's soft voice called him aside. "I think he wants to see you."

He entered the dimly lit room and walked over to the frail figure. "Hi, granddad," he said, the words barely able to get past the lump in his throat.

"Good boy," his grandfather whispered.

"What?" Joshua urged gently. "What?"

"Eloise would...proud...you," he barely said.

Holding the chill hand in his warm ones, Joshua watched as his grandfather's life slipped away. Kissing his fingertips, Joshua whispered, "Goodbye, granddad."

The next few hours were lost in a bustle of activity as arrangements were made and release forms filled out. Finally, at seven-thirty in the morning, Joshua strolled into the bright sunshine and headed toward his hotel. Everything that required immediate attention had been tended to and he was free to catch up on the sleep he'd lost. He was also free to grieve.

Alone in the impersonal hotel room, he mourned his loss. How he wished he could curl up with Anna and share his loneliness with her. Instead he tossed around and thumped his pillow every other minute. He knew all of his sorrow was not for his grandfather.

Eventually exhaustion conquered him and he fell into a troubled stupor, but Anna's face kept appearing on the horizon of his dreams and her mocking laugh echoed in his sleep.

Joshua woke in a groggy fog and was confused for the first few minutes. He searched the room for a clue as to where he was and the piercing California sun cleared his mind. It also put his losses in sharp clear focus.

Douglas had always been his source of refuge and without hesitation he dialed his number.

"Glad I caught you in," Joshua said solemnly.

"What's the trouble I hear in your voice?"

"Granddad is dead. We lost him last night."

A long silence was held before Douglas said, "He was a fine gentleman. We'll miss him."

"Douglas?"

"What, son?"

"I was wondering if . . . ."

He hated to ask if Douglas would leave his business and fly down to San Diego, but he desperately needed his friend's support.

"No need to ask" was the older man's answer to his unspoken request. "I'll juggle things a bit and see you for dinner."

"Thank you."

"Before you ring off, Anna called askin' for you. Shall I let her know where she can reach you?"

"What? Anna?" He sounded puzzled. "What kind of game is she playing?"

"She sounded worried," Douglas said. "Not like she was playin' a game."

A bitter hollow laugh echoed across the miles. "She's a mistress of deception."

"I know you two had a slight fallin' out, but is that any reason to keep her in the dark?"

"Do not call her," Joshua demanded.

"Okay, son. I'll do as you say, but don't be tellin' me it's right. You should have the decency to let her know you're at least safe and sound."

"As if she would care," he sneered.

"What?"

"See you tonight," Joshua said, ignoring him and ending the conversation.

That evening, Douglas agreed to help Joshua with the funeral arrangements.

"Mudger is unable to cope with the details of the funeral," Joshua told him over dinner. "He is superb at handling annuities, arranging mergers and the like, but he can't deal with life-and-death matters."

"Even as a kid," Douglas reminisced, "if one of your pets died, Mudger wouldn't have anything to do with the rites you and I performed."

"He inherited it," Joshua said. "Even now, mother and father have abdicated their responsibility to someone else: me. That's going to leave me trapped in San Diego to make all the arrangements. I'm glad to do it but I'd better call my boss."

Joshua reached his supervisor the next morning and was granted a week's leave of absence. He was kept busy with a mountain of paperwork.

Early one morning, as he was stepping out of the shower, he heard the phone ring. Dripping water, he raced to answer it. It was the nurse from the hospital asking him to pick up some personal effects of his grandfather's that had been left behind.

"I'll pick them up this afternoon," he promised. "Thank you for calling."

This was the day the family would gather to hear the reading of the will. Joshua and Maurice met for a game of tennis and were lounging around the pool afterward when a curvaceous redhead strolled by, eyeing the two brothers with a bold appreciative stare.

"Hey, Josh, catch the redhead," Maurice said to Joshua, who was reading a book.

"Which redhead?" he asked.

"The one in the form-fitting maillot."

"Oh, her" was Joshua's disinterested response.

"Have a thing against redheads?"

"Skip it, Mudger. It's time we got changed for the party," he said, sarcastically referring to the reading of the will.

"You sure have been acting strange the past few days. What's eating you, Josh?"

"Well, let's see," he snapped irritably. "Grand-dad died. Mom and dad are furious with me because I refuse to give up my job to work with you. I have a new career I'm neglecting in Seattle. And the rest of the family is circling around like a flock of vultures waiting for the will to be read. Then I have a stupid brother who has the audacity to ask me, 'What's eating you?' Need I comment further or do you catch the drift?"

"Okay, okay. I'll drop it."

"Good. Let's get cleaned up and finish this business so I can get on with my life." He clamped his book under his arm the way an officer would a riding crop and marched angrily off to the locker room.

After changing they grabbed a quick bite to eat in the country-club restaurant and then headed for the hospital to pick up their grandfather's personal articles. It took longer than Joshua had expected to corner one of the harried staff. Finally a young orderly handed him a brown paper bag.

Joshua waited until he was in the car before checking its contents. He reached in and fished out the photograph of his grandparents that had been next to the bed. The smiling faces seemed macabre considering the loneliness his grandfather had lived with for sixty years. The picture reminded Joshua of the fruitless search his grandfather had made for a woman to replace the void that Eloise had left.

As Maurice wound his way through the heavy downtown traffic, Joshua felt an overpowering sense of loss. How could this old snapshot make him feel so depressed? he wondered.

He searched for an answer but he was stymied. As they pulled into the parking garage, he carefully wrapped the picture in the creased tissue paper and put it away. Turning to Maurice, he asked, "Ready for this, Mudger?"

"I don't know what you're so uptight about, Josh," his brother complained.

"I think the old man had something up his sleeve none of us knows about."

"Like what?"

"Like he had a new will drawn up about two months ago. Said he had some minor changes to make. Any idea what they were?"

Worried, Maurice answered, "No. It's the first I've heard of it."

Climbing out of the car, Joshua flashed his brother a wide grin and said, "Don't worry, Mudger. I don't think he left you out."

They were ushered into a conference room and Joshua mentally ticked off the expectant faces. Everyone was present and accounted for. The preliminary declarations of state of health and mental condition at the time of the signing were dispensed with rapidly. Next, the lawyer related the various trust-fund arrangements and direct inheritances to the assembled group. As each person's name was read, his face took on a look of undisguised relief as he realized he'd been generously remembered.

Finally the attorney came to Joshua's name, and he paused for a moment to adjust his glasses. As he wiped them off, he glanced over at Joshua and shot him a strange look. Joshua couldn't determine what hidden message the man was trying to convey but was surprised that his name wasn't simply included with the list of other family members.

"'And to Joshua Brandon III, my beloved and firstborn grandson, I bequeath twenty-five percent of my stock in CAN-AMER-MEX,'" the deep rumbling voice of the lawyer intoned.

"There is a personal note from your grandfather,"

he added, and read aloud. " 'I know how sensitive you are about family wealth, Joshua. I want you to use the proceeds from my stock to benefit the charitable organizations of your choice. And don't feel guilty, boy, I do know the true meaning of altruism.' "

As the vast implication of his grandfather's legacy sunk in, Joshua realized that he would be able to help many people and provide funding for agencies that desperately needed backing. A dozen worthy recipients occurred to him as he sat groping for words.

"You look stunned," the attorney said.

"I . . . I am," Joshua tried to respond.

"Didn't you know that he was one of the most generous philanthropists in this country?"

"No, I had no idea."

"Well, he was a great man and there are many who are going to miss him sorely."

"Do you know which organizations he supported?" Joshua asked.

The portly man rose out of his chair, walked over to Joshua and sat next to him. "He didn't want you to know how he distributed his money. He specifically told me that he wanted you to make the choices based on your own evaluations. He had a great deal of trust in your judgment and didn't want you bound to follow in his exact footsteps."

The remainder of the day Joshua walked around in a daze. He struggled to comprehend the import of what had transpired.

Douglas cornered him in his hotel room late in the afternoon. "Can you spare a few moments?"

"Sure. What's up?"

"Have you called Anna yet?"

Douglas had steered, goaded, pushed and shoved him through his formative years, and his parenting hadn't stopped just because Joshua was grown.

"I don't want to discuss her."

"Don't you think you owe her an explanation?"

"I owe her nothing," he snapped. "I'd appreciate it if you'd let me handle my own life."

It was the first time Joshua had ever reproached his friend and Douglas recoiled as if he'd been slapped. To hide his pain, he quickly turned and left the suite.

Feeling guilty and miserable, looking for solitude, Joshua went to the beach and stripped the shoes and socks off his feet. Hot and tired, he rolled up his trousers, revealing his tanned calves. He wandered the deserted sands and eventually sat down on a log. He found that digging his toes into the cool wet grains was soothing. Finally relaxing, he watched the small waves break offshore and serenely ripple toward him. Carrying the paper bag from the hospital, he withdrew the photograph again and stared into his grandparents' faces.

As his tension flowed out to sea like flotsam, he called out, "Oh, Anna, what happened to us?"

Something about the faces, barely discernible in the moonlight, nagged at him, and he studied them for a clue. Then the truth he'd been looking for struck him with a startling revelation. If he let Anna go without a fight, he would spend the rest of his life searching for a woman to replace her. He'd end up just like his grandfather. A lonely, misunderstood and misjudged old man.

"Anna Provo," he shouted to the stars, "I love you and I'm not going to give you up!"

Finally admitting his love for her and determined to end his misery, he ran to his car and raced to the nearest phone booth. His heart pounded with anticipation and dread as her phone repeatedly rang. "Please be home," he whispered. At last the ringing stopped.

"Hello?"

Joshua's anger nearly exploded as he heard that same deep voice answer the phone. The same voice that belonged to the giant in her doorway.

Struggling to control his strained emotions, he said, "This is Joshua Brandon. Is Anna home?"

"Nope, but I'm not supposed to tell you that."

Joshua was confused by the childish comment. Was his rival trying to be funny?

"Could you give her a message for me?"

"Sure could. But how come you didn't want to play the other day?"

"What?" Joshua barked into the receiver.

"I only wanted to meet one of Anna's friends. She doesn't get much company and I like company."

A faint light began to dawn. Somehow he'd gotten his image of her brother wrong. He'd pictured Niki as a frail young man, possibly with a physical disability, confined to a wheelchair.

"Is this Niki?"

"Yep, it's me. How come you didn't come in?" he persisted.

"I'm sorry, Niki. I was in a hurry. How about if I come over real soon?"

"Hey, that's super. When?"

"Oh, maybe tomorrow night. How's that sound?"

"Great. Can I tell Anna or do you want to surprise her again?"

"I think we've had enough surprises for a long time. Please tell her that I called and I'll call back at ten-thirty."

Before Joshua could rebound from his shock, Martin took over the phone.

"Looking for someone, old buddy?" he teased.

"What are you doing there?" Joshua asked, unable to figure out what was happening.

"Once more trying to repair the damage you've wrecked."

"Don't you mean wreaked?"

"No, if you had spoken to Anna lately, you'd know I mean wrecked."

Martin explained that Anna had stepped out for a few minutes and he was entertaining Niki while she was gone. He'd dropped by after she'd called him on the pretext of asking something about Elizabeth but he'd suspected she was searching for Joshua.

"I told Niki I'd call back about ten-thirty. Will you see she gets the message?"

"Better late than never," Martin jabbed.

They hung up promising to get together soon.

He stepped out of the cramped interior of the phone booth and inhaled the fresh night air almost like a drowning man who has just surfaced. The nightmare he'd been living in was ended. All his ranting and raving had been directed against a totally innocent victim. Ashamed of himself, his relief was marred by the horrible injustice he'd done to her.

She'd forgiven him once but it had been for a more trivial error. Would she be as fair this time? Would she be as patient? He knew one thing for certain: he couldn't plead his case adequately over the telephone. It would have to be done in person. For now, he would just ask her to give him another chance. When he got back home, he'd present the facts and hope that she had her father's sense of humor. He fervently prayed they'd be able to laugh about the whole incident.

Back in his suite, he threw open the lanai doors and breathed the night air, trying to calm himself and gain control of the joy that filled him. She didn't have another man in her life. She hadn't replaced him. He hadn't lost her.

Then reality sobered him. Maybe he had? He'd hurled ugly words at her like sticks and stones, and they could cause irreparable harm.

With shaking fingers, he dialed her number.

Anna let the phone ring a few times even though she was sitting right next to it. She'd waited a week; he could wait a few seconds. What was she going to say to him? What did she want to hear him say?

Clearing her voice, making sure it sounded cool and indifferent, she picked up the receiver. "Hello?"

"Anna, it's Joshua."

"Niki said you called."

"Before you say anything, I want to explain. But I can't do it this way. I'm in San Diego." He was talking fast. "I'll be on the first flight out of here tomorrow and I was hoping I could come over to see you."

"Are you sure you want to?" was her cool reply.

"If you'll let me."

She was filled with doubt. After a week he was calling from San Diego tenderly asking to see her. Should she just hang up and end their relationship? She had believed he'd cast her aside when he'd made no attempt to reach her, and the pain of rejection was still too raw to handle. Now he was scratching those wounds by calling.

"I don't know, Joshua...."

"Please, Anna," he interrupted. "Just hear me out tomorrow, and then if you never want to see me again, I'll leave you alone. I promise."

"All right. Call me when your plane lands and I'll meet you at Freddy's."

She wanted the meeting in a neutral place where he would have to keep his distance. She would stand a better chance of maintaining her cool reserve there, too.

"Anna?" Joshua's voice sounded so clear. "Anna, I love you." He hung up the phone before she could respond.

She cradled the receiver thoughtfully before putting it to rest. His words still rang in her ear and tears of repressed joy brimmed over her lashes. Hugging herself, she danced across the room repeating, "I love you. I love you." The words were music for her soul and she waltzed to the rhythm until Niki came into the room.

"How come you're dancing all by yourself?" he asked.

"Because I don't have a partner. Be mine?"

The two of them jigged around the furniture to a catchy commercial blaring from the television set and they laughed in mutual merriment.

"Do you always dance to ads?" Niki asked.

"Only when I'm happy, big brother."

Rumpling her hair, he said gaily, "I think you're kinda weird, but I won't tell anybody."

CHAPTER TWELVE

THE GRATING NOISE of cowboys and Indians battling each other on television jarred Anna out of her private reverie. She'd been busy envisioning her reunion with Joshua and rehearsing exactly what she wanted to say. It was hard to concentrate on their reconciliation with war cries screeching in the background. She enjoyed having Niki stay at her house, but his programs played on her nerves like a bow being drawn across an out-of-tune violin.

"Turn off the set," she ordered. "It's time for work."

"Don't bug me," he protested. "Nobody's won yet."

"If you are late and have to stay late to finish your work," she pointed out carefully, "you won't be able to come for dinner and see Joshua."

"Anna." Niki stood up, turned off the TV and spoke very slowly. "Sometimes you're an aspirin."

The way he stressed the first syllable told her what he really meant, and it wasn't the word *pill*. Pursing her lips to keep from laughing, she watched him stomp off to his room to put on his boots.

The ensuing silence was a blessed relief. Now she could think. The past week had been draining, leaving her with little patience and no vitality. She'd been suffering in an emotional purgatory, impatient for some kind of word from Joshua that would parole her from the vague underworld he'd tossed her into.

Joshua had once joked that he'd been searching the obituary column for her name when she hadn't called him. But her search was not a joke. She'd scanned the paper but his name hadn't appeared. Finally, after hearing no word from Douglas, she'd phoned Tom and asked him if he'd heard anything.

"Sorry, Anna," he'd replied. "I haven't heard a thing. Want me to ask around?"

"Would you mind?"

"No problem. I'll call you."

That night he called her at home. "Anna, I found out why Joshua hasn't been answering the phone. He isn't in town. Apparently something came up quite unexpectedly and he took the week off to straighten it out."

"I know what came up. I was just wondering where I could get in touch with him."

"Can't help you. Nobody seems to know where he is."

"Thanks, Tom."

"Is there a problem?"

"Yeah, he met Niki. He thought Niki was a boyfriend."

Tom tried to smother his chortling. "I can see how a man might get that idea. Niki makes Adonis look like a pip-squeak."

"I thought it was funny, too. But Joshua failed to see the humor."

"Don't worry, babe. He'll be back with roses, begging your forgiveness."

"I doubt it. But thanks for checking. Say hello to Sue for me."

As the days passed, Anna's fears and frustration had been replaced by righteous indignation. How dare he treat her in such a cavalier way! Who did he think he was? Granted, she had told him to get lost, but she hadn't really meant it.

And when he had called, she'd forgotten all the things she had wanted to say. Surrendering to the effect he had on her, she flitted merrily around the apartment straightening things up. The thought of talking things out excited her. If things went well, they could resume their relationship where they'd left off. The idea of touching him once more brought a flush of anticipation to her cheeks.

"Hey, Anna—" Niki took her burning cheeks in his cool hands "—I think you got a temperature. Where's the thermostat to take it?"

"I'm fine," she reassured him. "I was just rushing around cleaning and I got overheated." Taking his hands off her face, she corrected, "Thermometer. A thermostat is that dial on the wall for turning the heat up and down."

Bewildered, Niki looked from her to the wall and back again. "I don't think it'll fit in your mouth," he said seriously, then walked away shaking his head.

"Get your coat," she told him. "You're making me dizzy."

"See, I said you were sick," he called from the hallway.

Defeated, Anna hurried him out the door to the bus stop. It was Saturday and she didn't have to go anywhere until Joshua called from the airport. She tried to keep a tight rein on her fantasies and her expectations. She and Joshua still had a lot to work out before they tumbled into each other's arms—if they tumbled at all.

While she toweled her damp hair, Joshua called on a layover in Portland to say he'd be landing in an hour. A bundle of nerves, she picked through her closet and pulled out a denim wrap skirt and a turquoise-and-white-striped knit top. To compliment her outfit, she threw a white sweater across her shoulders and tied the sleeves into a knot that rested on her chest. She slipped canvas-topped espadrilles on her feet, draped a delicate gold serpentine chain around her neck and put small gold hoops in her ears. To please him, she left her hair cascading down her back like a frothy red waterfall.

Glancing at her watch, she estimated she still had time to shop before she went to Freddy's. A quick spree through the market would provide all the ingredients for dinner.

Bustling from counter to counter, she selected the beets, cabbage, onions and ground chuck she'd need to create her borscht. Her next stop was the bakery to buy some heavy black bread and rich cheesecake. Deviled eggs topped with black imported caviar would round off the menu.

The Lubki was the only place to get Seattle's best caviar so she headed there. Mama's back was to the door when Anna walked up behind her and wrapped her arms around the stout woman's waist.

"Hi, mama," Anna said, giving her a squeeze. "How's the world?"

"*Vsyo proidyot*. God willing, everything will pass."

Anna loved that her mother always responded to any question beginning with "how" in the same manner. It reassured her to know mama was so predictable.

She took a jar of caviar off the shelf and handed it to her mother to ring up on the cash register.

"Niki's having dinner with me tonight, but I'm going to bring him home afterward. Is that okay?"

"Certainly, but why? He always spends the night with you when he eats at your place."

"Tonight I'm busy," Anna parried.

"So that's why my girl looks so good, eh?" Mama's face radiated. "You are seeing that Joshua again."

"Maybe."

"No maybes. You are seeing him."

"Yes," Anna admitted and prepared herself for one of her mother's well-meant scoldings on how to behave, how to catch a man, how to be a real woman.

"That's nice." She handed the caviar to Anna in a small paper bag.

Her almost complete silence was too much for Anna, who was prepared for a barrage of advice.

"Is that all you're going to say?"

"No. . . have a nice evening."

"Mama! Are you well? Why aren't you bullying me with your wisdom?"

"Because what I say will be very important and you must not turn off your ears. So I must close my mouth until you tell me you are listening," she answered softly.

Her mother's sudden reticence was unsettling. It was also awe-inspiring. She'd never once been reluctant to voice her opinion in Anna's entire life.

Reaching across the counter and taking her mother's rough chafed hands in hers, she said, "I'm listening, mama. Tell me what's on your mind."

Mama was hesitant for a minute, and then looked her daughter straight in the eyes before speaking. "A woman cannot spend her life not taking risks. If she wants to be complete, she must take chances. So far, my little daughter, you have taken none. Tonight, with this Joshua, gamble."

"Gamble?"

"Yes. Tonight. Tomorrow." Her hands pulled out of Anna's and she counted the future on each finger. "Each day from now on, gamble. Now get out of here. I have lots of work and I can't be talking to you all day."

Dismissed with a peck on her cheek, Anna drifted out of the shop feeling baffled. What in the world was mama talking about? But Anna didn't really want to answer that question. Deep in her heart, she knew very well what her mother was saying. But it was too much to face at present. She'd think about it later.

Right now she was going to pop home and put the soup on to simmer for the afternoon. Right now she was going to wait for Joshua to call and say he was at the airport and heading for Freddy's. Right now she was not going to take any risks, do any gambling. Her mother may have gone crazy but Anna Provo still had her sanity.

While Anna peeled beets, Joshua looked at his notebook as the plane circled Seattle. He'd outlined exactly what he wanted to say to her. He analyzed his position and prepared his speech as if he was fighting for someone's life before the Supreme Court. It dawned on him that in actuality he was fighting for a life. His. And he hoped it would be with Anna. For without her, he would become a mere shadow of himself, going through the motions of living but not really feeling alive. He'd learned that in San Diego.

The more he thought about his abominable behavior, the more convinced he became that he had no recourse other than to simply admit that he'd been a pompous, insensitive, addle-brained fool.

After the plane nosed into the terminal, he collected his gear and called Anna. She said she'd meet him in twenty minutes.

He had no trouble finding a parking spot at Freddy's and pulled up to the curb right behind Elizabeth. His legs felt like lead as he slowly walked into the pub and scanned the booths for her face.

Out of the darkness came a quiet greeting, "Joshua, over here."

He followed her voice and slid into place beside her. Reaching across the table, he picked up her hand and kissed the palm.

"Thank you for coming," he said.

She pulled her hand away and fiddled with her bracelet. "What would you like?" she asked.

"A cup of coffee."

Anna maintained her aloof posture. She was not going to make this too easy for him. She would be fair and listen with an open mind, but her feelings were still too sore to ease his discomfort.

Joshua drummed his fingers on the table while he waited for their order to arrive. He didn't want to start talking and then have to stop while a waiter hovered over them. Finally he gathered up the threads of his courage and plunged in.

"Anna, I'm sorry I haven't called you. My grandfather died and I was in San Diego clearing up his estate."

He looked tired and drawn and her heart thawed. His loss seemed to have sapped his life force and she wanted to hold him, to replenish his normal exuberance. Her father had been right when he'd said, "The truth has seven sides."

"I had no idea," she commiserated.

"How could you? I came to tell you that morning but I didn't let you get a word in edgewise."

He idly ran his fingers around the rim of his cup while he searched for a way to express his feelings. All his prearranged speeches were contrived and inadequate. He was more afraid than he'd ever been, too fearful to look into her amber eyes lest he see her anger.

"Anna, I love you. I made some nasty accusations for which I will be eternally sorry. I now know the man I met was Niki. I believed the worst."

Anna couldn't bring herself to reprimand him. She just nodded, unwilling to interrupt him, to let him know she was listening.

"To be brutally honest, I reacted to the green-eyed monster called jealousy and I behaved hideously. The thought of sharing you with another man made me go crazy."

"I'm at fault, too," she admitted. "You came back up the stairs to ask me, didn't you?"

"Yes. But I don't blame you for not giving me the chance. I'd probably have done exactly the same thing."

"Neither one of us," she said with a smile, "acted like adults."

Gazing into her eyes, he said remorsefully, "When you laughed, I thought I had all the answers."

"Did you?"

"No, but in my defense, the reasonable part of me kept saying you weren't the kind of woman to enter into casual one-night encounters. I knew what we shared was more than that to you."

"So why didn't you call?"

"Ego. Confusion. I thought maybe the tall handsome fellow on your doorstep was Niki, but I pictured him younger and somewhat physically handicapped."

"I can't fault you. A lot of people make the same mistake."

Hesitantly, he reached over and wrapped his fingers around her slim ones. "I love you, Anna."

Unable to resist, she brushed the hair back from his forehead. "What am I going to do with you?"

Bolstered, he brashly asked, "Love me?"

Running her fingernail lightly along the outline of his mouth, she said, "I do." Then she kissed him, trying to erase any traces of anguish or guilt he harbored.

"Let's go home," she murmured, wanting him all to herself for the afternoon.

"Do you know how lovely that sounds after days in a hotel?" he asked wistfully.

"No, but I think I can guess," she answered.

He followed her in his car. Seattle has hills to rival San Francisco's, and as he crested the last hump of Capitol Hill's back, he felt like he was finally nearing home.

As Joshua stepped into her house, Anna felt wanton. She threw her coat on the sofa and ran her hands from his stomach to his neck just to feel his muscles quake at her touch.

Joshua's breath took a quick sharp intake at her advances. "It's been a long week," he barely managed to say.

"Forever," she whispered as she ran her tongue along the curves of his ear. "Mmm, you taste luscious."

Her hot breath on the cool trail her tongue made sent shivers to his toes. He had to focus on his knees to keep them from buckling.

"It's warm," she teased, slipping his jacket off and dropping it into a heap at her feet. "It's claustrophobic," she said as she unknotted his tie and flung it into a corner. "It's too clinging," she mumbled as she unbuttoned his shirt and pulled the tails out of his slacks. "Too binding," she dictated as she unbuckled his belt, drew it languorously through its loops and pitched it into a chair.

He was exposed and nearly denuded. She stepped back and gazed at him. Her sudden distance made him feel more urgent, more aroused. It was as if the air had been taken away briefly and he was experiencing an induced headiness. He reached out to pull her back, but she gently repelled him.

"Let me look," she pleaded. "I thought I'd never see you again."

With a smile she circled him, occasionally drawing a light touch to his skin with her hand. He felt like Michelangelo's Adam on the Sistine Chapel being given life.

There was music between them that only they could hear. Time was nonexistent, the room was invisible, and the world, except for two people, had dissolved.

"He don't look dirty to me," Niki said with a mouthful of apple.

"What?" Both Anna and Joshua exclaimed at the same time. Totally startled by Niki standing in the living room watching them, they tried to adjust to his unexpected intrusion.

"Joshua don't look dirty so how come you're making him take a shower?"

To Niki, the only logical explanation for Joshua's state of undress was Anna's insistence on a shower.

"What are you doing home?" Anna demanded angrily.

"I done my work and got the rest of the day off," Niki answered as he blithely walked past her to turn on the television.

Joshua, who was normally a rich golden color, was distinctly pink. He awkwardly tried to stuff his shirt back into his trousers. He'd never had a mood shattered so swiftly, nor had he ever felt so compromised.

"Don't turn it on," Anna ordered Niki as he reached for the dial on the set.

"If you're going to yell at me," Niki hollered back, "yell at him." He pointed at Joshua.

"Why me?" Joshua already felt as if he stood out like a sore thumb.

"'Cause you threw your clothes all over the room." Niki pointed to the tie in the corner. "Anna hates a mess."

Anna held her breath, waiting to see how Niki and Joshua would interact. So far, their encounters had been distorted and outrageous. Would Joshua be resilient?

Her apprehension evaporated as Joshua laughed benignly. He collected his clothes adroitly and started putting them on.

"You're right, Niki. I'm a terrible slob." He winked at Anna mischievously. "I think I'll take that shower later."

Grinning, Niki sidled up to him and said softly, "If you can get away with it. She—" he pointed to Anna "—never lets me get out of washing."

"Well, I'm new around here," Joshua said conspiratorially. "Maybe she'll give me a break."

Anna saw that Joshua was obviously fighting back his laughter, for there were tears glinting in the corners of his eyes. He was valiantly suppressing his reaction to the comic situation and she appreciated his control. He was being sensitive to Niki's feelings at the cost of his own embarrassment.

"I guess you two don't need an introduction," she said.

"Nope," Niki said. "I know who he is and who I am."

"Do you know who you are?" Joshua teased her. "For a while there, I thought you were Aphrodite."

"Naw," Niki said. "She's just old Anna."

"Well, ol' Anna," Joshua said, "how about something to eat? I'm starving."

"Me, too," Niki chimed.

She smiled at the two men and said, "Why not? You two set the table and I'll dish up."

Conversation through dinner was easy and relaxed as Joshua talked about sailing. He explained the basics of boating safety and promised to take both Anna and Niki out on his sloop very soon.

Clearing his dishes away, he said, "My compliments. That was excellent borscht."

"Thank you." She accepted the compliment graciously. "Would you like some cheesecake?"

"I would," Niki answered first. "How come you didn't tell me you got that for dessert?"

"I was saving it for a surprise."

"She must like you a lot," he told Joshua.

"Why?"

" 'Cause Anna hardly ever buys cheesecake. You must be special, but you look just like a regular guy to me."

Anna felt her mouth hang open as she listened to Niki's theory. He had a full-blown thesis on "The Merits of Cheesecake in Judging the Importance of an Event." Throughout her family history, cheesecake had been served on only the most important occasions.

Looking at the afternoon from an unbiased viewpoint, she was amazed to see that she had unconsciously honored the meal by selecting the family's favorite dessert. How foolish of her not to have realized it and how wise of Niki to have picked up the unconscious signal.

Tonight was the beginning of her new life with Joshua and she was celebrating their new understanding. She walked over to Niki, kissed his cheek and said, "You're absolutely right. This is a celebration."

"Is it somebody's birthday?" he asked excitedly.

"No. We're commemorating a friendship. Don't you think Joshua is worth celebrating?"

Immediately she regretted her question and tried to cover her tracks. Niki was totally guileless. She wasn't sure if Joshua was ready for a large dose of his honesty. Skillfully intervening before he had a chance to answer her question, she directed Niki to finish clearing the table while she cut the cake and poured the coffee.

As she passed Joshua's chair, he caught her arm and whispered, "Afraid to let him answer?"

His power of observation was disarming and she stuttered for a response. "I uh. . . ."

"How could he think I'm great? He barely knows me. Don't push too hard, Anna. I like him and you don't have to keep running interference. I won't be scared off by an opinion."

"Sorry. I just didn't know if you could handle his blunt comments."

"They're refreshing," he said. "Give me a chance to prove myself. I don't have to be treated like a piece of fragile crystal. Usually I roll well with the punches."

"Yes, I recall how well you rolled right down my front steps about a week ago."

"So, I stumbled that time. Nobody's perfect. Just relax and let Niki be Niki."

"Okay, but remember, you asked for it."

"Hey," Niki called from the sink, "whatcha whispering about?"

The telephone rang and let Anna off the hook. The call was for her so she left his question unanswered.

A detective was on the phone who needed her to come down to the court and issue a search warrant. He believed a house contained evidence crucial to the solution of a serious case. Occasionally it was necessary for her to be summoned on a weekend.

"Can you two manage alone for a while?" she asked. "I have to run to my office for a few minutes to verify that some detective has justifiable cause for a search warrant."

"Sure, we'll hold down the fort," Joshua said.

"Are there Indians coming?" Niki sounded worried.

"No, Joshua was just using..." she started to explain but then remembered that Joshua wanted to take care of himself. "Let the counselor set you straight. I'm leaving."

She kissed them both goodbye and grabbed her coat. Comfortable that they would learn to understand each other, she headed for her office.

"I was using a form of speech," Joshua explained to Niki. "You know, a different way of saying things."

"I know," Niki said. "Anna does the same thing. I'm always making a fool out of myself 'cause I'm dumb."

His scathing assessment of himself shocked Joshua. It also blew to shreds another of his stereotypes. He'd always assumed that the retarded are blissfully happy because they are unaware of their shortcomings. It never occurred to him that they could be frustrated with their limitations.

"I'm dumb, too," Joshua consoled.

"How?" Niki was incredulous.

"Once I used hair spray instead of deodorant. I thought my armpits were glued together permanently."

"Me, too." Niki laughed. "I mixed up one time and filled the sugar bowl with salt."

"See?" Joshua emphasized. "Everyone makes mistakes."

"I guess," Niki grudgingly agreed. "But sometimes I wish I learned easy like."

"Want me to teach you how to tie some knots? You can help out when we go sailing."

"Think I can do it?"

"I know you can. Get two pieces of rope and we'll start."

Joshua slowly showed him the basic overhand knot and explained that it was used to keep a cord from unraveling, slipping or pulling through a hole. They progressed to the cat's paw, a simple knot used to suspend a load from a hook.

The two men were deeply engrossed in completing a complicated-sounding knot, the studding-sail halyard hitch, which in truth was very simple, when Anna came home. They were oblivious to her as she entered and she noted that it was the second time she'd found Joshua totally absorbed with one of the Provolosky men in a mutual interest. This time Joshua was the teacher rather than the student, but he seemed equally adept in either role.

Niki spotted her first and jumped up to show her his accomplishment. "Look!" He shoved a wad of rope in her face. "Bet you can't name this knot."

"I don't even know what the one I use to tie my shoes is called," she answered. "Can you teach me this one?"

"You betcha," Niki bragged and he slowly worked his way through a fairly accurate rendition of the cat's paw.

While he was still flushed with success, it was the perfect place to end the day with Niki. She took his coat out of the closet and brought it to him.

"Time to drive you home, big brother. Mama and papa are expecting you."

"Do I have to?"

"Yes. Joshua and I'll take you. No arguments."

"Hey, Niki," Joshua said. "Take this home to papa and teach him. Maybe you can make a sailor out of him."

Pleased at the prospect of flaunting his newly acquired skill, Niki happily slipped into his jacket and ceased his arguing. He chattered all the way home and raced up his front steps, anxious to show off.

Joshua had enjoyed the time with Niki but his patience had begun to wear thin. His irritability had nothing to do with Niki personally. He was just anxious to be alone with Anna and finish what had been interrupted earlier.

As soon as her front door was closed, he enveloped her in his arms and clutched her yielding body close to him. He could feel her soft breasts billowing seductively against him.

Anna could barely breathe as he continued to melt his demanding body into her receptive contours. She could feel his growing rapacious need and dropped her purse to the floor as she entwined her arms around him, lightly running her fingers through the soft curls at the nape of his neck.

"Do you have a dead bolt on your door?" he whispered in her ear.

"Yes."

"Good. Lock it. This time no power on earth is going to stop you from finishing what you began this afternoon.''

He carefully removed her coat and lazily hung it in the hall closet, then slipped out of his jacket, hanging it next to hers. With deliberately measured movements, he picked up her purse and dropped her keys into it.

She watched as he meticulously tended to these insignificant matters and wondered if somehow she'd misunderstood or misread his intentions. He didn't seem as if he was a man possessed by the same erotic hunger that had left her almost physically aching. But as he turned back to face her, she saw that the vein on the side of his neck was throbbing and her doubts vanished. He was damming the flow of his passion, intentionally reserving his ardor.

She felt him unwrap the belt of her skirt with shaking fingers until the fabric was lying in folds at her feet. Nimbly, she stepped out from the swirl of denim. She was left cloaked only in her revealing ivory satin camisole and lace-trimmed panties.

Emboldened, she removed his tie and added it to the mound on the floor. His eyes were hooded with desire as she punctiliously unbuttoned his shirt and peeled it off him. Stepping back with a triumphant look, she silently pleaded with him to undress her.

He denied her. ''Don't stop there, little one,'' he cajoled. ''Finish your work.''

A feeling of brazen power spurred her on to remove all his clothes. He stood absolutely still while she slid his trousers down and eased him out of his restricting garments. She was amazed that he was completely at ease with his nudity. What she didn't realize was that his passivity was calculated to erase any shyness and assure her that she could set the pace of their lovemaking.

Guided by the desire to explore every inch of his muscled torso, she took Joshua's hand and led him to her bathroom. She turned the shower on and while he stared at her, she purposely removed her camisole and panties with a teasing hesitancy.

The room was filled with clouds of steam as she stepped into the spray of warm water and led him in beside her. The moisture whetted their appetites as they lathered each other and gently slid exploring fingers over slippery surfaces.

Joshua fought for command as she magically orchestrated her movements, and when he was certain that the time was right, he took the soap from her and began to glide his anxious hands over her breasts. Massaging the full crescents, he lifted them up to the spray and marveled at how their peaked nipples quivered at his touch. They reflected her intense arousal and he couldn't resist kissing them, pulling them tauter.

His probing tender fingers sought the patch of auburn hair between her thighs, and he painstakingly kissed a path to her fervid triangle. She responded by groaning and leaning against the tiles, widening his access and increasing her pleasure.

"Love me, Joshua," she moaned.

She was no longer in control. Joshua acted on her request. He turned off the shower and carried her to bed. They both ignored the rivulets dripping from their heated bodies as they tumbled onto the velvet spread.

Anna thought she had reached the ultimate height of desire but soon learned that her joy had just begun. The prickling touch of Joshua's tongue as he removed every trace of water from her tingling skin sent spasms surging through her.

In delightful retribution, she lightly flicked her fingers across the golden hairs of his chest and loins. She kept a steady progression of movement going with one hand and made stimulating surprise attacks with the other.

Through her haze, she heard him call out, "Anna, oh, Anna," in a husky voice, and she increased her advances.

He suspended his body above her welcoming form, bringing himself home in her hot moist center. She shuddered at the meeting and he reacted with an uncontrollable thrust.

Each move was like a wave building offshore, not ready to crest but growing larger in intensity as it raced onward.

Anna felt delirious and begged, "More. . . ."

Entwining her legs around his waist, she surged up to meet him and clamped him tighter to her. Her whole body was wildly clutching at him, screaming to be fulfilled.

He lifted her hips, drawing her even closer, piercing her even deeper and he groaned, "One. We're one, my love."

They rode the wave of passion as a single entity. The universe was their union, their love. The intensity of their pleasure was like an earthquake, rocking them to their depths.

For a long time they were silent. The profoundness

of their passion left them awed. Anna just rested her head on his chest and their legs were left tangled together in clutching closeness. She lazily drew circles on his thighs with her fingernail as she envisioned her life with him. It would be bliss, pure bliss.

"Anna?"

"Yes?"

"Do you know how fantastic you are?"

"No, but I know how magnificent you are."

She raised her head to look into his glittering eyes and added, "Want to form a mutual admiration society?"

"I think we've already completed the initiation rites," he said, laughing.

"But there are membership dues."

"Oh, they'll be easy to pay." He kissed her forehead. "Night after night just like this."

CHAPTER THIRTEEN

JOSHUA'S SPORTS CAR was packed to the hilt with camping gear and Anna could just barely squeeze the small trunk shut. The day was sunny and clear. Every thing had been washed clean by the midnight shower that had popped over the mountains and then turned itself off before morning. She relaxed in the leather seat and securely fastened her safety belt.

They were getting an early start for the annual family camp-out. *Family* meant the Provoloskys and all their accumulated friends. When Anna was a child her parents took her and Niki across the mountains every year to seek the birchbark Papa used. Over the years friends had asked to come along and help in the harvest. The event was now a tradition and this weekend was to be Joshua's initiation.

Most of the other people had left early Friday evening for the Naches River but Anna had been detained by last-minute judicial problems. She and Joshua had postponed their departure till early Saturday morning.

She reflected on the past week with a sense of contentment. Both she and Joshua had been busy with their work but, despite the hectic activity, things had gone well. Very well. Joshua had spent the evenings establishing a friendship with Niki and she was pleased that the two men seemed to be developing a close bond.

There had been a few difficult moments, such as the time Niki wanted to spend the night and she had had to take him back to mama and papa. But otherwise, Niki had instinctively known that he needed to curtail his demand for her undivided attention. As a result, Joshua and Niki seemed to be able to share their interests and her as if they had always done so.

Anna studied Joshua's profile as he drove. Behind the rugged exterior was the most considerate and tender man she'd ever known. The eye belied the heart.

He wound their way through the Auburn Valley, and the sweet aroma of strawberries was heavy as they passed acre upon acre of the ripening fruit. It had been years since he'd been out to the valley, and it brought back the lazy June afternoons he'd spent with Douglas picking succulent berries.

"You know," he told Anna, "Mudger never liked to go picking with Douglas but I always loved it. Of course, I filched as many berries as I put into the boxes. I can still taste them."

"Let's stop and buy a quart," Anna suggested. "That can be breakfast."

Joshua grinned boyishly and she knew she'd hit the right note. He pulled over at the next stand and she rinsed their purchase off at the farmer's garden faucet. As Joshua followed the road up past truck farms and out of the valley, she popped a huge juicy red treat between his waiting lips.

"Umm," he moaned and rolled his eyes. "Best breakfast in the world...besides you, that is." He jokingly leered at her.

"Stop ogling me, Counselor. I don't want to end up in the ditch." She laughed and pushed his cheek lightly, forcing him to look back at the road.

After they finished the box of berries, she poured a cup of coffee from the thermos and shared it with him. The two-lane highway led them to Enumclaw and soon they were passing through the Muckleshoot Indian Reservation. Joshua slowed the car and curiously glanced at the unique characteristics of the Indian territory. He'd forgotten about the area he'd known as a child.

As the houses and farms became more scattered, his attention drifted away from the surrounding countryside and he recalled a funny incident with Niki.

Laughing, he asked Anna, "How's the chicken?"

She choked on her coffee. She'd asked Niki to wash the chicken so she could fry it for the outing, and he had obliged. While she was busy rounding up sleeping bags, he promptly filled the sink with hot soapy water and scrubbed the drumsticks and breasts with a scouring brush. It had been her fault for not having told him to rinse it in cold clear water. She should have anticipated his litcral interpretation of her directions.

Once she swallowed the coffee, she said, "I really appreciate how you handled that."

"Well, I almost blew it. I could barely keep from laughing out loud. He was trying so hard to do a good job."

"But you let him maintain his dignity."

A loud roar of laughter erupted from him and between chortles he said, "You should have seen your face. It was priceless."

Anna giggled. "He still has the remarkable ability to take me completely off guard."

"At least it keeps life from being boring."

The powerful Jaguar began climbing the steep grade of Chinook Pass. Silence descended on them as they made their way through the towering Cascades. The narrow road was a curving intricate pattern drawn five thousand feet through the tall mountains, and Joshua's full attention was needed to negotiate the many twists and turns.

Anna drank in the pristine beauty of the snow-capped spires and made a mental vow never to take life's treasures for granted again. Joshua had renewed her zest for living and she witnessed the unfolding panorama with a deep reverence.

At the summit, he pulled off the road and grabbed his camera from the glove box.

"I can't resist," he said. "You stand over there and let me get a picture of you framed by all this grandeur."

She flashed him a smile and he clicked the shutter several times before he was satisfied he had the perfect shot. A group of elderly people filed out of a crowded motor home and Joshua was drawn aside. They asked him to take a few pictures of them in front of Mount Rainier. Happy to oblige, he merrily snapped the cameras and recorded the day on film.

Anna was struck by how easy it was to please people, people one didn't even know, by just showing a little kindness and understanding. Traits that Joshua had in abundance.

The temperature at that elevation was quite cool despite the summer weather and Anna's teeth were chattering before they finally got back to the car. Joshua handed her his heavy sheepskin coat and turned on the heater.

Joining the flow of traffic, he focused his attention once more on the serpentine road. They passed a small icy alpine lake ringed by patches of snow. It was graced by a stand of stunted trees.

"Look at that." Anna pointed to one particularly gnarled fir. "Bet it's at least five hundred years old and no taller than I am."

"The whole place looks like an oversized bonsai garden," he said.

He was right. The scenery was amazingly like one of those Japanese dish gardens where the shrubbery was intentionally dwarfed.

As they descended the face of the pass, he asked, "How much longer?"

"About forty-five minutes."

The heavy undergrowth faded and was replaced by dry timbered country. The change was abrupt and Joshua enjoyed the contrast with the lush dense forests of western Washington. The road now paralleled the Naches River and Anna spied her father's pickup truck parked at his favorite spot. He always returned to Squaw Rock.

Everyone was gathered around the campfire and they didn't notice Anna and Joshua pull in. With their arms wrapped around each other's waists, the two wandered up and casually said, "Hi, everybody."

Anna's mother jumped out of her chair, grabbed Joshua's arm and happily introduced him to the assembled group. "This is my Anna's beau," she said proudly.

A barrage of greetings, all in different accents, bombarded Joshua and he felt overwhelmed. The Provoloskys' friends must have represented half the nations of the world.

Papa came over and gave Anna a kiss. "We were worried you might not make it," he said.

"I wouldn't have missed this for the world, papa."

"I thought Joshua might be reluctant to share you with your family."

"Joshua? He was more excited than Niki about the trip."

Anna watched her father relax and he whispered in her ear, "He's a good man, and all Nikolae can talk about is Joshua this and Joshua that."

"Yes, he is a good man, papa. Can you keep a secret?"

"Always, Firebird."

"I love him and he loves me. Are you surprised?"

A tender light shone from her father's eyes and he said, "Surprised? No. I've known it since I first met him. It just took you two longer to figure it out."

She hugged him tightly and whispered back, "You always were smarter than I was."

Joshua was adeptly fielding questions and she rescued him from the boisterous group by offering to show him around the private resort. The area was dominated by a log cabin structure that housed a combination general store, gas station and office. Overlooking the water was an open-air cabana with a massive stone fire pit in the center. There were rustic cabins up and down the riverbank with more primitive camping spots scattered between them.

They strolled along the dirt path and stopped to

greet other vacationers and to investigate the empty
cabins. They ended up on the riverbank skipping
stones across the swirling water. Niki caught sight of
them and came loping over.

"Where ya been?" he asked.

"Showing Joshua around. He's never been here before."

"Wanna see my favorite fishing hole, Josh?" he offered.

"Well...." Joshua looked to Anna for help. He
was enjoying being with her and didn't relish following Niki all over camp. She either didn't notice his
look or chose to ignore it. "I'd like that," he
capitulated. "Most fishermen aren't willing to share
their secrets."

"Well, I only show special people."

Joshua smiled halfheartedly. "Do you mind, Anna?" he asked, hoping she did.

"Not at all. You two check out the trout and I'll
head back to camp. See you later."

Anna lost track of the time while she sat and gos-
siped with her friends. Even though their backgrounds
were as diverse as the produce and goods they sold in
the market, she felt they all shared a common history.
Everyone was a first-or-second-generation immigrant
who had adopted a whole new country without losing
the unique heritage of his homeland. Age differences,
wealth or the lack of it, stature of occupations or
marital status failed to inhibit their easy conversation.
They swapped stories, exchanged tidbits of information and planned out the itinerary for the weekend,
hoping to crowd as much pleasure into a short time
span as they possibly could.

Dinner preparations had begun by the time Joshua and Niki came trudging back to the group. Niki sighed deeply as he plopped into the nearest vacant chair.

"Joshua sure does like to walk a lot," he groaned. "We musta hiked a thousand hundred miles."

"Where did you two go?" Anna laughed.

"The fish didn't like the way our worms tasted, so Joshua said we were gonna find some mountain goats."

"Did you find any?"

"Nope, but we found this old cabin and it was fallin' apart. Woodpeckers ate it—"

"Look what we found," Joshua interrupted him.

He proudly displayed a tiny pair of high-topped women's shoes. The dry weather had preserved the black leather and the only marks of age were the pieces of nesting material some bird had deposited on the insides. Spears of prairie grass and tufts of baby's breath were wrapped around the small metal buttons.

Anna inspected their treasure. She was fascinated by the detailed stitching and the delicate workmanship.

"Where did you find these?" she asked, rubbing the dust off them with the corner of the dish towel she was holding.

"Oh," Niki answered, "in a corner covered by dust. I thought it was something alive and I made Joshua check it out. You know bears could be hiding."

"No bear would be covered with dust hiding in a corner," she said.

He argued indignantly, "Well, I'm not taking any chances. No bear or Big Foot is gonna catch me."

Niki had never forgotten the movie he once saw in which the legendary Sasquatch gobbled up poor unsuspecting campers. The creature is supposedly a ten-feet-tall cross between a primate and man. Indian legend says he lives in the forests between northern California and the Yukon. Anna had had to sit up with Niki many a time over nightmares generated by the film.

"Big Foot doesn't exist," she said emphatically.

"Prove it," he demanded.

"Anyway," Joshua said, breaking the tension, "we brought these back for you. We thought you'd like them."

"Thanks, to both of you," she said, kissing Joshua and Niki's cheeks. "They're fantastic. I'll take them to a shoemaker and have them cleaned."

Niki's pout vanished when he saw how pleased she was and he turned his attention to his growling stomach.

"When can I eat?"

"Nikolae, you hungry hunter," mama scolded as she joined them. "Don't you ever think of anything but food?"

"Only when I'm sleeping," he answered, completely deadpan.

"Well, you won't have to take a nap," mama reassured him. "Just wash up because dinner is almost ready."

Anna drew Joshua aside before they sat down to eat. Kissing him, she asked, "What did you do? Drag him over the hills to wear him out?"

"You got it, babe." He tried to laugh good-naturedly. "That guy seems to think I'm his personal playmate."

"You do kind of look like a golden teddy bear."
She laughed back.

"Grrr," he growled and lunged at her. "Feed me,
I'm starving."

Heaping platters of food were loaded onto the picnic table and soon everyone drifted over and helped
themselves. It was a gastric challenge to leave enough
stomach room so each dish could be sampled. Joshua
managed to eat his way through each offering, but
ended up a moaning figure stretched out on the picnic bench.

"It'll take me a week to burn off all that delicious
food," he complained with his head cradled in Anna's lap.

She stroked the hair from his forehead and differed. "I'd say we'll have it digested in about three
hours."

"How?" he groaned.

"Sit up and look," she said as she pointed to their
friends who were strolling back to the table with instruments. One of them carried his violin, another
toted a classical guitar, and papa was strumming and
tuning his balalaika as he walked. "Now the fun
begins."

The men serenaded the women as they quickly
cleared the food and did the dishes. Then everyone
headed to the cabana, which they reserved every
year, to start the real singing and begin the dancing.

The musicians broke into a lively tune that prompted a circle dance. The women spaced themselves evenly in a small circle while the men formed an outer circle
and pranced around them with lively steps. The
women twirled left and the men spun right and the

various colors they wore swirled in opposing blurs making the dance look like a huge kaleidoscope. The tempo became faster and faster until the dancers were shouting, encouraging the musicians to pluck their strings even more quickly.

Joshua was unfamiliar with the set pattern of intricate movements but he did his best to keep pace with the others. When the music abruptly ended, he was panting for air and gratefully sank onto a wooden bench.

"What was that called?" he asked Anna in halting gasps.

"It was a French bourrée. Does knowing the name make your heart slow down a little?"

"No," he heaved, "but knowing what could have killed me is comforting."

She retrieved a handkerchief from her pocket and patted dry the streams of perspiration that were edging down the sides of his face. "Over the years we've all borrowed a little from one another's cultures and now we have quite a repertoire of international dances," she said.

"Repertoire?" Joshua smiled ruefully at her. "Is that what you call this insane collection of lung busters?" He was watching the group pair off into couples to begin a Spanish fandango. The wild stomping of their feet shook the earth and he thought the seismograph at Mount Saint Helen's must be scribbling off its paper.

"Come on," Anna said, dragging him to his feet. "By the end of the evening you'll be an expert."

"I doubt it, but by midnight I'll be ten pounds lighter for sure," he complained but happily followed her onto the dance floor.

Anna put him through a choreographed wringer as she goaded him to tackle one lively jig after another. Occasionally when Anna danced with another man, mama grabbed Joshua and took up the slack. Joshua stomped, dipped, shagged, bransled, skipped and strutted his way through the night.

When he was rarely allowed to catch his breath, he leaned back and watched Anna spin and whirl around the floor. Her long hair was flying out behind her like an auburn silk scarf in the wind. Her face was happily animated and she tossed her head back often to laugh gaily.

Anna threw herself down next to him and he kissed her flushed cheeks. The music stopped and the musicians packed their instruments and tucked them into their cases. As everyone shuffled off to bed, Joshua and Anna walked to his car, arms curled around each other's waists. Earlier they had decided to sneak off to another campground down the road so that they could spend the night together without placing Anna's parents in an awkward position. It was obvious they were together, but Anna felt that everyone would be more comfortable if she and Joshua were discreet.

The stars were out and the night had taken on a definite chill so Joshua was hurrying to unlock the car and get the heater going. Niki caught up with them and clapped his arm around Joshua's shoulder.

"I got the tent up, Josh," he said.

"Great," Joshua complimented him.

"Your sleeping bag is next to mine but I couldn't find your pajamas to put under your pillow."

"What?" It was beginning to sink in that Niki expected Joshua to be his tent companion.

"You're gonna sleep with me in my tent," Niki said.

"I had other plans, pal," Joshua said firmly, his voice edged with indignation.

"But that's how we always do it," Niki explained. "Anna sleeps in the back of papa's truck and I use my tent. There's enough room for both of us," he begged.

Eyeing the tiny one-man tent near the campfire, Joshua stammered searching for an excuse to avoid spending the night crammed into it with his giant companion. He turned to Anna, hoping she would bail him out, but he was only met by her amused grin.

"Looks like Niki has thought of everything," she said, smothering a giggle.

"Well...I...uh...guess it'll work okay," he hedged. "Sure there's enough room?"

"Oh, yeah, Josh," Niki guaranteed. "You'll love it."

"Too bad you forgot your pj's," Anna whispered in his ear.

"I don't own a pair," he mumbled.

"I'll give you a pair of my old ones for Christmas," Niki said magnanimously. "They got blue-and-red stripes on 'em."

"Whoopee." Joshua's voice was as flat as a punctured balloon. "Let me say good night to Anna and I'll be right with you."

As soon as he was out of sight, Joshua scooped her into his arms and headed for papa's truck.

Shrieking in mock protest, she laughed, "Put me down this instant."

"Ssh, you might wake someone."

"Then put me down."

"Listen, lady. Unless you save me and think of some way to make Niki understand I won't sleep with him, this is the closest I'm going to get to you all night. Believe me, sleeping with him in his toy teepee is not my idea of a fun night."

"Oh, poor baby." She offered false consolation. "Will you survive?"

"Probably not," he growled. "With my luck, your brother will roll over during the night and turn me into a grease spot."

Holding her captive in his arms, he kissed her neck and breathed in the gentle sweet smell of her soft skin.

"It's going to be a long night with you so near and yet so far away," he complained. "Can't I just say no?"

"Not without a scene," she whispered. "But that's what happens when you hitch up with a Provolosky. Love under the stars but...long distance."

Setting her down, he pulled her close and locked his arms around her waist. "I don't know if I can let you go, Niki or no Niki."

She put her hands on his broad chest and pushed him away. "Simmer down, Counselor. Just think. This way everyone will believe I've fallen in love with a gallant gentleman. I won't tell them what a truly lecherous villain you really are." Kissing him on the end of his nose, she added, "Leave them with a good impression. False, but good."

Giving him another quick kiss, she dove into the truck and slammed the door. Smiling, she blew Joshua a kiss and watched as he trudged off to crawl in with Niki.

EVERYONE WAS UP at the crack of dawn and fishing the river for breakfast. A few had good luck so they all feasted on pan-fried trout. Joshua and Anna had had no chance to spend any time alone and by late morning they were anxious for a few private moments together.

Stealing off, they hid under the spreading branches of a giant tamarack tree and hungrily joined their lips. Both felt as if they'd been separated for months, and they thrilled at the touch of each other's hands. Anna's heart quickened as Joshua firmly thrust his tongue between her parted lips, engaging her with his fierce starving demand. His breathing was labored as he mined the sweet interior of her mouth and his hands roamed her body, promising sweet relief to the ache she was feeling.

The sharp snapping of branches alerted them that they were no longer alone and Anna hastily pulled away from his lovemaking.

"Anna?" Niki's deep voice called out. "Where ya hiding?"

Reluctantly she answered, "Over here."

Following her voice, he soon joined them under the tree. "Whadda we do now?" he asked. "I'm bored."

"I thought you went with mama and papa to collect some bark?" she asked.

"Naw, I've done that too many times. I wanna stay with you and Josh."

To hide his exasperation, Joshua kept his face

turned away and watched the river rush headlong through the forest. Eddies lined the banks every few feet and huge boulders broke the water flow creating fluffy whitecaps on the blue glacial surface. The river was angry looking and turbulent. Joshua identified with it. Niki's lousy timing had often forced him to change course. Just as the river had to work around fallen trees and landslides, he had to shift, adjust and redirect himself past Niki's intrusions.

Anna understood Joshua's reaction and covered his silence by asking Niki, "What did you want to do?"

"How about going into town?" he prompted.

The small town of Naches had a few quaint shops and Niki enjoyed prowling through them. Kissing Joshua on the back of his neck, she asked, "Would you like to look around Naches?"

In control of himself again, he responded brightly, "Sure, let's go."

They drove into town and lazily wandered the boardwalks and snooped through the gift shops and antique stores that lined the main street. At one end was a photographer's studio that specialized in costuming its customers in period clothing. Drawn by the pictures displayed in the window, the trio decided to go into the studio. Each photograph was done in the yellowed tones of the old tintype pictures and people looked as though they had stepped out of time and into the past.

An inspiration flashed through Joshua's head as he spotted an elegant flapper's dress hanging on the rack of available costumes. He remembered the picture of his grandparents and was seized by a desire to have a similar pose of Anna and himself. He wanted to place their picture in a double frame next to that of his grandparents.

Anna was fingering a velvet-and-taffeta dance-hall dress when he called her over to his rack.

"How about this?" he asked.

She looked at the blue-beaded chemise. "Is that your favorite?"

"Yes. Would you mind?"

"Of course not. Let's change."

As they were selecting an appropriate suit for Joshua, Niki asked, "What about me? Can I dress up with you guys and be in the picture?"

Joshua had the sudden image of their "son" balanced on his knee. The idea of holding huge Niki on his lap made him chuckle and he fought to keep from bursting into a full-blown laugh.

"Not this time, pal. Do you mind if I have one with just my best girl and me?"

"Yeah, I guess," Niki said, but Joshua could see that he wasn't too pleased.

On the sidelines, Anna held up a pair of chaps and a large cowboy hat. Seeing the solution, Joshua suggested, "I have a better plan for you."

"Yeah, what?" Niki sounded petulant.

"How about you getting all decked out like a real cowpoke for a picture by yourself?"

"Do I have to stand next to a horse?"

"No." Joshua laughed. "I don't think the man has any horses."

"All right." Niki marched off to change into his leather chaps.

Afterward, they sat outside on the bench of the

studio licking ice-cream cones while they waited for the film to be developed. It had taken only a few minutes to snap the photos and Joshua was trying to figure out what to do the remainder of the day. He wanted to spend a little time alone with Anna, but he couldn't come up with a plan without risking a scene with Niki.

"Well, gang, what's next on the agenda?" he asked.

Anna looked down at the ground and scraped her toe back and forth across the rough boards. She seemed distracted and unconcerned when she said, "How about going horseback riding?"

Joshua hadn't ridden a horse for years, but it sounded as good a way as any to pass the time. "Sure," he said. "I'm game."

"Well, I'm not," Niki objected loudly. "I hate horses," he hollered.

Joshua immediately understood Anna's ploy and took over. "You do?" he asked.

"Yes, they stink and they bite. No way. Not now, not never are you gonna get me on one."

"But all cowboys ride horses," Joshua said.

"Didn't you hear me ask about that before? I'm not a cowboy, Josh. I was just pretending."

"Oh," Joshua added some mock disappointment to his voice.

"But you two can go without me," Niki insisted. "I don't mind."

"Are you sure?" Anna questioned him. "We don't want you to be bored."

"No problem," he said. "As long as I don't have to go near any dumb horses, I'll be happy."

Driving back to deposit Niki at the campground, Joshua inwardly applauded how skillfully Anna had maneuvered Niki and created their escape.

THE WRANGLER saddled two slightly spirited mounts for them and Anna guided Joshua across the road and up into the surrounding hills. Where the trail permitted, she rode next to him and gave a running commentary on the rides she had taken as a girl.

They were riding through an area where the ground was covered by large boulders facing south into the warm sun, so she cautioned him to not get off his horse without first checking for rattlesnakes.

"There aren't any snakes this close to the water," he argued.

"That's what I always thought, too."

"You have to get farther east," he insisted.

"When I was about twelve," she recounted, "I dismounted my horse without the trail guide's permission and he proved to me that there are some pretty big rattlers in this area."

"Really?"

"Really. He shot one about three feet away from where I was standing and draped it across a tree limb to drum home his point." She indicated a jack pine off to their right. "That one over there. He said snakes like to sunbathe on these rocks. Ever since, I've been very cautious when I ride through this section of the hills."

"You've convinced me," he conceded. "I'll be careful."

She reached across the short span between them and ran her hand up and down his arm. "Just when

I've found you," she said, "I don't want to lose you to some snake in the grass."

"Rocks." He corrected her pun and laughed. "Don't worry, Annie Oakley, I'm not going anywhere without you."

They left the boulders behind and the higher they climbed the more wild flowers she was able to point out to him. Wild strawberries blanketed the lower slopes interspersed with the variegated colors of blooming Scotch broom. Trees stunted by heavy winds cast distorted shadows on the yellow daisylike petals of the flashy black-eyed Susans. Farther up the slope, she picked out Indian paintbrush with their spear-shaped salmon-colored blossoms blazing in the sun.

When she and Joshua finally reached the crest, the hills were treeless but far from barren. The ground was covered by tiny dots of flowering moss and blue bellflowers and hundreds of other mountain flowers she couldn't name. Dozens of shades of color spread before them, and there appeared to be an intricately woven Oriental rug at their feet.

From their lofty vantage they had an unobstructed view of the deep green forests surrounding Mount Rainier, and they could see the heavy growth diminish as their eyes traveled eastward. To the north, the land was tinted by acres of golden wheat and emerald alfalfa. The once-arid region had been reclaimed by successful irrigation and now many families made their living harvesting the abundant crops.

Cutting through the territory like a wide blue ribbon was the mighty Columbia River, winding its way to the Pacific Ocean and nourishing the thousands of orchards that lined its banks. Later in the fall, millions of bushels of apples would be picked and shipped around the world.

To the southeast stretched a dry, sparsely populated country that ruggedly defied man's permanent civilization. Dotted by sagebrush, lava rock, tumbleweed and huge basalt boulders, even the wildlife seemed to avoid the area. Yet the arid land was magnificent in its defiance. It was like mother earth had said, "You can only have a part of me. Only a part."

Joshua had never stood in such a place where he could contemplate such richly diverse country. The panorama forbade him to speak and he silently absorbed the individual beauties of the land spread out below him.

Finally Anna moved. When she took his hand the spell was broken and he finally felt free to talk.

"Breathtaking, isn't it?" she offered. "I wanted to share this with you."

"The view is staggering" was all he could manage to say.

They continued to ride the ridge and she pointed out a tower in the distance. "That's a Forest Service lookout for fires," she said.

"Seems like it would be lonely way up there."

"I don't think so," she said. "As a teenager, I tried to get a summer job manning one of them, but I never could manage it. It doesn't pay well and I always needed more money than they offered."

"Would you settle now for a cabin with a view?"

She smiled. "Wouldn't that be something?" she said dreamily. "A little log cabin with a big brass bed and a window right at the foot of it? You could snuggle under an eiderdown, watch the sun set and be all cozy and warm."

"Let's try to make your wish a reality," he said. "Somewhere there has to be a piece of mountain property for sale. We could buy it and build a small place." He doubted he could find anything as grand as the land on which they stood, but he vowed to search. The pleasure they'd find in combing the hills together and loving the nights away beckoned to him.

"If you get to have a brass bed," he teased, "I get a huge potbellied stove."

"How do you plan on getting it up a mountain?" she retorted. "Airlift it?"

"If I have to," he answered, and she didn't doubt his seriousness.

"We'd better head down before dark sneaks up and catches us," she warned.

Planning and designing their cabin, they slowly worked their way out of the hills. It was almost dark when they finally reached camp, and almost everyone had gone. Mama and papa were still waiting.

"We were getting worried," papa said. "What took you so long?"

"Sorry," Anna apologized. "It's a long way up and back."

"You went all the way to the top?" papa asked.

"We planned Anna's dream cabin on the way down," Joshua said.

Mama chuckled and hugged her daughter. "Got your head in the clouds, eh? Good. Keep it there."

Papa Provo asked Joshua to follow him over to his

truck while Anna and her mother rolled up some sleeping bags.

"I finished that tea box for your parents," papa said, reaching into the cab of his pickup. "Here." He handed a burlap-wrapped package to Joshua.

Joshua unfolded the cloth and held the most beautiful object he'd ever had the privilege of touching. There was nothing to compare the box to, since nothing had ever been created quite like it. Papa Provo had carved wispy but intricate scenes. On the top a troika was being drawn by a team of prancing horses. The animals were so clear, so perfect that Joshua could see the muscles flexing as they high-stepped through the snow.

"I know I owe you something for this," Joshua said, awed, "but whatever price you ask wouldn't nearly be enough."

"You like it then?"

"I think it's the loveliest piece I've ever seen."

"Then I'm paid."

Joshua was about to protest, but he realized that by insisting on payment he would ruin the gift he'd received and insult Anna's father.

"Thank you very much, Papa Provo," he said as sincerely as he could.

Anna's father just patted him on the shoulder and smiled.

Joshua and Anna were the last ones to leave Squaw Rock. Even though they made the pretense it was to check around to see that all fires were doused and that no one had left anything behind, they were actually reluctant to end the weekend.

"I've been coming here my whole life and I've

always loved it," Anna told him. "But this year it is different. This year it's taken on a special significance. Showing you the town, the river, the hills, introducing you to my family friends, has broadened the experience—enhanced it. I could never come back here alone."

"The weekend was special to me, too," he said. "Thank you for including me."

He drove wordlessly back over Chinook Pass as the radio played strains of soothing music. Absently, with her head resting on his shoulder, she danced her nails up and down his leg as if her fingers were little puppets putting on a ballet. Unconsciously she pliéd, demi-pliéd and made piqué turns higher and higher up his thigh.

Suddenly he snatched her hand away. "Do you want to get home tonight or did you plan on spending the night at the nearest motel?" he growled in a husky tone.

Confused, she asked, "What are you talking about? We both have to work tomorrow."

"Then quit skipping your fingers along me," he said, clearing his voice with a slight cough. "You're driving me crazy and I'm likely to seduce you before we make it back to Seattle."

Suddenly aware of the havoc her touch had caused, she leaned over and ran her tongue around his ear.

Whispering, she said, "Patience, Counselor. The wait will be worth it."

They pulled up to her condo at ten o'clock and rapidly unloaded their gear from the trunk. She noticed he was moving a little stiffly and she offered him the shower first while she put some things away.

"Thanks." He smiled. "I don't know which got the best of me, the dancing or the horse." Rubbing his backside as he meandered down the hall, he mumbled, "Or maybe it was the old dry riverbed Niki lay my sleeping bag over."

By the time she entered the bedroom, he was sitting up in bed with only a sheet covering him. The way the linen clung to his still-damp body accented his sinews and curves. He might as well have been naked. Anna wished she'd already had the dust showered from her body. If so, she would have thrown aside the sheet and crawled into bed beside him.

Smiling at her as if he could read what was on her mind, he beckoned to her without saying a word, without lifting a finger or flicking a muscle.

She forced herself to ignore his unspoken command and stripped in front of him, taunting him, making him ache for her as she did for him. With a deliciously wicked smile, she sashayed her magnificent body out of his sight and into the shower.

As she turned on the faucets, she heard him call out, "I'm unhooking the phone in case Niki decides to call and invite me over to a pajama party."

CHAPTER FOURTEEN

JOSHUA AND ANNA settled into a comfortable pattern of living. They took turns cooking. He specialized in baking breads and creating casseroles. Her forte was soups and salads. And like their menus, they complemented one another in most ways until it seemed they'd always been together. Their days fell into a smooth flow of work, play and love. Time winged its way through the weeks, and the cooler evenings of early summer heated up into the balmy nights of August.

They established a rhythm in their lives and both found gratification in its easy predictability. Like most couples, each made concessions. One of Joshua's was to join Anna for her early-morning runs.

He'd jog up Capitol Hill from Portage Bay to her place and they'd run along the vacant sidewalks, through the uncrowded center of Volunteer Park, around the perimeter of the reservoir, past the Seward mansion and then they'd encircle the Seattle Art Museum.

They usually talked as they ran and on a Tuesday morning, Joshua asked, "Want to head up to Rosario on Saturday?"

"Will you take me dancing?"

"I think I can handle it now that I've been running like a maniac for weeks."

Anna laughed. "I didn't have folk dancing in mind."

She was remembering the Fourth of July weekend they'd sailed around the San Juan Islands. Joshua had anchored off the elegant resort on Orcas Island and they'd rowed into the main dock. Strains of ballroom music beckoned them to the hotel. It had housed an opulent dining room and adjacent to it was a lounge with a large dance floor. A small orchestra outfitted in tuxedos was playing oldies-but-goodies music. Couples dressed in evening clothes danced to "Sentimental Journey."

It was like stepping back into time or watching an old movie. Neither Joshua nor she was properly dressed in boating clothes to join the other couples, but Joshua had promised to bring her back another day.

Slowing down and walking the last block back to her place, he asked, "Did you plan on asking Niki?"

"I thought maybe we would. Any objections?"

He sounded hesitant as he answered. "Not really."

"What's wrong?" She stopped and took his hand.

"Let's wait till we're home to talk about it," he said.

While they cooled down with large glasses of orange juice, Anna broached the subject of Niki spending two days with them.

"It's not that I mind him coming along with us. I just wondered—" he paused, reluctant to talk "—how comfortable we'd be. Remember how much fun I had sleeping with him in his pup tent?"

"He can't pitch a tent on the water," Anna joked.

Ignoring her, he persisted, "What will we do with him at night?"

"The couch makes into a bed. There'll be plenty of room."

Exasperated, he snapped, "Don't be so dense. How will we explain that you and I are sleeping together in the bunk?"

Smiling, she teased, "Afraid of what my brother will think?"

"No," he said decisively. "But he isn't totally naive."

Anna stopped her ribbing. There was more bothering him than she realized. It wasn't the question of who slept where.

"There's something else on your mind, isn't there?" she asked.

He pulled off his T-shirt and mopped his brow before answering. Tossing it aside, he faced her squarely. "I'm tired of us being Niki's entertainment committee. Do you think it's unreasonable for us to spend some weekends alone?"

"Are you saying you're burned out?" she asked point-blank.

"No," he said. "I like and really enjoy him, but not as a steady diet."

"What do you suggest I do with him?" she asked testily. "Hire a permanent baby-sitter? Adopt him out to a childless couple? Disown him?" Her sarcasm had a razor's edge to it.

"Knock it off, Spitfire," he ordered. "You always spew garbage like that when you get defensive."

"And you stay so calm, so cool?"

"You're turning this into an argument. Why? We were discussing Niki's constant dependence on us," he reminded her dispassionately.

"Objection sustained, Counselor," she snappishly conceded. "So what are *your* suggestions? What do you propose we do with Niki?"

Joshua ran his hand through his hair and tried to think of an answer. Taking her in both his arms and pressing her to him, he said, "I don't know. There has to be a solution somewhere. What do other people do with retarded adults?"

Anna's anger evaporated in his hold. She could understand how someone who had not grown up with Niki would find his company claustrophobic. He was demanding but she'd never had any reason to search for alternatives to the life-style she'd always known. What did other families do?

"I don't know," she admitted. "I guess I've never thought about it much."

Joshua didn't want to generate any more anger so he suggested, "Let's take him with us this weekend but start exploring different avenues. This issue must be resolved. I don't want to continually battle with you about him."

Anna nodded her head. "Deal. And next weekend we'll have all to ourselves. No Niki. Think you can handle that?"

While she pledged her undivided time and attention, she mischievously nipped at the sensitive spot on the side of his neck. His bare chest felt delectable as he gripped her closer. She hated to remind him that they both had jobs waiting, but duty called and she mentally answered the plea.

"My turn for the shower first?" she whispered in his ear.

"Only if you can beat me to it."

They were like two young children at play as they raced for the bath. Joshua won but willingly relinquished his victory to Anna. He had purchased an extra set of grooming supplies and left them at her home. When they had first started exercising together, he had returned to his houseboat to change for the day. It cut into their time together and she suggested he simply leave fresh clothes in her closet so that they could spend the entire morning with each other.

While she showered, he waited on the terrace and pondered their situation. They had reached a stalemate. Both of them wanted more time alone but neither of them knew where to turn. But there was a solution. Somehow he'd find it. He had to.

They were both neatly groomed and ready to face the day when Anna waylaid him.

"Let's make a pledge," she decided. "Instead of trying to second-guess what the other is feeling, let's be honest, always. It'll be a lot easier and save us time and worry."

"Agreed." He laughed and playfully shoved her out the door.

Driving to work they planned a quiet solitary evening together, but the day turned everything upside down. Joshua phoned to say he'd be held up because he had to serve a subpoena to a bouncer on Skid Road and he couldn't ask his intern, Tiffany, to do it. Anna assured him that it was just as well. Spring quarter was over and although she hadn't taken on a summer class, the instructor of the summer group was sick and Anna was going to cover for him. Joshua offered to drive her to the community college and pick her up afterward.

The class was a breeze. This was their last night and all Anna had to do was pass out the final exam. Deep in thought, she leaned back in her chair and gazed at the ceiling while the students answered the essay questions. It was the first opportunity she'd had all day to think about the conversation she and Joshua had had that morning. Everything he'd said was valid, but what could either of them do about it?

She wished she could answer that question as easily as the class in front of her could answer theirs. There were no books or guidelines to rely on to tell her what to do.

Joshua was in the same quandary. As he exited the bar where he had served the subpoena, he found his mood was black. He wanted Anna more than he'd ever wanted anything in his life. But he was beginning to understand that he might have to compete for her love forever. Was that the way a relationship was supposed to be? No. They should be the center of each other's lives, but somehow the rules were warped because of Niki. Anna had tried from the beginning to warn him that the dues for loving her would be high.

But he'd promised her that they would tackle things a day at a time. He would pick her up tonight, plan a quiet evening for tomorrow and they'd start to work out the problem. As he unlocked his car, his frame of mind was considerably brighter.

The following day was sultry. Anna and Joshua came home together literally drained. As she stripped, took a cool shower and put on a light little sun dress, Joshua cut up a bagful of fresh lemons to make lemonade.

She found him leaning against the drain board, his tie off and his shirt open to his waist. He was brushing the tall frosty glass against his cheek.

"Hi," she said, kissing him and feeling renewed. "Let me have a sip."

"What's for dinner?" he asked as he handed her his glass.

"Why don't you go put on some shorts." She played with the hair on his chest. Cooing, she continued, "Lie out on the chaise, bake for an hour and I'll serve you."

"Are you bringing me dinner?" he said, laughing. "Or am I the main course?"

She barely nibbled his chin and pretended to dine on him. "My preference is you."

"Only if you're the dessert," he bantered.

Moments like this made up for any doubts he had about loving Anna. Everything was perfect when she teased him, when they were alone and free to demonstrate their need for each other.

"Anna? We brought you a watermelon!" Niki bellowed from the living room. "Mama and papa are bringing in the rest of the dinner."

"Damn," Joshua muttered under his breath. "We left all the doors open."

"What do we do?" she whispered.

"I don't know about you," he seethed, "but I'm going to take a shower and cool off!" He shoved a kitchen chair angrily aside and stormed past Niki who was just coming into the room.

Anna masked her embarrassment and anger with her family for just dropping in.

"It was so hot today," mama said as she put a

bowl of coleslaw into the refrigerator, "we decided to picnic around your pool."

Anna forgave her mother's assumption that she need not call before visiting. For years it had been acceptable for the family to simply come and use the condominium's facilities.

"That's fine, mama," Anna said. She decided not to say anything now to her mother. She didn't feel she should ruin their fun. But Anna intended to have a talk with her very soon and tell her to please give some warning before visiting.

A kind of bedlam reigned. Niki was searching for his lost thongs and hollering about how stupid they were to hide from him, mama was banging through Anna's pots and pans searching for one large enough to boil corn on the cob, and papa was watching the evening news, repeatedly turning up the volume to override all the other noises.

Joshua came up to Anna and kissed her on the temple. "Sorry about the fit of temper," he apologized. "But tomorrow night we go out to protect ourselves."

Surveying her family, she said, "Anywhere that is private."

"Bush Gardens?"

"Great. Make the reservations," she said with a smile.

Joshua retreated to her bedroom to make the call. He reserved a tatami room and hung up. But before he had taken his hand off the receiver, the phone rang.

A few minutes later, he found Anna loading a tray to carry down to the pool. "Is there enough food for one more mouth?" he asked.

"Sure, but for whom?"

"Douglas just tracked me down. He sounded a little low so I invited him over. Do you mind?"

"Of course," she joked. "I think it's unreasonable of your friends to just drop in. My family wouldn't think of doing such a thing." She flashed him a broad smile as she headed down the stairs.

After dinner everyone went swimming except Douglas, who didn't have a suit. Joshua swam a few laps of the pool and climbed out. He dried off and sat in a chair next to his friend.

"You seem pensive tonight," Joshua probed.

"I am." Douglas sighed. "I put my place on the market today."

"Your restaurant?"

"Yes, both my inn and my house."

"Why?" Joshua was astonished.

"Why not? There's nothin' keepin' me here." Douglas sounded indifferent.

"What do you mean you have nothing here?" Joshua almost ranted. "You have your friends, your business and me."

"Yes, but no family. I'm gettin' to a time in my life when I need family."

"I thought I was family," Joshua said softly.

"That you are, son, but you've grown up and you don't need me anymore. Since you and Mudger have gone off, I thought I'd see what I could find waitin' for me back in Ireland."

For a long time Joshua didn't speak. What could he say to his lonely friend? *Stick around and I'll visit you once a month? I'll wedge you between Anna and Niki? I'll find time for you on Christmas Day?* There was nothing really solid Joshua could offer Douglas.

The man had devoted his life to him and now there was no one who needed Douglas.

"Think about it," Joshua pleaded. "Really think about it before you sign any papers."

Niki heaved himself out of the pool and started to shake the water off his body like a puppy. His gyrations sent a cold spray all over Douglas.

Feeling depressed and cranky, Joshua barked, "Niki, stand over there if you're going to shake your-self like a jack—"

Douglas's hand grabbed Joshua's arm, warning him not to explode. He tossed Niki a towel and said, "Here, Niki, dry yourself properly."

Niki sauntered off and Douglas turned to Joshua. "People who fly into a rage always make a bad landin', son." He stood up, adding, "Now I thank you and Anna for your hospitality, but it's time for me to be leavin'."

His departure set the precedent for everyone else. Mama, papa and Niki loaded up their things and said goodbye.

Joshua considered leaving as well, but decided that even though it was late he needed to discuss some of his feelings with Anna.

"Firebird," he began as he helped her unload the dishwasher, "Douglas is selling out and going back to Ireland."

"Back home?" she asked.

"No," Joshua barked irritably. "This is his home. It has been for nearly forty years."

"Don't bite my head off," she countered. "Just tell me what's eating you."

Joshua took her in his arms and held her. "I've

never known him to be so depressed, so lonely. He says there's no reason for him to remain here."

"You really love him, don't you?" she said.

"Yes. I expected to lose my grandfather someday. I'm resigned to the fact that I won't have my parents forever. But Douglas? No, I thought I'd have my mentor, my guide, my confidant permanently."

"I'm sorry," Anna whispered. "I wish there was something I could tell you to help."

"Thanks—" Joshua kissed the top of her head "—but I think I'll head home and mull it over."

When he reached the houseboat he was far from tired. Douglas's loneliness ate at him. All the men he had loved and cared for in his life had been lonely. Then it struck him that for the first time, he, Joshua Brandon, wasn't. He had Anna. He just hadn't secured her yet. It was foolish of him not to grab her right now.

He suddenly wanted to start building his own life. The thought erased his sadness. Tomorrow he was going to ask her to marry him.

JOSHUA WOKE EARLY, feeling a lovely sense of expectation. He prolonged seeing Anna by not jogging with her. He called her, begging off and saying he'd meet her that evening. Like someone who waits to open a gift, Joshua increased his pleasure by extending his special moment.

By the time he met Anna at Bush Gardens, he was beyond bridling his eagerness. They kissed hello in the reception area and the feel of her was intoxicating.

"You look wonderful," he said, holding her at

arm's length and eyeing her completely. He was feeling so good that he could have picked her up and twirled her around.

"You're in a marvelous mood," she said. "Something happen today?"

"Yes," he said with a laugh, "and no. I'll tell you all about it."

They followed the kimono-clad waitress across the small bridge that spanned a trickling stream, then wound their way past several screened rooms until they came to their tatami room. Slipping off their shoes, the couple walked on the woven straw mats and sank onto the brightly colored pillows scattered around the inlaid lacquer table. The deep well under the table accommodated Joshua's long legs but Anna chose to curl hers up gracefully under her and sit Oriental fashion.

He ordered some warm sake and they toasted each other with a gentle click of the small porcelain cups.

"What's up?" Anna asked, feeling invigorated by just being around him. He was so happy it was contagious.

He took her hands in his, kissing each slowly and carefully, and never took his eyes off her. Joshua had looked at her many times, but never like this. There was something behind his gaze that made her tremble.

"What is it?" she insisted, sure that it must be something good the way he was smiling.

Squeezing her hands, he asked, "Will you marry me?"

Anna inhaled deeply and held her breath to still the upheaval in her. She had been afraid from the beginning of their love that he was going to abandon her, reject her some day. Now he was asking to marry her and she was more afraid than she'd ever been in her whole life.

He cupped her face in his hands. "Say yes and we'll get married immediately."

"There's nothing that I want more or anything that could please me more," she whispered. "But...." She hesitated. The words were too hard to say.

"But what?" She wasn't reacting at all like he had planned or wanted. She was acting as if she was afraid. "Can you tell me what's bothering you?" he asked.

Pulling out of his grasp, she swirled the sake in the tiny cup and stalled for time. A child's cry seeped through the thin paper walls and it was like her conscience wailing, and then she realized it wasn't a child at all. It was the music of a Japanese zither being played. She had to tell him but it was harder to say the words than she'd expected. Maybe speaking her thoughts aloud was too much. She was afraid to speak the truth: the fact that her heart hesitated but ached to hold their own small baby in her arms.

Joshua sensed Anna's tension, sensed also that what was troubling her was something extremely significant. Patiently, he allowed her all the time she needed to summon the courage to speak.

Finally, with a lump in her constricted throat, she asked, "Joshua, you want a family, don't you?"

"Of course, I do. Don't you?"

With a rush of pained words, she answered, "Yes, but I can't give you one."

He immediately assumed that for medical reasons

she was unable to bear a child, and he was stunned. Why hadn't she confided in him earlier? Was she afraid he would love her less?

Looking across the table at her downcast eyes, he said, "I'm sorry."

Then the image of her popping the small yellow pill into her mouth every morning came to him. "Wait a minute," he almost stammered, "I don't understand. If you can't have children, how come you're on the pill?"

"I didn't say I couldn't have them," she corrected, looking him directly in the face. "I said I can never give you one."

A note of anger slightly tinged his voice. "What the devil are you driving at? Be more specific."

She instantly lashed out, "How would you like to have a house full of Nikis?"

Joshua immediately regretted his tone of voice and said, "I shouldn't have been abrupt. I just didn't know what you were talking about. What makes you think our children will be retarded?"

"Niki is my brother," she said in exasperation. "Isn't that reason enough?"

"Have you seen a geneticist?"

"No, but—"

"Then why are you borrowing trouble?"

"I just know, that's all." She felt herself steeling for the argument. "My parents have always told me that Niki was born the way he is. He wasn't sick in infancy; he didn't fall down a flight of steps. He was born that way. I don't need a geneticist to tell me there's a genetic flaw in the Provoloskys."

Tenderly, Joshua took the cup out of her grip and

rubbed the back of her hand. "Listen to me, Anna. There are a lot of reasons for a child being born retarded and most of them are not inherited. You should know that."

"I guess I do," she admitted, "but I've always assumed I couldn't take the risk of finding out if it applied to me or not."

"Life's a risk," he said, sounding just like her mother. "Look at you. You are younger than your brother and there's nothing wrong with you...except for being very foolish. Tomorrow I'll make an appointment for us to see a specialist at the University of Washington. We'll find out if there is a problem or not. Who knows? Maybe my side of the family is rife with flaws."

"What if there is something wrong?"

"Then we'll adopt."

"You mean you'd really consider adopting a baby?"

"No," he teased. "Babies. I'd like to have more than one. Listen, Firebird, there are a lot of options available to us. But even if fate determines that we can never have a child, I want to marry you. Once and for all," he said, squeezing her hand to emphasize his words, "I want you to get it through your thick skull that I love you. That's all that really matters."

"I adore you," she said wistfully, "but I can't say yes while the jury is still out."

"Why not?" he demanded impatiently.

"Because you'd end up hating me. I saw the way you looked when Julie's babies were being born," she reminded him. "I couldn't deny you the experience of seeing your own children entering the world."

Joshua's frustration began to turn into anger and he started to say, "You're not listening to me. I—"

"Besides—" Anna halted him by placing a finger on his lips "—we haven't even solved the problem of Niki yet. I think you are asking to bite off more than either of us can handle."

He swallowed whatever arguments he had. Bullying her was not the way to get her to accept his proposal. Hadn't he learned that by now? All right, he was willing to let it go for a while and resume a slower pace.

"Anna—" he held her by the chin "—I'll give you room if you'll at least take the tests and settle that question. Niki is something we'll work out later."

She couldn't focus on his face. Her eyes were misted by tears and she had to blink rapidly to focus. "You like me that much, huh?"

"Maybe a little bit more."

She searched through her purse for a tissue and after carefully wiping her eyes, she looked over at him. He took the tissue and dabbed gently at her cheeks and winked at her. She grinned back. He'd been able to deal with her terror so easily and in such a calm rational manner. How had she been so lucky to have found him?

"What are you smirking about?" he asked.

"About how lucky I am."

"You're wrong again."

"Why?"

"It's how lucky *we* are."

For the rest of the evening she was filled with

wonder at how readily Joshua had worked out their options. Her trust in him was magnified and her appreciation of what a unique person he was had grown.

Maybe it was the warm sake or maybe it was natural euphoria, but later when they were in bed and Joshua clutched her with fierce hunger, she willingly gave herself to him and matched his need. Her fingers urged him on until he pleaded for her. "Anna," he begged. "Anna...."

She slowed her touch and held him on the brink of release while she shifted herself above him. Little by little her movement decreased and she let him enter her as she became as still as a leaf on a windless afternoon. Small spasms quivered deep inside her and she let them ripple over him. Then, without warning, she thrust her whole being at him, forcing him deeper in her until he cried out.

His voice whetted her appetite even more and she tucked her heels under his buttocks, drawing him as close as she could.

Joshua responded by grabbing her with his hands and forcing her breasts to press into his golden-haired chest. Without warning, he rolled her onto her back and held her arms above her head.

"My turn," he said.

He didn't move, making her tremble with expectation. Her chest heaved, thrusting her peaked nipples at him. Involuntarily he shuddered at their touch.

Leisurely they led each other to the peak of loving by giving, taking and sharing. At the apex, all constraint evaporated as they gave themselves over to their wild delicious union. Sinking into each other's arms, they descended, exhausted, their bodies entwined.

On Friday morning, Anna attacked the day jubilantly. She and Joshua began crowded preparations, and by seven-thirty they had loaded all their gear and were heading off to join the other sailing enthusiasts at Rosario for two carefree days.

Anna and Niki attempted to follow Joshua's orders, but more often than not, Joshua was forced to have her take the helm and adjust the sails himself. But with all the Provo siblings' bungling, he never lost his patience. He seemed to be the perfect teacher.

Once they were free of the crowded waterways around the marina, Anna went below deck and dished up their dinner of cold cuts and potato salad. They sat on the cushions around the stern and enjoyed the fading daylight. The sunset was a vivid rose splashed across the horizon. The tired sailors were bathed in the ethereal glow the sunlight cast upon them.

They anchored in a small cove off Port Madison and spent the rest of the night rocked by the gentle lapping of the waves. Saturday morning was damp and overcast, but the sun had scorched off the covering of clouds before noon, when they tied up at Rosario. They spent the remainder of the day basking in the sun, eating light snacks of fresh fruit and anything else that took their fancy.

While Anna oiled her skin and read a book, Joshua took Niki out in the dinghy to teach him how to handle the oars.

"Now—" he demonstrated, holding both oars in his grip "—if you want to go forward, pull like this. If you want to go backward, you shove." Again, he showed Niki what to do.

Niki jumped up eagerly to switch places with Joshua, and the dinghy nearly capsized with his hasty movements.

"Sit down!" Joshua barked, and Niki again nearly threw them into the water by abruptly shifting his weight.

"Never," Joshua emphasized, "never stand up in a small boat."

"Okay, Josh," Niki promised.

"Good. Now move slowly and stay low to change places with me."

Niki obeyed him, but even so he rocked the small dinghy dangerously. He sat in Joshua's seat and took the oars. He had a difficult time getting both of them going in unison, and Joshua's patience was tried.

"Together, pal," he encouraged Niki. "Together."

Niki worked them wholeheartedly and the boat surged forward. But he failed to let up as they crested out of the water, and as a result Joshua took a cold saltwater bath.

Joshua hollered at Niki as he wiped sea water off his face. "Let up on the oars when they start to come out of the water."

"Here, Josh," Niki started to stand up to hand him his handkerchief.

"Sit down!" Joshua bellowed at the top of his lungs. "How many times do I have to tell you? Never, never stand up in a small boat!"

Niki looked wounded. "I'm sorry. I forgot."

"There are some things you can't afford to keep forgetting, Niki."

"Are you mad at me?"

"No, and I'm sorry I yelled. Let's get back to rowing."

Joshua felt guilty. He thought that during the past couple of months he'd learned how to be patient with Niki, but this was the first time he'd ever spent two uninterrupted days with him. He didn't seem to be able to maintain a constant degree of understanding. Where was he failing? Why wasn't it easy for him? Niki never seemed to get on Anna's nerves, but this afternoon it felt like Niki was a giant pain in Joshua's neck.

Taking a deep breath, he lowered his voice and once more tried to teach his soon-to-be brother in law the basics of handling a boat. Half an hour later, Joshua had taken more cold-water dousings than he ever wanted to experience again, traveled in more circles than his stomach could handle and decided it was time to finish the lesson and head back to The Docket.

Just as they were drawing near the ladder dangling over the side of his sloop, Niki pointed excitedly and shouted.

"Look out, Joshua," he yelled at the top of his lungs and stood up impetuously.

In fear he made a quick movement backward and the dinghy swung to the left and scooped in a huge gush of water. To counterbalance, Niki lurched to the right, and the next thing Joshua knew they were both in the bay. The oars and the buoyant cushions floated away slowly. Niki was thrashing in the water and his panic made his motions useless.

Angry, Joshua took a few strong strokes toward him and grabbed him by the collar. Snapping the commands, he ordered, "Relax and start swimming."

Spitting water, Niki answered, "Oh...I forgot how," and stopped flailing.

By now Anna had approached and was reaching over the side of the sloop. She had her hand extended for Niki. "Come on," she coaxed. "Take my hand and climb aboard."

Grabbing it and the ladder, he hauled himself onto the deck. Joshua swam out and retrieved the oars and cushions.

Throwing them up to Anna, he told her, "Drop the rope with its hook so I can attach it to the dinghy and winch it back aboard."

With everything righted and stored and still dripping, he asked Niki in an extremely calm manner that disguised his fury and frustration, "Why did you stand up again? And don't tell me you forgot."

"I saw a monster," Niki answered.

"Where?" Joshua searched the bay even though he was sure Niki was covering up his absentmindedness with a sea monster.

"Over there," he pointed to a flag attached to a buoy. He had seen a scuba-warning flag alerting boats that someone was diving below.

"That was no monster," Joshua tried to explain as nicely as he could manage. "That was a man or woman with scuba gear on."

"No, it wasn't." Niki was adamant. "It was a killer whale."

Joshua gave him the benefit of the doubt. "If it was, you were perfectly safe. They only eat fish and they wouldn't like the taste of you," he barked sarcastically.

Avoiding Anna's eyes, he went below to dry off

and change his clothes. Back on deck, Joshua buried his nose in a book. His patience had evaporated and he was feeling angrier at himself than he was at Niki.

The three of them silently lay on deck and after a short while Niki's gentle snoring allowed Anna the opportunity she'd been searching for.

"Joshua," she whispered. "Let's go below."

"Why?" he asked, knowing she was probably going to lecture him about his nasty temper.

"I want to talk to you," she said sweetly.

Following her down the narrow stairs, he slid around the small table and sat next to her.

She said, "Don't be so hard on yourself. I get frustrated with him, too."

"What makes you think I'm on my own back?"

"Because you're tense and all knotted up," she said and gently turned him away from her so she could knead the muscles of his lower neck. "Anger turned outward has a releasing effect. Inward, it preys on you."

"Mmm, that feels wonderful. But Niki's not bothering me. It was all that rowing and swimming," Joshua lied.

Stopping her massaging, Anna made him look her in the eye. "I thought we weren't going to be afraid to share things with each other?"

"Okay, you caught me," he conceded.

"Listen—" she wiggled his earlobe affectionately "—you're doing a great job with him. I get as mad as hell sometimes, so don't feel so guilty."

"I never see it."

"I've just had more practice. Give yourself some

time alone if you find him too much. I'll understand.''

Smiling, he kissed her forehead. "I'm okay now. I guess I just felt like I shouldn't show my irritation with him.''

"Why not? Because he's retarded?''

"I suppose.''

"What makes him so special he can breeze through life that easily?'' she demanded. "He's human and you have every right to blow your cork when he's out of line. He doesn't need to be handled with kid gloves.''

"I never thought of it that way.''

"Just relax. Be natural with him and it'll be easier for both of you.''

"Firebird?'' He tried to stand up but the low cabin kept him from straightening his neck. He pulled her up so he could wrap his arms around her and pat her fanny.

"Yes?'' she answered.

"Niki's got the right idea.''

"What's that?'' she asked, lazily playing with his mustache.

"About taking a nap. The bunk's empty.'' Keeping a firm hold on her, he inched toward the bed while planting kisses from her ear across her shoulder and down the warm oiled skin of her chest that swelled gently to her breasts.

"I am terribly tired,'' she pretended to yawn.

"Then let me tuck you in,'' he said with a leer and carried her to the bunk.

IN THE EARLY EVENING, they dressed for dinner and dancing. After they ate, Joshua gave Niki a roll of coins and took him to a video arcade. He told him to have a good time and that he and Anna would be close by.

They danced until Anna saw Niki come in, obviously out of money, and then the three of them headed back to The Docket. As Joshua rowed in the moonlight, Anna remembered an old song she and Niki used to sing with her parents.

"We were sailing along," she sang, and Niki immediately echoed the lyrics.

"On Moonlight Day," she continued. Niki again repeated the line.

"We could hear the voices singing," she led, and Joshua picked up the words and resang them with Niki.

"They seemed to say," Anna led. "You have stolen my heart. Now don't go 'way."

As a trio they chorused, "As we sang love's old sweet song on Moonlight Bay."

Delighted with themselves, they applauded one another and laughed. The peal of their gaiety echoed in the harbor as they tied up to the sloop. The echo contained their shared joy. Joshua listened to it and it made him feel better than he had all day. It reassured him that, despite his anger and frustration, everything was still on keel. Niki might sometimes rock the boat but nothing would knock him and Anna off course.

CHAPTER FIFTEEN

JOSHUA AND ANNA felt the constraints of their job
during the next week. He had either been buried
under a mountain of papers to be processed or closet-
ed with hysterical clients whose lives rested on his
assistance. Anna was deeply involved in a lengthy divorce trial that included a bitter struggle for the custody of the separating couple's children. With cases
like the one before her, she was forced to look at the
law from a new angle. In this instance, the man and
woman were trying to use innocent victims, their children, as pawns in a spiteful game of revenge. It took
all of Anna's emotional strength to retain her sense
of impartial justice and weed through the angry accusations that were flung before her bench.

By Friday she was almost convinced that she
should place the children in a foster home and
grant only limited visiting privileges to both parents.
Then an advocate who had been assigned by the
Child Protective Services, presented an unbiased
fresh viewpoint. The young woman had voluntarily
taken over the role of seeing that the rights of the
children were protected at all costs, and she held no
allegiance to either parent. She was simply there as a
safeguard for the children's welfare. Impressed with
the social worker's observations and suggestions,

Anna placed a great deal of weight on the woman's judgment.

After awarding custody to the father, Anna recessed court and gratefully headed home. She hadn't seen much of Joshua all week because of his own professional obligations. He'd been tied up in court with several time-consuming cases.

It was ten o'clock before she heard Joshua rap on the door. He had a key but she'd thrown the dead bolt. She quickly unlocked it and he perfunctorily kissed her on the top of her head as he came in.

"You look bushed," she said as he crossed the room, yanked his tie off and tossed his coat on the closest available piece of furniture.

"I am, babe," he agreed, sounding close to exhaustion.

She patted the spot next to her on the sofa and he flopped down.

"Have you eaten?" she asked.

"Yeah, I picked up a sandwich about seven. What I need is a real kiss."

His fatigue made his shoulders droop. As requested, she fondly sought his lips.

"Rough day?" she questioned.

"I don't even want to think about it. Let's forget the world for a while. Okay?"

"You got it, Counselor."

With his head in her lap, they watched the light-hearted movie, *Tootsie*, on Anna's VCR. By the time the film was finished, Joshua had drifted off to sleep. She carefully slipped a pillow under his head and covered him with an afghan. He looked too peaceful to wake.

The next morning they both agreed that the nicest way to spend the next two days would be cloistered in the condo. The need to replenish their depleted reserves was their primary concern. So Saturday coasted by and the most vigorous tasks they tackled were lathering each other's bodies in tanning oil and refilling their glasses of iced tea.

By Sunday morning they were beginning to feel renewed. As they lounged in bed with the paper, they poured over the large spread in the Travel section that was devoted to sailing adventures.

Joshua pointed to an article on British Columbia's Queen Charlotte Islands. "How about sailing up there this fall?"

She glanced over the column and they started to plan how they would juggle their schedules to give them the two weeks they wanted.

He folded the pages up and pulled her close to him and nuzzled the soft flesh just below her ear. "Want to take a shower?" he suggested.

"How about filling the tub and soaking in some bubbles?"

"That sounds a little too risqué," he kidded and continued to work his lips further down her neck.

Throwing the covers back, Joshua sat up on his heels and looked at Anna lying in front of him with her nightgown twisted and curled around her. He ran his hands up her silky calves lightly, then over her knees and along her firm thighs.

"You're exquisite," he whispered, as he slipped her gown off.

She started to rise up to him but he gently pushed

her back. "No, just lie there and let me look at you. You're a feast."

She shivered—a pleasant tingling that traveled from her toes to her head and back down to her auburn triangle. She felt a warm pleasing moistness, a harbinger of rapture. His gaze was a powerful stimulant. He didn't need to touch her to make her body respond.

Slowly he turned her over onto her tummy and lightly ran his fingers from her heels to her scalp, exploring, probing, kissing each freckle, tracing every mole, feeling every curve of her. Nothing was left uncaressed. Inch by inch, he savored her essence.

The momentum of his adoration and her hypnotic submissiveness was suddenly shattered. Someone was pounding on the front door.

"Who in the hell is that?" he exploded.

"Stay here. I'll get rid of whoever it is," she told him, slipping into her robe.

Hurrying to answer the relentless banging, she fought the fear that threatened to shatter their blissful morning. She was certain that she would find it was Niki pummeling her door, demanding to be included. Desperately she racked her brain for a tactful way to shoo him off.

Her prediction was accurate. He stood there grinning in complete ignorance of his rotten timing.

"Hiya, Anna," he beamed. "What took so long?"

Barging past her into the hallway, he asked, "Is Josh here?"

"Yes, he's just reading the paper and relaxing."

"You know," he informed her, "it's ten o'clock. Mama said I can't come over and bug you before ten anymore."

Anna appreciated her mother's attempt to shield them from Niki's early-morning visits. She'd had that little talk with mama about giving her and Joshua more privacy. Niki had probably walked the block a dozen times, checking his watch until it was the right hour to come visiting.

"Where's Josh?"

"I'm in the bedroom, Niki," Joshua called out to him. "Be right with you."

"It's okay. I know where Anna's room is," and he promptly headed down the short hall and perched himself on the end of the bed.

"What are we gonna do today?" he asked.

"Nothing," Joshua answered. "Absolutely nothing. Your sister and I are tired and we're just staying home. We both had a hard tough week and we need to rest up."

Niki furrowed his brow and cast accusing glares at both of them. "But I wanna go somewhere today," he almost whined.

Anna came up from behind him and wrapped her arms around his shoulders. "Sorry. Joshua is right," she patiently explained. "We're not doing a thing."

"What am I supposed to do while you guys stay home?"

Joshua slipped his robe on and patted Niki on the biceps as he walked over to the dresser to comb his hair. "Look," he said, "we'll go somewhere next weekend."

"But I want to go to Fort Nisqually *today*."

Turning to Anna, he begged, "Please, Anna, please? You haven't taken me there for a long time."

Anna felt guilty. Niki was having a difficult time

learning how to share her with Joshua. She had two
men in her life now, but she didn't want Niki to feel
that he'd been cast aside. She'd never desert him.
Maybe if she explained to Joshua what it would mean
to Niki if they relented, he'd reconsider. She knew
how much her brother loved scaling the gun towers
of the old fort. He enjoyed inspecting the ancient Indian war canoes in the middle of the large stockade
and could spend hours wandering through the trad-
ing post, granary and blacksmith shop. Fort Nisqually was the highlight of the many afternoons that
they'd spent at Point Defiance.

While she wavered and pondered Niki's hopeful
face, Joshua patiently waited. But when he saw her
resolve start to fade, he stepped in. "No, Niki. You'll
just have to wait. Anna and I took you out last weekend on the boat. We spend a lot of time with you."

He was amazed, even aghast, at the anger that
erupted from Niki. Yelling at the top of his lungs,
Niki hollered, "I hate you, Joshua Brandon! You're
stupid!"

As he madly rushed out of the bedroom, he
screamed his ultimate insult. "You're selfish!"

Stunned, it was a moment before Joshua spoke.
Finally he said, "I've never seen him like that."

"Welcome to the family," Anna laughed humor-
lessly. "You've just had your first fight with the dark
side of Niki."

"Well, he's acting like a spoiled child," Joshua
barked. "There's no reason we have to accommodate
his every whim."

She tried to placate him. "You're right, but he's
never had to share me before. It's going to take him a

little while to get used to not being the center of my affection.''

"I forget—" Joshua's tone became softer, acknowledging the legitimacy of her statement "—that he has a hard time adjusting.''

The closing of a car door sounded from the street and he wondered aloud, "Who's here now? Your parents?''

The sound of someone grinding unmercifully on a starter until it howled in protest at the damage being done to its innards pierced the air.

"Some nut doesn't have the brains to know when a car's been started," Joshua laughed. "The poor machine is taking a beating.''

The horrible high-pitched whining finally stopped but was replaced by the dreadful clanking of transmission being shifted without the driver using the clutch. Joshua couldn't stand the din and walked out onto the verandah to see who the devil was ripping some vehicle to shreds.

At first he couldn't register what he saw. That *couldn't* be Niki. What would he be doing in Joshua's Jag? Dashing to the entry table, Joshua saw that Niki had taken the keys on his way out.

Charging out the front door, he yelled at Anna, "Your sweet little innocent brother is stealing my car!''

Anna ran to the railing and yelled, "Get out of that car, Nikolae, right this minute!''

As Joshua raced down the front steps, Niki locked the door and shot Anna a triumphant grin. He wasn't going to listen to her and she flew after Joshua to help.

Joshua reached the closed driver's window and pounded on it as Niki madly stepped on pedals and ground the gears, trying to get the car in motion.

"Get out of there immediately," Joshua ordered.

Niki responded by finding first gear and making the car lunge forward. Defiantly he shouted, "I'm going to Fort Nisqually by myself."

The car jerked slowly down the street and Anna ran with Joshua to try to keep pace with it. "Turn it off, Niki, and I'll take you out for lunch," she pleaded, hoping to bribe him through his bottomless stomach.

"Stuff it!" he answered and stepped harder on the accelerator.

Gaining speed, the car veered back and forth on the narrow crowded street, passing several parked vehicles. Niki tried to steer the Jag straight but the more he handled the steering wheel the more he overplayed it.

Straining to keep astride of his careening car, Joshua saw that fear had erased the gloating on Niki's face. Holding on to the door handle, he tried to give Niki instructions that would bring the car to a halt.

"Turn the key off," he yelled. "Turn off the engine!"

Niki was too frightened to respond. He clenched the steering wheel, fingers frozen in place. Immobilized by terror, he couldn't even turn his head.

"Step on the brake," Joshua commanded, but Niki hit the gas pedal instead, making the car surge forward. Joshua was thrown loose of the grip he had on the door and was sent smashing onto the asphalt.

As he picked himself up, Anna reached him, and

before they could start after Niki and the car again, they watched Niki bounce off a parked van's fender and then rebound into another car's passenger door. The path of destruction was almost incomprehensible. Joshua's Jaguar sideswiped half a dozen vehicles, smearing its ice-blue paint on all of them like the ugly swathe of a vandal.

Running faster than she ever had in her life, Anna saw Niki heading for a busy intersection. A sickening horror clutched her heart as she realized there was no safe way that Niki was going to get through the four-way stop, the busiest in the neighborhood.

To her horror, instead of trying to head straight through the intersection, Niki swung the wild car up onto the sidewalk, scattering terrified pedestrians. Sunday strollers were leaping left and right as he plowed between them. In desperation, Niki piloted the car over a bus-stop bench and back onto the main road. Somehow he'd managed not to hit anyone.

Suddenly he swerved left, cut across the opposite lane, jumped another sidewalk and smashed through the plate-glass window of a store. The car chugged to a halt and its engine expired.

Joshua tore past Anna in a sudden surge of speed and reached Niki before she could. Niki pulled up the lock and slowly crawled out of the driver's seat.

The odor of paint filled the air and Anna saw that every color in the spectrum was oozing off the Jaguar's hood. Niki had driven into a closed paint store. The burglar alarm was clanging at a decibel so loud she couldn't even hear her own panting.

Ignoring Joshua, the acrid smell of exhaust and paint and the mounting crowd of curious bystanders, sne reached out to Niki to see if he was hurt. He seemed to have only a little bruise on his forehead where the steering wheel had bumped it. But she was afraid there might be internal injuries.

Joshua brushed her aside, grabbed Niki by the shirt-front and shook him vigorously. "What the hell did you think you were doing?" he demanded. "Look at my car. It's ruined."

Niki grabbed Joshua's hands and tried to pull away. But Joshua only increased his furious shaking. Anna watched in mute panic as Joshua pushed Niki beyond the point of his thinly held reason and her brother's powerful fist slammed into Joshua's stomach. As Joshua released his hold on Niki and grabbed his mid-section, Niki thrust a powerful uppercut to Joshua's undefended jaw.

A look of surprise crossed Joshua's face. He was being battered by a giant and he responded with the natural instinct of self-preservation. Dodging Niki's next blow, Joshua wrapped his arm around Niki's neck and spun him against his body by tightly yanking Niki's arm behind his back. Niki was powerful but he was incapable of reacting to such skillful moves. Joshua contained him.

Anna expected Joshua to calm Niki down and then release him, but he only increased the pressure on her brother's bent arm. Afraid that he would do serious harm, she screamed at Joshua, "Let him go. You're hurting him."

Joshua had been totally consumed by a blind rage. Panting heavily, he released Niki and said, "Hurting him? What about me?"

Anna ignored his question and turned her attention to her brother. "Are you all right?" she quietly asked as she gently ran her hand across the bruise on Niki's head.

"Is he all right?" Joshua's earlier ranting was now replaced by a seething, controlled, white-hot fury. "What about my car? What about the other fifteen or twenty vehicles he decimated?"

"Don't worry about your car. We'll get it fixed. Just be glad no one was hurt."

"Oh, I am," Joshua said sarcastically. "I'm delighted." Then he yelled at the top of his lungs to overcome the alarm system, "Your charming brother is damn lucky he didn't kill a hundred people."

Someone turned off the power to the alarm and the sudden silence was unnerving. She placed her hand on Joshua's arm and whispered, "Can we talk about this later? People are watching."

"So what?" he bellowed, his face turning a deep mottled red. "We've been running down the street like madmen and you're concerned about people overhearing us? Your brother just did thousands of dollars of damage to who knows how many cars and a store and you're worried about making a scene? You actually think no one has noticed us?"

Someone in the huge crowd laughed and hollered out at him, "That's right, buddy, tell her the police have been called. Explain to them, lady, this is no big deal."

Embarrassed, she spoke with measured tones to hide her feelings, "I'll figure out a way to pay for all this."

"You'll pay for it? Why not him?" Joshua pointed his finger at Niki who was standing there looking so pathetic and sorry.

Seeing Niki looking so stricken, Joshua began to regret his words. But before he could recant, a series of snickerings distracted him. Some young children were unable to hide their mirth behind the hands covering their mouths. The way they were looking at him and Anna stymied him for a second. Then it dawned on him what they found so funny. He and she were standing there dressed only in their bathrobes with the wind blowing around their bare legs.

The realization that she was almost nude hit Anna at the same time. She and Joshua wrapped themselves further by cinching their belts and drawing their necklines closed.

Clutching at her throat modestly, she saw the police trying to get through the crowd. She had never felt so exposed, so completely on display. Trying to fill out an accident report while a mob watched to see if her flimsy red robe might disintegrate was too much.

Fortunately, the older policeman, a sergeant, ordered, "Show's over, folks. Go on your way."

He took out his notebook and demanded, "Explain what happened."

His kindness and professionalism made the ordeal easier than Anna could have expected. The hardest part was trying to explain that Niki was retarded without hurting her brother's feelings. If he heard her describe him that way, he would be crushed. He'd spent too many years coming home from playgrounds after other kids wouldn't play with him because he was a "retard."

She turned to see if Niki was within earshot, but he wasn't behind her. Pivoting, she looked all around. No Niki. He wasn't anywhere.

"Where did he go?" she asked Joshua, who looked about as amenable as a man-eating tiger.

"Probably home to tell your parents what a wonderful time he had this morning."

"Maybe," she agreed, but she wasn't sure. At least she could talk freely without Niki being offended.

After the report was finished, a wrecking truck called and a carpenter found to board up the storefront, the sergeant drove them home. Neither she nor Joshua spoke a word to each other until they were in the house.

Joshua checked the bedrooms to see if Niki was sulking in a corner somewhere while Anna looked in the kitchen and den.

"Find him?" she called.

"No," he hollered from her room. "And it's a damn good thing he isn't here. I'm ready to kill him right now."

She walked into the room. "Joshua, you don't understand. I think he took off because the police were coming."

"I would too, if I were him."

"But I'm worried."

"Why? He'll come back."

"I'm going out to look for him," she announced, starting to dress.

"Just let him think this through. Let him worry for a while. It won't kill him."

"You really don't understand," she said in icy tones. "He is probably frightened and wandering around downtown somewhere. I've got to find him."

"Fine," he said, literally throwing up his hands. "Go search for him. But I think you overprotect him. I always had to face the music when I was a kid."

"Oh, yeah," her voice sparked with challenge. "Just like the time you had Martin fix your dad's car so you wouldn't get into trouble?"

He reeled at her words and he walked over and stared deeply into her blazing eyes. "That was a low blow, Spitfire."

Angry retorts swirled through her head but she was unable to voice them. She had stepped beyond the bounds of clean fighting and broken the cardinal rule of relationships. She should never have used Joshua's secret against him but she was too proud and too angry to apologize. The only thing to do was leave, so she shrugged her shoulders and left to search for Niki.

Furious with Anna, Niki and himself, Joshua threw on his clothes and stomped around the house in a fit of temper. Eventually he simmered down enough to call the insurance agent and then Martin. He told him the bare details of what had happened to his car, and asked him to take the Jaguar back to Vashon.

Feeling out of place at Anna's, he went to the impound yard and waited for Martin to arrive. Only two hours earlier he'd been at home in her house, content to love and be loved. Now he felt like a ship in a storm that had been torn loose from its anchor.

Anna drove first to her parents' to see if Niki had come home. She wasn't surprised to discover that he hadn't. She filled her parents in on what had happened and put their minds at ease. She was sure, she said, that she would find Niki within thirty minutes so they shouldn't worry.

Thirty minutes turned into three hours as she combed Seattle's streets, checked out alleys, scanned darkened movie houses and walked through some of the city parks. Her nerves became as taut as piano wires and she began imagining all sorts of horrible things. She called her mother from a phone booth, hoping Niki had wandered in hungry as a bear and ready to plop down in front of the television to watch his beloved Muppets.

"No," mama said, her voice nearly cracking, "he hasn't come home. Papa's out looking now."

"Has he checked the stalls at the market?" Anna asked.

"Of course," mama snapped angrily. "We can't find him anywhere."

Anna knew her mother was frightened and she wasn't stung by her sharpness. "I'm going to continue looking," she promised. "I'll call again in an hour."

She tried everywhere she could think of—the waterfront, the zoo, the Ballard Locks, the International District—still no trace of him. Praying she'd find him back at her place, Anna went home. The house was empty. Joshua had returned and left her a short note saying he'd talked to the owners of the paint shop and they weren't going to press charges if all costs were paid. He'd gone to meet Martin and didn't know when he'd be back.

She made herself a quick cup of tea and left again. Niki had to be somewhere and she had to find him. It would be dark soon.

By nightfall, papa had asked all the family friends to help. But everywhere they went, they received the same reply: "Sorry, we haven't seen him."

Gnawing cramps in her stomach nearly caused Anna to double over. She wasn't sure if the pains were from hunger or worry. Willing to try a bite to ease her discomfort, she went to her parents' home to fix a sandwich. Mama didn't hear her come in and Anna found her with her face buried into a sofa pillow, sobbing.

She tiptoed over and consoled her. "Don't cry, mama. We'll find him."

"Oh, Anna," she wailed even louder. "He never stays out this late."

"I know. He's just hiding somewhere. I'm sure he's safe and sound holed up in a corner."

"But he's scared. Niki is always getting scared."

"It's my fault. I should have watched him and realized he'd be upset when he found out the police were coming."

Blowing her nose and sniffing loudly, mama rose and consoled her. "You aren't to blame. No one is."

"But if only I—"

"If only what?" mama demanded. "Can you make your brother whole? Can you always be there? No. No one can. You do a good job with him. Don't ever blame yourself."

JOSHUA LET HIMSELF into his dark houseboat. It was still unfinished and it felt uninviting. He'd spent the day with Martin assessing the damage to his Jag, and he was tired. His emotions were once again under control and he'd tried several times during the afternoon to call Anna, but he'd received no answer. Looking up her parents' number in the directory, he dialed it, hoping they'd know where she was.

"Hello?" Anna answered it on the first ring. Her voice was strident.

"Anna?" He was startled to hear her. "Where have you been all day?"

'Oh, it's just you." She sounded disappointed and irritated.

'What's wrong? Still angry?"

"No," she snapped. "I'm not mad."

"Listen, I'm sorry for losing it all this morning. I'll apologize to Niki. Put him on."

Joshua's ignorance cracked her control and she sobbed into the phone.

"Hey, little one," he soothed. "What's wrong?"

His real concern was clear and she fought to stop her tears. "Niki's lost, Joshua. We can't find him anywhere."

"You mean he's been gone since this morning?"

"Yes. I've been searching all day."

"Stay there. I'm on my way."

Joshua slammed down the phone, grabbed a jacket and bolted out the door. He'd considered selling his motorcycle earlier in the summer but now he offered a prayer of thanks that he'd kept the giant beast. He'd outgrown his days of cruising on his bike but tonight it was his only source of transportation. He was grateful he'd put off parting with it.

Anna and her mother sat rigidly, sipping cups of tea, staring at the phone, willing it to ring. The relentless silence was torture.

Anna jumped when she heard Joshua's powerful Goldwing pull up and she went out to meet him. Her eyes were ringed with dark circles and her mouth was drawn tight. She was preoccupied with Niki's disappearance and she made no reference to their earlier fight.

"Any word?" he asked as he followed her into the house.

"No, nothing."

He joined the two bereft women at the table and they told him what had been done, who formed the search party and where they had looked. He mentally listed the places mentioned and then said he had a few ideas of his own. Anna wanted to join him but he rejected her offer.

"Stay with your mother. I'll call if I find him."

Ten minutes later he was questioning the desk clerk of a seedy flophouse. "Have you seen a very tall dark man in his midthirties tonight?"

"No one like that has been through here," was the reply, and so it went as Joshua made his way through every flophouse or mission along First Avenue.

He was about to give up on that track and start a new one when he spied the small unlit entrance to a particularly decrepit hotel flanked by two adult movie houses. He glanced around as he climbed the steep flight of stairs to the second-story lobby. A rheumy-eyed woman was perched on a tall stool behind a greasy reception desk. She was leafing through a well-thumbed magazine.

"You a cop?" she demanded, eyeing him suspiciously.

"No," Joshua assured her. "I'm just looking for my friend."

After he described Niki in more detail, he saw a light of recognition glimmer in the woman's watery eyes, but she denied having seen him.

"I think you know where he's at." Joshua fished his billfold out of his back pocket.

"How much is it worth to you?" She smiled.

"This much," he said, and slid a twenty-dollar bill across the grimy counter.

Stuffing the money into her blouse, she said, "Check Room 314."

There was no elevator so Joshua sprinted up the rickety stairs and found the door he wanted. Rapping on it, he called out, "Niki, you in there?"

"No, I'm not. Go away!" a voice hollered back at him.

"Niki," Joshua spoke loudly and slowly, "I guess I'll just have to find someone else to take out to dinner."

A faint movement was heard from inside the room and Joshua heard someone whisper, "Thought you said you were all alone."

"He just wants to take me to jail," Niki answered in a low voice.

"Hey, you didn't say you were in trouble with the cops."

Joshua detected footsteps shuffling to the door and slowly it opened. A pair of bloodshot eyes peeked out at him.

"You looking for this guy?" the old man asked.

"Yeah, open up."

"All right. I don't want any trouble. I was just trying to help him out."

He unhooked the chain that stretched across the door and allowed Joshua to enter.

Niki was crouched in the corner, sniffing loudly and wiping his face with the back of his huge hand.

Joshua walked over and squatted down in front of him. Taking Niki's hand in his, he said, "Hey, it's okay, pal. You don't have to be scared."

"I don't wanna go to jail," he cried.

"Nobody's taking you there. I promise."

"I heard that man say the police were coming."

"Sure, just to make out an accident report, not to get you."

"You still mad at me?"

"No. What you did was wrong, but I'm not mad anymore."

The elderly man interrupted. "Saw him wandering around the streets like a lost Saint Bernard puppy. This ain't no place for a fella like him to be alone."

Joshua rose and shook the man's hand. "I really appreciate what you did. He could have gotten into a tough spot. Thank you."

"That's okay. Glad to bail the poor kid out."

"You know, there's a reward for finding him."

"Yeah?"

Niki stopped his sniffling and stood up. "A reward for me?"

"Yes," Joshua convinced them. "A fifty-dollar reward."

"Wow!" Niki grinned. "Fifty dollars. You guys musta been really worried."

Joshua patted him on his broad shoulders. "Worried sick. Anna's been searching all day."

He pulled out his wallet, peeled off five ten-dollar bills and handed them to Niki's newfound friend. "Thanks. You took great care of him."

"Ah, wasn't nothing. You guys get out of here and give an old man some peace."

"Bye, Bud," Niki said as he shook the man's hand. "Come to the market and see me sometime."

"Just might do that, kid. Now go on."

The fresh night air was a relief after the dank interior of the Maynard Hotel. Joshua was anxious to get Niki home and end the Provolosky's suffering. He handed Niki the spare helmet.

"Put this on. Wrap your arms around my waist and don't let your feet drag. Keep them on those foot-rests." He pointed to the bars on the rear of the motorcycle.

Niki whistled. "Is this bike yours?"

"Yep. Hop on."

"Where we stopping for dinner? You promised."

"Okay, we'll call your house and tell them you're safe first."

Joshua found a pay phone and spoke with Anna. "He's sitting over there on my bike perfectly safe and sound."

"How long before you get here?" She sounded relieved but anxious to see for herself that Niki was fine.

"I'm going to take him for a hamburger. I think we need to square things away between the two of us."

"Why don't you just bring him home and we'll all talk to him?" She was doubtful that Joshua could handle Niki properly.

"We've got to work it out between us, man-to-man. I'll have him home in an hour." Without waiting for a response, he hung up the phone.

As they ate their food, Joshua quizzed Niki. "Why did you really run away? You know your sister and I would never let you go to jail."

Niki fiddled with his french fries and silently refused to answer.

"Talk to me," Joshua prodded.

Niki continued eating. He wouldn't look at Joshua. Finally Joshua broke the silence. "Did I hurt you?" he asked.

"Naw. I'm okay. 'Sides, I hit you first. How's your belly?"

Glad that he opened the lines of communication, Joshua answered, "Fine but you pack a pretty good wallop."

Encouraged by Joshua's good humor, Niki said, "I got a new tetterous shot the other day."

It took Joshua a minute to figure out that Niki meant tetanus. He was about to tell Niki to quit changing the subject, but something in Niki's face warned him to hold his tongue.

"You got all your shots, Josh? I mean when you was a kid, a baby?"

"Yes. I think so."

"Me, too, I guess. They got 'em for everything. Measles, mumps and stuff I can't remember." Munching on a french fry, he continued, "Mama says they even got 'em to make you better after you get sick. Them doctors can just 'bout fix anything. Anything but me."

Joshua didn't dare speak. Niki was probably telling him something he'd never told anyone.

"They couldn't fix my head. It gets all mixed up and I know I'm not as smart as Anna. Not even as smart as some little kids I know. Isn't that right?"

What could he say? The man was asking for an honest answer and Joshua didn't know if he should give him one. What would Anna say?

"I feel like a sixth wheel, Josh. You got Anna. Papa has mama. I'm always in the way."

"That's not true. Everyone loves having you around."

"Oh, yeah?" His eyes reflected his skepticism. "Then why did you wanna get rid of me this morning?"

Guiltily, Joshua admitted, "You're right. I was trying to get rid of you and I should have been honest. I wanted to spend some time alone with Anna."

"How come I can't have a place of my own?"

The honesty of Niki's question forced Joshua to look at Niki's life from his vantage point. What would it be like to be thirty-two and still dependent on your family?

"I get tired of waiting for you guys to take me places. How come I can never go by myself?"

"I can't answer these questions, pal. Why don't we go home and talk about them with the family?"

Niki's seriousness vanished as they rode home. By the time they entered the house, he was beaming happily.

"I got to ride on Josh's big bike," he bragged.

Mama rushed over and hugged him fiercely. Then she stepped back and bawled him out with gentle words.

"Don't you ever scare your poor old mother like that again, Nikolae Alexandrovich Provolosky."

Contrite, Niki promised, "I won't, mama."

Anna and papa kissed and hugged him until he protested. "I'm all right. My friend, Bud, took real good care of me."

Mama fixed them a fresh pot of tea and they all sat

around the coffee table. It was a good time to bring up the questions Niki had asked.

Acting as Niki's advocate, Joshua said, "Niki told me he'd like to live on his own. Make his own way. Do his own things. I agree with him, but how it could be arranged is the problem."

"That's ridiculous," Anna said. "He has us. Why would he say a thing like that?"

"Because he wants to be like everyone else," Joshua argued, wishing he didn't have to say anything. He'd rather stay out of the debate altogether and let Niki speak for himself. But Niki was letting him do all the work, and he knew that Anna was seeing him as a kind of enemy to the pattern she and her parents had established.

"But you know you need extra help," Anna patiently explained to Niki, ignoring Joshua.

Joshua sat back and listened to Anna and her parents try to reason with Niki's bid for independence. He sympathized with the man's dilemma, but he could see no earthly way that Niki would be able to survive alone.

With no concrete solutions offered, mama finally ended the conversation by announcing, "It's the middle of the night. We'll talk tomorrow. You go to bed now."

Niki made his way around the table kissing mama, papa and Anna good-night. When he came to Joshua, he approached him and then dropped back, unsure what to do. Joshua ended his indecision by wrapping his arms around the other man and giving him a hug.

"Sleep well," he said as he released him.

At peace, knowing he'd been forgiven by everyone, Niki went to bed.

Anna was numb with exhaustion and she slowly rose to leave. "Talk to you tomorrow," she told her parents. "I'm going home."

The Provoloskys thanked Joshua profusely for having found their son, but he waved away their gratitude. "Don't thank me. It's the least I could do."

He glanced at Anna out of the corner of his eye. He detected no flicker of approval or even acknowledgment. The only thing he read in her face was utter fatigue.

"Want me to drive you home?" he asked.

"No, thanks. I can make it."

"I'd be glad to," he coaxed.

He followed her to her car but she still refused his offer. Shaking her head, she slipped behind Elizabeth's steering wheel.

"See you in the morning," he called as she drove off.

She was unable to face him and his unreasonable expectations. His last words indicated that nothing had changed between them, that they could simply pick up the fractured pieces of their hearts and mend them with a kiss.

Joshua's expectations for Niki were totally unrealistic. Niki could never live alone, could never meet the standards Joshua expected from him. How could he? And if Niki fell short, where would that leave her? Would Joshua's impossible dream continue to widen the gap that loomed between them?

CHAPTER SIXTEEN

JOSHUA GAVE ANNA a wide berth for several days. His instincts told him that following a hands off policy would be wisest. When he finally did seek her out one afternoon for lunch, she politely begged off, saying she was staying in her chambers to do some research. It wasn't what she said that infuriated him, it was what she didn't say. Her silence accused him of failing, with her, with Niki, and it also implied that she held a grudge because he hadn't lived up to his promises.

Both of them made a few halfhearted attempts to keep the lines of communication open, and outwardly they observed the polite amenities, treating each other with the utmost civility. But the warmth, sharing and spontaneity between them had faded. They were actors on a stage they had designed and neither one of them knew how to end the scenario in which they had cast themselves.

Anna reacted to her inner confusion in her usual manner: she immersed herself in her work. Joshua racked his brain for a way to break through the facade she was hiding behind, but each time he tried, she built the wall of silence a little higher.

Like Anna, Joshua was beginning to let work dominate his life. Activity helped offset his urge to throttle some sense into her stubborn head. Every time he broached the subject of Niki, she shut him out. He wanted to batter her with words to try to thaw her icy reserve.

One morning his boss inadvertently forced the issue. "There's a pretrial conference scheduled in Judge Provo's chambers this morning," he said. "Your witness on the Carroll case is in the hospital."

"Anna Provo?"

"Yeah, the case is on her docket."

Great, he thought. *If I can't talk to her about personal things at least we'll always have business to discuss.*

IN HER CHAMBERS, reading her schedule for the day, Anna scanned her docket. She was to meet with Joshua Brandon and Dione Seim from the prosecuting attorney's office. Looking at Joshua's name, she was secretly pleased that he had drawn the short straw. If she allowed this case to go to trial, she and Joshua would have to see less of one another. It wasn't in the client's best interest for her and Joshua to have too much contact. Unwittingly, the public defender's office had given her an excuse to postpone any immediate confrontations with him. Maybe the time would help her sort out the dilemma she was in.

At ten o'clock her assistant, Miriam, informed her that all the principals had arrived for the pretrial conference.

"Please show them in, Miriam," she instructed.

The first to enter was Dione Seim from the prosecuting attorney's office. She was a petite and extremely attractive woman. Joshua held the door for

her and she flashed him a dazzling smile. Anna sensed
the woman's signal was more intense than a mere
social courtesy. Dione wanted Joshua to know she was
not only a lawyer but a woman, as well.

Following Joshua and Ms Seim was the court reporter. She discreetly set up her machine in the corner. Each motion, each decision was to be put on
record.

"Please be seated," Anna told the assembled
group. This was an informal meeting and protocol
was relaxed.

Introductions were made and then they went over
the charges, limiting the issues and witnesses.

"Your Honor," Joshua said, "I'd like to request a
six-week postponement of the trial."

"Your reason?"

"One of my major witnesses is in for major sur-
gery. Without his testimony I have no defense."

Anna nodded her agreement. "I see no reason
your request should be denied." She turned to the
court reporter and said, "Let the record show that
the defense attorney has been granted a continuance
of six weeks."

All other business was quickly dispensed with and
the court reporter departed. Anna was left with
Dione Seim and Joshua Brandon in her chambers.
There was no professional reason for either attorney
to remain. Joshua undoubtedly had something personal to say but Dione didn't know that. She appeared to be waiting to talk to him.

"Is there anything else, Mr. Brandon?" Anna
asked.

"Yes, there is," he started to say, but then realized

that he was not in a position to speak privately with her. He had an audience, one that he did not cherish. "Yes, there is," he repeated. "But it can wait."

He started to leave but Dione caught him by the elbow and he turned to her.

"How about a cup of coffee?" she offered.

"We've covered everything that needs to be handled for now," he snapped irritably. "If something comes up, I'll contact you." Without glancing over his shoulder, he abruptly left.

His rudeness took a moment to register on Dione's face. Embarrassed, she looked at Anna and said meekly, "Touchy, isn't he?"

Tucking a strand of hair back into place, Anna mumbled offhand, "I wouldn't know."

"Well, he's certainly gorgeous," Dione said with a sigh, "but I think it would take a lion tamer to handle him."

As Anna ambled home, an early-evening shower sprinkled water droplets on her face like a fine mist from an atomizer. The weather had been dry for the past two weeks and the cleansing drizzle was a pleasant relief. Having left Elizabeth at home, she leisurely strolled up the hill, electing to walk rather than catch a bus. She enjoyed the opportunity of passively losing herself in the inner-city anonymity.

Taking her time, she glanced through windows at families gathered around dinner tables sharing the events of their days. They heightened her loneliness. Anna wondered if she'd be forever on the outside looking in.

The shifting breeze carried a fresh clean scent and

Joshua's image floated before her. That was the way
he smelled. He was the key to ending her solitary ex-
istence, but was she brave enough to reopen the door?

Her house was stuffy, harboring the heat of the
day, and she flung open the doors and windows to
banish the stale air. She hoped that Joshua wouldn't
try to reach her this evening. She wanted to delay
dodging his questions.

Turning on the television, she lost herself in a light-
hearted situation comedy. The ringing of the phone
ended her retreat and she considered not answering
it. But she knew she couldn't stall forever and finally
picked up the receiver.

"I've been trying to reach you for two hours,"
Joshua complained. "Where were you?"

His voice rang with irritation and she was tempted
to snap back, but she curbed her temper.

"I stopped off for dinner on the way home."

"So much for my idea of bringing over some
Chinese food."

"I thought I'd go to bed early tonight. Do you
mind?"

"Mind? No, I can tell you're tired. But tired of
what? Me?"

"There's no need to be cranky," Anna retorted,
losing her composure.

"Why don't you be honest?" he said nicely.
"You're still brooding about Sunday."

"No, I'm not."

"First you tell me it's perfectly natural to get angry
with Niki, and when I do, you shut me out." He took
a deep breath before admitting, "I don't know what
to do."

Anna couldn't deny his truth. But she still found the right words evading her. She stumbled over disjointed phrases. "I, uh, guess that...."

"Are you the only one with the privilege to correct him?"

She weighed his words carefully. "Maybe you're right. I have been isolated with him so long that it rankles me when someone else criticizes him."

"Like a mother protecting her child?"

"Yes," she agreed. "I can chastise him all I want, but I won't let an outsider find fault."

"Since when am I an outsider?" he asked, stung.

"You're not. That was just an unfortunate choice of words."

"The way you've been treating me I feel like one."

"I didn't mean to give that impression. I really didn't."

"Anna, I don't believe you have enough perspective to really understand how indulged and overprotected Niki is. How can he mature or fulfill his potential when no one gives him the opportunity to try?"

Anna's temper flared at his accusation. "You simply don't want to admit that Niki is too much for you to handle. He'll never advance beyond his current level. You can't face facts."

"I face them better than you do, but I can't accept the way you baby him. People rise to the level expected of them. You only reinforce Niki's feelings of inadequacy when you tell him he *has* to be taken care of."

"I do not!" she shrieked.

"Untie the apron strings," he hollered back.

"I have devoted my whole life to helping raise him. He doesn't have a sister, he has two mothers. He needs me," she furiously informed him.

"Quit being a martyr. It's unbecoming. He needs attention and affection, yes. But you treat him like the child you've always been afraid you'd have."

"He is a child."

"No, he's not. He is a man who wants independence. Quit hiding behind his retardation. Quit using him as a shield to protect yourself," Joshua said.

"I'm not hiding," she objected quietly. "You want Niki to grow up, but I don't think you've ever tried to imagine what it feels like for him." Then her voice took on the bite of a viper. "You're so damn smug, so self-righteous and pompous with your opinions. Well, you're a Johnny-come-lately, Counselor, and your advice isn't worth two bits."

Joshua wasn't sure who slammed the phone down first. It didn't matter. The conversation was fruitless and he'd blown it by losing control. He'd attacked her and that was the worst way to get to her. Not only that, but she'd scored a point or two, as well. He was self-righteous and pompous, yes, and he hadn't spent his whole life with Niki, either.

He envisioned a lifetime of battling over Niki, and it wasn't a happy prospect. Never in his wildest imagination had he ever thought he'd be in such a mess. He adored Anna and he wasn't going to lose her. But how in the world was it going to work out?

He picked up a book to read, hoping it would distract him, then flung it aside. He switched on the television, but turned it off after ten seconds. He combed his unfinished and cluttered houseboat desperately looking for something to divert him. Nothing worked. The last thing in the world he wanted to do tonight was spend the evening alone staring at four blank walls. Any project he started to take his mind off Anna would be of little or no purpose.

Slamming the front door, he headed for Vashon. Something drew him to Douglas. The old Irishman was the only one Joshua knew he could always count on to be there. He did a mental double take at the thought when he remembered that even Douglas was moving out of his life. He'd forgotten about him selling out and returning to the old sod. Forgotten? Joshua had also forgotten how he'd treated Douglas in San Diego. A blanket of guilt descended. He'd been short with him when he'd tried to help. Like an ungrateful child, he'd thrown Douglas's love in his face.

Joshua wanted to mend the emotional breach he'd created. Now was the best time to make his apology and offer an explanation for his rude behavior.

The dinner rush was over by the time Joshua reached the inn. He wandered into the kitchen.

Douglas was busy stirring one of his sauces when he walked over and asked, "What are you concocting?"

"Brandy sauce."

The simple reply was unusual for Douglas and Joshua knew that he'd been right about the other man's hurt feelings. Douglas was distancing himself.

"I never gave you a peace offering after the way I spoke to you in San Diego," Joshua said.

"A simple apology will suffice, son."

"How about a sincere apology? It was no way to repay you for all you've given me," Joshua said. "Is my ingratitude the real reason you are leaving?"

"Perhaps," Douglas answered. "Joshua, everyone needs to be needed. I'm no different."

"But I do need you."

Douglas patted his shoulder. "I wish you did. But you're grown now and there's no way you could fill the space of a family."

"I'm really sorry for yelling at you in California," Joshua said.

"Thank you, son."

"I'd like to explain my behavior that night."

"Only if you're willin'."

Joshua pulled up a stool and, while Douglas blended the liquor into the sweet sauce, told him about the fight he had had with Anna before leaving for San Diego. He was candidly honest in recounting the story and didn't spare any details. He was meticulous about not coloring the facts to make Anna appear in a less than favorable light. He told the truth as it had actually happened.

"So you handled it poorly, did you?"

"I handled it like a jackass. Now can you understand why I bit your head off?"

Douglas smiled at him and forgave him with his eyes. "Things goin' smoothly again?"

"For a while. Just when things were promising, her brother decided to go for a Sunday drive. The fact that he'd never driven a car before muddied the waters once more."

Joshua filled him in on what had happened right up to their angry phone call of that evening.

"She's been hidin' from the world. It's a painful burden she bears," Douglas sighed.

"That's where we're stuck." Joshua sighed, defeated. "She refuses to let him grow up and I don't know how our relationship can survive if we can't work it out."

"I'm sure Niki doesn't mean to cause you grief."

"No, he doesn't. But he's struggling for some independence and she keeps holding him back."

"Holds him back or holds you back?"

"Both of us, I think."

"It's a beast to let go of someone you love. I shed a tear or two when you and your brother jumped the pasture fence. I never tried to bring you back, though, 'cause I knew you were capable of runnin' to where the road led."

"I'm aware that Anna doesn't have such faith in Niki," Joshua said. "But she has to trust it'll work out. Somehow."

"Trust. That's the crux of it right there." Douglas wiped his hands on his apron. "Niki's trusted her to take care of him and she took it very seriously. Now you're askin' her to abdicate that care without any guarantees. 'Somehow' is a weak plan."

"I guess so. She doesn't put it in words like that, though. Anna says I don't know what Niki really feels. She thinks I'm putting words in his mouth. Maybe she's right. There's no way I can put myself in his place. I've tried but it's impossible."

Douglas carried the sauce to the refrigerator. He poured himself a cup of the strong tea he always kept brewing on the stove. After adding a dab of sugar and a spot of cream, he rejoined Joshua.

He held out one of his hands and turned it slowly in front of Joshua's face. "Ever thought about the job your thumbs do?" he asked.

Joshua saw no purpose in the question but allowed him to continue. "My thumbs?"

"One time my father strapped my thumbs to my palms."

"What in the world for?" Joshua was trying to follow the reasoning.

"I'd fallen in with a hive of bullies when I was eight or nine. The gang of us was tormentin' a poor bewildered boy, someone like Anna's Niki," he explained. "Father caught me and hauled me home by the gristle of my ear."

"He strapped your thumbs down as a punishment?"

"No, for a learnin' experience. He said I had to wear the tape for a full twenty-four hours to find out what it feels like to be handicapped."

"And?"

"I couldn't tie my shoes without makin' a mess of it. I struggled with my buttons till the sweat rolled off my face. Turnin' a doorknob was hell. It was humiliatin' tryin' to write my name, or to have to ask someone to pick up a coin or a raisin."

Douglas lowered his hand after flexing each finger, and touched each to the thumb. "I never took for granted the miracle of that thumb. I went weepin' to my father long before the time was up, beggin' him to take me out for a whippin' rather than leave the tape on."

The story painted such a vivid picture that Joshua had no trouble grasping what Douglas meant. "And that's how Niki feels," he said in a hushed tone.

"Only for him it's not temporary."

The path that Douglas had gently led him down brought Joshua out of his maze of confusion to a new awareness and understanding. Niki's behavior was a result of pleading for dignity, and Joshua was reminded of Niki's story about the doctors and their shots.

"Thanks," he said, patting Douglas's arm. "You always have the answers. What do I do now?"

"That's a more difficult question. But why are you askin' me? I'm not the one they sent to that fancy university. You are."

Once more Douglas had prodded him to get busy, solve a problem, find a solution, work out alternatives, just as he had for the past three decades. Being told to get to work snapped Joshua out of the depression he'd been wallowing in. He felt revitalized and the first thing that hit him was his incredible hunger.

"Anything around here to appease my stomach?" he groaned. "I'm starving."

"There's a table by the window," Douglas offered, indicating the main dining room.

"Still mad at me? Can't I stay in the kitchen?"

Douglas smiled. " 'Course you can. Grab a plate and help yourself."

Joshua ladled up small portions from the steaming kettles and sat with the kitchen help. It reminded him of when he was a child and had dinner at home with the cook, Douglas, Mudger and himself. They used to gather around the large work table and talk about the day. It was a far cry from the formal meals they ate in the dining room when their parents were in town. When they ate in the kitchen, the boys were expected to do the dishes while Douglas spun yarns about Ireland.

Joshua purposely prolonged the meal, sampling the tasty morsels Douglas prepared for his guests. A steaming mug of blended Arabian coffee capped the dinner perfectly.

"Eatin' me out of house and home?" Douglas teased.

"If you weren't such a culinary wizard, there'd be no problem."

Douglas smiled at the compliment. "While you were eatin', did you come up with anythin'?"

"Just more questions."

"Well, keep searchin'."

Douglas was closing up shop, scrubbing the grills, stacking the clean dishes for the morning crew, and Joshua knew it was time to go home. He'd escaped back into his past for the warmth and encouragement that Douglas had always lavished on him. But it was time to move on. It was time to build instead of dream.

Joshua slept well, more at peace than he'd been in weeks.

ANNA AWOKE after a restless night. Hurling her words at Joshua hadn't given her the release she'd hoped. Instead, self-doubt clung to her like a wet blanket. Was she hiding behind Niki? Had she been giving Joshua mixed signals? Was she undermining Niki's growth by making him too dependent?

Her misgivings pervaded the morning like smog hanging overhead. By lunch, Anna was ready to hibernate in her chambers to avoid everyone. She looked forward to sitting in her chair and regaining some tranquillity. After sending Miriam out for an extended lunch, she kicked off her shoes and tried to relax.

What Anna really needed to unload were the nagging questions that burdened her. She went to her window and pondered her future. Clouds scudded across the sky like the little toy boats she watched on Green Lake. Their white sails caught the wind and the children spent hours making them tack back and forth on the water.

"I'm probably sailing off the end of the world," she said aloud.

"That's hard to do when the world is round," Martin laughed from the doorway.

She jumped at the sound of the mechanic's voice, and spun around to make sure she hadn't lost her mind and started answering herself. She saw him leaning against the doorjamb with a mischievous grin on his face.

"My mother always said there was something wrong with me because I talk to myself," he said.

"Mine, too." Anna laughed.

"You should hear what I tell a stubborn bolt when I'm angry. It isn't fit for a lady's ear."

Smiling, happy to see him even though she had thought she wanted to see no one, she asked, "What brings you up here?"

"I was in the building transferring a title on a car," he explained, "so I thought I'd say hello and invite you to lunch."

"Hello," she said. "How about sharing my sandwich and cookies instead?"

"Peanut butter?"

"The sandwich is. But the cookies are oatmeal."

"Then I'll join you." He came into the room and pulled a chair up to her desk.

Miriam had left the door between their offices open and when Martin had come in, he had peeked into her chambers to find her.

"The only time I start babbling at the walls is when something is eating me," he said, taking half her sandwich. "Times like that I wish someone would ask me what's on my mind."

His unsubtle probe made her smile again. From the moment she had met him, something special had happened between them. Maybe he was like the brother Niki would have been if he'd ever really grown up. She knew she could talk to Martin. She'd known that from the moment she'd said anything about the Maserati he'd repaired for Joshua. He'd held that secret for years.

"Things have been a little rough since Niki side-swiped most of my neighborhood," she said.

"Between you and Josh?"

"Yes."

"It's not like him to hold a grudge. He might rant and rave, but he usually cools off and starts to laugh about things like that," Martin said, shaking his head.

Anna flinched. Martin had automatically assumed it was Joshua who was being stubborn. The truth was they were both guilty. "Actually," she admitted, "he got over the damage done to his Jaguar in a couple of hours. It's more complicated than that."

"Feel like making it simple for me?" Martin asked.

She felt like unloading the whole tangled mess, so she forgot about eating and began talking. She found herself waxing verbose like a love-struck girl when she talked about how Joshua and she had found so much to love in each other. And she discovered herself waning when she explained the drain Niki had caused on the relationship. It was difficult keeping her feelings impartial but she gave it a brave try.

"And that's where we are now," she ended. "Butting heads over Niki."

Martin wiped his face with a napkin and sat back. He didn't say anything. Instead, he just smiled at her.

"Am I being foolish?" she asked.

"Who knows?" he answered. "I haven't walked a mile in your moccasins."

"How about Joshua's moccasins? Have you ever borrowed them?"

"No," he hedged. "But I know that sometimes when I'm working on a car, I start to dream about what I'd do with it if I owned it, not what the customer wants done. I lose track of my first priority. I forget what it is that I started out doing."

"In other words you get sidetracked?"

"Something like that." He stood up and pulled the chair back to where it had been. "I have to stop and remember where I'm going. That the job is really a partnership between me and the customer. If I do it right, we're both happy."

"I'm not sure I really understand," Anna said, trying to analyze what it was Martin was really telling her.

"You see, I get hung up on remaking, remodeling,

redoing the car. But that isn't the important part. What counts is the respect I receive, the pride I feel by making the relationship between me and the other fellow the best it can be. Sometimes that means compromising.''

The idea of compromising over someone as important as Niki was disturbing to Anna. All her life she'd gone out of her way to protect him and fight for him. Compromising sounded like treachery. Was Martin suggesting she throw her brother to the wind in favor of Joshua?

''I have to get back to the island, Anna,'' he said as he headed for the door, ''but I have an offer to make. I'd enjoy having Niki some weekends at my place. I could use a strong guy like him to help me in the shop.''

Martin's offer was a bolt out of the blue to her. Here she was accusing him of suggesting she abandon Niki and now he was offering to have him over. ''Thank you,'' she said. ''That's a nice gesture, but you don't have to try—''

''Anna!'' he snapped. ''It wasn't a gesture and I resent you taking it that way. I can use a man like Niki. Now either accept my offer or reject it, but don't go around labeling it.''

''I'm sorry, Martin,'' she said meekly. ''It's just that I thought you were being kind and trying to give Joshua and me more free time together.''

''You know, kid, you think too much. I should make you an apprentice, then by the time you'd mindlessly sanded a dozen vehicles you'd know how to just do something *without* thinking.'' Abruptly, he gave her a thumbs-up sign and left.

Anna wasn't sure if unloading herself on Martin had been good or not. He'd left her wondering if maybe she'd lost track of what she was doing. Did love mean you sacrificed everything and everyone for it? Was she wrong for not compromising? He'd left her with more doubts than she'd originally had.

Miriam returned to work and mercifully rescued her from any more thinking. Once more she stuffed the problem into a neat little corner of her mind with the resolution that she'd figure it out later.

As ANNA FACED GOING BACK to work, Joshua was looking forward to his meeting with Tom Randolph. Tom was waiting for him in front of the small open-air café in Pioneer Square. They had made arrangements to plot their proposal over lunch. Both men were core members of a group of activist attorneys who were campaigning for more stringent security measures in the courts. Tom was heading up the task force and Joshua had volunteered to assist him.

After the perfunctory handshakes, Tom reviewed the current status of their petition. The cause was being backed by a few influential politicians and they had good reason to hope their campaign would be successful.

When he was finished discussing strategy, Tom asked, "How's Anna? Sue and I haven't seen much of her lately."

"Neither have I," Joshua admitted.

Tom unsuccessfully masked his surprise. "You aren't joking. What's going on with you two?"

"A war of wills. The struggle between the big bad Joshua who wants to throw Niki out into the street and let him starve, versus the sweet saintly Anna who wants to keep her brother a spoiled and over-protected little boy for the rest of his life.''

Tom nodded. ''So it's come to that? A misunderstanding over Niki. I suppose it was inevitable. What are your plans?''

Joshua laughed like someone who's heard a bad joke. ''Throw her over my shoulder caveman style and hit her on the head with a club because she won't do what I want.''

Tom chuckled. ''I don't think that worked even in the caveman's day.''

''I don't know,'' Joshua said. ''I've been racking my brains for a way for Niki to have a life of his own that Anna will buy. This isn't just my idea. It's Niki's. That night I found him he poured out his frustration about being dependent on everyone. But Anna doesn't believe it. She thinks I'm dreaming it all up.''

Scratching his jaw pensively, Tom said, ''How about a group home? It's a fantastic concept.''

''Group home?'' The idea was so simple and so brilliant that Joshua felt stupid for not having thought of it. ''That's perfect. Why didn't it occur to me?''

''Probably because you've been trying too hard.'' Tom poked fun at him. ''For a long time Sue and I have thought it would be a great idea for Niki, but we were never in a position to suggest it.''

Elated, Joshua said, ''You know, Douglas, a friend of mine, used to say some people can see at a glance what others can't see with flashlights and telescopes. How do we go about finding a group home for Niki?''

"Well, from what I understand, you go looking for one for several months. Then you put him on a waiting list that is about three-to-five-years long," Tom said sadly. "It's a great idea, but the truth is there are very few of them and they're all full."

"You know something, pal," Joshua said sourly, "you have a way of lifting a guy up and then dropping him on his head."

"Sorry. The only other thing is to start one yourself, but that means an incredible amount of work and planning."

Joshua brightened. "Start one? That's a wonderful idea. How do you go about doing it?"

Tom had to smile at his enthusiasm. "I can only guess. It means money, a board of trustees, finding a house, meeting fire codes, health standards, hiring a houseparent, buying furnishings...and a thousand other things I can only imagine. Are you serious about taking on such a project?"

"Will you help? Be one of the first trustees?" Joshua asked.

Tom didn't respond immediately. He studied Joshua for a few seconds and finally said, "I'd be honored. And as an added bonus, I'll ask Sue. I won't commit her to the project but I'm pretty sure you can count on her. She has some pretty strong feelings about children, no matter what their age."

"Children?"

"We always think of Niki as a child."

Joshua bent into Tom. "See, that's the problem. Sorry, but I feel you're wrong. Niki is not a child. He's a grown man with needs, desires, frustrations and joys. Sure, he has limitations the rest of us aren't burdened with, but he's not a child.''

Tom didn't say anything for a few moments and Joshua wondered if he'd just lost his first board member.

"I guess we've all inadvertently denied him his dignity. It's nice to see you're trying to give him some,'' Tom admitted. "You've convinced me, but how are you going to convince Anna? She's a tough cookie, especially when it comes to her brother.''

"Leave that to me. I think she'll love the idea when she understands what it'll mean to him.''

"Want some advice?''

"Sure.''

"Talk to Papa Provo. If he likes the idea, you've won the battle. He's been sidestepping his women for years. He's a master.''

"Sure, I'll talk to him after I bounce the idea off Anna. He is Niki's father, after all. Without his co-operation, the idea's dead.''

They discussed the group-home plans for another hour until they both had to rush off for appointments. Before parting, they solemnly pledged to see that Niki got his chance at life and shook hands.

A few hours later Anna was about to fix herself a light dinner when Joshua came by. She opened the door and was visibly surprised to see him after the fight on the phone the previous night. He drew her into his arms like a man who was starving and, as much as she wanted to resist him, she couldn't. Her body betrayed her cool resolve to keep him at least at arm's length. The evenings were becoming shorter and the dim light playing on his hair accented his golden coloring. He seemed to possess a luminesce that radiated like an aura.

He released her long before she was ready to let go of him and she was embarrassed by her eagerness to make love to him. She stepped back shyly and tried to compose herself.

"Hello, Counselor," she said, clearing her throat.

"Firebird," he whispered lovingly. "I've missed you."

"What brings you here?" she asked. "I got the distinct impression we were hardly on speaking terms after last night."

Reaching out for her, he said, "That was last night."

She darted away from him before he could hold her, before he could make her melt in his arms again and forget their major differences. "You're in a good mood. What's wrought this sudden change?" she sneered sarcastically, stressing the word *wrought*.

Joshua fought back his angry reply and said, "I had an idea today and I wanted to share it with you. It's a great one and I thought it might please you, too."

Something warned Anna that she wasn't going to be nearly as pleased as he thought. Lately, anything that made one of them happy only upset the other. That was how badly things had become between them.

"Okay, let's sit down and you can tell me about it," she said, indicating the sofa.

He made room for her next to him but Anna walked right past Joshua and took an armchair facing him. Her move was like a slap in the face, but he kept his reaction neutral. This was going to be like trying to convince a queen to give up her realm, he realized. Not the easy task he'd hoped and wanted it to be.

"Tom and I had lunch together today," he began slowly, haltingly. "And we were discussing Niki."

"I suppose you two came up with some marvelous idea?" she said icily.

"As a matter of fact, we did. A group home."

"What?" Her voice rose nearly an octave. "What group home?"

"The one Tom, I and a board of trustees want to set up."

"And you took it upon yourself to thrust Niki out of our lives by placing him in this institution disguised as a group home?" she demanded sharply.

"No!" He nearly shouted, but he curbed his temper. "I thought you'd like to help set it up. Make sure it was what Niki wanted." He took a breath, letting it settle his temper. "Besides, it will be a warm, loving, caring home, not an institution."

"Niki would despise the idea."

"How do you know? Have you asked him?"

"I do know my brother," she angrily said as she stood up and marched around the room. "He'd be lost without us," she threw back over her shoulder.

"Yes," Joshua agreed. "He might be for a while. But that's the entire premise. To allow him to grow and develop."

"I don't agree. Mama and papa would never send Niki away."

"He wouldn't be sent away," he said curtly. "It isn't a prison. You'd call him whenever you wanted to and he'd call you. There would be Sunday dinners, family outings, holidays—all of the natural interaction.''

''He'd be lonely,'' she objected, stopping her walking and looking out to the lanai.

''If he wasn't retarded, he'd be living in his own place. Possibly married with a bunch of kids. This way he'd have an extended family. I don't think he'd be as lonely as you suspect. He'd have friends that enjoyed his company, and most importantly, he'd feel as if he had finally grown up. What man wants to live with his parents when he is thirty-two?''

''He's happy now,'' she insisted.

''Not as happy as you'd like to believe. He was trying to proclaim his emancipation that Sunday from the moment he climbed into my car until I found him in that wretched hotel. You're not listening to him.''

Anna glowered at Joshua and he knew it was pointless to continue. He stood and came up behind her. ''I don't want to fight with you, Firebird. Why don't we let your parents decide this? And let Niki have his say?''

She felt his arms curl around her and she kept herself rigid. ''How is anybody going to pay for all this? My parents on their retirement money? Is that the price they have to pay for this grand idea of yours?''

''I haven't worked it all out yet,'' he admitted. ''But my grandfather left some money to be used for any cause I thought worthy.''

Anna spun out of his embrace and turned on him in a fury. Slamming her fists against his chest, she yelled, ''You're buying Niki off with Brandon money. How dare you think that you can manipulate me and my family with your wealth!''

He grabbed her wrists and kept her from striking him again. "That's not what I meant," he yelled back.

"Get out!" she screamed. "Get out! This whole thing is just a scheme of yours to dispose of Niki." Her voice became low and loathsome. "You want only part of me so you're offering to buy off the part you don't want. Well, you can go to hell, Mr. Brandon."

Joshua released her wrists and watched the hatred in her beautiful amber eyes. If her glance could have pierced him, it would have been a mortal wound. Looking away, he walked to the door and stopped.

He threw his shoulders back and tightened the knot of his tie. Anna had never seen him so elegant, so imperial. His anger was almost tangible and she could feel it fill the distance between them. His contempt permeated the air and she thought she would choke on it.

"Thank you for the sentence, Your Honor." His voice was cold. "You've just proven that justice *is* blind."

CHAPTER SEVENTEEN

ANNA'S WORLD WAS TURNED UPSIDE DOWN. She seemed to be moving through the sluggish weeks like a snail. She went from one task to another, lifeless and indifferent while everyone else was rushing around at full speed. She was out of sync with the universe, with her family, with her friends. After their confrontation, she never saw Joshua again. But he must have gone to her parents and presented his idea, for papa and mama were suddenly in a bustle setting up a group home. They added themselves to the board as trustees, along with Tom and Sue.

Mama Provo didn't even have time to nag Anna or pry into her life. It was as if Anna had been abandoned by everyone and she reacted by becoming more lethargic.

Papa sought her out and found her still sitting in her chambers one day after work. The courthouse was nearly empty and Miriam had been gone for an hour. His little girl, his Firebird, had her chair turned to the window and was looking out at the city lights beginning to flicker on.

"Anna," he called her name from the shadows, "I came to check on you. Mama and I haven't seen you at the shop or at home."

"I've been very busy, papa," she answered without turning around to look at him.

"You've always been busy, but you used to find the time to come see us."

Anna suddenly became angry. Lately someone always seemed to be telling her what to do and what to feel. It had started with Joshua. He'd corrupted all the people in her life.

"All right," she said scathingly to her father, "you've sold out. You sold out Niki's life to that rich man's dreams. You never bothered to ask me what I wanted, what Niki wanted. You just bought Joshua's proposal. Why?"

Papa turned her swivel chair around so she could see his face. "Joshua didn't come up with anything mama and I hadn't already discussed a thousand times. We didn't buy anything," he insisted firmly. "We finally acted, that's all. Sure, we didn't have enough money until he made his generous offer, but he isn't supplying everything. Mama and I are contributing what we can, so are other parents we've met who want this home for their children. Don't you see, Firebird, it's a wonderful group commitment."

"I wonder if you'll be so confident when you dump Niki on the doorstep and see how miserable he'll look."

"Niki is excited about the idea. Talk to him about it," papa suggested.

"Now he is because he still has his own room and you and mama. Later he'll understand he's been betrayed."

"Is that how you really see it?" papa demanded. "Betrayal?"

"Yes," she answered, looking him directly in the face. "That's how I see it."

He turned away from her accusing eyes and stood at the window. "One time when you were a little girl, I gave you a lovely tea set for a present. You adored it and played with it every day, drinking hot milk out of the tiny cups. Then I discovered it had been glazed with lead paint and I had to take it away because it would harm you. You were very angry. You thought I'd betrayed you then because you didn't understand. You don't understand now."

"I'm not a little girl anymore, papa."

"No?" He turned back to her and put his hands on her shoulders. "You'll always be my little girl." He kissed her on the forehead, brushed her auburn locks back from her temples with his gnarled hands, then walked out of the dark chambers.

She heard the door close and she slipped further down into her chair. The tears flowed in silent streams down her cheeks and she didn't even try to halt them. Everything was wrong and it was all Joshua's fault. He'd made promises and then distorted them.

Papa had left to go to a board meeting of the group home. He had hoped to change Anna's mind and talk her into coming along, but he had been so discouraged by her attitude, he hadn't even issued the invitation.

Tom and Sue were having the meeting at their home so they wouldn't have to hire a sitter for the kids. Papa arrived to find everyone present, including Joshua, who had been doing most of the legwork behind the scenes. He'd battled the bureaucratic requirements for weeks and finally felt confident that every base had been covered.

"Sounds good," Sue said after he had summarized his progress. "We've got the eight applicants already picked."

The board had set guidelines for eligibility of the residents, such as a minimum age of twenty-one and only those who were ambulatory and without serious physical problems. The trustees had selected male adults they felt would form a cohesive family unit.

"Now all we need is a house and a houseparent," papa said. "The two biggest obstacles so far. Any luck, Joshua?"

He shook his head. "Not yet. I've interviewed a dozen men and women for the job, but none have quite fit."

"What qualities are you looking for?" Sue asked. "I mean outside of the ones we already outlined?"

"It's hard to define," Joshua answered. "The person who lives with the residents has to have that special touch. The kind you give to your family, Sue," he said, smiling at her pretty face. "The kind all of you give and the kind I got from Douglas."

"Who's Douglas?" Sue asked.

"He's the man who raised me. He lives on Vashon now but he plans on moving...." Joshua let his words trail off. Douglas! He was perfect for the job. A smile lit Joshua's face. "I think I've just found our houseparent," he announced to the group.

"This man you were just talking about?" Sue inquired.

"Yes, and if he'll accept, all of you will like him. I'll go over and see him tomorrow."

"Great," Tom said. "Now all we have to find is the right house. How's that going?" he asked everyone. It had been an effort to find a place and each person had taken it upon himself to look. So far the results had all been negative. Each possibility was either too small, too run-down, surrounded by too little land, or too far away from any potential jobs for the residents.

Mama gave her report. It was negative. Papa added his nothing. Tom and Sue shook their heads and Joshua just gave them a rueful smile.

"Nichevo." Mama sighed. "Never mind. We'll keep looking."

Tom nodded. "Is there any other business?" he asked.

"Yes," Joshua said. "I brought some papers setting up the trust fund. Each month money will be transferred into it. I need your signatures."

He passed the papers around but did not affix his own name to them.

"Aren't you signing?" Tom asked.

"No," Joshua said. "After tomorrow when I talk to Douglas, I'm leaving all of you on your own. I'd like to stay involved but it's best I back out."

An awkward silence hovered. Everyone knew Joshua's reasons for leaving and they couldn't argue with him without making his position even more difficult.

Papa filled the empty silence by saying, "We'll miss you, son."

Joshua rose and put the papers in his briefcase. "I'll call you tomorrow, Tom, to let you know what Douglas says." Closing his case with a sharp click, he added, "I'll forward these to you through the mail. Good night."

As he strode out of the room, there was a rigidity to him that seemed alien to his natural grace. It was as if a ramrod had replaced his spine.

The next day, as he drove to Doug's Island Inn, he was pleased at the way his repaired Jaguar handled. Martin had done a superior job. Even the insurance agent had been impressed. As he pulled up to the familiar establishment, he felt uneasy. At first he thought it was just because there were no cars in the parking lot. Unusual but understandable if it was a slow day or there had been a lull between rushes. It wasn't until he tried the door and found it locked that Joshua realized something had changed. A sign taped to the window read Closed for Remodeling. Under New Management.

So Douglas had sold out. Had his friend already left the country without word? Would Douglas do that? It didn't seem likely, Joshua reasoned. He must be at his house down the hill.

Driving faster than the speed limit, Joshua raced the sleek Jag around the island road's curves, squealing his tires. He hoped he wasn't too late. He'd been too late for everything important. Too late to bridge the distance between himself and Anna. Too late to think of Douglas as a houseparent. Too late to realize he'd given Douglas a reason to pack up and leave when he'd snapped at his friend in San Diego. Too late to understand what the independence of Niki would mean to the woman he loved. Too late to grasp how loyal she was to her brother.

When he crested the knoll at the top of Douglas's driveway, he screeched to a halt, almost afraid to go any farther and discover he wasn't there. He searched the windows for a glimmer of life, a flicker of a curtain telling him the house was still in use. But the huge white house with its bright red composition roof stood like a solitary mammoth sentinel on its bluff above the bay. Like a well-worn spouse of the home, the barn stood to the rear, weathered but impressive. Douglas's llamas were grazing in a pasture to the east and the vegetable garden was tilled under where the summer crops had already been harvested. Only the pumpkins on their vines remained, sprawling down a gentle slope toward the brawling brook that rambled below.

Everything looked the same as it had the last time Joshua had visited, but there was no indication that Douglas was around or even still owned the place. Then Joshua's eyes saw the For Sale sign posted on the latticed porch. He'd never been so pleased not to see a Sold sticker splashed across the face of a sign in his life.

He felt like a man who'd been given a reprieve. Stepping on the accelerator, he headed down the driveway. If Douglas wasn't home, he'd wait. He'd wait all night if he had to.

He snapped off the ignition, and just like he had as a little boy, he started calling out, "Douglas, Douglas, where are you?"

"By the saints," Douglas said quietly as he opened the screen door and came out onto the porch. "No need to be rattlin' the window glass with your bellowin'. I'm right here."

"I thought maybe you'd flown the coop without telling me," Joshua said.

"I'm no chicken, son, if that's what you're accusin' me of. Besides, I haven't sold my house yet. I can't leave until I do." He motioned Joshua inside. "I'll fix you a spot of tea and we'll visit."

Joshua followed him into the large old-fashioned kitchen and took a stool at the huge chopping-block table that dominated the middle of the room. It should have been a comfortable room, but it wasn't with only two men occupying it.

"What brings you out here?" Douglas asked.

"You."

"Me? I'm flattered, but what use do you have with me?"

Joshua was struck by the tinge of bitterness that had crept into his friend's voice. Such acridness had never been there before and it only reinforced his belief that Douglas was hurting.

"A few friends and myself have had a problem lately and I thought you might help us out," Joshua said, choosing his words carefully, knowing that Douglas liked nothing better than to "help out."

As Joshua expected, Douglas sat up a little straighter and his interest cleared some lines from his face. "How?"

"We're looking for someone to be the houseparent of some retarded adults in a group home. One of them is Niki."

"And you're askin' me? That's a mighty big job, Joshua," he said, shaking his head. "Do you think I'd be right?"

"You'd be perfect," he answered.

"Where's this home to be?"

"We don't know yet. We haven't found a place big enough."

Douglas slipped off his stool and walked around the cavernous kitchen. He kept his thoughts to himself as he brooded, "letting his gears grind," as he liked to say. After a few minutes, he took his place back at the chopping block.

Joshua knew his answer just from the way he smiled. Douglas always curled up one side of his mouth when a pleasant thought or a good idea took hold of him. "The answer is yes?"

"Under one condition."

"What?"

"If this house is suitable, we'll use it for the home."

For the third time in weeks, the answer to a problem had been directly under Joshua's nose and he hadn't even seen it. "I think I'm going to throw away that flashlight and telescope now." He laughed. "I've been hanging on to them for too long."

"Then it's a deal?" Douglas said, grinning.

"Deal. How much do you want for the place?" Joshua gestured all around him, indicating the house, the barn and the land.

"The price of the job," he said. "The price of the job."

"I don't understand."

"The house is for the young men, so it goes to them free. It's my contribution to the cause."

Joshua knew better than to argue. When Douglas made a decision it was irrevocable. Besides, it was a gift and the gesture made the whole concept of communal living seem more valid. "Thank you, Douglas," he said as sincerely as he could, hoping Douglas understood his profound appreciation.

"It's my pleasure, son."

Joshua didn't doubt it for a second.

He wasn't able to escape Douglas for hours. His friend insisted on outlining the things that needed to be done to the house for it to meet fire regulations. Then he wanted to discuss what could be done with the third-story room, how the rooms should be divided between the men, who could be contacted on the island to hire the residents and a hundred other considerations. Douglas was, without dispute, in his element.

Finally, about midnight, Joshua headed home. As he drove onto the ferry, he blocked out the last time he'd ridden across the sound this late at night. He rested his head on the back of the seat and attempted to catch a few winks. He drifted off but woke with a start. Was that Anna he'd heard laughing? No, he was dreaming. Or maybe he was just remembering. Either way, the mind was unforgiving when it was left untended. Anna had sentenced him to hell in a rage, but she didn't know how accurate she was. Each day was a new form of damnation and he wondered if he'd ever get used to it.

Forcing himself not to think of her, he finished the ride home by thwarting any thoughts he had of smoky topaz eyes, hair the color of cinnabar, skin as smooth as ivory and lips that melted at his touch like butter. Instead, he thought only of her pummeling his chest and wounding him with her words. Such memories sealed his decision to have nothing more to do with the woman he'd once thought he could tame into a kitten.

THE INDIAN-SUMMER DAYS of September chilled into the cooler days of October. Anna felt as if a frost had settled on her soul, so why shouldn't the weather be in step? She pulled a handwoven alpaca cape around her shoulders and shivered. The heat was cranked up in her condo but she couldn't get warm. Grudgingly she conceded that perhaps she was just reacting to Niki's departure today by trembling, not with cold, but with fear. Was he as happy as he seemed? She didn't know.

Her brother was in the bedroom packing up his things for Eloise Manor, his new home. Mama and papa had dropped him off saying they'd come back to take him to Vashon when he finished. He'd flown into the house higher than the dragon kite she and Joshua had launched in Gas Works Park. At first she'd thought his soaring spirits were a smoke screen to hide his apprehension. But after listening to Niki babble about the llamas he was going to care for and the new job he had at Martin's garage, she decided maybe he was excited. Maybe.

"Anna," Niki called from his room. "Where'd ya hide my medals?"

"I'll get them," she said, getting up from the sofa. "I put them away in my room. I was going to have them framed for you as a present."

She rummaged through her chest of drawers and took them to him. "Here," she said, handing them to him.

"Naw, you keep 'em," he decided. "Get 'em framed and I'll put 'em in my new room. I didn't mean to spoil your surprise by asking for 'em."

Pocketing the medals in her cape, she watched him boxing up his precious belongings. Each poster he peeled from the wall was like a layer of her heart

being removed. The bare walls were a naked testament
to how empty her life was going to be. At one time,
she'd thought her career, her teaching and her jogging
had been enough. Now she knew they'd only be props,
flats and scenery for an empty stage.

"Anna?" Niki asked. "Can I trust you with a
secret?"

"Sure," she said. "What is it?"

"I don't want mama and papa to drive me to the
house today. I want you to."

Anna didn't know how to answer. He was asking
her to enter the scene of her bereavement; to walk
through Joshua's nightmare.

"Please," he begged. "Mama and papa have been
there but you haven't. I want you to see my new home.
Please?"

Maybe this was Niki's way of telling her he wasn't
sure. Maybe if she took him to Vashon and he changed
his mind, she could take him back home. Perhaps his
plea was his way of hedging. Is that what he meant by
secret? He didn't want to go? Or was his secret just
that he wanted her, not their parents?

"All right, Niki," she said. "I'll take you."

"Great." He laughed. "You're gonna love it."

"I bet," she said dourly. "I'll call papa and let him
know."

Niki was a jabberwocky the whole trip. He went
from one topic to another without ever completing a
single idea. He was as hyper as a newly caged wild
monkey. Anna's mood was as sullen as an aging
lioness who'd known nothing but confinement.

She followed the directions papa had given her and
she found Eloise Manor. Like Joshua before her, she

stopped at the top of the drive and looked over the vast compound. She had to admit that the house and its environs looked appealing, like a Grandma Moses painting of a rural farm.

She was pleased to note the fire escapes going from the third story to the ground. Every safety precaution had been thought of. She silently complimented Joshua, but then remembered her parents telling her how this had been Douglas's home, how the trustees and parents had all pitched in to help. Joshua had started the ball rolling, making sure that the home's financial stability had been secured. Then he had resigned from the board.

She pulled up to the house and saw a young man slowly sweeping the porch steps. Douglas was showing another man how to trim some bushes.

He set the clippers down and walked over to greet them. He extended his hand. "Hello, Anna," he said. "I'm glad you decided to bring Niki."

"He twisted my arm," she said.

"I did not!" Niki vehemently objected. "I never touched you." Then he reasoned the expression out. "I did it again, didn't I?" he laughed at himself.

"That you did." Douglas patted him on the arm.

The blond man on the porch joined them and Douglas put his arm around his shoulder. "Hi, Niki," the man said, and then laughed.

"Hi, Robert," he said. "This is my sister." He mimicked Douglas's gesture and hugged Anna so hard she nearly fell over.

"Let's give Anna the grand tour," Douglas said, and he led the way with the silent man following them.

"Here's the living room. We don't have a television yet but we're hopin' to get one soon," Douglas informed as he ushered them through the huge room, which was still nearly empty.

"Do you play video games?" Niki asked Robert.

"I'm not very good," he answered.

"I love Pac Man," he informed him proudly. "I'll show you sometime how to get away from those mean ghosts."

Robert gave him a small laugh and Anna observed that it seemed to be his main form of communication.

To the left of the living room was a large dining room with a long oak table centered under a gleaming brass chandelier.

"This is where we all eat," Douglas explained.

"Who cooks?" Anna asked.

"All of us. Everyone takes turns helping."

"I can't cook. No way. I always burn my fingers or spill stuff," Niki admitted.

"You could learn to make a grand salad, Niki. Ever try?"

"Nope."

Anna followed Douglas and the others up the broad stairs to the second floor.

"Mind if I show them your room, Robert?" Douglas asked.

Robert chuckled his consent.

Opening the door, Douglas asked, "Don't you think he picked a lovely shade of lemon?"

"Here's the bathroom," Douglas explained when they went back into the hallway, "and there is another one down there."

"Scott and I are going to bunk together," Niki explained.

"Who's Scott?" Anna asked, and Niki pointed to the man who'd been trailing them.

Scott pulled out a harmonica and blew a few notes. He looked to Niki and Anna wondered why.

"He wants you to see our room," Niki announced. "He don't talk regular but I know what he's sayin' on that thing."

"How?" Anna asked.

"You just gotta listen, that's all," he explained. "Listen real good."

Cheerfully he led his sister down the hall. As she followed him, her fear that he would be unhappy in the home eroded. Niki was bursting with pride.

Maybe she hadn't known how to listen to him after all. Joshua had accused her of that and now Niki was innocently vindicating his opinion.

Scott flung open the door to his and Niki's room and Anna was hit by the bluest walls she'd ever seen. Painted sailboats with gigantic white sails were scattered over the walls and they broke up the intensity.

"Scott and I painted it ourselves," Niki boasted. "We wanted blue. Of course we didn't do those sailboats," he admitted. "Sue did. She worked real hard on 'em."

"It's wonderful," she complimented the two men.

"My first place of my very, very own," he smiled.

Anna choked back the lump in her throat. If only she had known what all of this had really meant to him. If only.

"Where do you sleep?" she asked Douglas to keep herself from crying.

"My room's at the end of the hall."

They finished the tour by checking out the third floor. t was a magnificent aerie encircled by small paned windows.

"Whose is this?" Anna exclaimed. Huge patchwork pillows were stacked on the floor, books lined the shelves, games were set up on tables and a telescope was aimed out one of the windows.

"It's the quiet room," Douglas said. "It's a place for relaxin' after a hard day."

"That wasn't here before. Is it a real telescope?" Niki was enthralled. "Can you look at the stars and spaceships and stuff like that?"

Douglas smiled. "I'd be glad to show you stars and planets and even the moon, but I'm not promisin' any spaceships."

They decided to sit a minute on the pillows and silently gaze out across the expanse of rough blue water. A stiff breeze had kicked up and was ruffling the bay's surface. Scott sat in a corner playing a mournful tune on a harmonica.

Douglas turned to Scott and requested, "Can you play 'Rainbow Connection' for us?"

"I know that," Niki offered. "You play and I'll sing the words. I listen to Kermit the Frog sing it all the time."

After their duet ended, everyone applauded.

"Good job, Niki," Douglas praised him. "You have a nice voice."

Niki sang a bit off tune and jumbled the words occasionally, but his effort was worthy of a sincere compliment.

"Robert," Douglas instructed, "why don't you

and Niki go outside and check on the llamas? Scott, you can go with them. Give them each a scoop of grain, but only one, mind you. I'll make coffee and we'll have cookies to go with it in a little while.''

The three men bolted out of the room like colts let loose in a pasture of clover. Niki was free and she hadn't even known he'd been corralled.

Anna followed Douglas down the two flights of stairs to the large antiquated kitchen at the rear of the house. She took a stool at the butcher-block table.

"May I ask some questions?'' she inquired as Douglas handed her a cup of tea.

"Fire away.''

"Where will these people work?''

"There are many small firms that have signed up to hire and train them,'' Douglas answered. "Martin wants another assistant at his auto shop, the orchid farm has requested two people to work in the greenhouses, and the firm that manufactures water skis wants to train as many people as we can supply. Our biggest problem is that we aren't able to meet the demand.''

Anna silently sipped her tea and pondered his reply. "How long can Niki and the others live here? Are there time limits or can this be a permanent situation?''

"The men can stay as long as need be. We would like to see them become somewhat independent, but there aren't any rules to say they can't stay with us forever.''

She looked at her hands holding the teacup and spoke. "It's no secret I've been against this thing from the beginning. In fact, I've detested the idea.''

"How do you feel about it now?"

"Well. . . ." She stopped. Had Joshua been right? Yes. But it hurt to admit that she couldn't give Niki everything he needed. It hurt to realize that maybe she had never taken proper care of him.

"Well," she repeated, "I think I should eat a little crow."

Douglas chuckled. "We don't serve that here, Anna."

Niki came crashing through the door like a fireman on a three-alarm fire. "Hey, Douglas," he bellowed, "Robert says he gets to have chickens. Is that right?"

"Niki," Douglas whispered, "are you deaf?"

Shocked, Niki shook his head.

"Am I deaf?" Douglas continued to whisper.

"No."

Using a normal voice, Douglas said, "Then there's no need to be yellin'. Now to answer your question, yes, Robert is going to raise chickens. He's going to have to do all the work, though."

"Chickens are dumb," Niki grumbled.

"Are not," Robert argued as he came through the door with Scott.

"Are so!"

"Stop it, you two," Douglas chided firmly. "Pour yourselves some coffee and help yourselves to the cookies."

Appeased by the platter of chocolate-chip cookies, Niki ended his taunting and rapidly consumed six of the biscuits. Robert only ate one, explaining he was on a diet. Scott drank coffee with three teaspoons of sugar in it.

After a little prodding by Douglas, the trio stacked their dishes in the sink and went back outside.

"Will Scott ever talk?" Anna asked.

"Who knows? He's been shunted from foster home to foster home since his parents abandoned him when he was a tot. He's not had much schoolin' but he's bright enough. Somethin' happened that's been locked up in his heart," Douglas answered. "The way I figure it, he's afraid to talk for fear it'll all come pourin' out."

Anna couldn't imagine anyone holding such a fear his whole life. "What are you going to do for him?"

"Give him lots of love and the first family he's ever had," Douglas answered. "Maybe someday he'll trust enough to let the words come. If not, we'll just let him be Scott and enjoy his music."

Such unconditional love was rare, Anna thought. She and Joshua hadn't been able to love that way. They had qualified, defined, ruled and regulated their relationship until it had died. Perhaps she'd been the guiltiest.

It was getting late and she rose to leave. "I'd better get going. The ferry leaves soon."

She called out the back door to her brother. "Nikolae, I'm leaving." He didn't answer and Anna felt a pang of pain as she realized that he was so busy, so happy, he didn't care if she came or went. Trying to hide her hurt, she turned to Douglas and masked her feelings. "This is a wonderful place. I'd like to help out. What can I contribute?"

"We need a television," he said.

"I'll bring one over. I'll also bring Niki's video games from my place. Anything else?"

"We'll always need somethin'. Keep comin' over and checkin' in."

He walked her to her car and Niki caught up with her to say goodbye. A two-man entourage was at his heels to help unload his things.

"Bye, Anna," he said offhandedly. "See you soon." He headed for the house with his gear.

"Bye," she called wistfully and took a deep breath.

She climbed in her car and rolled down the window. Douglas leaned in and put a hand on hers.

"Have you seen or talked to Joshua lately?" he asked.

"No. I doubt our paths will cross except in the courtroom," she said curtly. "At least, I hope not."

"Consider seekin' him out," he advised.

"No, we said some pretty angry things to each other. There's no way to erase the past."

"Anger is a wind," he counseled. "It blows out the lamp of the mind."

"It also blows out the lamp of love," she added.

"You're wrong, darlin'." He smiled. "Love is a golden vessel. It bends but never breaks."

Starting the engine, Anna smiled sadly. "I guess ours was made of glass, then. Bye, Douglas. I'll be back."

She didn't head directly for the dock. Instead she meandered around the back roads of the island. She couldn't go home yet. There was no one to go home to and there never would be.

CHAPTER EIGHTEEN

UNLOCKING THE DOOR to her condo, Anna felt like one of those old-fashioned dolls whose arms and legs are filled with sawdust. She was more than tired, she was lifeless. It had been one of those weeks. The coup de grace was that she'd had to face Joshua over her bench today. It was only an arraignment but, in his presence, even the shortest procedure seemed too long.

Joshua had directed his statement with detached authority and he'd never made eye contact with Anna. He looked through her as if she didn't exist.

"Your Honor," he said, "my client's plea is not guilty."

"Is he requesting a trial with or without a jury?" she asked him.

"With one, Your Honor."

"Then I recommend that bail be set at ten thousand dollars," she decreed.

Joshua packed his briefcase without glancing over his shoulder. Gone were the looks that used to strip her. Gone was the smile playing at the corners of his mouth. Gone were the old flashes of anger he used to demonstrate. He was more handsome than most attorneys who stood before her, but that was all.

She knew then that even if she had wanted to approach him, to grovel at his feet and apologize for not giving his idea a chance, it would have been fruitless. He was gone from her life for good.

But she didn't want to seek him out. He had come into her life and turned it upside down, then discarded an important part of it, namely Niki. He had remodeled her world and she didn't like the results.

When he walked out of the courtroom through the swinging double doors, she wished he had walked out of her professional life. She rapped her gavel and took a fifteen-minute recess to regain her composure.

Now, hours later, she was washed out. Unable to face the emptiness of her quiet house, she made a spontaneous decision to head for the ocean. It had been her refuge for years, a sanctuary where she found peace of mind wandering the empty stretches of sand. The sound of the sea gulls as they circled overhead spying for crabs and starfish to feed on; the deafening roar of the mammoth breakers as they broke offshore before racing in to wash the beach clean; all the sights and sounds of the waterfront would drum the silence from her ears. And there would be the wind. Joshua had once said the wind helped him "shed the city." Now she craved to shed some of the oppressing weight that was robbing her of peace.

She quickly packed some jeans, a sweater and a heavy parka into a bag. At the last minute she grabbed her boots. She loved to wade in the incoming tide but hated having her feet freeze. The current off Washington State is not warm and the water bites back at a person even on the hottest days.

It was two and a half hours to the coast and she paid little attention to the passing scenery until she turned west. The massive dome of the state capital in Olympia alerts travelers to take the exit off Interstate 5 and she headed into the dense timber of the Black Hills. Miles of forest stretched around her creating a landlocked sylvan ocean. Only an occasional break in the forest marked an isolated house or an exit to a little town.

Anna smelled the salt air and knew she was close to her retreat. She could feel the muscles in her neck begin to loosen as she pulled up to Pirate's Alley, a wonderful old motel in Grayland. The establishment's sign was hand painted and unmarred by neon lights. Individual cottages with little lawns and well-tended flower beds lined the private road to the dunes. It was like stepping back in time to a more restful age.

She went to the office, which also served as the owner's home, to register. Knowing Anna well, her hosts welcomed the judge warmly.

She looked at the names on the cottage keys hanging on the wall. Captain Kidd, Bluebeard, Jean Lafitte, Anne Bonny and Calico Jack. Each cottage was named for a pirate. Each had a different floor plan and as unique a character as the man or woman it had been named after.

"Is Anne Bonny vacant?" she asked.

The owner's wife checked her reservation book. "Let's see," she said. "I know she's your favorite." Scanning the column, she had to juggle units before she could free the cottage for her.

"I really appreciate this," Anna thanked her.

"Glad to help. What brings you down? For the storm they say might hit this weekend?"

"I just need a little R and R. Long week."

"Say," the kind woman said, "I've got some fresh salmon steaks. Want a couple for dinner?"

One of the rea ns Anna kept returning to this spot was that the wners made her feel special and they were forever offering her some little delicacy to enjoy.

Repeating her thanks, she strolled to her cabin. The surf roared in the distance and the sound of the crickets sawed the air with their racket. She opened Anne Bonny and went in.

The first time she'd lodged in the cottage, she'd asked, "Who was the real Anne Bonny?"

"She was one of only two known women pirates in history," the owner had answered. "She and Calico Jack were lovers."

While Anna unpacked, she thought about the buccaneering paramours and wondered if Anne Bonny had been tough about the loss of her love—Calico Jack had been hanged by the authorities. Anna couldn't decide. If Jack had been anything like Joshua, Anne Bonny had probably turned him in, she thought wryly.

Exhausted, Anna put the salmon in the refrigerator and went to bed. It was too much to even think of cooking. At least tomorrow was Saturday and the most important task she had to face was whether or not to roll over in bed.

BY AFTERNOON the wind on Washaway Beach was up a knot or two but Anna was still comfortable combing the strand. She had a dufflebag draped over her shoulder and she'd been putting shells, pieces of driftwood and perfect sand dollars into it. What she was really looking for, the elusive Japanese glass fishing balls, were nowhere to be found. She'd been searching for a couple of hours but her luck was bad. A good storm tonight might improve things tomorrow. Then all kinds of treasures might be washed up.

Skirting the very edge of the water, she kept scanning the surf for a glimmer of color, a flash of light that would tell her she had found a treasure. The tide was going out and more sand was being exposed. The drag was powerful, so Anna was careful not to allow any more than the tips of her boots in the water.

Unexpectedly the wind increased and a violent gust blew her scarf off. She tried to catch it but it was sucked under by the dangerous water. Two forces were at war—the ebb of the ocean pulling away the water and the might of the westerly wind trying to push it back toward shore. The result was a forward churning rush of water and a mad backward rolling.

The noise of the breakers was louder, more thunderous than she could ever recall, and she couldn't even hear the gulls screeching. Anna knew she was going to have to go in, for the weather was becoming too rough to stay on the strand.

Hefting her awkward and heavy bag of treasures over her shoulder, she turned to shore and froze in place.

Joshua was coming across the beach directly toward her. What the devil was he doing down here? She had already been hurt too much, too deeply, and to have another meeting with him would only worsen the pain.

He kept coming and she angrily yelled over the

pounding of the waves, "Why are you barging into my life again?"

As he neared, she screamed, "Go away!" but the roar of the ocean ate her words and she flagged him off. "Go away!"

Fragments of his own words caught her. "Talk!" and "Understand" barely survived the raging wind.

Anna felt an icy rush suddenly spill over the top of her boots. She was in the water! She had unwittingly stepped into a deep pothole and lost her balance. There was no longer any footing and she was pitched into the foaming brine. She couldn't get back up. Her boots were full, dragging her like an anchor, and her heavy down parka was waterlogged.

She struggled with the bag that was latched to her by a flap and button on the shoulder. The frigid water almost instantly made her fingers numb and she couldn't get them working right.

Joshua waded into the surf and grabbed her by the collar. He hauled her out of the pothole to shore.

Anna felt freezing cold. The wind worked on her wet clothes and she was chilled to the bone. Her teeth started to chatter and her legs had almost no feeling.

"You're all wet," he teased.

"No," she chattered. "You're all wet for tracking me down here. I don't want to talk to you. Leave me alone."

"Whether you want to talk or not is a moot point," he said. "Both of us are wet and we need to get warm and out of these clothes."

"All right," she conceded. "You can come back to the cabin and change before you leave."

The heat of the cabin was exquisite. She stripped

off her clothing, rubbed her body down with towels until the feeling came back to her skin, and then wrapped herself in a robe.

Joshua brought in a change of clothes from his car and put them on before restoking the fire in the little potbellied stove.

"How are you feeling?" he asked gently from the doorway. "Would you like a cup of coffee?"

She nodded mutely. Slipping on a pair of socks, she went into the cabin's main room, a combination kitchen and living room. He was standing at the stove pouring steaming coffee into a mug.

"What are you doing here?" she snapped.

Smiling, he handed her the mug. His dimples were deep, his smile arresting. "Is that any way to talk to a man who just saved your life?"

"It's your fault I ended up in the brink," she answered irritably.

"As usual," he said, "you twist things around." He sat in the armchair near the potbellied stove.

"Why are you here?" Her words tumbled out of their own volition. She felt threatened and remained standing. There was something about towering over a sitting person that gave command and presence to a bad situation. "Did you come because Douglas told you I liked the group home? Are you looking for an apology from me? Well, you're not going to get one."

The smile faded from his ever-changing face and a saturnine look washed over him. Anna wasn't sure if the light in the room had shifted or if something within him had caused the difference.

"Firebird," he said her name sweetly, "if all I

wanted was an apology, I wouldn't have driven a hundred twenty miles.''

"Then what is it you want?" she insisted.

"Your father came to see me this morning," he continued.

"Why would he do that?" she asked.

"He received a phone call yesterday. He decided to stick his nose in things and approach me."

"What about the call?"

"It was from the genetic clinic. Remember you made an appointment after I'd given you the number?" He looked at her softly, willing her to sit down.

"Yes?"

"You didn't keep it."

"I had no reason to," she answered. "It was over between us. Why did they call papa?"

"You gave them an alternate number in case they needed to reach you. Remember?"

"Yes."

"They called him wanting to know why you didn't show. It made your father curious," Joshua explained. "He wanted to know why you'd ever be interested in genetic counscling."

"That's silly," she said. "Because of Niki. Why didn't he just ask me?"

"First of all," Joshua said, "he knew you'd come down here. Secondly, he wanted to clarify things with me since we were obviously considering marriage at one time."

"Clarify what?"

"Why Niki is retarded," he answered.

"Because he was born that way." Anna was exasperated.

"Yes, in a way that's true."

"What do you mean 'in a way'?"

Joshua sat back in the chair before speaking. "You know how you said how your parents have always been vague about Niki's mental handicap?" he asked.

"Yes?"

"Your father's words to me this morning were 'Niki should have been perfect.'"

Anna was shocked. Papa had never said anything like that to her. "Should have" implied something had gone wrong. She sat down on the sofa.

"What happened?" she asked.

Joshua put his coffee cup down. "Your parents were new to this country and they wanted to make their new life the best it could be. They worked from dawn to midnight."

"I know."

"When your mother was pregnant with Niki, she continued to work just as hard. She was lifting and hauling heavy boxes into their new shop. She painted and scraped and scrubbed until she was exhausted," Joshua said.

"She's still like that," Anna whispered.

"Your father feels that he should have stopped her. Taken better care of her. Your mother went into labor early and they had to settle for the first doctor they could find." Joshua moved from his armchair and sat next to Anna. "It was an accident. The doctor overanesthetized her, cutting off the oxygen supply to the baby. It caused brain damage."

"I had no idea. Do they feel guilty?" she asked, shaking her head.

"Yes," Joshua said, rubbing her arm. "It was an unspoken emotion but you picked up on it. Both your parents tried hard to make up for what they believed was their fault."

"Why didn't they tell me?"

"Mama and papa are old-fashioned. Maybe Niki would have been born early anyway. Certainly the lack of oxygen was the doctor's fault, not theirs. But—" he played with her hair "—they assumed all responsibility. No one, especially people like your folks, like to speak about something they feel was their error."

"I've spent all these years believing that it ran in the family?"

"Yes. It was understandable. Like your parents, you were afraid to really look into it."

Sweeping her into his arms, he held her tightly. "I love you, Firebird," he said slowly, then released his hold. Cupping her face in his hands, he held her head back and looked deep into her eyes. "I love you very, very much. I came to tell you that and to tell you that there's no reason for you to be afraid anymore."

"I love you, too," she whispered. "Thank you for not giving up on me."

Joshua stood up, pulling her with him. He took her hand, but didn't take his eyes off her, and led her to the bedroom.

He slipped her robe to the floor and stripped out of his own clothes. The silence was wonderful. The storm had passed and peace surrounded them like a satin comforter.

Joshua lifted Anna up and placed her on the bed as if she were a precious jewel being nestled on a mound of velvet. He stroked her hair back from her face, thinking of it as the plumage on his magical Firebird. The song he was going to make her sing would last in his ears for a lifetime.

Anna let out a sigh as his fingers played her body. A melody drifted through her head as he orchestrated their lovemaking. Her hands drifted across him and she felt him trembling at the rhythm. Sweetly and patiently, the symphony reached crescendo after crescendo.

A cry rang from Anna as he brought them together. She couldn't distinguish between the real and the ethereal. Nothing would ever separate them again.

When their lovemaking reached its apex, they descended together, exhausted, into a snug embrace. He tucked her under his arm as he lay back on the pillow and kissed her forehead. There were many more songs to be played for the rest of their lives together.

"Anna," Joshua whispered in her ear, "feel like talking some more?"

"Sure," she said softly. "What about?"

"Us." Rising up on one elbow, he looked directly into her face. "Will you marry me, Firebird?"

Without any hesitation, she answered, "Yes, my love, as soon as possible."

Joshua softly chuckled. "Is this week soon enough?"

Running the gold chain around his neck through her fingers, Anna said, "No, but there's a three-day waiting period for marriage licenses in this state."

"When you say soon, you really mean soon!" He

laughed. "Why don't we pop down to the courthouse license bureau on our lunch hour Monday and tend to it?"

"Great," she agreed. "Who do you want to perform the ceremony?"

"Know any judges?" he joked.

"I think I might know one or two. How about Ben Walker?"

"You go straight to the top, don't you?"

"You," she said, and lightly kissed his forehead. "Only the best will do."

"Who shall we invite? Shall we keep it very small or would you like to invite some friends?"

"Mama and papa would never forgive me if they missed my wedding. I don't want to start our life together with them mad at us."

"Good idea," Joshua said. "There's been enough regrets to last a lifetime."

"But do you think your parents could make it on such short notice?"

"They're somewhere in the Outback of Australia right now, so I doubt it. But Douglas would be honored to represent my side of the family. He's the one I'm closest to, anyway."

Joshua shifted his weight and pulled Anna on top of him. As she settled her head over his heart, she nuzzled the golden hair on his chest.

"When should we tie the knot? Next weekend?" she asked.

"A double celebration? Next Saturday is the open house for the group home. Why not plan a surprise wedding?"

Delighted by the idea, she said, "Perfect. Everyone we care about will be there."

"Have we left anything out?" Joshua asked.

"Only this," she murmured as she kissed her way up his neck.

Joshua flipped her quickly onto her back, greedily looked at all the beautiful aspects of her body, and huskily added, "We wouldn't want to forget any details."

He drew Anna's slim thighs apart and traced the curves that he relished. Using his fingers, he gently rubbed the soft inner flesh of her thighs. She responded by tipping her hips up.

She sighed, "Don't stop," and ran her hands through his hair, pulling him closer.

"Loving you? Never," he groaned. "Never."

They continued to reveal themselves to each other, discovering, exploring and fulfilling their love. They had no sense of time, and it was hours before they stopped satisfying each other. Eventually, they slept serenely in each other's arms.

DURING THE NEXT WEEK, both Joshua and Anna had a hard time keeping their news secret. They succeeded, but by Saturday they were bursting with excitement. The weather cooperated gloriously for the house-warming at Eloise Manor. The sun was brilliant, the leaves on the trees were a rainbow of autumn hues, and the air held the slight nip of fall that had sprinkled the grass with white crystals in the morning.

The guests were to arrive at noon and Joshua and Anna drove up at precisely twelve o'clock.

"Now don't you two make a fetchin' pair," Douglas complimented them as they walked in with their arms filled with boxes of appetizers.

"Thank you, Douglas." Anna kissed his cheek.

She displayed their contribution to the party on the dining-room table and went to the living room to see if the television she'd ordered had arrived. Niki came in and hugged her.

"Hiya, Anna. What kinda food did ya bring?"

"Lots of your favorites, but no nibbling until all the guests arrive," she warned him.

"I know," he said. "Douglas told us that nobody better pick at his little pies or we'd have extra kitchen duty. You don't need to remind me."

She hugged him tightly. "Sorry. It's going to take me a while to remember you've grown up. But be patient, I'm catching on."

As she released him, she noticed Robert standing in the hallway. "You look very handsome today," she complimented him. "Is that a new shirt?"

He bobbed his head up and down and smiled broadly.

The rest of the guests arrived in small clusters. They toured Eloise Manor and raved about the special touches. Patchwork quilts had been contributed by one family, paintings by Sue lined the walls, crisp curtains for the rooms had been sewn by Mama Provo, a workshop set up and stocked by Papa Provo, and dozens of other special touches had gone into making Eloise Manor a home.

People broke into groups as everyone chatted happily about the goals of their children and their friends. The energy level in the house was electric.

Joshua looked around at the party. All his life he had wanted to be surrounded by loved ones. Now he had more family than he'd ever dreamed possible. Douglas, Niki, mama and papa, and of course Anna.

And they would add their own children to this extended family. Picturing Christmas and all the other holidays to come made him smile.

Anna saw his smile and wondered what he was thinking. "Did you bargain for all this?" she asked, indicating the roomful of people.

Joshua hugged her. "No, I dreamed of so much less and got so much more."

"Ready to make it official?" She kissed him.

"Yes," he said. "Kiss me again for the last time as Anna Provo. The next time you'll be Mrs. Brandon."

Pulling him close, she gave him a sweet quick peck on the lips. "That'll have to hold you till later."

Joshua rapped a piece of silverware against a glass and said, "Friends and family, may I have your attention, please?" He waited for the din to subside before he proceeded. "Anna and I have a surprise. We have our marriage license and Ben Walker is going to conduct the ceremony now."

A jubilant uproar broke loose and people swarmed around and congratulated them.

"But, dear," someone called out to Anna, "the bride needs a bouquet."

"Solved," Joshua said, and took a large bunch of mums from a vase and wrapped a linen napkin around the wet stems. He handed the gorgeous blossoms of bronze, burnt orange and pale yellow to Anna.

Mama began weeping. "What kind of a bride has no veil?"

Smiling, Anna drew her mother's babushka off her head and tied it around her own. "See? No more tears."

Papa kissed her and said, "Every mother should cry

at her daughter's wedding. They're tears of joy, Fire-bird.''

An expectant hush fell over everyone as Ben Walker stood in front of the mantel. They stood back to make room for Anna and Joshua.

But they weren't ready yet. Joshua called out, "Niki? Would you be my best man? And Sue, would you be the matron of honor?''

"Sure thing, Josh,'' Niki hollered back. Sue nodded her accent.

Joshua instructed Niki when to hand them the rings. Then he took his place at the mantel. Papa walked Anna across the room. Before he stepped back, he took one of her mums and sprinkled the petals over the heads of the bride and groom. It was his adaptation of the Russian tradition of crumbling gingerbread over the couple for luck.

Anna and Joshua solemnly repeated their simple vows. Using plain gold wedding bands to symbolize the equality of their union, they placed them on each other's fingers. After they sealed their marriage with a kiss, the room remained silent.

It was broken by a slow haunting melody from Scott's harmonica. No one could place the author or origin of the piece. It was probably something only Scott knew, but he made his humble instrument draw out each exquisite note like a master.

Encircling Anna's waist, Joshua waltzed her around the room. Soon other couples joined in the dance. Joshua and Anna's marriage began with what would become a tradition of being in step with each other and their families and friends.

EPILOGUE

THE WEEKS, the months passed into nearly a year. In August, Joshua drove the new van he and Anna had purchased for the group home up over Chinook Pass. Anna sat in the front seat between Douglas and himself. Niki, Robert, Scott and the other family members of Eloise Manor were crammed into the back. The luggage rack on top of the van was packed to the hilt.

As Joshua began descending the pass toward Squaw Rock and the annual Provolosky camp-out, he recalled the last time he had made this trip. He hadn't known what to expect. Now he was looking forward to the happy mayhem he knew would occur.

The gang in the back seat had just finished singing one of those hiking songs that barely made sense. The silly tune, "The Other Day I Met a Bear in Tennis Shoes," drove Joshua crazy. He could never figure out if the bear or the hapless hiker was wearing the sneakers. The only thing worse was enduring a dozen verses of "Ninety-nine Bottles of Beer on the Wall."

"I'm scared," Robert said as he looked out the window. "That's an awful long way down." He pointed to the edge of the road where the cliff plummeted nearly a thousand feet to a large river that looked just like a silver thread.

Douglas said, "Switch places with him, Niki. Let him sit in the middle. You've been over this pass many times and I know the height doesn't bother you."

"Okay Boss," Niki said.

Anna smiled at the nickname the fellows had given Douglas. Niki had started the trend and, as usual, his pals had followed suit. There was no doubt that "Boss" was appropriate. Douglas was definitely in control with five charges to push, prod, cajole and goad.

Robert stayed in the center until they pulled into Squaw Rock. Douglas put the whole crew to work unloading and setting up tents. Joshua had reserved a cabin for himself and Anna. There would be no tenting with Niki this year.

After they stowed their luggage in their cottage, Anna suggested, "Let's wander around and see if the Hewitts have arrived. I haven't seen the twins for weeks."

As they stepped out the door, Niki came charging up. "Hey, Josh," he bellowed, "take me fishing."

"Not right now, buddy," Joshua said. "Anna and I want to look for Julie and her family."

"Ah, Joshua," Niki whined. "I wanna go now."

"If you keep that up," Joshua warned, "I'm not taking you fishing the whole weekend."

Niki started to pout and then reconsidered. "Okay, I'll do what Douglas tells me. Hold my tongue."

Anna and Joshua burst out laughing. The first time Douglas had used that expression, Niki had taken him literally and hung on to the end of his tongue for about five minutes. Finally, Robert had asked him if he was crazy or something. Niki had gotten the point.

They found the Hewitts sitting around their picnic table. The twins were toddling after chipmunks.

"I'm glad you could make it," Anna said to Julie.

"Two more weeks and we wouldn't have. Gary's new orders came in. We leave for Alaska by the end of the month," Julie said.

Anna watched as Joshua romped with the twins. He was going to miss them. She knew how much they meant to him, but she had some news that would cheer him up. She was planning to tell him tonight.

As they walked along the edge of the Naches River, however, she couldn't wait any longer. Holding his hand, she shared her joy.

"I missed lunch today," she began.

"Why?" Joshua asked. "Too busy to take a break?"

"No. I had a doctor's appointment," she answered, intending to explain why.

She didn't need to. Joshua whisked her up into his arms in a split second.

"We're going to have a baby?" he impatiently demanded.

"Yes." Anna laughed. "Yes."

He peppered her with kisses and squeezed firmly while twirling her around jubilantly. He was making her dizzy, but that was nothing new. Her life had been a heady experience from the first moment she'd met him.

Niki saw them in each other's arms, swaying to their happiness.

"Whatcha doing dancing?" he asked. "There's no music playing yet."

Anna looked at him and smiled. "Oh, yes there is, big brother. You're just not listening."

Niki looked puzzled and listened intently. "I don't hear nothing. Whadda you mean?"

Joshua clapped him on the back. "You're going to be an uncle, Niki. Anna's going to have a baby."

"Really?" Niki was pleased. "I sure hope the poor kid isn't as weird as you two are," he mumbled as he walked away.

Arm and arm, Anna and Joshua strolled back to camp to tell everyone that the size of the family was going to increase. As the setting sun glowed behind the shadowed trees, Anna knew that her life was complete. Fear would never again cast its shadow over the love she and Joshua had found.

Begin a long love affair with

HARLEQUIN SUPERROMANCE.™

Accept LOVE BEYOND DESIRE **FREE.**

Complete and mail the coupon below today!

- -

Harlequin reaches into the hearts and minds of women across America to bring you

Harlequin American Romance ™·

YOURS FREE!

Enter a uniquely exciting new world with

Harlequin American Romance ™·

Harlequin American Romances are the first romances to explore today's love relationships. These compelling novels reach into the hearts and minds of women across America... probing the most intimate moments of romance, love and desire.

You'll follow romantic heroines and irresistible men as they boldly face confusing choices. Career first, love later? Love without marriage? Long-distance relationships? All the experiences that make love real are captured in the tender, loving pages of **Harlequin American Romances.**

What makes American women so different when it comes to love? Find out with **Harlequin American Romance!**

Send for your introductory FREE book now!